last
seen

Novelist, traveller and fresh air enthusiast, Lucy Clarke, is the author of four novels, including the Richard & Judy Book Club pick, *The Sea Sisters*. Lucy is married to a professional windsurfer and, together with their two young children, they spend their winters travelling and their summers at home on the south coast of England. Lucy writes from a beach hut.

Keep in touch with Lucy:

www.lucy-clarke.com
@lucyclarke_author
@lucyclarkebooks
/lucyclarkeauthor

Also by Lucy Clarke

The Sea Sisters
A Single Breath
The Blue

last seen

LUCY CLARKE

HarperCollins*Publishers*

HarperCollins
PUBLISHERS
Since 1817

This novel is entirely a work of fiction.
The names, characters and incidents portrayed in it are
the work of the author's imagination. Any resemblance to
actual persons, living or dead, events or localities is
entirely coincidental.

HarperCollins*Publishers* Ltd
1 London Bridge Street
London SE1 9FG

www.harpercollins.co.uk

First published by HarperCollins*Publishers* 2017
1

MIX
Paper from
responsible sources
FSC
www.fsc.org
FSC™ C007454

FSC™ is a non-profit international organisation established to promote
the responsible management of the world's forests. Products carrying the
FSC label are independently certified to assure consumers that they come
from forests that are managed to meet the social, economic and
ecological needs of present and future generations,
and other controlled sources.

Find out more about HarperCollins and the environment at
www.harpercollins.co.uk/green

To Darcy Wren,
the newest addition to the family.

Acknowledgements

Firstly, thank you to my editor, Kimberley Young, who has an extraordinary knack for reading a manuscript and posing revealing questions that always push the story – and me – further than I thought possible. Thank you also to the rest of the HarperFiction team, who are a truly gorgeous bunch to work with – with particular thanks to Charlotte Brabbin, Jaime Frost, Claire Palmer, Katie Moss and Heike Schüssler.

Huge thanks to my incredible agent Judith Murray at Greene & Heaton. Your advice is always pitch-perfect and I feel very lucky to have you at my side.

A big hug of gratitude to my friends who have read and offered feedback on the manuscript during various stages of the drafting – it's proved invaluable. Thanks also to Andy King for his expert help on the policing front, particularly missing persons procedures. Any mistakes are, of course, my own.

Heartfelt thanks to my parents, Jane and Tony, for their continued support and championing, AND for buying a beach hut twenty-five years ago. None of us knew how that little wooden hut would shape our lives, but it has, hasn't it?

Finally, thank you to my husband, James, who will always be the boy in the beach hut next door.

The character name of 'Lorrain' in this book was a winner of the *Get In Character* charity auction raising funds for www.clicsargent.org.uk – the UK's leading cancer charity for children and young people, and their families. The prize winner was Claire Russell, who won the prize for her lovely niece, Lorrain. I do hope you enjoyed your fictional turn as a beach hutter, Lorrain!

Prologue

Salt water burns the back of my throat as I surface, coughing. My legs kick frantically, trying to propel me nearer the boat. The hull is close, whale-sized, solid. I lash out, white fingertips clawing at the side, but there's nothing to grip and I go under again, mouth open, briny water shooting up my nose.

Suddenly there's an iron hand around my arm, pulling, dragging me upwards. My kneecap smashes against the side of the boat as I'm hauled on board, a pool of water spilling from me. I blink salt water and tears from my eyes, staring into a face half hidden by a beard. A dark gaze meets mine; the man speaks quickly, asking questions, draping a blanket over my shoulders.

I say nothing. My whole body shakes beneath the stiff fabric.

I look down at my feet. They are pressed together, white, bloodless, impossibly pale. Beyond them, stacked in the centre of the boat, is a tower of briny, dark cages, where lobsters writhe, tails and claws snapping and clacking.

'What happened?' the man asks over and over, his voice sounding distant as if it's an echo in my head.

I don't answer – won't take my eyes off the lobsters. They are not red as you see them in pictures, but black and shining, huge claws flecked with white. Can they breathe out of the sea, I wonder? Aren't they drowning, right now, here in front of me? I want to throw them back into the water, watch them swim down to the sea bed. Their antennae quiver and flit as we motor towards the shallows.

There's a sudden roar of a boat engine close by. My head snaps up in time to see a blur of orange flashing past: the lifeboat. For the first time I notice the small crowd gathered on the shoreline. My fingers dig into the blanket as I realize: they are looking for us.

Both of us.

I am shaking so hard my teeth clatter in my head. I look down at my hands, then slide them beneath my thighs. I know everything is different now. Everything has changed.

1. SARAH

DAY ONE, 6.15 A.M.

In the distance I can hear the light wash of waves folding on to shore. I lie still, eyes closed, but I can sense the dawn light filtering into the beach hut, slipping beneath the blinds ready to pull me into the new day. But I'm not ready. An uneasy feeling slides through my stomach.

I reach out to find Nick's side of the bed empty, the sheet cool. He's in Bristol, I remember. He has his pitch this morning. He left last night with a slice of birthday cake pressed into his hand. At that point Jacob was still smiling about the presents he'd been given for his seventeenth birthday. Nick has no idea what happened later.

A low flutter of panic beats in my chest: *Will Jacob tell him?*

I push myself upright in bed, my thoughts snapping and

firing now. I can still feel the vibrations of Jacob's footsteps storming across the beach hut, then the gust of air as the door slammed behind him, his birthday cards gliding to the ground like falling birds. I'd picked them up, carefully replacing each of them, until I reached the last – a home-made card with a photo glued to the front. I'd gripped its edges, imagining the satisfying tear of paper beneath my fingertips. I had made myself return it to the shelf, re-arranging the cards so it was placed at the back.

I listen for the sound of Jacob's breathing, waiting to catch the light hum of a snore – but all I can hear are the waves at the door. I straighten, fully alert now. Did I hear him come in last night? It's impossible to sneak into the beach hut quietly. The door has to be yanked open where the wooden frame has swollen with rain; the sofa bed has to be skirted around in the dark; the wooden ladder to the mezzanine, where Jacob sleeps, creaks as it is climbed; and then there's the slide and shuffle of his knees when he crawls to the mattress in the eaves.

Pulling back the covers, I clamber from the bed. In the dim haze I scan the tidy square of the beach hut for clues of my son: there are no trainers kicked off by the door; no jumper tossed on the sofa; no empty glasses or plates left on the kitchen counter, nor dusting of crumbs. The hut is immaculate, neat, just as I left it.

I ignore the faint pulse of pain in my head as I cross the beach hut in three steps, climbing the base of the ladder. It's dark in the mezzanine – I'd pulled the blind over the port-hole window and made Jacob's bed before going to sleep myself. Usually the distinctive fug of a teenage boy lingers up here, but this morning the heaped body of my son is absent, the duvet smooth.

I squeeze my eyes shut and swear under my breath. What did I expect?

I don't know why I let it happen, not on his birthday. I shouldn't have risen to his challenge. I went too far. We both did. *Diffuse, not antagonise*, Nick is fond of telling me. (*Thank you, Nick. I'd never have thought of that myself.*)

When Jacob was little, Nick would always ask my opinion on what Jacob needed, how best to dress a cut on his knee, or whether he could do with a nap, or what he might prefer to eat. But, in the last few years, my confidence in knowing what my son needs has slipped away. In his company, I often find myself at an utter loss as to what to say – asking too many questions, or not the right ones. On the odd occasion that Jacob does confide in me, I feel like a desert-walker who has come across a freshwater lake, thirsting for closeness.

Last night, as Jacob swung round to face me, I couldn't think what to say, what to do. Maybe it was because seventeen is like a line in the sand; he'd just stepped over it into adulthood – but I wasn't ready. Maybe that's why I said the things I did, trying to pull him back to me.

I descend the ladder now, feeling the full weight of my headache kicking in. I'm sure Jacob will have stayed out with his friends – he'll probably roll in at mid-morning, a hangover worsening his mood. Yet still, I feel the tentacles of panic reaching, feeling their way through my chest.

Coffee. That's what I need. I pump water into the kettle, then light the hob, listening to the rush of gas. As I wait for the water to boil, I have a strange, uncomfortable sensation that this is going to be my life one day: just me, alone, making coffee for one. It makes sweat prickle underarm, dread loosening my insides.

I reach out and snap on the battery-powered radio. A song blares into the hut – Jacob and I are always having radio wars, he switching it from Radio 4 to a station he likes, knowing I've still not learnt how to use the *Memory* button, so I must manually retune it to find my station again. But this morning, I like the noise and the thrash of guitars. I'll leave it on. That way, when he comes back it'll be playing.

Once I've made myself a coffee, I use the rest of the hot water to wash my face. There's a toilet block nearby, but the sinks are usually mapped with sand or the white trails of spat-toothpaste. Diane and Neil next door have installed a water tank beneath their hut, and rigged up a heater from their solar panels so they can have hot running water at the flick of the tap. Isla thinks it's an extravagance – another sign of the beach huts becoming too gentrified – but I'd laughed and said I'd be adding that to Nick's To Do list.

I pat my face dry, then move to the windows, pulling up the blinds. Sea, sky and morning light spill into the hut and my breathing immediately softens. The early sun lies low to the horizon, the glassy sea tamed beneath it.

Stepping out on to the deck, the air is fresh and salted. I love this time of day before the breeze picks up and stirs white caps, when the light is soft against the water and the sand is empty of footprints. If Nick were here, he'd take his daily swim before leaving for the office, but right now he'll be waking in a hotel room. I picture him shaving off the weekend's stubble in a windowless en suite, then making an instant coffee with one of those silly miniature kettles. I don't feel sorry that he's there; he thrives on that kick of adrenalin that will be firing through him as he runs through the pitch for a final time, making sure he's got just the right blend of humour, professionalism and hard facts. He'll be brilliant, I know he will. His agency is pitching for the print advertising for a confectionery company that he's been wooing for months. I'm keeping everything crossed for him. I know how much Nick needs it.

How much *we* need it.

Standing at the edge of the deck, I glance across to Isla's hut. It stands shoulder to shoulder with ours – exactly five feet between them. In the summer that our boys turned seven, Jacob and Marley had fastened sheets above the shaded pathway running between the huts, calling it their Secret Sand Tunnel. Their games usually involved wanting to be in the water, or making dens in the wooded headland at the far end of the sandbank, so Isla and I were delighted to have them playing close by where we could hear the soft murmur of their chatter through the wooden walls of our huts, like mice in the eaves of a home.

In the clear morning light, I notice how tired Isla's hut looks. The plywood shutters, which were hurriedly fixed across the windows last night, give the air of eviction, and the deck is empty of her faded floral sun-chair and barbecue. Several planks of decking are beginning to rot, mould lining the grooves. The yellow paintwork of the hut is peeling and flaking, and the sight saddens me, remembering how bright and vivid her hut was the first year she owned it – *sherbet lemon yellow*, she called the colour.

I feel my throat closing. Everything felt so fresh at the beginning. That first summer we met, I remember my father asking hopefully, 'Is there a boy?'

I'd laughed. In a way, meeting Isla was like falling in love. We wanted to spend every free moment together. We would call each other after school, and have long, laughter-filled conversations that made my cheeks ache from smiling so hard, and my ear pink from being pressed close to the phone. My exercise books were filled with doodles of her name, and I'd find ways to bring her into conversation, just so she would feel present and real to me. Our friendship burst to life like a butterfly shedding its chrysalis: together we were bright and beautiful and soaring.

What happened to those two girls?

You didn't want me here, Isla hissed last night before leaving to catch her flight.

I wondered if I'd feel guilty this morning. Regret the things I'd said to her.

I pull my shoulders back. I don't.

I'm relieved she's gone.

2. ISLA

It was so close to being perfect.

We were best friends.

We spent our summers living on a sandbank in beach huts next door to one another.

We fell pregnant in the same year – and gave birth to sons three weeks apart.

Our boys grew up together with the beach as their playground.

It seemed impossible, back then, to imagine that anything could come between us.

Yet perfect is a high spire to dance on – and below there's nothing but a very long drop . . .

Summer 1991

A strong briny scent rose from the stacks of blackened lobster pots, where a flock of starlings hopped and chattered, iridescent feathers catching in the sunlight. At the harbour edge, the water gurgled and slopped. Sarah crouched down and dipped her forefinger into the water, then brought it to her lips and sucked it. She thought for a moment, then said, 'Notes of engine oil, fish guts and swan shit.'

I grinned. I'd known Sarah for precisely one hour and forty-five minutes, but already we were friends. She had a good laugh – mischievous and surprisingly loud – yet there was something almost apologetic about the way she lifted a hand to her mouth as if to contain it.

Right now we were meant to be crammed into a sweltering studio taking part in a week-long drama workshop. I had my mum's Reiki clients to blame for losing a whole week of the summer holidays; Sarah said she'd signed herself up as it was better than being at home. During the first break, we'd sat on the sun-warmed steps outside, drinking cans of Cherry Coke, and decided we wouldn't be going back indoors.

Sarah placed her hands on the railings. Her bitten fingernails were painted pink, the polish faded at the edges. She looked across the water to the golden stretch of sand ahead of us. 'Where's that?'

'Longstone Sandbank.' It was flanked by a meandering natural harbour on one side, and on the other by the open sea. 'You've never been?'

She shook her head. 'We only moved here a month ago. Is it an island?'

'Almost.' The sandbank was no more than half a mile long, and was separated from the quay by a fast-moving channel of water. Dotted along its spine were a rabble of brightly coloured wooden beach huts. I always thought it looked as though the sandbank had tried its hardest to escape the mainland – and it had succeeded, except for the slimmest touch of land still tethering it to a wooded head-land at its far end.

'How do you get there?'

'By boat,' I said, nodding towards the ferry that was bobbing across the harbour, orange fenders strapped to its sides. The engine growled against the running tide as it motored towards the quayside. We watched as the round-faced captain leant out to loop a rope around a thick wooden post.

'Wanna go there?' I asked.

Sarah's green eyes glittered as they met mine. 'Yes.'

We climbed on to the wooden boat, handing the captain our fifty-pence pieces, and moved to the bench at the back. Kneeling up on the seat, we rested our chins on top of folded arms so we could watch the wake the ferry created as it pulled away.

I glanced across at Sarah. The sun illuminated her clear, smooth face, and the delicate curve of her small mouth. She grinned at me. 'Who knew drama club would be so much fun?'

The ferry crossing only took a few minutes and we hopped from the boat and moved down the rickety jetty, our sandals clanking against the wooden planks. Reaching the beach, Sarah's gaze flitted over the huts as she exclaimed, 'They're like little houses. Look! They have proper kitchens – and beds!'

'You can sleep in them during the summer,' I told her, pointing out a hut with a wooden ladder leading up to a mezzanine. 'Imagine waking up here!'

A low, rhythmic boom hinted at the sea that lay on the other shore of the sandbank, so we left the harbour behind and squeezed between two huts, stepping over a set of oars and skirting a deflated dinghy. Immediately the breeze was stronger, blown onshore in salty gusts. Whitecaps ducked and dived, driving small waves to break on the shore. Rocky groynes punctuated the beach, creating a series of small bays.

We kicked off our shoes and walked with our arms linked, tramping through the thick, warm sand. Sarah was a head shorter than me, but she walked with long strides and our steps fell into an easy rhythm. There were pockets of activity everywhere: two young girls buckled into life jackets were dragging a kayak to the shore; an older woman standing in the shallows threw a stick for a muscular, bounding dog; a man in a panama hat struggled to put up a windbreak in the fine sand, using a pebble for a hammer. We passed a family eating brunch at a picnic table, their bare feet dug into the sand, a pile of napkins secured from the breeze by a large pebble. At the hut next door a group of teenage boys lounged bare-chested and tanned, two guitars leant against sun-chairs. I nudged Sarah in the ribs and she smiled into her chin.

Surprisingly, many of the huts were closed, their blinds drawn. I wondered where their owners were – what they could possibly be doing that was better than being here. They looked odd, those shuttered huts, secretive shadows in the brilliant midday sun.

After some time, a craggy headland ended the row of huts and the beach thinned as it wrapped around crumbling sandstone cliffs. We scrambled over a rocky groyne that separated one deserted bay from the next, and walked on the shoreline, avoiding the dark piles of seaweed flagging on the sand.

Sarah paused, turning to face me. 'Shall we swim?'

I glanced around us; the bay was empty, the water a tantalizing blue. I grinned as I wriggled out of my T-shirt and cut-offs, leaving me in mismatched underwear.

Sarah shrugged off her dress, grabbed my hand, and together we ran towards the water.

My breath caught at the first grip of cold around my ankles. Sarah squealed as a rush of white water engulfed our middles. When a wave came, I dived through it, cold squeezing a scream from my lungs. Beneath the water I glided, the rest of the world closing out. My skin came alive with the bite of the sea, the sting of the salt.

When there was no more air left in my lungs, I broke through the surface, hair slick to my head. The sea fizzed and breathed around me.

Sarah was laughing with her head tipped back.

We let the sea toy with us – lifting us up, then sucking us back with each shelf of water.

'Let's catch this wave,' I said, paddling for a small peak and trying to bodysurf into shore, but I wasn't quick enough and it passed beneath me. I trod water waiting for the next and, when it came, we both kicked feverishly whilst striking out with our arms. We were rewarded as the wave propelled us forwards, Sarah whooping as we travelled. The wave broke early in a charge of foam and we were sent flailing, legs tangled about arms like rag dolls. I

13

felt myself rolled along the sea bed, my underwear flimsy protection against the ride, and we both surfaced gasping and laughing. We waded out, staggering up the beach.

An older boy with thick dark hair, who I hadn't noticed earlier, was fishing on the rocks at the edge of the bay. He watched us closely, his gaze both serious and curious. I glanced sideways at Sarah and found she was staring right back at him.

I shivered. We didn't have towels, so we stood with our arms outstretched to salute the sun, like my mother did in her yoga practice.

Looking towards the beach huts, they seemed like tiny colourful homes whispering of sun-swept holidays. High on adrenalin and the bloom of a new friendship, I announced, 'One day I'm going to buy a beach hut. I'll fill it with books and candles and board games and music – and I won't leave all summer.'

'Except when you walk over to my beach hut,' Sarah added. 'Because I'm going to buy the one next door.'

It was a girl's wish, that's all. Beach huts next door, long summers spent on a sandbank.

But neither of us could know that our lightly cast dream would come true – or what it would cost us both.

3. SARAH

DAY ONE, MIDDAY

I wait until midday before I call Jacob; it gives him long enough to sleep off the worst of his hangover, and enough time to feel he's proved a point by not returning to the beach hut. When I pick up my mobile, I see that I missed a call from Isla last night. There's no message and I wonder vaguely if she was ringing to apologize.

I scroll to Jacob's number, press call, and then hold the mobile to my ear, my fingers drumming the kitchen counter.

Oddly, there's no ring tone – just a recorded voice informing me that they're unable to connect me, and I should try again later.

Jacob would never switch off his phone. His mobile is like a fifth limb, which he uses with an instinctiveness that eludes me completely. He can point his phone to the sky and name star constellations, or take over the car stereo with a swipe of the screen. It's unlikely he's got no signal either, as everywhere on the sandbank is in range. I suppose it's possible that he's run out of battery, although we all charge our phones from an attachment that Nick rigged up from the solar panels.

I wonder what to do now. I don't like the idea of stewing in the beach hut, waiting for him to return. I keep replaying our argument, pausing on the narrowness of Jacob's dark gaze, and the way he'd yanked his rucksack from the floor, then slammed the beach hut door so hard that the panes of glass rattled in their frames. I'd gone to the window, pressing my fingertips against the cool glass. The beach was in darkness, except for the lantern of a night-fisherman setting up for the evening and the glow of Neil's boat going out, and I'd watched Jacob slide away into the night, a stranger to me.

What happened to the little boy I used to hold in my arms as a baby, with his inquisitive brown gaze that fixed on mine, the button nose that wrinkled when I made him laugh? It had been so much easier then. There were fewer mistakes to make.

I pick up my mobile again, passing it from hand to hand. Part of me is desperate to call Nick and tell him what's going on, but he'll still be in the pitch and, anyway, if I tell him that Jacob's stayed out overnight, he'll want to know why.

No, I need to handle this myself.

I slip the phone into my pocket, then leave the hut.

Luke's beach hut is on the harbour side of the sandbank, near the wooden jetty where the ferry docks. I've known his parents for years: they are a lovely couple, both GPs, who take on gruelling schedules. Luke is the youngest of four brothers and I think, by now, his parents' rules have relaxed so greatly that Luke spends the majority of the summer in the beach hut on his own.

A shining cloud of starlings rises from a hut roof as I pass, wings beating a bewitching pattern in the sunlight.

As I near Luke's hut I pull my sunglasses down and go to smooth my hair back – forgetting I've recently had it cut so it now rests just above my shoulders. The space where it has always hung down my back feels strangely exposed, naked. Nick assures me he likes the change, but I worry I look too severe, the blonde bob sharpening my features.

Luke is sitting on the deck in his board shorts, opposite a girl who wears a black bikini, her skin tanned and tight. I glance beyond them, inside the dim hut, and can make out a cluster of young people sprawled across the sofas. I have no intention of embarrassing Jacob with a lecture about why he didn't come home last night – I simply want to see him, know he's okay.

'Luke!' I smile, lifting a hand.

He sits up a little straighter, squinting. 'All right?'

He's turning into a handsome young man, with his thick sandy blond hair and an open smile. 'Good party?'

'Yeah,' he says, getting slowly to his feet. He climbs down from the deck and stands on the beach, leaning a hand on a weathered picnic bench as he squints against the sun. I don't flatter myself that he's come to greet me – he just doesn't want me to enter the hut. It's a space for teenagers, not mothers.

Up a little closer, it's clear he's hung-over. He's got that glazed look, and a slumped, low energy, as if everything is a little too bright, a touch too vivid. His hair sticks up at one side of his head, and his eyes are bloodshot. I can smell the alcohol fumes rising from his pores. 'Jacob still here?'

'Jacob?' he repeats, surprised.

'He didn't stay here last night?'

'No.' Luke glances back inside the hut, my gaze following his. Through the gaggle of teenagers I spot empty cans of beer, bottles of spirits, cigarette butts. I notice a plastic drinks bottle with the nose cut off and tin foil wrapped around one end of it, and can guess what they've been using it for.

I keep my tone light. 'He did come to the party?'

'Yeah, course. It was for him.'

Jacob has always dismissed any suggestion of a birthday party, which is why I was thrilled this year when he said he was going to Luke's hut for drinks. I offered to buy some beers for them, and a few packs of burgers in case they were hungry later, but he said, 'It's sorted.' Which meant, *Don't interfere.*

Despite myself, I ask, 'What time did he leave?'

Luke rubs the heel of his hand across the side of his head. 'I dunno. Maybe around eleven, I guess.'

Early – especially as it was a party for him.

'He said he was gonna come back here.'

Then I realize. I smile lightly as I say, 'I should probably be looking for him in Caz's hut, shouldn't I?'

One of the young men in the hut adds with a smirk, 'Maybe they were making up!'

Luke narrows his eyes at the boy.

I want to ask more, but instead I say, 'Cheers, Luke.'

Cheers? I never say cheers.

I leave the hut feeling like an idiot. Of course Jacob will be at Caz's hut! Robert, her father, must be away.

As far as I can intuit, Jacob and Caz have been a couple since the start of summer. I've known Caz since she was a little girl. She's always been pretty – petite and blonde with sharp green eyes – and I've watched her bloom into a confident, beautiful young woman, but there's a knowingness in her eyes that doesn't escape me. Earlier in the summer I'd come across the pair of them lying on a rug by the shore, listening to music. A song they both knew was playing loudly and Caz began to sing. I was surprised to see Jacob joining in at the chorus. Their singing grew louder and more raucous as they half shouted the lyrics, nodding their heads, laughing together, the sun on their faces. Caz had jumped to her feet, the rug becoming her stage as she danced and sang. Jacob pulled out his phone and snapped pictures, Caz posing with a hand on her hip, laughing, pouting. As I watched, a spike of doubt stabbed the scene: *Do not hurt my son.*

As I'm walking away from Luke's hut, I catch one of the girls saying, 'Caz was a total mess.'

I slow my pace enough to catch someone else adding, 'He didn't need to march her out. She was just having fun.'

I strain to hear the rest, but the conversation swims away from me. Did Jacob have to help Caz back to her hut? Was she so drunk that he didn't want to leave her? I like the idea of my son being the responsible one.

*

Caz's hut is at the furthest end of the sandbank, near the headland. The walk from one tip of the sandbank to the other should only take fifteen minutes, but in summer it feels like you can't go more than ten paces without a hut owner calling out a greeting, or inviting you in for a drink. I have to pass our beach hut on the way, so I pop my head in briefly just to check Jacob hasn't returned in the mean-time. I'm not surprised to find it empty still.

As I'm moving on, I notice Diane, our next-door beach hut neighbour, standing on her deck. Despite the warmth of the day, a navy fleece is zipped to her chin. She stands with her hands planted on her hips, staring out into the bay where her husband, Neil, is boarding his boat.

'Neil going fishing?' I ask.

She looks at me for a long moment. 'The boat's been dinged. He's checking the damage.'

'Oh, what happened?'

'No idea.'

Neil will be on the warpath, then. The boat is his pride and joy. He spends more time tinkering with it than fishing from it.

Although Diane and Neil have owned the hut next door for over ten years, I've always found it disappointing that we've never grown close. Nick and Neil sink the odd beer around the barbecue – but I just can't imagine sitting out late on the deck sharing a bottle of wine with Diane. I honestly don't know what we'd talk about.

I ask, 'You haven't seen Jacob this morning, have you?'

Diane looks at me through the corners of her eyes. 'Jacob? Why? Is something wrong?'

'He didn't come home last night,' I say with a loose wave of my fingers, as if it is no big deal.

There's something odd about the way her gaze travels searchingly over my face. 'No. I've not seen him.'

'He's probably at his girlfriend's.'

Her gaze still doesn't leave me. 'I do hope so.'

It's an odd remark – although perhaps not in the context of Diane. As I move on, I think that, if Diane were one of my other friends with teenagers, I'd already be turning this into an anecdote: *Jacob stayed out all night on his birthday. He didn't bother to text, didn't answer his mobile the next morning – nothing! I was in a total panic. I found him eventually – with his girlfriend, of course!* I can picture the other mums doing that reassuring little roll of their eyes, which means: *teenagers.*

I'm a good sharer among friends; I trade just the right balance of lamentable parenting tales, with the occasional golden highlight thrown in for good measure: *Jacob cooked for us all yesterday. Spaghetti bolognese. Without being asked. I had to stop myself demanding to know what he'd done.*

But I am careful not to share *everything*. For example, it's only Nick and I who know that Jacob's head of sixth form called us in halfway through the term to talk about Jacob's poor attendance. My hands trembled as I left the office. 'Truancy? Where's he been going? Do you think something is wrong?'

Nick had slung his arm around my shoulder, just like he used to do when we were younger, and said with a grin, 'I seem to remember you and Isla bunking off your drama classes.'

'That was different. It wasn't school.'

Nick only grinned more.

I also didn't tell my friends how Jacob broke two toes in the spring. He didn't injure them in a skateboarding accident, but because he'd kicked the skirting board in our hallway when I'd told him he was too young to go to Glastonbury with his friends.

Just before I reach Caz's hut, I become aware of Isaac at the periphery of my vision. He's crossing the beach, his gaze fixed on me. I keep my eyes lowered, pretending not to notice him.

'Sarah!' he calls.

I flinch at the sound of my name from his mouth – but I don't turn.

I can hear his footsteps hurrying through the sand. Heat suffuses my skin as I march on.

'Sarah! Wait!' he calls when he is almost at my shoulder.

I have no choice but to turn. 'Oh, Isaac! I was miles away.' I keep pace as I say, 'Sorry, I can't stop. Meeting Jacob. Already late!'

It's a lie, of course, but at least Isaac doesn't say anything further. From the corner of my eye, I see him hesitate. He looks anxious, his hands fluttering at his sides. Then thankfully he nods his head and lets me go.

Caz and Robert's hut, painted a fresh sky blue, is raised slightly above the neighbouring ones. I scan the harbour to see if I can spot Robert's boat – a large grey RIB with an oversized engine (which, to me, screams *Penis extension!*). I can't see it moored up today, which most likely means he isn't on the sandbank.

I call out as I climb the wooden steps leading on to the deck, not wishing to surprise Caz and Jacob if they're together. I find Caz curled into the sofa with her headphones on, eyes closed. Her clear skin is deeply tanned, and her hair, bleached to a white-blonde, looks wild and mussed. I glance beyond her, looking for traces that my son is here. I suppose he could have left by now, deciding to see one of his friends, or to take a walk up on the headland. I am turning to leave when Caz's eyes suddenly flick open. She sits up, startled, yanking off her headphones. There's a red mark across her cheek from where she's been lying, and I notice a slight glassiness to her eyes.

'Sorry, I just came to see if—'

'I was just . . . going out.'

'Out?'

'To catch up with a friend.' Caz puts a hand to her head and ruffles her hair around her face.

I hover in the doorway, giving no indication of leaving.

'I've got a minute though.'

I move into the hut, lowering myself on to the sofa opposite her. I take in the cream tongue-and-groove panelling, the expensive striped navy blinds, the antique barometer fixed above the sink. Caz's mother decorated the hut before she left Robert to live in Spain with the manager of the timeshare she owned. I've not been in the hut since she left and I'm reminded how serene the view of the harbour is on a still day; only sailing boats and sea birds dot the water, the fishing quay visible in the distance. I do enjoy crossing to the harbour side of the sandbank to watch the sun go down in the evenings, yet it's the sea view that I love; it's wilder, more exposed.

'Want a drink?' Caz offers half-heartedly.

'Thank you, but no. I was just passing and wanted to catch Jacob. But obviously he's not here.'

'No.'

'He stayed last night, didn't he?'

She shakes her head. 'No.'

The word is clear and firm. It drops like a pebble into my chest, causing a ripple of panic. *Then, where did he stay?*

I look closely at Caz, wondering whether she is telling me the truth. She is perched on the edge of the sofa, as if she's about to spring up – disappear. Perhaps she thinks I'd be cross if she admitted that Jacob spent the night. She reaches a hand to her left ear lobe, toying with a silver earring she wears in the shape of a seahorse. I watch as she turns it lightly through her fingers, over and over, like a rosary bead, and then removes it. She does the same with the second earring, placing them both on top of a pile of *Coast* magazines that are stacked neatly on the rustic coffee table between us.

I have the strongest desire to reach out for the earrings, feel the warm weight of the silver in my palm. I keep my focus on Caz though, asking, 'Do you know where he is?'

'No. No, I don't.'

'But you saw him at the party last night?'

'Yeah, for a bit.'

'I heard you left together.'

Colour spreads up Caz's neck. 'Oh, yeah. That's right. We walked back together.'

'But Jacob didn't stay here?'

'No,' she says tightly.

'Where did he stay?'

She sighs, exasperated now. 'Look, we walked back along the beach. Stopped by the rocks near his hut to talk for a bit. Then I came back here. That's it.'

'Was he planning to return to the party?'

'Maybe. I don't know.'

I think of the conversation I overheard in Luke's hut – Caz was a 'mess' and Jacob practically had to 'march her out'. 'Did the two of you argue?' I picture Caz standing close with one of the other boys at the party, looking up through her long lashes, while Jacob waited at the edge of the hut, watching.

It's clear I've overstepped the mark by the way Caz lifts her chin and glares at me. 'Jacob wasn't in a brilliant mood last night.' She pauses. 'I'm sure you know.'

The comment, delivered so innocuously, holds a clear accusation. Heat builds in my cheeks as I wonder what exactly Jacob told her.

Caz's barbed remark seems to have returned her composure, set her on some ledge above me that I didn't know we were vying for. She uncrosses her bare legs and stands. There is an empty glass on the coffee table, and she collects it, carrying it towards the sink. 'If I see Jacob, I'll be sure to let him know you're looking for him.'

I'm about to rise to my feet, but my gaze catches again on the silver seahorse earrings, lying right there in front of me.

As Caz fills her water glass, I stand, and as I do so I find my fingertips brushing the earrings. I tell myself I am only looking. I just want to see the detail of them. Touch them once. But, before I can stop myself, I feel my fingers closing tightly around them.

I feel the burst of energy filling my chest, the heat roaring through me.

Caz turns to look at me.

I meet her eye, smile. Then I leave her beach hut, heart thudding.

4. ISLA

My thoughts wander back through the events of this summer, turning each one through my mind, like a collection of pebbles I'm trying to arrange. I need to understand how I'm here. How any of this happened. Where everything went wrong between Sarah and me.

There was an evening jog in the mosquito-clouded air; a bottle of wine shared in the wrong beach hut; a stinging remark made on the deck of Sarah's hut; a photo removed from a wall. Were those some of the events that led to this?

It wasn't just this summer when things began to unravel – the first thread came loose years before. I meander further back through deep sands and beneath cloudy, salt-bitten skies, pausing on a boat returning to shore with only one boy on deck – not two.

There. That is the moment.

Maybe there's a sense of inevitability, because how do you recover, pick up your friendship, after something like that?

Yet there was a time when Sarah was everything to me. When she was my family. Back then, I thought nothing could break us.

Summer 1997

My knees were pressed against the metal frame of my mother's hospital bed, my hands squeezing hers. I was scared: scared by the smell of decay in the thick, still air; scared by the lightness of my mother's fragile, bony fingers that had once danced with silver rings; scared by her tissue-thin eyelids that hadn't opened in two days; scared by the watery rasp of her breath that dragged through her body like the tide drawing over rocks. I wanted to pull my hands away, clamp them over my ears. I wanted to run. I wanted to be anywhere but in the curtained space of a Macmillan ward watching my mother dying.

This could not be it. I wasn't ready.

Our life together was walking at night through the woodland that backed on to our bungalow. It was reading books in front of the fire, me lying on the faded rug, my mother sitting in the oak rocking chair. It was picking elderflower heads and making thick sweet cordial that we stored in glass bottles in the pantry. It was strangers coming in and out of the house for Reiki appointments and reflexology. It was the smell of lavender and rosehip and orange blossom. It was the sound of laughter.

Cancer is a wicked thief. In four short months it had stolen almost everything my mother had: her energy, the songs she used to sing, the quickness in her steps. I'd watched her fade away until all that was left was her shadow. I knew the thief wouldn't rest until it had that too, but I sat there, clinging on, not ready to let my mother go.

I squeezed her hand tightly, silently begging, *I am nineteen years old. Don't leave me, Mum. Please . . .*

But she did.

She slipped away from me even while I was holding on.

A night-shift nurse with cropped black hair pulled the curtain back a little. Maybe that nurse had learnt to tell death from the expression on the living's faces, or from the silencing of the hospital machines, or from that certain stillness that pervaded afterwards. She padded softly across the lino floor and gently placed her hand on my shoulder. 'It's all right, sweetie. You're going to be all right.'

I didn't move. Didn't speak. Didn't let go of my mother.

I screwed my eyes shut and gripped tighter, already beginning to feel her fingers cooling within mine.

On the afternoon of my mother's funeral, I stood in the hallway, watching people trampling across our rugs, smearing our glasses with their fingerprints, leaving their scents of perfume and aftershave lingering in our home – wiping away the final traces of my mother.

I squeezed into the kitchen, skirting a group of my mother's yoga friends, searching for Sarah. She'd slept at the bungalow with me every night since my mother died; we'd grab a stack of blankets from the lounge and sit on the mildew-ridden swing-chair in the garden, smoking and talking. I had no siblings to grieve with, and my father – a Scottish chef who'd met my mother during a retreat – had never been a fixture in my life. Sarah was everything, now. It was easy being together because she'd loved my mother, too. She'd tried on wigs with us, striking silly poses in front of the shop mirror; she'd artfully wrapped bright scarves around my mother's neck to hide the tumours that had spread there; she'd smoothed blusher across her cheekbones before hospital appointments. My mother called her 'Sarah Sunshine'.

I saw her across the room carrying a tray of drinks, smiling, thanking people for coming – doing the things I hadn't the heart to. Seeing me, she tapped the pocket of her trousers where I could make out the rectangular shape of a cigarette packet, then signalled towards the garden with a grin. *A smoke outside.* That's exactly what I needed. We'd pull down the hood of the swing-chair and light up with our heads bent together, shutting out the rest of the world.

As I started to make my way across the lounge, a heavyset man with tufts of white hair sprouting from the crown of his head lowered himself into my mother's rocking chair. The oak spindles protested beneath his weight as he rocked it back and forth, the back of the chair clipping the wall with each motion. He lifted a hand to his mouth, inserting a forefinger to work something loose from his teeth, flashing his thick pink tongue at the room. He sucked his finger clean, then drummed it against the polished arm of the rocker, leaving a glistening smear of his saliva on the wood.

My throat burned with red-hot outrage as I bellowed, 'No!'

The room fell instantly silent. Every head swivelled in my direction.

'Get out of my mother's chair!'

The white-haired man looked horrified. His brow dipped uncertainly, shock making his mouth hang slack. He pushed himself unsteadily to his feet, apologizing. His eyes darted around the room, as if looking for someone to help him.

A hand wrapped around my arm. Heart thudding, I turned to find Sarah looking at me, worry etched in her high, pale forehead. 'Isla?'

An enormous pressure was building within my chest. 'I . . . I just . . . need to go.'

'Okay,' she told me. 'Okay.'

I spun round, crossed the living room and raced along the hallway, bursting out of the back door. A blast of cool air hit me, and I ran with my head down, my red pumps flashing along the damp pavement in quick bursts of colour, like a heartbeat.

Some time later, I found myself at the quay, my dress stuck to the small of my back, my breath coming hard. I gripped the metal railing, sucking in the salt-tinged air.

The beach huts sat quietly on the distant sandbank, a comforting presence with their pastel-light colours cutting through the grey, rolling sky. When the harbour ferry arrived, I didn't pause to think about the guests abandoned in my home, or worry that Sarah would be left to lock up; I simply climbed aboard.

Within minutes, I was standing on the shoreline of the sandbank before a grey, restless sea. Tears ran down my face, dripping from my chin into the neckline of my dress. I had no coat, not even a cardigan, and I could feel the cold beginning to seep into my bones as I hugged my arms around myself, shivering into my sobs. When the first drops of rain began to fall, I stood firm thinking I could outlast them – that I would dance in the face of the cold, of the rain, my grief burning like heat inside me – but after a few minutes, the dark romance of the idea waned, and I hurried for cover beneath the pitched wooden roof of a beach hut.

Sheltering from the rain, I noticed a handwritten advert was tacked to the window, the blue ink faded: *Beach hut for sale.*

I stepped back, considering the hut. It had once been painted a brilliant blue, but the paint had peeled and flaked over the years. In places the wood had rotted, and the deck I was standing on had moulded in the corners, long fingers of dune grass reaching up beneath the planks.

There was a small gap at the base of the blinds, and I pressed my face against the damp glass, peering in. Through the dimness, I could see the deckchairs, a barbecue and a windbreak cluttering the small space. A sun-bleached sofa bed was piled with a rabble of patterned cushions. Above it was a driftwood shelf that had been emptied of the previous owner's belongings, hardened candlewax pooled in two spots. At the back of the hut there was a small kitchen area with an ancient gas oven and a two-ringed hob. An old wooden spice rack was tacked to the wall, and an array of mugs hung from hooks below it. The mismatch of colours and patterns reminded me of my mother's bungalow – and I wanted it.

I wanted that beach hut more than I'd ever wanted anything.

I could picture it: the hut would be a place to retreat to;

somewhere I could rebuild myself; a place where I could watch the weather moving across the horizon and begin to make fresh memories.

As I stood on the deck of that old hut with the roar of the sea at my ear and the fresh breath of salt air on my skin, the sandbank seemed to stretch around me, holding me tightly, anchoring me.

Back then, I had been certain that buying the beach hut was the right decision. I used the money from the sale of my mother's bungalow, though everyone had told me I was mad. Keep the inheritance in brick-built property – not a beach hut! *But I was nineteen. I didn't want mortgage repayments, council tax bills, or responsibility. I wanted the sea. I wanted space. I wanted to do something for myself.*

Summers I'd live in the beach hut. Winters I'd rent one of the cheap holiday lets that always stood empty in the winter months.

It was a plan. It was the best I could do.

'Go for it!' Sarah had said to me as we ate Chinese take-away sitting on the floor of my mother's bungalow, surrounded by boxes marked for charity shops. 'That's what your mother would have told you to do, isn't it?'

I nodded because she was right.

I remember how Sarah had put down her plate and slung her arm around my shoulder, pulling me in close. 'The beach hut will be a fresh start, Isla. It's going to change everything.'

Sarah was right about that, too.

5. SARAH

DAY ONE, 6 P.M.

I pour a large glass of wine and drink it watching the clock on the hut wall. Alone in the beach hut, the ticks seem to sharpen the silence. Still no Jacob. The panic is growing louder and louder, like an insistent guest who won't be silenced.

My phone beeps with a message. I snatch it from the kitchen side, stabbing at the screen – but it's just a text from a friend about her upcoming fortieth. I don't bother reading the full message. Instead I check the call log on my mobile and see I've rung Jacob a dozen times today – and each time I've been greeted by the same recorded message telling me I can't be connected.

I gulp back my wine, then pour a second glass, reminding myself to drink it more slowly.

All day I've been hoping that Jacob will roll in at any

moment – but it's six o'clock now. I try to breathe slowly, but a rising tide of fear is building in my chest as I look at the facts: I haven't seen or heard from Jacob in almost twenty-four hours. He didn't stay at Luke's hut after the party, and he didn't stay with Caz, either. There's no possibility that he could have gone back to our family home since it's rented out for the summer. So where the hell is he?

A movement on the shoreline captures my attention. I narrow my gaze, focusing on the figure. I recognize the long, loping strides, the slight roundness of the shoulders: Isaac. He must sense my gaze on him because his stride abruptly falters and he turns to face this direction. He's too far away to make out his expression, but I know he is watching me. Watching this hut.

I swallow, turning away.

I give myself a moment, then I pick up my mobile and call Nick.

He answers to a rush of noise and I guess he's in the car with the windows down.

'You driving?'

'Yes. Only just left Bristol.'

I hear the electric whine of the windows being closed. 'It went on that long?'

'Yeah,' he says, and I can't tell whether his tone suggests it was a good pitch or not.

I picture him in his shirt and tie, his jacket thrown across the back seat. He'll have undone his top button and pushed up his sleeves. He'll park near the quay, then catch the ferry to the sandbank. He loves the unusual commute, tells me it's his wind-down time in the evenings – allows him to shake off the day. When I see him striding across the beach in his shirt and tie – everyone else in flip-flops and cotton shorts – I feel a swell of pride that he's mine.

For three months of the summer, we rent out our house and move into the beach hut. We used to go back and forth between the house and hut, but for the past couple of summers we've stayed solely on the sandbank. It's a huge amount of work having to clear out the wardrobes and cupboards of our home, and lock away our possessions in the garage. Jacob thinks we do it so we can spend more time at the beach, but the truth is, we need the money.

I know Nick will be expecting me to ask how his pitch went, but I need to tell him about Jacob first. 'Listen, it's probably nothing, but I haven't seen Jacob since last night.' My words sound more clipped than I'd intended.

Nick is always telling me to give Jacob a bit more space. He never uses the word 'smothering', although I sense it is there on the tip of his tongue. 'Last night?' His reply is sharp with surprise. 'Well, where is he?'

'He went to Luke's hut for drinks – but didn't stay over. And I checked with Caz, and she says he didn't stay with her either. I've no idea where he is.'

'Not like him.'

'I know.'

I don't mention the fight between Jacob and myself, yet. Instead I say, 'I think he and Caz may have been arguing.'

'Ah,' Nick says, as if this explains everything. 'He'll be letting off steam. Licking his wounds. He'll be back when he's hungry.'

I want, so much, to believe that's true. Yet I think about Jacob's mouth twisting with anger as he faced me, and the way the hut shook as he slammed the door on his way out.

From my pocket, I pull out Caz's seahorse earrings. Up close they look a little tacky; the curves are blackening, and one of the butterfly clasps is gold and must have been mixed with another piece of jewellery. I wonder whether Caz will even look for them.

If I had my ears pierced, I would try them on. As I hold them up to the light, I picture Jacob walking in – seeing me with them. I can't begin to imagine how I'd explain it. The buzz that hummed through me is already quietening. In its place, I feel the steady rise of shame. I cross the hut and stuff the earrings into a cotton bag at the back of one of our drawers, trying not to think about the other items in there.

I move to the food cupboard and take out three baking potatoes, choosing the smaller one for myself. I scrub them, pierce the skins, then dust them with salt, before placing them in the small gas oven. I've made chilli for dinner, as I know it's a favourite with Nick and Jacob, and I can only hope that the three of us will be sitting together to eat.

I pick up my wine glass and move to the doorway. It's a warm evening with little wind. All along the sandbank, children have been put to bed and parents take chairs and drinks on to the beach, sitting together in groups as the yawning shadows of huts stretch down to the water. Our dear friends, Joe and Binks, who have owned the tired green hut on the other side of Isla's for over thirty years, huddle around a barbecue, the food long cooked, driftwood keeping the fire stoked for warmth. They look subdued this evening, perhaps missing their much-adored grandchildren who returned home yesterday after spending the week with them. Lorrain, who is new to the sandbank, sits between Joe and Binks, leaning close to the flames to light the cigarette pressed between her lips. She calls them her 'summer treats', buying just one pack and making them last the season.

The sight of the red ember glowing in the dusk makes me yearn for a cigarette, too. I haven't smoked properly in years – not since I fell pregnant with Jacob. Occasionally I share the odd cigarette with Isla, pressing it to my lips like a delicious secret. If Nick's with us, he'll make a show of protesting, but in truth, I think he likes the nod to our youth. That's one of the special things about old friends – you never quite let go of the memory of who you used to be.

What was I like at Jacob's age? It's so easy to forget who I was at seventeen as the years keep stacking, one on top of the other; the girl who wore silver platforms and drew flicks of liquid eyeliner at the edges of her eyes getting compressed beneath the weight of the past. I know that at Jacob's age I wasn't close to my mother, that's for certain. It was Isla who I spent every free moment with.

A memory swims back to me . . . an evening when we were seventeen and cycled into town with fake IDs stuffed into our handbags. We'd fluttered our way into a club and danced for hours in a bar built into a disused church. Discs span. Our bodies curved to a beat that thundered from two speakers, our dresses stuck to the small of our backs.

Isla had slipped her hand into the tiny single pocket on

the front of her dress, then uncurled her fingers in front of me, eyes glinting. I peered at her palm, then looked up at her smiling.

We put gold tablets on the end of our tongues and swallowed.

The rhythm sped up. My pulse flickered in my throat.

A boy danced with his knee through mine – and I tipped back my head and laughed. Isla jumped into the air with the music, long hair catching in a flash of light. A strobe played over us, distilling our movements into a hundred frames.

Later, much later, we tumbled out on to the street, hearts thumping, minds buzzing. We squeezed through the doorway of a kebab shop together, watching meat spin in a blizzard of overhead lights. We ate on the pavement, glittering heels kicked off, grease and mayonnaise dampening our lips. We stuffed wrappers in a bin and walked with our arms linked, hips knocking, to where our bikes were chained together.

Heels were thrown in baskets and we carved through the night on our bikes, the wind behind us, tanned legs pedalling fast circles. I raced to the top of a hill, standing up on the pedals, feeling my dress billowing around the tops of my thighs. At the brow, breathing hard, Isla and I were shoulder to shoulder.

I turned.

She looked at me. Grinned.

Before us the dark road unfurled. We leant forward, gave a dozen hard pedals, and then the momentum caught us. We felt the pull of the wheels as they began to roll. We went hurtling down, wind whipping our hair back from our faces. No bike lights, no helmets, bare skin inches away from the rough scrape of tarmac. Isla lay across the handlebars, legs outstretched behind her, screaming a single high note. I kicked out my legs so they sailed like wings away from the pedals.

The stars rained down as we glided.

Together we felt free. Invincible. Brave.

I was young once, I want to tell Jacob. *I haven't always been this person you see now.*

I love you. I'm sorry. It was the wrong decision. Those are some of the other things I need to say.

Forgive me.

'No Jacob yet?' Nick asks the moment he walks in.

I shake my head.

Nick moves towards me and I know he'll press a quick kiss on my cheek. I can't remember when we stopped kissing each other on the mouth – but I realize that I miss it. As he bends towards me, I turn my face into him so his kiss lands on my lips. We bump chins, like uncertain teenagers, and Nick raises his eyebrows slightly.

I catch the smell of his fading aftershave, and a hint of air freshener from his car. He is forty-three in autumn and I think he looks good on it; he still has a thick head of light-brown hair, and the lines on his face trace a pattern of smiles rather than frowns. He goes to the fridge and pulls out a beer, then sinks down on to the sofa.

I pour another glass of wine for myself, but remain standing. 'How did the pitch go?' I ask, although all I really want to talk about is Jacob.

'Okay. I think. God, I don't know. It's so hard to say. We

were there all day. But they're seeing three more agencies. It'll come down to figures in the end, I suppose.'

'Three more?' Nick had thought it was just his agency, and a London firm.

He shrugs, surprisingly relaxed about it. Since he heard about the pitch, he's been working flat out. He's grinding his teeth again in his sleep. I haven't mentioned it; I know he sees it as a weakness – a sign that he can't handle the stress.

'When will you hear?'

'Friday.'

I take another sip of wine, then direct the conversation to Jacob. 'I'm surprised there's still been no word from our boy.'

'What did Luke say?'

'Just that Jacob was at the party until about eleven, and then he and Caz walked along the beach – had an argument, I'm gauging – and then she left him and went to her hut alone.' I tell Nick about the remarks I overheard at Luke's hut about Caz's drinking.

'Sounds like the two of them had a bust-up. He was happy enough earlier on in the day, wasn't he?'

I hesitate, thinking of our argument.

Nick knows me too well. 'Did the two of you have a fight?'

'It was ridiculous, really. Something and nothing.'

'What started it this time?'

I make a show of trying to remember what we argued about, although I know exactly how it began. I remember the way Jacob turned to face me, the accusation in his eyes as Isla's name came hissing out of my mouth. But I don't tell Nick that. I say, 'I asked Jacob whether he had enjoyed the barbecue – I was fishing for a thank you, I suppose. But he missed the hint entirely, just got out his phone and ignored me. I don't mind doing all the work – I really don't – but I'd just like him to notice sometimes. I nagged him about not being glued to the screen all day. He flared up. I fired back. That was it. I should have left it – it was his birthday.'

'Doesn't give him the right to be rude to you.'

I shrug lightly.

'And then what, he left?'

'Stormed out.'

Nick's brows draw together, annoyed. He doesn't ask a lot from Jacob – but good manners are high on his list.

'I'm worried,' I tell Nick, truthfully. 'It's been almost twenty-four hours since we've seen him. We don't even know where he stayed last night. He wasn't with Luke, or Caz, so where was he?'

'He could've crashed in another friend's hut – or even slept on the beach. It's warm enough.'

'Yes, but surely he'd have come back today? And he's not answering his phone – it keeps on telling me that I can't be connected.'

'He's switched it off, then.'

Why? Why would Jacob keep his phone switched off all day? Even if he was angry enough to not want to speak to me, surely he wouldn't want to be cut off from everyone else? He could have just ignored my calls – but left his phone on.

Nick asks, 'Do you think it's serious between him and Caz?'

'I think *Jacob* is serious. He's in love with her, I can see it. He's just been so . . . changeable. One moment he's on top of the world – practically skipping around the hut. He was even singing yesterday morning. Jacob. Singing.' I shake my head. 'Then the next minute, he's a moody bugger. Probably because they've had a fight or he's seen her talking to another boy.'

'And you don't think she feels the same?'

I sigh. 'To be honest, I've no idea. She just seems more . . . *together* than he does.'

'So maybe they had a fight, like you suggested, and he's just taking some time to cool down. Let's give him another hour or two. You know what us Symonds men are like: when we get upset we like to just disappear, take ourselves off into the woods. Maybe this is Jacob's way of letting off steam. He's dealing with a lot of emotions, right now. He's in love. His first love. That's life-changing.'

Before Nick realizes what he's said, the words are out there.

Colour spreads across his cheeks. He meets my gaze and I can see the apology in the widening of his pupils.

I wasn't Nick's first love.

Isla was.

6. ISLA

Nick was mine before he was Sarah's. It's one of those oddly uncomfortable, yet incontrovertible pieces of history that Sarah, Nick and I pretend to ignore. We flit around the subject, never quite brushing the edges of it, like moths scared of getting too close to a flame.

I met Nick the summer I bought my beach hut. His parents, David and Stella, owned the newly built hut next door, which had modern windows and a brand-new cooker that was fancier than the one in my mother's old bungalow. They talked to me mostly of their three sons. Two were doctors, both on secondment in America, and their youngest son, Nick, was completing an MA in Business Studies – and was due to return to the sandbank for summer.

I was expecting someone pale-skinned and bookish from a spring spent studying, but when Nick arrived, he was tanned and athletic-looking. I liked his easy manner, and the smile that lit up his whole face when he shook my hand for the first time.

We were friends for two days – lovers by the third.

Summer 1998

'Sherbet lemon yellow,' I said to Nick as I balanced on the stepladder, dipping the paintbrush into the tin, the sun-warmed rungs of the ladder hard against my bare feet.

Nick, a glue-gun in hand, glanced up.

'That's how my mum would've described this colour. She painted my bedroom door in the same shade.' I worked the brush across the hut in smooth strokes. I liked the steady rhythm of painting, the soothing repetition, the heat on my back.

'You had a yellow bedroom door?'

'All our doors were different colours. Mum's room was new-leaf green,' I said, thinking of the smear of my child-sized fingerprints from where I'd pushed the door open before the paint had dried. 'The bathroom door was iceberg blue, and the kitchen was plum-pie purple. The estate agent who valued the bungalow said, "You might want to think about more neutral tones before putting it on the market."'

Nick laughed. I could see he was going to ask something further about my mother, but I pointed to the radio and said, 'Oh, I love this song! Turn it up.'

Sometimes I liked to talk to Nick about her, but more often than not I kept her for myself. It felt like an impossible task to try and pin her into words. He wouldn't have been able to picture the violet flecks of her irises, or the way she sometimes slipped a pencil through the loose twisted knot of her hair. He didn't know that when she played the flute, her eyes fluttered closed and her head would dance with the notes. He would struggle to understand that, in our house, we didn't have a dining table – we brought mugs of tea and biscuits into bed in the mornings; we took jam sandwiches in our pockets when we were walking; we'd make thick soups over a fire in the garden. He wouldn't know that sometimes my mother disappeared inside herself for long periods of time, and I would bring her food and books, and she'd run her fingers through my hair and call me, 'My darling, Isla-la.' She was a mother of colour and inconsistencies – and I wasn't ready to share her.

In Nick's family there were older brothers, a host of cousins, and two sets of grandparents; there were family meals and trophies on shelves; there was laughter and ribbing and family jokes. I loved being a part of it. His father treated me as though I was an exotic, intriguing patient he was still trying to diagnose. His mother looked at me through the corners of her eyes and spoke carefully. 'She adores you,' Nick would assure me with his easy smile, believing it. 'How couldn't she?'

I looked across at Nick, his top lip beaded with sweat as he concentrated on filling the cracks in the wood. I loved the confidence he had in the world – and his place in it. He belonged in a way I never would. If my mother had met him, she'd have held his face in her hands and said, 'Well, aren't you something special?'

He glanced up. 'What?'

I smiled. 'I wish Mum could have met you.'

46

He moved towards the stepladder where I still balanced, placing his lips against my bare ankle.

That evening, Sarah arrived at the hut with a sleeping bag stuffed underarm. 'Can I stay?'

'Course.' I pushed myself up from Nick's lap and crossed the hut, wrapping my arms around her. 'Maggie's birthday, isn't it?'

She nodded. Maggie was her older sister, who was killed in a road accident the year before I met Sarah.

I took Sarah's hand and pulled her across the deck, into the hut. 'Watch the paint. It's wet.'

'Sherbet lemon yellow,' she said with a smile. 'I love it.'

Nick gave Sarah a warm hug, then told us he was going to The Rope and Anchor on the quay. I loved him in that moment for his tact, his sense of knowing when Sarah and I needed to be alone.

That night the air was warm and windless, and we built a fire near the shoreline and sat around it drinking cheap French beers and smoking.

As I shuffled closer to the flames, holding my palms up to the heat, Sarah said, 'I threw the ball.'

There was no introduction, no explanation. In the darkness I couldn't see her expression, but I knew exactly what she was talking about. Maggie was chasing after a ball when she was hit by the car that killed her. Sarah had told me before how she remembered Maggie lying on the roadside, an arm behind her back, her school skirt twisted around her waist. 'Her knickers were on show – pink cotton ones with a mouse on the front that were too babyish for her. I

47

thought, *How embarrassing! Everyone can see your knickers!* Honestly, that was my very first thought.'

Sarah poked at the fire with a stick, sending orange sparks crackling into the night. 'I threw it,' she said again. 'It was this bouncing ball, as big as my fist, and when it bounced, silver glitter swirled like falling snow. I loved it – it was my favourite thing.' She shook her head lightly. 'I didn't even mean to throw it. I was just holding it one moment . . . and the next I must have let it go without thinking. The ball started bouncing away from me, glittering in the sunlight. Maggie chased after it for me. She didn't trip, didn't stumble. She literally stepped right off the pavement without looking, her hand reaching out for my ball. I saw the car coming. It was bright red with a flat shiny bonnet and those pop-up lights. Do you remember? Some of the older sports cars had them. They were so square and sharp. I screamed at her to look out, but . . .'

I laced my fingers through Sarah's, squeezing tight.

'I threw the ball,' she whispered, leaning against my shoulder. Her hair smelt of wood-smoke and dewberry shampoo. 'I wish more than anything I hadn't. She'd be twenty-one today.'

'It wasn't your fault,' I whispered back. 'It was an accident.'

A trail of tears glistened on Sarah's cheeks. 'You know what my mum said on the morning of the funeral? We were sitting at the kitchen table waiting for the hearse, listening to my father pacing on the landing above. He must have paused outside my sister's room as we both heard the creak of the door handle being turned, then a gulp as if a sob was being swallowed. Mum pressed the heels of her hands into her eye sockets. She shook her head, hands twisting into her face. I could smell her lipstick, and the heat of tea on her breath as she said, "You should never, ever, throw a ball near a road! Remember that, Sarah! Remember!" She couldn't even look at me.'

That night, as on many others, Sarah and I fell asleep on the beach, the stars watching over us. We crawled into my hut at dawn, dewy and shivering, and fell asleep on the sofa bed, a pile of blankets pulled over us.

Nick found us the next morning, curled together like a clasped shell around our secret pearls of grief.

Seven months later, I found myself at Heathrow Airport. I was standing at the departures gate, with Sarah facing me, arms folded. 'You know Nick's heartbroken?'

I tipped my head back, closed my eyes. 'Don't.' I felt the weight of my backpack on my shoulders and against my pelvis. It was comforting, like a solid hug. I liked knowing that, for the next year, everything I needed was right here on my back.

'He would've gone with you.'

I straightened. 'I couldn't let him give up his job. He loves it.' He'd just started working as a marketing executive for a large agency that was young and forward-thinking and worked with some great clients. Nick practically bounced out of bed in the mornings, excited to get to the office.

'It wasn't only that, was it?' Sarah said, her gaze still pinned on me.

'I need to do this alone.' I reached out and took her

fingers in mine. 'I'm sorry,' I said softly, understanding that Sarah was hurt that I was leaving her, too. It was difficult to explain why I had to go on my own. For the last few months, the idea of travelling had become intoxicating. Every time I pictured it, there was no one else in the frame. It was me I saw riding a bus, my head leant against the sun-warmed window. It was me who would be getting lost in the dusty heat of a city. It was me who would be swimming in a lagoon on my own.

I needed time for myself. If Nick came with me, he'd keep me safe, plan routes, book accommodation, look after me – when I didn't want any of that. I wanted to put myself in the hands of the universe and see what happened.

'I'll wait for you,' he'd told me last night as I'd locked up the beach hut.

'You mustn't. Please,' I'd begged him, burying my face in his neck.

When we'd stepped apart, he'd placed a final kiss on my forehead, almost reverently. He'd cleared his throat and told me, 'Even though we're not together now, Isla, if you have any problems – anything at all – you call me, okay? Whatever it is, wherever you are, whatever time of day or night – please don't be too proud to call. If you need anything, I'm here. Okay?'

I'd felt tears prick at the base of my eyelids. I'd wrapped my arms around him one last time and wondered why the hell I was letting him go.

A flight delay was announced over the airport Tannoy, and I listened to check it wasn't mine. Then I reached into the side pocket of my backpack, and slipped out a silver key that was attached to a small stone by a browning piece of string. 'Here,' I said, handing it to Sarah. 'This is for you.'

'Your beach hut key?'

'I want you to look after it while I'm gone. Use it. Stay there.'

'Really?'

I couldn't bear the thought of the hut standing empty. I wanted it to be used, enjoyed, loved. I looked Sarah squarely in the eye and asked, 'Take care of Nick for me, too?' I paused. 'I want him to be happy.'

Sarah stared at me for a long moment, her gaze moving searchingly across my face. 'Okay.'

I sometimes think about that request and wonder exactly what I meant by it.

What Sarah thought I meant by it.

It's easy to start pondering the possibilities of how life could have turned out differently. What if I'd kept my beach hut key safely tucked in my pocket? What if I'd asked Nick to wait for me? What if I'd never left at all?

They are questions without answers. Beginnings without ends. I don't waste time in that place, not any more. I once thought it was answers I was looking for – but now that I've found them, I realize they're not enough.

I want something far more.

7. SARAH

DAY ONE, 8.15 P.M.

Nick and I eat dinner in silence. Each mouthful of chilli feels like an effort, but I force myself to chew, washing down the food with sips of wine. When we're finished, I clear our plates, grateful for the activity. Jacob's meal is still left on the side, the jacket potato already slumping, the chilli congealing with a dark red film of oil. I stretch clingfilm over the plate and, even though the gas fridge in the beach hut is tiny and already crammed with food, I spend a minute or two crouched down rearranging everything so that I can make room for Jacob's meal. I need everything to be normal.

Yet nothing is normal. Jacob has never disappeared like this. There've been arguments in the past where he's taken himself off for a whole day. Once he didn't come home at all – but he'd at least messaged Nick to say he was staying at a friend's. I let myself hope he's done something similar this time.

I turn to find Nick looking at the clock, his expression serious.

'What are you thinking?'

'We should probably let the police know.'

The knot in my stomach pulls tight. *Police.* Nick – who is always the calm to my storms – is taking this very seriously. He's right, though: the police do need to be informed. I don't know why I'm hesitating. I think it's because it suddenly switches Jacob's disappearance from being a protest by an angry teenager to being potentially worse. Far worse.

'It's quarter past eight,' Nick says. 'Let's give it until nine o'clock.'

Waiting forty-five minutes will make no difference, but we make these small rules and deadlines to give ourselves control in a situation where we have none. 'Okay,' I tell Nick. 'Nine o'clock.'

Nick tells me he's going to get some fresh air. I'm about to say I'll join him, when I catch the tightness of his expression and realize this isn't an invitation. He wants to be alone.

As the door closes behind him, I have a sudden sensation of being trapped here, sealed within the four walls of the hut. Night seems to push right up to the windows. On the sandbank there are no streetlamps or car headlights to diffuse the thick blackness and, on a moonless night like this, the dark is so heavy that it feels like I can't breathe.

Out on the water I catch the flicker of a light, the faint shadow of a boat sliding past. I find myself wondering if it's Isaac's boat – whether he's out there, looking back at me. I shake my head, pull the blinds down, then set about lighting extra candles, placing them on shelves, the kitchen counter and the windowsills. I can't bear to sit down, be static, so I decide to check through Jacob's belongings. I know he took his rucksack with him to Luke's – I remember him slinging it over his shoulder before he stormed out – and I wonder whether he'd packed anything that would indicate he was planning to stay away.

I kneel down and pull out Jacob's drawer. A musty, boyish smell immediately hits me. His iPad is still here, and beside it are a heap of crumpled clothes: unwashed T-shirts mixed in with clean ones, balled-up socks, a pair of jeans with the belt wagging from the loops. Tangled among them is a damp beach towel that sprinkles sand across my lap as I shake it. Out of habit I begin folding things. I set the neatened pile of clothes aside, then pull out an old shoebox that is stuffed with odds and ends: a fin for his paddleboard, a piece of downhaul rope for his windsurfer, a pair of ancient goggles that washed up on the shore a couple of summers ago, a pack of cards that have softened with salt, a collection of bottle tops.

Behind the shoebox are a pair of binoculars housed in a tired black leather case that used to belong to Marley. I remember the times I'd see Marley sitting at the end of the rocks, the binoculars pressed to the bridge of his nose, watching the shorebirds, rapt. He'd run up the beach and I'd hear him on the deck excitedly recounting to Isla what he'd seen. 'A herring gull caught a spider crab in its beak! I saw it, Mummy! Plucked right out of the sea. The crab was almost as heavy as the gull – but he got it. I saw him!'

Isla had gifted the binoculars to Jacob, wanting him to have the thing that Marley treasured the most. I was apprehensive that Jacob wouldn't use them or treasure them in the way she'd hoped – but I was wrong. Jacob loved looking through the lenses, watching the horizon for yachts or passing ships, or seeing a weather front blowing in.

I open the case now and find a slim book tucked inside. *Shorebirds of the Northern Hemisphere.* On the inside cover, I see Marley's handwriting: *Marley Berry, age 8½.* He would be turning seventeen soon. I picture that flyaway blond hair, the dreamy look in his eyes, the way he'd politely touch my hand and say, 'Auntie Sarah, please may I have a drink?' He was a beautiful little boy. My godson. Jacob's best friend. Even as a toddler – when Jacob was bombing around, yanking everything he could reach from cupboards and drawers – I remember how Marley would sit quietly, sucking his fingers, watching with a thoughtful, observant expression. He was a quiet boy – *My little thinker*, Isla used to say – but he was wonderfully happy, too. He could spend hours turning the pages of his storybooks, or playing make-believe with the set of plastic dinosaurs I gave him for his third birthday.

I glance back down at the binoculars in my hands. A lump forms in my throat as I remember Isla using them to search the sea for Marley for days and days after he disappeared. She sat inside her beach hut with the doors closed, her gaze tracked to the rolling water.

I slip the book of shorebirds inside the leather case and return the binoculars to the drawer. Next I pull out Jacob's wash bag. I unzip it and find a toothbrush with worn bristles and a bar of soap stuffed in a plastic bag. Although he hasn't taken it with him, it doesn't mean Jacob didn't plan to stay out overnight, as the small detail of not having a toothbrush or soap with him wouldn't have mattered. There are other things too – a can of deodorant, a razor, a bottle of shampoo. At the bottom there is an open pack of condoms.

I try not to be surprised. I tell myself he is seventeen. He has a girlfriend. It's perfectly fine. I'd be naïve to think they weren't sleeping together.

But, still.

He's my baby.

I zip up the wash bag and pretend I haven't seen.

I'm good at pretending.

In fact, Jacob was the one who pointed that out.

I've almost finished going through Jacob's drawer, when I find something hard nestled in the bottom of a sock. I slip my hand inside and pull out a small metal tin. I used to have a similar tin myself when I was his age, so I know exactly what I'm going to find when I open it.

Inside are a pack of large Rizlas, a pouch of tobacco, and a small polythene bag of what I'm guessing is weed.

I lean back against the foot of the sofa and open the bag, pinching a small amount between my thumb and forefinger. I've never caught him with a joint – but it doesn't come as a surprise to me that he smokes the stuff. Only a fortnight ago he'd returned to the hut one evening with the smell of smoke on his breath. His eyes had that slightly hazy, blood-shot look to them and he'd raided the biscuit tin, and then the crisp drawer.

'Have you been smoking?' I'd asked from the sofa, where I'd stayed up reading.

'Mum, you might wanna hold your application for detective school. The thing about beach fires is that sometimes there is . . . *smoke*.' He gave me a wide, easy smile.

Even though I knew he was lying, I didn't call him on it. Those smiles were rare. He flopped on to the sofa beside me. Up close, I could see his widened pupils, the light slackness to his face. 'Living in a beach hut – we're lucky, aren't we? The sea is just right there. Literally there.'

I let my questions drift away. Stoned or not, I'd liked that pleasant version of my son who sat next to me and actually held a conversation. We talked for a few minutes, reminiscing about past summers. But then I ruined it. 'Was Caz at the party tonight?

'Yeah.'

'She's nice. I like her.' I told myself I should edit my next thought, but it slipped out so quickly, I didn't have the chance. 'Take things slowly, won't you?'

I was worried Jacob might scare Caz off. I'd overheard his last girlfriend telling him, 'You're too possessive, Jacob. You need to back off. I'm your girlfriend, not your wife!'

As Jacob looked at me, his expression changed. He leant towards me, his face pressed up close to mine. I could smell the smoke and alcohol on his breath. He stared at me, eye to eye. His voice was low as he said, 'Intense. Me?'

I opened my mouth to say something, but Jacob burst out laughing. Then he patted me on the shoulder as he stood, saying, 'Great chat, Mum. Really great.'

Now I bring the weed towards my face and inhale.

The nutty, pungent smell takes me back to long evenings lying on the beach with Isla. We'd put a rug down by the shore and lie with our hair fanning around us, blowing smoke rings to the stars. On rainy nights, we'd bundle into her beach hut – Nick, too – and we'd smoke in there, the fumes so strong that we'd be stoned for hours.

It's been years since I skinned up, and my fingers itch to make those practised movements. I almost laugh at the thought of Jacob walking in now to find me smoking a joint. At least it'd be an icebreaker.

I put the weed back in its bag, and return the tin to Jacob's drawer. I'm surprised he didn't take it with him to the party. I commend myself for being relaxed: there are condoms and drugs in his drawer. It's not a parenting dream, but it could be worse.

I have a final rummage to see if I've missed anything, and my hand meets a white envelope. I pull it out, turning it over in my hands. There is no writing anywhere on it. The envelope is not sealed, so I simply lift the flap.

Inside is a wad of cash.

I count out the money. There's exactly five hundred pounds in a mixture of denominations, the notes dirty and used.

Over summer Jacob's been working part-time on the harbour ferry. He does three afternoon shifts a week and makes £70 at the end of it, but I know he's recently spent much of that on a new skateboard. I wonder why he'd need this amount of cash at the beach, when there's nothing to spend it on.

I look again at this envelope of money, wondering what he's doing with it – and why it's in a blank envelope.

I put everything back into his drawer and get to my feet, standing in the centre of the hut. My heart is beating harder now as the facts hit me, one after another: Jacob has not been seen in almost twenty-four hours; his phone isn't connecting; he doesn't appear to have taken any belongings with him. He has condoms, weed, and an envelope filled with money.

I don't commend myself about being relaxed any more.

The moment Nick returns, I show him what I've found.

It's the money that concerns him most. 'Is there anything he'd talked about buying? I don't know, like a new music system? A bike, maybe? Or something he knew we wouldn't want him to get – like a moped?'

'No, nothing.' I've already been through this in my mind, and I can't think of anything Jacob particularly wanted. I've even wondered whether the money was for Caz – to buy her a piece of jewellery, perhaps. She's a girl of expensive tastes, used to being indulged by her father.

'Maybe my parents gave him the money?' Nick suggests.

'No, they gave him twenty pounds,' I say, showing him the birthday card propped on the shelf, a cheque fastened inside. I feel impatient with Nick as he tries to catch up. I hurry him through my thoughts: 'It doesn't make sense that Jacob would have that amount of money here. There's nothing to buy at the beach. Anyway, most people make big purchases by card. Plus the money was in an envelope. Doesn't that strike you as odd? It's as if . . . I don't know . . . as if he was going to give it to someone.'

'Or,' Nick says, 'someone gave it to him.'

I press my lips together. I've told Nick about the weed, but neither of us have verbalized the possibility that the money could be linked to Jacob *selling* drugs – although the thought hovers in the back of my mind.

It's past nine o'clock when we finally ring the police. Nick makes the call on speakerphone at my request.

I stand with my back pressed against the kitchen side, my hands clasped as I listen to Nick answering their questions. As soon as he utters the words, 'male, seventeen', I can practically hear the sense of urgency slipping from the officer's tone.

If Jacob were a girl, I can't help but think the officer would be sitting up straighter, listening harder.

Then I have to ask myself, if Jacob had been a girl, maybe I would have called the police sooner, too. Maybe I'd have called first thing in the morning when Jacob didn't come home – rather than waiting all day.

Why the hell have we waited? I wouldn't forgive myself if Jacob has had an accident and Nick and I delayed until now before doing anything about it. My mind fires with images of Jacob trapped between the rocks, with his ankle bent at an unnatural angle, or crumpled at the base of the headland, tonnes of earth and sand heaped on top of him.

The officer tells Nick that they'll send someone out tonight, so Nick has to explain for a second time that he's phoning from a beach hut on Longstone Sandbank. 'The earliest you can reach us is first thing in the morning when the ferry starts running at eight o'clock.' It always seems strange to me that many local people don't visit the sandbank – often don't even know where it is.

When the call is over, Nick places his mobile on the kitchen counter. We look at each other – but neither of us speaks.

So now a missing person's file will be opened. There will be a case number. Officers at the beach. It feels as if I've been swimming away from the shore, being pulled unknowingly by a current, and now that I've turned to look back, I can see how very far away I am.

8. SARAH

DAY TWO, 7.15 A.M.

I sleep fitfully, listening for the sound of the beach hut doors opening, Jacob's feet moving across the floor – but the footsteps never arrive. I wake unrested, my heart heavy.

Nick is already out of bed, looping a beach towel around his neck and slipping outside, disappearing into a shaft of light. He'll swim out to the yellow buoy and back, then rinse the salt from his skin at the shower block. Usually he'd catch the first ferry to the quay at eight, and be in the office before the rest of his employees. Today, though, he won't be going into the office. He'll return to the hut and wait for the police to arrive.

I climb out of bed and set the kettle on the hob, in need of a hit of coffee. When I pull up the blinds, dust motes dance in the spill of sunlight. Outside, I can see the wind is up, the sea choppy. The patch of blue sky hovering above us will soon be swallowed by the thickening clouds.

I fold the sofa bed away, going through the motions of plumping the cushions and positioning them the way I like them. When Nick puts the bed away, the cushions are slung on to the sofa in any order – his silent protest that there are too many. Cushions. Did I really care about the positioning of cushions?

I hook back the beach hut doors so that the breeze can wash in and out. The sandbank is slowly yawning awake; two young girls from a few huts away are already playing by the rocks in their pyjamas, hair tangled over their shoulders. I try not to envy their parents: *Your children are there. Right there!*

Once I've made myself a coffee, I set the steaming mug beside the notebook I've dug out. The police will be here soon and I want to use the time I have productively. I fetch a pen and begin writing a list of all the people who could have seen Jacob on the day he disappeared.

Disappeared. Is that even the right word?

I start by listing the people who were at the family barbecue. There were only six of us: Me, Nick, Jacob, Isla, and Nick's parents, David and Stella.

Next, I think about his friends at the party at Luke's hut. I sip at the scalding coffee, realizing I only know the names of four or five of them, so I add a note to speak to both Luke and Caz again today. There are now eleven names on my sheet of paper, and I like looking at the neat structure of it – it gives me something practical I can work through.

I want to speak to each of these people and find out if they noticed anything unusual about Jacob's behaviour that evening, whether he gave any clue as to where he was going.

I will need to spread the net wider than the sandbank, as he could have hidden out for the night, then taken the first ferry off the sandbank in the morning. *I must ask the ferryman, Ross Wayman, if he remembers seeing Jacob*, I think as an aside, adding his name to the list.

It's also possible that Jacob left the sandbank in the middle of the night without using the ferry; if you know the route through the wooded path, you can walk across the headland, which takes just over an hour on foot.

If Jacob has left – who would he choose to visit, and why? His closest friends are here on the beach. There's family, I suppose. Jacob gets on well with his aunties and uncles – but both Nick's brothers live in America with their families; east coast for Ted and Linda, west coast for Brian, Sally and their twins. The only family member who lives nearby is my mother and, although she's very fond of Jacob, I don't think she'd have been his first choice of refuge. Apart from our visits on her birthday and at Christmas, we see very little of her.

I glance down guiltily, picturing my mother sitting at the large mahogany dining table, with a crystal water jug on the table and the best silver cutlery laid out ready for a breakfast for one. The house is far too big for her now. I imagine the clink of her spoon against her china bowl, the sound ringing out in all that deafening silence. I don't know how she can bear it.

I suddenly want to call her – to tell her about Jacob.

I take out my mobile, not caring that it's early.

When she answers, the sound of her voice causes a lump of emotion to rise in my throat. 'Oh Mum,' I begin . . .

The police said they'd arrive on the first ferry, but they don't. It's ten o'clock when they finally trudge across the beach, their dark uniforms looking incongruous against the backdrop of the sea.

'Sarah Symonds?' the male officer asks, approaching our hut.

'Yes, that's me.'

Next door, Diane pauses from sweeping the deck to watch, eyes narrowing with interest.

I glare at her, irritated.

'I'm Police Constable Steven Evans.' A thin man with delicate, almost effeminate features, and a round nub of a chin, steps on to the deck, stretching out a pale hand, which I shake. 'And this is PC Jacqui Roam,' he says, introducing the woman at his side. She is about ten years younger than me, with thin brown hair in a plain bob, and pencilled-in eyebrows. There are dark circles beneath her eyes and the purple traces of acne scars around her chin and mouth. Her cheeks are flushed from the walk and, when she smiles, her eyes show warmth.

'Come in.' I usher them inside and point to the sofa. I imagine Diane will be lingering on her deck still. I want to pull our beach hut doors shut so that there's nothing to overhear, but it's already too warm inside.

PC Jacqui Roam whistles through her teeth. 'Beautiful beach hut. I didn't realize they were so spacious inside. And there's an upstairs, too?' She glances up at the wooden stepladder leading to the mezzanine.

It's what always surprises people the first time they step inside the huts. From the outside, the beach huts look little more than colourful sheds, but inside they are like miniature homes. Usually I would chat easily about the layout of the beach hut, or show them the view from the porthole window upstairs – but the only thing I want to talk about right now is Jacob.

Sensing this, PC Evans takes out his notebook and a black biro. 'Let's start with the details.'

'My husband will be in shortly. He's just finishing up a call,' I say glancing towards the shoreline, where Nick is pacing. He's on the phone to his office and looks tense, preoccupied. He stares at the ground as he moves, his right hand gesturing blindly at his side. Occasionally his hand travels to his hairline, which he half-heartedly rubs. He should be in this beach hut with me, his hand holding mine. I try to catch his eye to let him know the police are here, but he doesn't glance up.

PC Evans begins by running through a long list of questions about Jacob – most of which Nick covered when he rang the station last night. He makes notes about Jacob's eye colour, whether he's right or left handed, the details of his social media accounts, his mobile telephone number, his access to funds. The list goes on and on.

PC Roam then takes over, asking, 'Sarah, why don't you tell us everything you can about the day of your son's disappearance?'

I sit up straight and clasp my hands together. I speak in

a clear, precise voice, wanting to give them all the facts as succinctly and exactly as possible. I tell them it was Jacob's seventeenth birthday and that we opened presents and had a family barbecue with Nick's parents and Jacob's godmother. Then I describe Jacob's plans to go to Luke's party that evening for some birthday drinks. I explain that I've talked to Luke, who told me that Jacob left the party at around eleven with his girlfriend, Caz, although Luke believed Jacob planned on returning to the party. I then repeat what I overheard – that Caz was very drunk – and that she and Jacob walked along the beach, then stopped at the rocks at the edge of bay, which I point to through the beach hut doors. I add that there may have been a disagreement, and that Caz then went back to her beach hut, leaving Jacob there. 'That was the last time he's been seen.'

I pass PC Evans the list of names I have written down, along with contact details, and – where relevant – the number of their beach huts. I have done my homework. I want to make things as easy as possible for the police.

PC Roam leans forward. 'How has Jacob seemed to you, lately? What sort of mood has he been in?' When she talks, her pencilled brows lift and dip above her eyes.

'He's been a little distracted,' I admit. 'I think it's his girlfriend. My husband and I think it might be *love*.'

'Things were . . . going well between them?' PC Roam asks.

Earlier in the week I'd been washing up breakfast dishes, while Jacob sat slumped in the deckchair, his feet resting on the balcony railing, binoculars pressed to his face. 'What are you looking at?'

Jacob whipped the binoculars away and turned to glare at me, as if shocked by my audacious attempt at communicating with him. 'Nothing. A cormorant.' He pushed himself up, his height still taking me by surprise. 'I'm gonna see Luke,' he'd grunted, then climbed from the deck and loped away across the beach.

Exhausted by the constant sensation that I needed to walk on eggshells, I'd settled into the deckchair he'd vacated and sighed.

Jacob had left his binoculars perched on the deck railing, so I picked them up and held them to my face, pointing them in the direction he'd been looking.

I squinted along the shoreline, looking for a cormorant. Joe and Binks were talking to Lorrain and Isla, who'd just come in from a swim and, beyond them, I saw what had caught Jacob's attention: Caz was sitting on the shoreline in her bikini, between two boys. She had her head tipped back, laughing. Then she playfully slapped one of the boys. I remember thinking then: jealousy can be a toxic emotion.

I knew that very well.

Now I answer PC Roam. 'Jacob doesn't talk to me about his love life. *Obviously*,' I say, imitating his gruff tone. I've no idea why I'm trying so hard to make the officers like me. Maybe I think they'll put more effort into finding Jacob. 'I imagine that there were the normal jealousies and arguments and make-ups.'

PC Roam nods, then asks, 'What about your relationship with Jacob? How were things between the two of you?'

'Fine. Everything was fine,' I say, and I wonder if I've answered too brightly.

PC Roam's mobile rings and she glances at the screen. When she flicks it to silent, apologizing for the interruption, I catch a glimpse of her screen saver – a picture of a round-faced baby smiling with a bib on. So she's a mother, too. I wonder who her child is with while she's at work, and how hard she must find it to leave.

When she looks up, I catch her eye and she seems to read my thoughts. She smiles.

'And where were you and your husband the night you last saw Jacob?' PC Evans asks.

'I was here in the beach hut. Went to bed early.'

'So the last time you saw Jacob was when he left for the drinks party at Luke's hut around –' he looks at his pad – 'eight o'clock.'

'That's correct. My husband left an hour before that. He had to drive to Bristol ready for a pitch on Monday morning and he wanted to miss the traffic.' As I'm talking about Nick, I hear the tread of his footsteps across the deck, and the three of us turn.

'Nick Symonds,' he says, offering his hand to both officers in turn.

'We were just hearing about your whereabouts on the night Jacob was last seen. Your wife tells us you were in Bristol.'

'Yes, that's right.' I pour Nick a glass of water while he gives the officers the details of his hotel and meeting.

I must have tuned out for a moment, because all of a sudden PC Evans is saying to me, 'You and your son had words, did you?'

I turn, blinking into the spotlight of his question.

I'm aware of Nick's brows drawing together as he looks at me, no doubt surprised that I have not shared this detail with the police. 'Oh, well, we did, I suppose,' I say to PC Evans, trying to smile. 'Nothing important – just curfew time. You know what teenagers can be like.'

Through the corner of my eyes, I can see Nick staring at me, bewildered.

I panic. I can't remember what I'd said the argument was about to Nick. It wasn't curfew time. Why did I tell the police that? I should have stuck to the same story. I can feel heat creeping up my throat, clawing into my cheeks.

Then it comes back to me: 'He also got a bit of a lecture about using his phone when I'm talking to him. Nothing serious. He left in a bit of a huff – but that's nothing unusual! He's seventeen!'

PC Roam saves me by smiling.

I daren't look at Nick, but I hope he's bought it, too.

PC Evans asks, 'Have there been any signs that Jacob may be depressed?'

'No, not at all,' Nick answers. 'Not to my mind, at least. Sarah?'

I shake my head. Jacob can be moody and challenging, but I wouldn't say he's depressed.

'And has he ever suffered from any mental health problems?'

'No,' we both answer.

'Have you been through Jacob's belongings?' PC Evans asks. 'Noticed anything missing? A laptop, passport, wallet, clothes – anything that stands out?'

'Jacob left the beach hut with his rucksack,' I tell them,

'but then he always takes it if he's going to a friend's hut for the evening.'

'What do you think was in it?'

'Not much – probably just his wallet and phone, and I think a blue hoodie. I couldn't find it in his drawer. I've checked through his things here, and no other clothes look like they've been taken, or his wash stuff. He doesn't have a laptop any more, just uses an iPad. That's still here, too.' I explain that our house is rented out during the summer holidays and all our other belongings are stored in the garage. The police suggest we visit this afternoon to be sure nothing is missing.

'If it's okay, we'd like to take Jacob's iPad with us. Just procedure,' PC Evans adds.

'Course,' I say.

Nick turns to me. 'Have you told them about the weed in Jacob's drawer, yet?

'Not yet,' I say tightly. *What is he thinking?* 'It was just a tiny amount,' I tell the police. 'We've never seen Jacob with any before. He's not into *drugs* – we'd know. I imagine he's just experimenting. He's at the age, isn't he?'

'Could we see?' PC Evans asks.

I move to the drawer, fuming with Nick. This gives completely the wrong impression of Jacob. I take out Jacob's tin and pass it to PC Evans. He opens it and looks inside, his expression giving nothing away.

'What I did want to show you was this,' I say, pulling out the envelope with the cash inside. 'There's five hundred pounds here. To be honest, I've no idea where it came from, or what Jacob is doing with it.'

I hand it to PC Evans, swapping it for the tin. He looks

through the money, asking whether Jacob had a job, or savings, or whether there's anyone who may have given him this sum of money. Nick and I share what we'd discussed, and the officer notes it down.

There are a few further formalities to go through, including the police conducting a brief search of the hut. They snap on blue plastic gloves, and move through the small space looking in the drawers and cupboards that I have already turned out.

'If you don't mind,' PC Evans says a few minutes later, as he climbs down the ladder from the mezzanine, his knees creaking, 'we'd like to take Jacob's toothbrush with us.' I must look surprised by the request, as he elaborates, 'It's just procedure. For his DNA.'

A flash of horror passes across Nick's face as he, like me, realizes why the police require this. I fetch the toothbrush, looking away as PC Evans takes out a clear plastic bag to seal it within.

PC Roam requests a photo of Jacob. Nick takes out his phone and shows them a selection of shots. The police choose one, and Nick emails the image straight over to them. It's a recent picture of Jacob wading in from the sea. His dark hair is pushed back from his face, and his skin glows in the way that it does after a day in the sunshine. He looks handsome in the photo, and I like it too, because he looks young. Not seventeen. Fresh-faced and innocent.

As they are closing up their notebooks, getting to their feet, PC Roam asks, 'Can you think of anyone who may have a grudge against him? Anyone who has ever threatened him, or would have a particular interest in him?'

The questions catch me off guard, and I open my mouth, but can't think of what I intended to say.

It is Nick who steps forward. 'No. Absolutely not. No one would want to hurt him.'

PC Roam looks at me for a moment and I wonder what she sees.

Then she nods.

Both officers thank us for our time and tell us they'll be in touch.

I stand in the doorway of the beach hut, watching as the police walk away.

Nick folds his arms across his chest. 'That seemed to go okay.'

'Yes,' I agree. In the hour the police have been here, I've only had to lie to them twice.

9. ISLA

Sarah never used to lie. Not to me, anyway. There was a time when we told each other everything. There were no secrets between us – it was what made us work. Maybe that's what it means to have a best friend – someone you can be wholeheartedly and unashamedly honest with. You can lay yourself bare to them – and they will love you, no matter what. That's how it felt for us.

I wonder when we stopped sharing everything. There wasn't a specific event, not that I remember, anyway. I suppose it's natural that over time allegiances shift. When we were younger, there was a large, clear space in our lives reserved solely for each other. But then other people moved into our worlds – a lover for me, a husband for Sarah, our children – and the space we'd carved for each other began to reshape, shrink, like a withering balloon that loses air so slowly that you don't notice until it is hanging limp, lifeless, a deflated reminder that the celebration is over.

Summer 2000

Sarah's fingers were gripped around the rope barrier, her head tilted forward, peering past the stream of people flooding through the arrivals gate.

I hesitated: it'd been eighteen months since she'd dropped me at the airport – and so much had changed. She looked different from the Sarah I'd left behind; this new Sarah was more sophisticated, with a sleek haircut that feathered around her face, sunglasses pushed on top of her head. Her skin was tanned and smooth and she was wearing an empire-line blue dress that flowed over her pregnant stomach.

I felt my fingers lightly brush the swell of my own stomach.

Yes, so much had changed.

When Sarah spotted me, she beamed, ducking under the barrier, hurrying towards me, squealing.

We held tight to each other, our pregnant stomachs adding a strange awkwardness to the embrace, as if we couldn't quite get close enough. 'You're here! You're here!' she kept on saying. Her hands moved to my bump, clutching it. 'I can't believe it,' she said, her voice choked with emotion. 'We're both having babies!'

Standing back on home soil, it suddenly felt very real. 'We're going to be *mothers*!' We hugged again.

'God, I missed you,' Sarah said. When I stepped back, she took my hand, turning me in a circle. 'Look at you, beautiful girl!'

My long skirt flowed around my ankles, and my hair had grown almost to my waist. My skin had tanned to a deep mahogany, the pregnancy bringing out a cluster of freckles across the bridge of my nose.

'I thought I'd never get you back. Nick and I were planning how we'd hunt you down.'

Nick and I. It felt painfully fresh, like the sting of soap on newly shaved skin.

I caught sight of Sarah's engagement ring glittering on her slim hand. I screwed my eyes up in mock bedazzlement. 'Check out that diamond!'

'I know!' she beamed, waggling her fingers.

On the drive home, we talked non-stop. I was relieved that there was no lull in conversation, no awkward pauses – we snapped back into our old rhythm as if I'd never been away.

'Tell me about Cubbie,' she said, one hand on the steering wheel, the other squeezing my knee.

'We met in Nepal. He's from Norway. God, Sarah, he was beautiful. Truly the most beautiful man I've ever seen. He had thick blond hair that he wore long, and this lovely regal nose – straight and long and perfect.'

'Good genes, then.'

'Here's hoping! Three days, though – that was all we spent together. We were staying in the same homestead. After that he travelled north, and I headed south.'

'You let him go?'

'I didn't know then. It was only a couple of months later that I began to suspect I was pregnant. We'd not swapped numbers, or addresses – nothing. I don't even know his second name. Is that awful? I travelled back to the homestead to track him down, and left messages on the pin-boards of hostels asking if anyone knew of him, but I couldn't find him.' I'd agonized over Cubbie, unsettled by the idea that he'd never know he was to become a father. Eventually I had to accept there was nothing I could do, no way of locating him. I pressed my palms against the tiny swell of my stomach and promised my baby that I would make it up to him or her. That I would be everything.

When we pulled up at the house Sarah now shared with Nick, she cut the engine, then reached across and squeezed my fingers hard. 'Nick and I. Are you sure?'

'I've told you a thousand—'

'I know. But I want you to look me in the eye and tell me. Not over the phone. Not by letter. Face to face. Are you certain?'

I pulled up her sunglasses, and pressed the tip of my nose against hers, staring her right in the eyes. 'I'm certain.'

She exhaled with relief.

'Anyway, bit late for me to change my mind, don't you think?' I said, pointing to her bump.

Sarah had talked to me about Nick from the start. When I'd called from a hostel in Goa, she'd told me about their first drunken kiss at The Rope and Anchor. Later, I think I was travelling north into the mountains, when she told me, 'There've been more kisses, Isla. If I told you I thought I was falling for him, how would you feel?' I was thousands of miles away, hiking through rice terraces, sleeping on overnight buses with my head on the shoulders of travellers I'd only known for hours. My relationship with Nick was a fond, warm memory. I cared about him deeply – but I didn't ache for him. 'I'd be happy for you both,' I'd told her, and meant it.

By the time I phoned Sarah again, three or four months later, she told me that Nick had proposed. 'He laid a picnic rug on the beach, and when he opened the hamper, there was a ring box inside! We're engaged.'

Engaged. The word caught me off-guard, like a fist in the stomach. I managed to catch my breath and smile as I said, 'Congratulations.'

At seven months pregnant, I knelt on the beach, scooping my hands into the damp sand. The sun was warm on my back, and I could feel the weight of the baby shifting within me.

I made two large holes, sculpting them smooth with my palms. 'Done!' I called to Sarah, who was walking towards the shore carrying a jug of cordial and a bowl of strawberries. In her bikini, her bump protruded so neatly it looked as if she'd swallowed a beach ball. I carried wide, and everyone told me I was having a girl because of the extra width at my hips, and the new thickness to my thighs.

I lay our beach towels side by side, covering the holes I'd dug. 'You go first.'

Sarah, who was eight months pregnant to my seven, put the tray down, then knelt forward, gradually lowering herself on to the beach towel, her rounded stomach disappearing into the bump-sized hole. She made a low sound of pleasure at the back of her throat. 'I will love you forever for this.'

I positioned myself next to her, my bump fitting snugly into the groove beneath my beach towel. It'd been months since I'd been able to lie on my front. At night, the only way I could get comfy was by lying on my right-hand side with a pillow gripped between my knees, and another wedged beneath my bump.

For a while, the two of us lay in silence, enjoying the bliss of stretching out flat. I lazily flicked the crescents of sand from beneath each of my fingernails, and every so often I'd feel the baby kick, a powerful little jab just below my ribs.

Sarah and I were spending most of our time at the sandbank. Nick's parents had bought a holiday home in Spain, so had gifted their beach hut to Nick and Sarah. I'd picked up a part-time job waitressing but, whenever I wasn't working, I'd be at the beach hut.

Sarah turned her head towards me, her cheek pressed into the beach towel. I could see the gold flecks in the green of her irises and smell strawberries on her breath. 'You, Isla Berry, are a genius. Thank God you're home.'

I grinned and squeezed her fingers. Sarah and I both looked up at the sound of Nick's voice. 'I'm looking for two pregnant women. I know they headed this way. Have you seen them?'

'Nope. Not seen them,' I said.

'Now stop blocking our sun,' Sarah told him.

He stepped aside, then stripped off his T-shirt and looked out over the water as if contemplating a swim. Then, as if he thought better of it, he patted his stomach and said, 'Reckon you can make me one of those sand holes?'

It would be easy, I'd thought back then. The three of us would be best friends. We could make it work.

And maybe we would have done if Samuel had stayed in

my life. If Marley had, too. Maybe, when they left, the space I carved for Sarah and Nick became too big – held too much weight – and it set the balance all wrong.

Or maybe it wasn't my fault at all.

Maybe it was Sarah's.

10. SARAH

DAY TWO, 11.45 A.M.

After the police leave, I step out on to the deck, my legs trembling. A sharp caw sounds above, and I glance up to see a solitary gull gliding, beady eyes watchful.

'Shall we walk?' Nick says from behind me.

I nod quickly. I can't bear to sit and wait in that hut for one more moment.

As we move off, we pass Joe and Binks's hut. Binks is dozing in her deckchair, her mouth slightly ajar. Next to her, Joe is squinting at a crossword that he holds at arm's length. The normalcy of the scene is disorientating – like stumbling out of a darkened cinema into the blaze of the foyer.

'Hello, both!' Joe chirps.

Binks wakes at the sound of our voices, lightly touching the corners of her mouth. 'Sarah. Nick.' Binks would hate anyone to catch her dozing; at seventy-seven years young she still takes her grandchildren kayaking, and swims several lengths of our bay each morning.

Nick pauses in front of their deck, and I can sense he is about to tell them about Jacob. I push my hands deep into my pockets, somehow unready for this to become public.

'Don't know if you saw the police at our hut earlier,' Nick says, 'but Jacob's missing.'

'What?' Joe sits forward in his chair. 'Since when?'

'He didn't come back to the hut after a beach party on Sunday night.'

I can see them calculating that it's now Tuesday morning. Joe gets to his feet, knees clicking. He stands with a hand on the deck railing. 'What do the police say?'

I lift my shoulders. 'That most missing people come back of their own accord.'

'They're going to make some enquiries,' Nick follows. 'You haven't seen Jacob since Sunday night, have you?'

Joe and Binks look at each other. 'Sunday night?' Binks repeats. 'It was Jacob's birthday, wasn't it? We saw you all out on the beach having that lovely barbecue in the afternoon. We commented on it, didn't we? Thought how nice it was that Isla joined you – what with it being the anniversary.'

There it is. *Anniversary.* The word that Nick and I haven't been mentioning. The word we didn't bring up in front of the police, because surely it is just a coincidence that Jacob disappeared on that day.

Everyone who's been on the sandbank for long enough knows about what happened seven years ago. Joe and Binks were there on the shoreline – they saw the lifeboat out in the water, felt the sand lifting around them as it was caught in the updraught of the coastguard helicopter.

Everyone remembers because what happened rocked the whole beach hut community.

'No, we haven't seen Jacob since that evening,' Joe confirms. 'But he'll turn up. Course he will.'

Binks asks, 'Is there anything we can do to help?'

'The police are taking care of things for now,' I tell them. 'Like you say, I'm sure he'll be back before we know it.' I say it with such ease that no one would guess my hands are shaking within my pockets.

The sandbank ends at the base of a wooded headland. We follow the weaving path of steps that are shaded by a canopy of rangy trees, ferns and brambles. I count the steps. I've always worked well with numbers. If I feel my thoughts starting to unravel, I count things – the number of tiles on one side of a shower, the bricks in a section of wall, the number of flowers on a patterned skirt.

Ninety-eight steps.

By the time we reach the top, the muscles in the backs of my thighs feel warm. The view sweeps open around us, the harbour lying silent beneath a heavy grey sky – just a whisper of brightness remaining on the horizon. The air, dense with moisture, hangs above the landscape, compressing it. I can feel the weight of it, as if it's squeezing the breath from my lungs, muffling the songs of the birds, quietening the sea. The purple tips of heather are still in the windless air, and the scent of gorse and ferns is thick. From here, the huts look no more than monopoly pieces. I can't help but wonder if Jacob is down there, stowed away in someone's beach hut, or camped out in the woodland.

I'd had such high hopes about this summer, imagining our family playing cards by candlelight late into the evening, or laughing around a barbecue cooking fresh fish. I pictured Nick with a tan, finally losing that pinched expression that has settled around his eyes. The beach hut, I'd thought, would be the answer. When mothers from Jacob's college asked about our summer plans, it was hard to explain why we chose to spend it in a beach hut, where the fickle British weather is master of our days. There are things I love – that sense of freedom when my shoes are kicked off, my feet pushed deep into the sand – and there are things I loathe, like the grit of sand in the bed, and cooking on a temperamental two-ringed hob. But what brings us back here, summer after summer, is that the beach hut unites our family. The three of us are enclosed in one space; there are no doors to hide behind; Jacob can't disappear to his room, or have his attention absorbed by the television. For a few weeks of the year, we step out of the rush of our normal lives and live outside-in, letting the rhythms of the weather and tides rule our days.

Our first weekend in the hut this summer had been beautifully warm. Jacob was in a bright mood – probably because college would be a distant memory for the next eight weeks. I'd been swimming and was pleased that I wasn't quite as unfit as I'd imagined. As I was about to wade out, I saw Jacob jogging down the beach in his swim-shorts. 'Mum! You're actually in the sea!' he laughed. With the sun on his face, he looked happy, handsome. 'Stay in?'

I hadn't planned to; I was already chilled to the bone, but it was such a rarity that Jacob wanted my company that I said, 'Okay.'

As he bounded into the water, I dived down to the sea bed and kicked my legs up in the air, performing a wobbly handstand.

When I surfaced, Jacob was laughing at my poor attempt. I smiled with my teeth together, then squirted water in his face, a trick I used to love playing on him when he was a boy. Jacob slapped his hand across the surface, sending a spray of water towards me.

Laughing, I splashed back at him.

Jacob rushed forward, gripping my shoulders, and ducked me under.

I hadn't expected his strength or the sudden weight of him. Salt water shot up my nose and burst into my mouth. I writhed beneath his grip.

I could only have been under for a matter of seconds, but when Jacob released me, I surfaced gasping, hair pasted to my face.

He reared back, the laughter gone. He lifted his hands in the air. 'Sorry, Mum. Are you okay? Sorry . . .'

I wanted to tell him, *It's okay, I'm fine*, but I couldn't catch my breath to speak.

We stood in the shallows facing each other. Then, without a word, Jacob turned and waded out.

'Jacob!' I called after him. 'Stay! I'm fine . . .'

He didn't turn back. He jogged up the beach and disappeared inside the hut.

By the time I was out of the sea and had made my way

into the beach hut, Jacob was gone, leaving puddles of salt water on the floor and a damp towel thrown over the deck railings.

'Should we have told the police about the anniversary?' Nick asks.

I don't turn, but I know my husband is looking at me. 'I didn't think it was important,' I say. The words sound like a lie – and I wonder if they are.

'Jacob might not show it,' Nick says, 'but he still takes it hard.'

A sudden image pops into my head of Jacob and Marley with their crab nets and buckets, sitting on the jetty, mud-streaked legs hanging towards the water, scoring the size of the crabs they caught. *That was a nine and a half. Look at its claws. It could tear boats out of the sea.*

'He blames himself,' Nick says.

My blood freezes. I'm not sure I've heard right.

'He doesn't talk about Marley, does he? But I'm certain he still thinks about him. Marley shaped his life. What other seventeen year old would happily use a pair of binoculars to study birds? He does it because it's his link to Marley.'

'He was ten,' I say. My voice is a whisper.

'I know. I know that. But Jacob probably feels guilty: he made it – Marley didn't. Isn't there some disorder that people who live through a tragedy can suffer?'

'Survivor guilt,' I say, having looked into it some time ago. Signs of it can include anxiety, depression and guilt, linked to an experience where an individual survived a traumatic event when others didn't. 'I don't think Jacob suffers from it. He's never struck me as depressed or particularly anxious.'

'Maybe not, but then would we even know? Jacob's not exactly a sharer, is he?'

'We'd know,' I say.

'Has he talked to you about Marley recently?'

My mouth turns dry. I shake my head.

'He hasn't mentioned his name in front of me – not for a while. But then,' Nick shakes his head, 'I never bring up Marley. Maybe I should. Maybe we should both be talking about him more. We don't want what happened to seem like something that should have to crouch in the shadows. It was a desperate, desperate tragedy, but really it's up to us to keep celebrating Marley's memory, isn't it?'

I manage to nod.

'We should ring Isla.'

I start. 'Why?'

'Jacob's close to her.'

The comment stings in a way it shouldn't.

'Jacob's confided in her in the past,' Nick continues. 'They often talk together about Marley, don't they?'

It was true. Sometimes I wondered if it wasn't good for Jacob. He would share a memory of Marley, and I'd watch the way Isla's face would light up with gratitude as if he'd given her the greatest gift.

Nick continues, 'I heard him this summer reminiscing with Isla about that time he and Marley found that old windsurfing board washed up in our bay.'

'When they cited scavengers' rights,' I add.

Nick smiles to himself. 'The boys were so close.'

My heart clenches. Could Marley's anniversary really have triggered Jacob's disappearance?

'Maybe Isla can think of something that'll help us,' Nick says. 'Jacob might have mentioned something to her.'

'I'm not sure if her mobile works over there.'

'Course it will.'

Isla has been living and working in Chile for the past four years. She originally went there on a hiking holiday to Patagonia – but fell in love with the country and ended up working as a teacher at an international school. When she's away, we rarely ring each other. We tell ourselves that ours is the sort of friendship that's unchanged by long distance: when she's back, she's back. But I can't help wondering whether, like me, Isla feels a sense of relief when we part. Summers on the sandbank have always had an intensity to them, our friendship blooming in the heat, living in each other's pockets for the summer stretch. When autumn arrives and the huts are swept out, boarded up ready for the winter, we each disappear back to our own lives, and I like that – the flow of the seasons mirroring our friendship.

I was definitely ready to see her go this time.

'Are you going to call her?' Nick asks.

I think of the things we said to each other before she left. But with Nick at my shoulder, I can't hesitate. I take out my mobile and turn so my back is to the wind. 'What's the time difference in Chile?' I ask. 'It could be the middle of the night.'

'I've no idea. Isla won't mind. This is important.'

I nod. Press *Call*.

There is long pause, and then the phone begins to ring.

I glance at Nick. He's watching, expectant.

I wait, a hand pressed to my other ear to block out the wind.

In my head I am silently pleading: *Don't pick up.*

11. ISLA

Sarah's name flashes across my mobile like a warning. I stare at the screen dispassionately. I can imagine what she's going to say. In truth, I'm surprised she's waited this long.

Eventually my voicemail intercepts the call. Sarah leaves a message, but rather than listening to it, I return the phone to the drawer. I don't want to hear her voice. I don't even want to think about her – because right now I'm back in a comfortable, warm place of memory. I'm with Marley. My beautiful newborn Marley, with the sweet scent of milk on his skin, a tiny pink fist gripped around my finger. All I want to think about is the moment he burst into my world. My light, my joy, my son.

Summer 2000

As the next contraction crashed through my body, I dragged my focus to my breath. I pushed the air from my open mouth, then sucked a new breath deep into my lungs. In. Out. In. Out. My fists were clenched rocks at my side, my skin licked with salt.

The contraction subsided, like a wave petering out. The midwife resumed rolling a pair of dark-green flight socks up my calves. 'The anaesthetist won't be long now.'

I pressed my lips tight, nodding.

Right then – more than anything in the world – I wanted my mother.

I'd been labouring for forty-two hours, but the baby's head had become jammed in the birthing canal. His heart rate was dropping with each contraction, and there was no way of pushing the baby out naturally.

'You'll stay with me?'

The midwife took my hand tight in her own and said, 'I'm going to be there until the moment that baby is put in your arms.'

I felt the next ripple of pain building and pulled my focus back to my breathing, jamming my fists into the bed as the full contraction ripped through my body.

When I was finally wheeled into the operating theatre, there was a room full of people in scrubs and masks. I didn't care that I'd envisaged giving birth in a water-pool with calming music playing. All I wanted was my baby safe in my arms.

I felt the blissful relief of painlessness as the anaesthetic flooded through me. It was seconds – that was all it took to cut me open. The midwife stayed at my side as she promised, keeping up a steady stream of conversation. Although I was numb from the chest down, I felt the exact moment when the baby was lifted out of me; it was astounding, I felt it, a strange lightness as the weight was removed. I waited, eyes tracked to the corner of the small room, listening. And then I heard it: a tiny mewing cry.

Someone said the word: *boy.*

He was brought to me, naked and red-skinned, his dark hair matted to his head. He was placed on my chest, a tiny squished creature with a swollen puckered mouth, and the love that rocked through me was fierce and primeval. I kissed his face, and through my tears and kisses words slid from my mouth – promises of love that I meant wholly. My newborn son – Marley – opened his eyes and looked right at me. In that moment it was perfect. He was perfect.

'Go carefully,' Nick said, holding open the car door.

I inched my way in, the wound from my Caesarean burning with each adjustment.

'Here, don't twist.' Nick leant across me to put my seat belt on. He closed my door, then rounded the car and got into the driver's seat, pulling the door shut, sealing the three of us inside. 'You ready?'

I glanced in the rear-view mirror. Marley, swamped in a fleece all-in-one, was fast asleep in his car seat. I smiled. My son. 'Ready.'

I'd spent four days on the antenatal ward watching the stream of fathers and grandparents flood in during visiting hours. Sometimes I pictured my mother padding in, a hessian bag filled with goodies swinging from her shoulder, the waft of a health food store lingering in her clothes. I wanted, so much, for her to tell me how well I'd done. That I'd be a good mother. She'd have scooped Marley out of his plastic cot, clutched him to her, and whispered, *You're the most wonderful creature I've ever set eyes on.*

Nick started the engine and we pulled out into a busy lane of traffic. As Nick drove, I looked at him properly for the first time; he hadn't shaved in days and there were deep bags beneath his eyes – yet he somehow looked happier than ever.

'How's Jacob?' I asked. He had been born three weeks before – a little dark-haired sprite who'd slipped into the world in a birthing pool, a week late.

Nick grinned. 'Beautiful. Exhausting. Mind-blowing.'

We both have boys, I thought, feeling a burst of emotion for the future I saw ahead for them.

'Thank you for collecting me,' I said to Nick. 'But don't think about going into the taxi business – we're going the wrong way.'

Nick smiled. 'You and Marley are coming to our house.'

'Absolutely not. You've got Jacob to—'

'No point protesting: the spare room is already made up. Sarah and I have talked about it; you've just had major surgery, Isla. You can't drive for six weeks. You can't lift. What are you going to do on your own in the flat? You shouldn't even be carrying him up and down the stairs yet. We *want* you and Marley to stay.'

I was renting a studio flat above a florist's on the high street. Yes, the stairs would be tricky, but the flat itself was comfortable enough, and the sweet scent of cut flowers drifted up into the landing. 'I won't put you out like that. I—'

'You don't have a choice. You made the mistake of giving

Sarah your spare key – she sent me in. Marley's Moses basket and clothes are already at ours, waiting for you both.'

I went to say something more, but Nick gently shushed me. 'The truth is, you'd be doing *us* the favour. I went back to work on Monday, and Sarah's all on her own with the baby. She needs you, Isla. Plus, the two little bruisers can keep an eye on you girls for me.'

My throat thickened with tears. 'Thank you.'

I sat propped against a throne of pillows on Sarah's spare bed, my toes curling as I tried to latch Marley on to my breast.

'Most natural thing in the world, they'll tell you,' Sarah said, who was feeding Jacob beside me. 'I'd say it feels about as natural as wearing bull-dog clips on your nipples.'

I laughed, then winced as my let-down came.

'Wine, paracetamol, and nipple cream: my breastfeeding survival kit.'

'Just like they recommended in antenatal class.'

I'd been at Sarah and Nick's for five days now, and we'd settled into a routine with the boys. If Sarah saw my light on at night, she'd slip into my room with Jacob and we'd do the night feeds together. In the mornings, if Nick had already left for work, we'd take turns in making a strong pot of coffee and we'd sit together, finding endless variations on discussions about cracked nipples and baby poo. When the babies napped, we'd put them in the same Moses basket, and coo at the way they curled into one another like kittens.

'Sounds like Nick's back,' Sarah said as the front door opened. 'Hope he's in a takeaway mood. Again.'

We heard him put down his keys and briefcase, then listened to the tread of his feet up the stairs.

'In here,' Sarah called out.

Nick walked into the spare room, then paused, leaning against the door jamb, arms folded across his chest. He looked between both of us and shook his head. 'There was a time when finding my wife and another woman in bed – with their breasts out – would've ranked pretty high on my list of fantasies.'

'Hold on to that fantasy tightly, honey,' Sarah said, 'because that's all you're going to have for the next few months.' She unlatched Jacob, then passed him to Nick to wind.

I watched Nick's eyes brighten as he looked at his son. 'How's my boy? I missed you today. Are you hot in all those layers?' He carefully removed Jacob's tiny woollen hat, then pressed his nose to Jacob's head, inhaling the sweet, milky scent, his eyes momentarily closing. 'God,' he sighed, 'don't you wish we could bottle that?'

Sarah smiled warmly.

Watching them I felt a stab of jealousy, which caught me by surprise. It wasn't that I wanted Nick, or that I needed someone to help me wind Marley or change his nappies; it was that I wanted someone to share the special moments with – to help keep them alive and fresh by remembering them together, over and over throughout a lifetime.

I wanted someone else in the world to love my little boy as fiercely as I did.

Four weeks later, I padded along the beach with Marley strapped to my chest. It was the end of October – one of those beautifully crisp sunny days that lured me into thinking that summer hadn't quite left us. It was Marley's first visit to the sandbank, and it felt like an auspicious occasion. I'd stayed at Sarah and Nick's for a fortnight, and although I wouldn't admit it to them, I was struggling in my rented studio flat. Negotiating the steep and narrow staircase was tricky with a baby, but far worse with a buggy, and I felt my scar tissue pulling tight with each ascent.

'Marley Berry,' I said, as I climbed the steps on to the deck. 'This is our beach hut.'

He'd looked up at me, his navy-blue eyes wise and alert.

I unlocked the door and we moved inside. The hut smelt exactly as I knew it would: of salt and books and damp wood. I threw the doors open to the afternoon sun. Autumn's golden light cast deep shadows down to the shore, the sand glowing beneath its touch.

I fed Marley sitting cross-legged on the sofa bed, looking out to sea. I told him the story of how I'd fallen in love with this stretch of beach for its rickety wooden huts, the sense of isolation, its big skies and wild seas. I whispered that I was looking forward to watching him fall in love with the place, too.

When the light faded to dusk, the temperature plummeted and I pulled the beach hut doors to, sealing off a draught that snaked beneath them with an old beach towel. I lit the hob – breathing a sigh of relief that I'd connected the gas bottle correctly – and heated a fish pie that I'd brought with me. I burnt my mouth eating the bubbling creamy sauce – too hungry and impatient to wait for it to cool; I'd learnt to eat fast, never quite knowing when Marley would wake next.

Before bed, I dressed Marley warmly, then laid him beside me beneath a huddle of blankets, watching the moonlight dance over the sea. I bent my mouth to Marley's ear and told him about all the adventures he and Jacob had to come – a lifetime of summers to run wild on the sandbank together. That night we fell asleep with the waves at our door.

Looking back, part of me wants to shake that young, naïve version of myself who assumed that life was going to hand out nothing but sunshine and love. Yet another part of me wants to hug her, to tell her, You were absolutely right. That should've been your life!

I thought the beach hut was going to be a sanctuary. A place tucked into the folds of sand, surrounded by horizon and water, next door to my best friend's hut. Of course, I'd had no idea back then what was to come. If I had, I'd have walked away from the sandbank – left our beach hut open to the elements to be hammered by the winds and driving rain until it was nothing.

12. SARAH

DAY TWO, 4.30 P.M.

Nick curses as he struggles to unbuckle a grey suitcase. It's one of a set we were given as a wedding present by his eldest brother.

'There's a lock on the side,' I tell him.

Nick heaves the case over, his jaw tight. 'It needs a code!'

'One, two, three.'

'Inspired.' He turns the digits and then the case springs open, the metal buckle snapping against his knuckle. 'Shit! Why do you even lock these bloody cases?' he fires. 'Bedding. You're locking away bedding? Jesus Christ!'

I ignore the remark. We're both exhausted and quick to anger.

We're searching through the boxes in our garage, like the police suggested this morning, to determine whether anything is missing. We've already spoken to the tenants renting our house, and they've not seen Jacob. It is possible that he's been in the garage unnoticed as we keep the spare key hooked beneath the bird feeder in our front garden, so it would have been easy enough for him to get in.

These past few summers, when we've rented out our house, I've cleared it of our personal belongings – and also put away the good things, too, like the special tablecloth my mother gave me, and the bed linen that I don't like to put in the tumble dryer – and stored everything here in the garage. Despite the effort involved, I find the process therapeutic, as it forces us to thin out our possessions. Minimalize. There's less *stuff* in our lives.

I step over a box of files that have tipped over. I gather them up from the concrete floor and place them back in the box. Beside it there's a bundle of post for us. We have an agreement with the renters that they gather our post and place it in the garage each week for us to collect. In amongst the bills are two birthday cards addressed to Jacob. I open them both. The first has a US stamp and is from Nick's brother. He's enclosed a generous music voucher and instructed Jacob to, 'Kill this on some new hip-hop tracks. Love Snoop-Teddy and the fam.' I smile to myself as I think of Nick's well-to-do doctor brother, who plays hip-hop with a thudding bass in his family sedan.

I pass the card to Nick, then open the second envelope, recognizing my mother's writing. A cheque flutters to the ground. The message reads, 'To my darling Jacob on your seventeenth birthday. Pop this in your savings and spend it on something important to you when the time comes.' I bend down to retrieve the cheque, my eyes widening.

'Five hundred pounds!' I turn the cheque to face Nick. 'My mother has given Jacob five hundred pounds!'

'Bit extravagant.'

I raise an eyebrow. That's exactly like my mother.

'What are you doing?' Nick asks as he sees me taking my phone from my pocket.

'Calling her.'

Nick lifts his hands. 'Listen, Sarah—'

She answers on the third ring.

'Sarah. Any news?'

'You sent Jacob five hundred pounds for his birthday?'

'His birthday. Yes. There's a card. I—'

'Don't you think it's a little over the top?'

'Well, I . . . I just thought it'd be nice for him to add to his savings. You know, he could put it towards university, or something, perhaps.'

'He doesn't have savings. He's seventeen.'

There's a pause.

Then I realize: 'This isn't the first big cheque you've given him, is it?'

'Well, no. I gave him the same amount for Christmas.'

'Mum!' I say, exasperated. 'You could have told me!'

'I assumed Jacob would have.'

The comment feels like a barb – a reminder that my son and I don't communicate. I'm seething, an anger that only my mother can ignite. 'Giving him a chunk of money won't buy his affection.'

'Sarah!' Nick is shaking his head at me. He extracts the phone from my grip, and says calmly into the receiver,

'Barbara, Nick here. Listen, Sarah and I are both just extremely tired and anxious right now—'

My mother will be speaking, as Nick is quiet. 'Yes. Yes, you're right. I know. I will, I will. Of course, of course. I know you were. Okay, yes, I'll do that,' he says with warmth in his voice. Sometimes I wonder if my mother likes everyone else in my family more than me.

When Nick ends the call, he says, 'At least we know where the cash in Jacob's drawer likely came from.'

'Yes, my bloody mother!'

'She's just trying to help. Give her a chance.'

I purse my lips, but say nothing further as I continue checking through our belongings. A few minutes later I come across a large red shoebox that has *Tights* scrawled across it in marker pen. I glance over my shoulder and see Nick is busy looking through a black sports bag of Jacob's, so I carefully open the lid. Inside there are a medley of items, but my fingers reach out to a small model of a horse, no longer than my little finger, cast from iron.

It's the first thing I ever stole.

I remember the way my fingers closed around it, like I was trapping a bird. My sister and I were both obsessed with *Black Beauty*, especially the scene where the horse gallops along the beach, wild and muscular, and is eventually tamed by a young boy. We imagined ourselves as that boy, and we'd practise our taming techniques on garden birds and squirrels – with limited success.

I'm not even sure who gave Maggie that tiny iron horse, but I do remember she wouldn't be separated from it. The horse came to school in the pocket of her uniform, and it watched over her as she slept. It took on a mystical presence in our young lives. Even when Maggie grew out of make-believe, she still kept it in the centre of her windowsill. I wasn't allowed to play with it, touch it, or even breathe too close to it. Those were the rules that older sisters enforced, and younger sisters obeyed.

When Maggie died, her room became a museum overnight: her toys were untouched, her clothes remained hanging neatly in the wardrobe, the bed was always made. My mother would spend hours in Maggie's bedroom with the door closed, while I sat on the landing, listening to her cry. I remember the taste of varnished wood when I'd touched my lips to Maggie's door, whispering, '*I'm right here, Mummy! I'm still alive!*'

One day, when my mother was downstairs, I went into Maggie's room and plucked the iron horse from her windowsill. I took it back to my room and climbed into bed, playing with it beneath the covers. My mother – who didn't notice when I went to school with unbrushed hair, or with a packed lunch empty of sandwiches – immediately noticed it was missing. She asked me point-blank whether I'd taken it, and I said, 'No, Mummy. I haven't.' The lie bubbled in my throat a little, but it was easier than I thought. You just need to keep eye contact, not look away.

There were lots of small thefts after that – nothing of my sister's, just minor things like a rubber from the girl I sat next to at registration, and a plastic necklace from the school costume wardrobe. My desire to take things fizzled out in my late teens, and I think a few years went by when I stole nothing at all. Then, one afternoon, I was visiting Nick's mother, Stella. She'd been a GP throughout her working life and, even now she was retired, she showed no signs of slowing down, her weeks filled with volunteer work, walking trips and various adult learning courses. She and Nick's father lived in a town house filled with the relics of a large family – rooms still made up for when their sons' families visited, photos on walls, a huge sagging sofa with a pile of books at its foot. Stella had told me more than once that she wasn't a homemaker, as if even the idea of it was distasteful to her. There was often washing up cluttered in the sink, piles of old newspapers and mail hunkered on the sideboard – but I found I liked the lived-in feel of their home. It was only my house that needed to be spotless.

When Stella was making tea, I wandered around her lounge and noticed a small placard perched on the window-sill. It read, *A clean house is the sign of a wasted life.*

It was just a placard, it didn't really mean anything at all, yet the words stung. Is that what she thought about me, my choices?

I reached out and plucked it from its position, looking more closely. As I did so, I heard the clinking of china mugs as Nick's mother returned carrying a tray of tea. I slipped the placard behind my back, pushing it out of sight into my jeans pocket.

As I drank my tea, making small talk about Jacob's schooling, my plans for redecorating our bathroom, I could feel the firm pressure of the placard against my skin. I had the opportunity to return it to the windowsill, yet there was something about the thrill of knowing it was right there in my pocket that stopped me. When I left Nick's parents' house that day, the wooden placard came with me. I felt oddly disappointed looking at it in my own home, so I shoved it at the back of a drawer in my *Tights* box, and didn't look at it again.

But, gradually, that box started to fill. Just small things. Nothing people would miss: a fountain pen from the snotty school receptionist's desk. A tube of scented hand cream from the bathroom of one of Nick's colleagues' homes. An ornamental spoon from a display in the dining room of the home of someone I've long forgotten.

I sometimes wonder what would happen if Nick looked through this box. How would I explain it? *Nick, sometimes I steal things.*

That's what it is: stealing. I've devoted hours and hours to justifying why I do it, telling myself I'm only borrowing the items and that I'll give them back. Only I never do. I don't plan to take the things I do, it's just that sometimes, this feeling sort of builds inside me, as if my blood vessels are starting to hum, to vibrate. The sensation spreads, travelling down my arms until I can feel my fingertips almost twitching with the need to take something.

If I was interested in seeing a therapist, I imagine I'd be paying someone to tell me that the theft is about seizing power over that person. Shifting it into my favour. The items I keep become trophies. A therapist would probably want to explore the steps I can take to stop.

But I'm not interested in therapy, or stopping.

I steal because I can, because it gives me a hit. It makes me smile privately because to the outside world I'm a mother who cooks wholesome meals and keeps an immaculate home, but I like to remind myself that there are other shades to me. Ones that no one else sees.

'It doesn't seem like anything is missing,' Nick says, looking up from the final case. 'Although it's hard to know what was here to begin with.'

I move to his shoulder and look into the case, too. It's scruffily packed – clothes bundled in haphazardly. I have a vague memory of sticking my head around Jacob's door, yelling, 'We need everything packed by the end of the *day*!' He'd glanced up with that easy smile, and said, 'Mum, it'll take me, like, half an hour.'

He was right – it clearly had done. Maybe I should pack like Jacob. All the folding and organizing and sorting I do is probably taking years off my life.

'It's a good thing,' Nick says. 'It means Jacob can't have intended to be away for a long time.'

We're both silent for some time. I can hear the scuffle of mice in the eaves overhead.

'When I was sixteen,' Nick says all of a sudden, 'I ran away.'

I turn and look at my husband. He is running a fingertip along the edge of a metal shelf, a strange expression on his face.

'I went to London – picked up work in a casino, cleaning the toilets.'

I blink, surprised. 'Did your parents know where you were?'

'I called them after four days. Came home after a fortnight.'

Four days. That's longer than Jacob's been missing for.

I cannot believe Nick has never told me this. I know he tells me this story to make me think perhaps Jacob has just run away too, but instead it makes me feel anxious. Like I don't know my husband or son. 'Why? Why did you leave?'

Nick looks at the garage shelf, his hands carefully adjusting the stack of plant pots and trowels, realigning them at angles that appeal to him. His gaze doesn't leave the shelf as he says, 'I came home from school early one afternoon. I had tonsillitis. My mother was in bed with another man.'

The confession is so incredibly surprising that I gasp. Stella is the head of their family, the planet around which her sons and husband orbit. 'What did she say?'

Nick gives the lightest shrug. 'My mother and I never talked about it. When my father asked why I ran away, I told him it was because of a girl. I think he was secretly pleased.'

I am staggered. I can't help wondering whether his mother was in love with that man. Whether she continued to have an affair with him – or whether she ended it in order to live the family life she had so carefully constructed.

I also can't believe that she and Nick have never once talked about it.

Or can I?

I look at my husband – the familiar curve of his neck, the line of his jaw, the stretch of his fingers – and I think of what I've been prepared to hide to protect my family.

13. ISLA

Summer 2005

I stood with a hip against the kitchen counter, talking to Sarah as she ladled hot stock into the risotto pan, stirring slowly.

I glanced over my shoulder checking on the boys; they were digging a huge hole on the beach ready to bury one or other of themselves in, sand flying everywhere. Suddenly the digging stopped, and their heads snapped up, like two little meerkats, followed by shouts of 'Daddy!' and 'Uncle Nick!'

Nick strode across the sand in his leather shoes, his white shirt unbuttoned. The boys launched themselves at him, attempting to drag him into their sand trap. I smiled, turning back to Sarah. She was watching too, something wistful caught in her expression.

A few moments later, Nick clambered on to the deck, a boy wrestled beneath each arm, his shirt straining. He had that look of relief: it was the weekend.

'Here are the extra ingredients,' he said, glancing down at the children. 'Think they'll fit in your pot?'

'We'll just need to trim them down to size,' Sarah said, using her hand as a chopping knife, making the boys squeal even more.

When Nick released the boys, they circled his legs, imploring him to help with the digging, to take them crabbing, to see if they could find fossils in the rocks.

'Give him a minute,' Sarah told them both, shooing them out of the hut. She passed Nick a beer from the fridge, kissing him.

Nick kept his head bent towards hers as he said quietly, 'You okay?'

She smiled. 'Better.'

I traced the base of my wine glass as he kissed her again.

'Good week, Isla?' Nick asked me.

'Blissful, thanks. It's this time of year that I remember why I do my job.' Since Marley started primary school, I'd been working as a teaching assistant. The pay was atrocious, but it was the only job I could find that meant I could be there before and after school for Marley. Plus, now that it was the start of the summer holidays, I was wonderfully free again.

'Joining us for dinner?'

'Sure am,' I said, then wondered whether Nick might prefer to celebrate the end of the week with his wife and son.

'Excellent.' His smile seemed genuine and I relaxed again.

Once Nick had wandered on to the beach with his beer, I turned to Sarah. 'Are you okay?'

She kept her back to me, stirring the risotto. 'Yes, fine.'

'I just . . . sensed there's something going on.'

Her shoulders lifted as she drew in a deep breath. 'We've just . . . we've decided we're stopping trying.'

For the past three and half years, Sarah and Nick had been trying for another baby. They'd changed their diet, stopped drinking midweek, started taking vitamin supplements, and using an ovulation kit.

'But, why?'

Sarah sighed. 'I'm just over it. The disappointment each month. It's exhausting. We have a healthy, beautiful son. Why are we obsessing over it?'

On the one hand, Sarah was right to be grateful for what they had, to enjoy Jacob rather than fixating on the next item on her life plan. Yet, on the other hand, Sarah had always said she wanted a big family. 'There's still the IVF route . . .'

'I'm not putting us through it. I've seen what it does to couples. The raised hopes, the crushing disappointments – it's too much.'

'A lot of people have success—'

'We had Jacob. Maybe he was our gift. I think there's a reason. It's time to just get on with enjoying our lives.'

'What does Nick say?'

'Oh, you know Nick. He says whatever he thinks I want to hear. He's probably secretly relieved. Now Jacob's at such an easy age, I'm not sure he's ready to go back to the night feeds and nappies.' Then she wiped her hands on her apron, brightened her voice and asked, 'More wine?'

I didn't see it then, the lie hidden in our exchange.

But it was right there all along, jagged and painful – like broken glass waiting in the sand.

109

14. SARAH

DAY THREE, 10.40 A.M.

My eyes burn with concentration as I read an article on my phone about missing persons' cases. More than a quarter of a million people go missing every year in this country – and two thirds of them are under eighteen. I press my thumb knuckle against my bottom lip, picturing Jacob within a sea of blank-faced teenagers. Gradually his shape begins to waver and fade, his features sliding away until he disappears into the crowd.

If Jacob is one of so many, how on earth are the police going to find him?

Stop reading! I tell myself. *Just stop!*

But I can't.

I read that in missing persons' cases, the police try to establish the risk of each individual. If the person's disappearance is out of character, it would immediately raise the risk. I visualize a seesaw, Jacob's name in the centre. On the high end of the seesaw, I picture the words 'out of character'. But then, on the low end, the words 'male' and 'seventeen' are stamped. I wonder which way the seesaw is balanced – is his case medium risk? Would it be higher if he were a girl? If he were younger?

I scroll down and a fresh fact snaps across the screen. I read it aloud to Nick, who is standing in the beach hut doorway, his back to me, a bowl of cereal in his hand. '*Vital clues are most often found in the first few hours.*' I look towards Nick, who still has his back to me. 'What clues do we have?' I ask, my voice rising. 'The police haven't found anything!'

He doesn't answer me. He continues to stare out over the water.

My throat begins to close as I read that the majority of missing people are located within the first forty-eight hours. It's Wednesday morning and Jacob was last seen on Sunday evening. Already we've moved outside of that vital time-frame, sliding into the minority.

There are quotes from parents whose children have disappeared, and my voice is a whisper as I read them: '*Elaine Chewsbury's son, Jack, was eighteen when he went missing in Derby twenty years ago. His case remains open. "It's the absence of knowing that is so impossible to deal with. When I wake each morning, the questions hit me afresh. Is he still alive? What happened to him? Will today be the day he walks through the door?" Elaine Chewsbury says.*'

The phone slides out of my grip and I place both palms

on the kitchen counter. 'That cannot be us,' I beg. 'Please, do not let that be us.'

From the other end of the beach hut, I hear Nick turn. There's the clink of a spoon against the rim of the china bowl as he sets it down, then I feel his hands sliding around my body, turning me towards him. The anxiety and tension I'm carrying makes my body rigid, as if it has hardened around my heart to protect the hole that has torn through it.

As his palms run in smooth, familiar strokes up and down my back, I press my face against his shoulder, threading my arms around him. It's the most tactile we've been in weeks, maybe months, and I realize how much I've missed it. Right now we need each other more than ever.

We stand together in the beach hut, the distant sound of waves rolling around us, as Nick's lips move against my hair. 'It's going to be okay.'

'This is the way I see things,' Nick says, pulling apart to face me. 'There are only two possibilities.'

His pragmatic, calm tone is reassuring, and I listen hard.

It's part of the story of why I fell in love with him – for his unstinting optimism, for his complete refusal of unhappiness in his life. I don't know whether his positivity is a product of a solid family upbringing, or whether it's because he's never had to deal with anything crushing before – but I love him for it. He radiates happiness and confidence, and it reaches me.

'The first possibility is that Jacob has *chosen* to go missing. We think he had a bust-up with Caz. We need to find out what the fight was about. What if she'd been unfaithful with one of his friends? Or vice versa. That'd explain his hurry to disappear. We should go and see her again, find out exactly what they were talking about.'

I nod.

'Or maybe it wasn't only the argument with Caz, but rather a combination of things: you guys had that little spat, then he argued with Caz. He could have fallen out with a friend, too, or maybe he was just struggling with the anniversary—'

'Any of those things are possible, but I just don't believe that Jacob wouldn't get in touch. He knows how worried we'd be – that we'd get the police involved. He wouldn't do it.'

'I know,' Nick says slowly, thoughtfully. 'That's what keeps snagging with me.'

'And the second possibility?' I ask, even though I know exactly what it is.

Nick takes a breath. 'Jacob *hasn't* chosen to go missing: something's happened to him. There could've been an accident. Or someone's hurt him.'

A hundred scenarios have already played through my head, each more unbearable than the last: he was walking across the headland at night and slipped into one of the ravines. He got so drunk that he passed out on the tideline. He took something at the party – had a bad reaction to it. I look at Nick. 'What do you think's happened?'

Nick has never been one for assumptions or speculations. He is a man who likes concrete evidence, facts.

I wait, looking into his face. His skin is grey, the corners of his eyes bloodshot with tiredness. Despite everything he's said so far, he looks like a man who is terrified.

Before Nick can answer, there's a knock at the door.

Luke moves inside, carrying a rucksack by one hand. He looks uncomfortable, awkward. I look at him closely, trying to work out what it is.

'Is there any news yet? Has Jacob been in touch?' he asks, glancing between us.

'Not yet,' I say with a shake of my head. 'Have the police been to see you?'

'Yesterday afternoon. They wanted to hear about the party. Find out who was there, what happened, when he left – that sort of thing.'

'You told them everything you remembered?'

Luke nods, then glances at the rucksack in his hand.

I suddenly realize what's wrong – why Luke looks so awkward. 'My God . . . that's Jacob's bag, isn't it?'

'I think so. Yeah. I had a look inside. Looks like his stuff.'

'Where did you find it?' I ask, heart racing.

'In my hut. Just now. He must've left it behind after the party. It was pushed to the back of one of the bunks. I didn't know it was there. I'm sorry.'

'Just now? You only thought to look through your hut now?' I step forward, snatching the bag from him. 'Don't you realize how important this could be?'

'Sarah,' Nick warns.

My hands feel damp, greedy, as I grip the sides of the rucksack, inspecting it. I know without doubt it is Jacob's: the zip pull on the front pocket snapped earlier this summer, so he'd fashioned a new one using a key ring. I open it and begin pulling out items, crouching down to lay them on the floor.

Jacob's dark-blue hoodie – the one I'd thought was missing.

A single bottle of beer, still housed in the cardboard six-pack.

A head torch.

An almost empty tube of sunscreen.

An old skateboarding magazine, the corners curling.

Jacob's wallet.

My skin prickles, as if it's itching just below the surface where I cannot reach. Jacob has been gone for three days, yet he doesn't have any of his belongings with him – not even his wallet. I let out a strange sort of wail, squeezing my eyes shut.

'This doesn't mean anything,' Nick says.

'Jacob had nothing with him. Nothing! Not even his wallet!' I swing around to Luke. 'He told you he was coming back to the party, didn't he?'

Luke nods quickly.

'See! That's what he intended! He left his bag there. He didn't run away, Nick!'

Nick goes to say something in response, but stops himself.

I can hear Luke shifting behind me. 'Sorry, you know, for not finding it sooner. I didn't realize it was in the hut, really.'

I kneel down, pulling Jacob's hoodie to my face, breathing in his boyish smell – deodorant, sweat and something sweet, too. Tears arrive hot and sudden, sliding from my face into the fabric of the jumper.

'Sarah, we're not doing this,' Nick says gently, trying to

peel the jumper from my hands, but I dig my fingers into the material, gripping harder. He crouches down beside me. 'We're going to find him. There will be a simple explanation, I promise you. We just need to think.'

He picks up Jacob's wallet and I watch his fingers search through old receipts, a five-pound note, a bulging pocket of loose change, two screws. Tucked at the back, Nick pulls out a small photo, faded and creased at the edges. I am expecting to see a picture of Caz, perhaps – but as the image comes into focus, I realize I'm looking at an old photo of Jacob and Marley. They must be about six or seven, and are sitting on the edge of Isla's deck in their pyjamas, brushing their teeth in the last of the evening sun. Marley is looking towards the camera, minty froth bracketing his smile, and Jacob is holding out his toothbrush to whoever is behind the camera. At least, I know it's Jacob – others wouldn't because his face has been scratched out using a coin or fingernail, a scribble of white lines zig-zagging his features.

'What is this about?' Nick asks.

I shake my head. I take the picture from him and rest it on my palm, deeply unsettled.

'Why would Jacob erase himself from the photo?' Nick asks, his brows drawing together.

'I've no idea.'

'There's something else here,' Nick says, pulling a folded piece of paper from the wallet.

As he smooths it out, I can see it's filled with Jacob's writing. A rogue thought snatches my breath: *Jacob's left a suicide note.* I read over Nick's shoulder, my heart in my mouth.

It's easier on paper. Maybe.

It's love. You said it wasn't, but I want you to know it is.

I LOVE YOU.

I think you need to know that.

I'll say it again in case you don't believe me: I love you!

Maybe this is too much. But it's the truth. So that's it, I guess.

Jacob xx
PS. Last night was amazing ☺

'A love letter!' My chest swells with relief. 'Just a love letter.'

'This is a good thing,' Nick says, tapping the letter. 'It means Jacob is seventeen years old and in love. So what if he didn't have his rucksack with him. He had a big fight with his girlfriend – the love of his life – and he took off.' He turns to Luke. 'It is serious then, with Caz?'

'I get that impression, yeah.'

Last night was amazing, I repeat in my head. If Jacob intended to give Caz that letter on his birthday, then he must have been referring to the previous evening they'd spent together. Nick and I had been having dinner at a friend's hut further up the sandbank – and I imagine the opportunity of a free hut would have been too good to pass up for Jacob and Caz. I remember putting a pizza in the oven for Jacob – and coming back to find a plate of crusts flagging on the kitchen side, and a large packet of crisps emptied, two glasses on the draining board.

What seems odd to me is that they had an *amazing* time one night – and then the next, they had a huge blow-up. Actually, no. Maybe that's anything but odd. Maybe those tempestuous highs and lows are a defining characteristic of young love.

I ask Luke, 'Why were Jacob and Caz arguing at the party?'

Luke lifts his shoulders. 'No idea.'

I glance towards Jacob's drawer and say, 'We've been looking through Jacob's things – and found an envelope with five hundred pounds inside. We think his grandmother gave him the money.' I pause. 'Do you know what he was planning to spend it on?'

'No,' Luke says, shaking his head quickly.

I wonder whether I believe him. 'Could it have been drugs?'

'Drugs. No, not Jacob.'

'We found some weed in his drawer.'

'He had the odd joint,' Luke admits, 'but he wasn't into other stuff.'

'You certain?' Nick asks.

'Well, he never took anything around me. That's all I can tell you.' Luke shoves his hands into his pockets. 'Guess I should head off.'

'Wait,' I say. 'It might sound like an odd question – but the police asked us, so I thought it'd be worth asking you, too – can you think of anyone who'd want to hurt Jacob? Anyone who, I don't know, had a grudge against him?'

He lifts and drops his shoulders. 'Like who?'

'Maybe another boy who was jealous about his relationship with Caz, or someone he'd annoyed for some reason or other.'

Luke pulls his lips to one side and I can tell that something has crossed his mind – that he's deciding whether or not to tell us.

'This is important,' I remind him.

He rubs a hand around the back of his neck. 'Well, I don't think Caz's dad is his biggest fan.'

'Robert?' I say, glancing over at Nick.

Luke nods.

Robert's made no pretence of the fact that he isn't thrilled about Jacob dating his daughter. He'd be happier to see her coupled with one of the boys from the private school she attends.

'He's pretty protective when it comes to Caz. Intense, you know?'

'In what way?'

'Never wants her staying out late. Doesn't like the idea of her having the odd drink, even though she's like, seventeen. He came by the party looking for Jacob.'

'Robert was looking for Jacob?' I repeat, goose bumps rising across my arms. 'Why?'

'Didn't say. Jacob and Caz were out the back of the hut at the time, so we told Robert that Jacob wasn't around.'

'What did Robert say?'

Luke glances through the open hut doors, then back to me. 'That he'd find Jacob later.'

15. SARAH

DAY THREE, 2.45 P.M.

'I'll go,' Nick says. 'If we both turn up at Robert's hut, it'll look like an inquisition.'

'Maybe that's exactly what this needs to be,' I reply.

Nick sighs. 'All Luke's told us is that Robert was looking for Jacob at the party. There's probably a perfectly logical explanation. Maybe Robert was actually trying to find Caz – and thought Jacob would know where she was.'

I raise my eyebrows at this. I'm not a fan of Robert's. Isla and I call him 'The Cockerel' (although the shortened version rolls off the tongue a little easier), as he spends the summer striding up and down the beach, chest puffed out, pecking into other people's business. He was one of those called on to help with the search for Marley – but Isla's never forgiven him for being the first boat to return to shore. Robert claimed he was low on petrol, but we all saw him roaring off the following day to visit his regular waterside lunch spot.

'You go then,' Nick relents, 'but Sarah? Tread carefully.' As I turn to leave, he passes me the love letter. 'If Caz is there, ask her about this. She might open up to you.'

I doubt it, I think, remembering our frosty interaction yesterday. 'Shouldn't we keep the letter? Give it to the police?'

'I'll photograph it – email it to them now.' He takes out his phone and snaps a quick picture.

I leave the hut and walk into the easterly wind, folding my arms across my chest. The bright sails of windsurfers race out towards the horizon, then tack back towards shore with a flick of the board.

I've not gone far when I experience the unsettling sensation that I'm being watched. I turn back towards our hut, but Nick has already returned inside, the doors pulled to. I glance along the row of open huts, half expecting to see a face pressed to a window, a pair of eyes tracing my path. Everyone will know by now that Jacob's missing. The news will be traded as gossip, updates blowing along the sandbank with the speed and force of a weather front. But there's no one there.

I tell myself I'm imagining it and press on, but the feeling doesn't disappear. If anything, it intensifies. The hairs on the backs of my arms stand on end and I feel my shoulders hunching protectively towards my ears.

I startle at a sudden rush of footsteps behind me.

A woman jogs past, apologizing for surprising me. She's my sort of age and wears a baseball cap. Her skin glistens with perspiration and two grey lurchers lope at her side. I press my fingers against my chest, trying to laugh off my jumpiness. My gaze follows the dogs as they bound towards the shoreline; they are beautiful – muscular and athletic looking, eyes bright. As I watch them race through the shallows, I become aware of a boat in the bay, turning lightly on its mooring. Isaac's boat. My skin tightens. I find myself searching for his figure at the wheelhouse – but I can't see clearly enough whether anyone is there. Isaac works on an offshore rig doing six days on, six days off. Over the years I've come to know the rhythm of his schedule – and he should be away right now.

I squint into the flat light, peering at the boat, wondering, *Could he be on the sandbank? Is he on board right now, watching me?*

I pull my cardigan tight around my shoulders, dip my head and walk on.

When I reach Robert's hut, I find the doors thrown open and Caz sitting in the corner of the sofa, legs tucked to one side, reading a magazine. She wears a long charcoal-grey top, shapeless and drab on most, but with her jutting hip bones and long legs, the top hugs her body in just the right places.

On seeing me, she sets down the magazine and emerges from the beach hut.

'Is your father here?'

She shakes her head. As she does, I notice a dark purple bruise across her cheekbone that looks angry against the even, tanned skin. 'Your cheek?'

'Oh.' Her hand lightly travels to her face. 'Embarrassing, really. Drunken tumble a couple of nights ago.'

Now I remember the fresh red mark on her cheek the last time I saw her. 'It happened on the night of Luke's party?'

Her eyes flick slightly away from mine. 'Yes. Tripped up the steps to the hut.'

There's something guarded about her expression that makes me wonder if she's lying. 'Could I come in for a moment?'

She shrugs, then turns and moves inside.

'Have the police been to see you yet?' I ask as I sit down. I already know they were here yesterday – PC Roam called to update us on their interviews so far. She said that Caz seemed nervous, cagey. Caz claims that she and Jacob had been arguing because she'd had too much to drink and was embarrassing him – although PC Roam felt there was more to it than that.

'I didn't have much I could tell them. I don't know where he is.'

'I've got something for you, actually. From Jacob. He left his rucksack at Luke's party. We found it earlier today. There was a letter inside for you.' I take the letter from my pocket, but don't immediately give it to her. I want her to wait.

Her eyes dart across my face. 'What does it say?'

I ignore the question, and instead ask: 'You've spent more time with Jacob than I have this summer. How do you think he's been?'

Caz shrugs. 'Fine, I guess.'

'One of the police's lines of inquiry is that something prompted Jacob to run away. Perhaps something that happened that night.' I pause. 'What were the two of you arguing about?'

'Just stuff. I can't even remember.'

'Then try,' I snap. The veneer of politeness that glosses my interactions with Caz is starting to thin. I will shake the truth from her if I have to.

She turns her head to look past me. Daylight hits the smooth planes of her face, and I remember how besotted Jacob was with her. I think of what I've learnt so far: the passion in his letter; his apparent jealousy; the way he marched her out of Luke's party.

'Were you cheating on him?'

Her head snaps around. 'No! Of course I wasn't! I loved him.'

There's a beat of silence.

'*Loved?*' I repeat quietly.

She presses her fingertips to her face, and I see once again that livid bruise.

I picture my son by the rocks with Caz – a beautiful girl he's wildly in love with – while alcohol courses through his system. I think of the anger I'd seen in his eyes earlier that night, and the way I'd flinched as he'd come towards me. My question is whispered, barely audible. 'Did Jacob hit you?'

'Is that what you think? That Jacob would hit me?' Caz looks at me with disbelief.

'I . . . I . . .' My throat tightens. I don't know what to say. I shake my head, shocked at myself.

'Jacob would never hurt anyone.'

'Yes. I know,' I say, heat flooding to my face. 'It was just . . . well . . .' I trail off, unable to finish. I am mortified.

'He's kind. Good.' Caz's eyes well with tears. She presses

a hand over her mouth, as if to contain a sob. Watching her, I'm certain she knows something important that she's not telling me: she was the last person to see Jacob; the one he confided in; the girl he loved.

'Why was your dad looking for Jacob the night he disappeared?'

Surprise registers in the widening of her eyes.

'Luke told us Robert interrupted the party looking for Jacob. He was angry.'

'I . . . I don't know . . .'

'Of course you do.'

Her gaze drops to her lap.

'I can ask your father about it, if you'd prefer?'

'Dad didn't even see Jacob. I promise.'

'Why was he looking for him?'

She shakes her head.

'Caz,' I say, softening my tone. 'I'm not angry with you – or your father. All I'm interested in is finding Jacob.'

I wait, giving her space to respond.

When she doesn't, I add, 'If you don't talk to me, you know the police will be back here to see you.'

There is the slightest nod, a relenting. She swallows and lifts her gaze to meet mine. Her voice is quiet, barely more than a whisper. 'I'm pregnant.'

My hands fall to my sides.

'That's what we were arguing about. Jacob and I got pregnant.'

My gaze trails to Caz's stomach, which is hidden beneath her loose grey top. 'Jacob found out that night?'

'No. We did the test together last month.'

I can't hide my shock. Jacob had known Caz was pregnant for a month, but said nothing to us. It is staggering. How had I missed it?

'Dad found out . . . I was talking to Mum about it on the phone. I didn't see Dad come into the hut.'

'That's why he went looking for Jacob.'

'Yes, but Dad didn't see him – so he went to the pub instead.'

'Perhaps he caught up with Jacob later – after the pub?'

'No, he would've said,' she tells me, although I catch a note of uncertainty in her voice.

Caz draws her knees towards her chest. She suddenly looks very young. 'Jacob didn't want the baby.'

'And you?'

'I want to go to university. I want to travel the world. I want to be *me* for a bit longer, you know?'

I do know. I know exactly what she means.

'But . . . it's a baby. An actual baby growing inside me. We're the ones who got pregnant. It's not the baby's fault.' She pauses, looking out over the water. 'I've booked it, though. Tomorrow.'

'An abortion?'

She nods.

I don't know how I feel. Everything's come too quickly. A few days ago the thought of my son as a father would have seemed utterly surreal and preposterous – a parent's nightmare. Yet right now, all I want is for Jacob to be alive, safe. Here.

'Why didn't you tell us any of this, Caz?'

'I . . . I thought Jacob would be back by now. That it wouldn't make any difference.'

Something comes to me. 'Did Jacob offer to pay for the abortion?'

Caz straightens. 'Yes, but that didn't even come into my decision—'

'We found five hundred pounds in Jacob's drawer. We've been wondering what the money was for.'

We're both silent for a minute or two. Then I ask, 'Jacob doesn't know, then, about your decision?'

She shakes her head. 'I've called him – but his phone is off.'

'Did you see where he went that night after you finished talking by the rocks? Did he walk towards the beach huts? Towards the headland?'

'He told me he wanted to be on his own. He was . . . crying.' Caz swallows. 'He kept telling me, *I'm not a good person. You're better off without me.* I didn't know what to do . . . what to say. When he told me to leave, I did.'

I'm not a good person. Is that how he felt? But, why?

I need to get out of here. Think. I stand, passing Jacob's letter to Caz.

'Thank you.' She smiles, grateful.

As I turn to go, I say, 'Caz, do you need someone to go with you? Tomorrow?'

She looks up, surprised. 'Dad'll be there. But, thanks.'

As I'm making my way back to the beach hut, Robert comes marching in the opposite direction. A salmon-pink polo shirt clings to his barrel chest, the collar pushed up so that it brushes the ends of his thick grey hair. 'Sarah! So sorry to hear about Jacob taking off,' he booms without breaking stride. 'Any news?'

'He's still missing,' I tell him, pointedly.

'Sure he'll turn up,' he says, with a flippancy that makes my jaw tighten.

'I've just been to your hut, actually. I spoke to Caz.'

'Oh yes?'

'She told me. About the pregnancy.'

Robert halts. His whole face changes, his mouth sliding downwards, eyes narrowing. He glances over his shoulder to check who is within earshot, and then he steps close to me. 'Seventeen,' he hisses. 'That's how old my Cassie is! For Christ's sake, what was Jacob thinking?'

'It takes *two* people to make a baby.'

'Yes – and I can bloody well imagine whose idea it was!' he says, hands clenching into fists.

I could point out that Caz isn't exactly a shrinking violet – rumour has it that there've been a series of older boyfriends before Jacob piqued her interest – but I'm not concerned with point-scoring. All I want to know is whether Robert saw Jacob the night he disappeared.

'You must have been shocked when you found out. Angry, even.'

Robert eyes me carefully.

'It was the night Jacob disappeared, wasn't it?'

The edge of his mouth lifts in a wry smile. 'Yes, I was angry. I was fuming. But I didn't tell him to sling his hook – disappear – if that's what you're thinking. I probably would've done, if I'd seen him.'

'Yet you went looking for Jacob.'

'Yes, *Detective*. I did. But I never caught up with him – lucky for him. Drowned my sorrows at The Rope and Anchor instead.'

'When the police interviewed Caz, she didn't tell them about the pregnancy.'

'Didn't she?' Robert says, although there's no hint of surprise in his voice.

'Caz withheld important information. It could be critical in finding Jacob.' I wonder if it was Robert who suggested that she keep quiet. I feel certain that there's something he's not telling me about that evening.

'I'll have a word with her,' he says, without a degree of conviction.

Robert looks over my shoulder as if something's caught his attention. I turn and see Neil, Diane's husband, coming towards us, his gaze moving warily over Robert. There's something in Neil's expression that I don't understand. I know there's a history between the two men, but I can't think where it stems from. I have a vague recollection of Diane once saying they were at the same school.

'Everything okay, Sarah?' Neil asks.

I nod quickly.

Robert uses the interruption as an excuse to disappear. 'Lovely to chat, as ever,' he says with a loose wave.

I bristle as I watch him stalk away.

When I turn back to Neil, he's looking at me closely. 'I heard Marley's missing.'

'Excuse me?' I say, stiffening, jarred by his mistake.

'Jacob! I mean Jacob!' Neil corrects himself.

A pulse of tension beats at my temple; I know people on

the sandbank will always associate Marley and Jacob together, but the slip somehow feels menacing, like the sharp point of a knife edging closer. The scratched-out image of Jacob's face alights in my thoughts, as I picture the unsettling photo we found tucked into his wallet.

Neil hurries on, clearly embarrassed. 'When was he last seen?'

'Sunday evening. It was his birthday.'

He scratches the back of his head. 'Sunday,' he repeats to himself. 'Right, well, I'll keep an eye out.'

Before he leaves, I take the opportunity to ask, 'What do you make of Robert? You've known him a long time, haven't you?'

He looks surprised by the question. 'Can't say I'm his greatest fan.'

'Did I imagine it, or were you at school together?'

'For a while, yes.' He blinks, looks at his hands. 'He managed to make those years hell. He was a bully back then – and I'm not sure that much has changed.'

'He was on the warpath looking for Jacob the night he disappeared,' I venture.

I keep my gaze pinned to Neil, ready to gauge his reaction, but all he says is, 'I see.'

Although I should go straight back to the beach hut where Nick will be waiting, instead I walk towards the water's edge. I need a moment alone to think. I slip off my sandals and plunge my feet into the cool shallows.

The sea bed eases out from beneath my soles, leaving me with the sensation that I'm gradually sinking. Questions dart through my thoughts, quick and slick as fish. It seems like Caz's pregnancy could be at the root of Jacob's disappearance. I wonder if it was simply too much for him to cope with – so he just upped and ran. Maybe that seemed preferable to having to tell Nick and me. Or did he run because he was scared of what Robert may do? When I tell Nick about the baby, he'll be shocked – but I wonder whether he'll be relieved, too: in a way it provides evidence, accreditation for Jacob's disappearance. The pregnancy could answer the *Why*: Jacob was scared, so he took off.

But I'm not sure it explains everything, because here's my question: why run? Why that night? Jacob knows that it'd mean the police would be involved. He knows the fall-out would be far bigger than if he just dealt with the situation head-on. He knows how much Nick and I would suffer.

Without thinking about it, I've slipped my mobile from my pocket and dialled Isla's number. I hear her voice asking me to leave a message, and suddenly I am talking. 'It's me. I . . . God, I really need to speak to you.' Our falling out is a distant memory in the face of what's going on right now. I need her. 'Jacob is still missing. You can't have got my message – he didn't come back from a party on Sunday night. The police are investigating . . . Jesus, Isla. *Police*. It doesn't feel real. None of this feels real. I've just been to see Caz – she was the last one to see Jacob that night – and she's told me, Jesus, she's pregnant. Jacob got her pregnant! They've known about the baby for an entire month, Isla, and he never told me.'

My gaze slides across the beach towards Isla's empty hut. Sunlight catches one side of it, illuminating a section of

16. ISLA

Yes, I knew about Caz's pregnancy.

*Sarah will hate the fact that Jacob confided in me – perhaps
more than the news that her son had got his seventeen-
year-old girlfriend pregnant. Or maybe that's unfair of me.
I'm not sure I trust my own perception of people any more
– not when I've been proved so very wrong.*

*The thing is, I didn't even want to know Jacob's news. I
certainly didn't ask to know – but Jacob came to me. What
could I do? Tell him to unsay it?*

This summer

'Mum's cooking,' Jacob told me as he'd flopped down on
the beach hut sofa, pushing his dark hair from his eyes.

'Ah.' *Mum's cooking* meant he was keeping out of the
way in case he was roped into helping. I put down my book,
emptied a packet of crisps into a bowl and poured us both

tall glasses of water. 'Did you get out on your paddleboard this afternoon?' I asked, sitting opposite, feet on the table. The sea breeze had dropped off and the bay had turned glassy and inviting.

'Didn't fancy it.'

I cocked an eyebrow, surprised. He was worrying the edge of his shorts between his thumb and forefinger, a habit he'd had as a child and never quite shaken. He took a sharp breath and began to ask me about the first trip I'd taken when I was nineteen. I thought he was building up to telling me he was going to take a gap year after college, but instead he asked, 'Were you travelling when you got pregnant with Marley?'

I nodded. 'I was in Nepal at the time.'

'Was it . . . planned?'

I laughed. 'No, it definitely wasn't planned.'

'Weren't you scared?'

'Terrified.'

He shifted. 'Did you ever think about . . . not keeping the baby?'

I reached forward, scooping a handful of crisps from the bowl and dropping one into my mouth as I thought for a moment. 'Yes, I did. I was halfway through a world trip – a baby was the last thing I thought I wanted. You know, I'd planned to travel as far as Australia,' I told him. 'I'd always wanted to learn to dive on the Great Barrier Reef.' I sighed. 'But then I just . . . I don't know. I felt different when I was pregnant – like suddenly I was a different person. I realized that if I was old enough to go travelling on my own, to get myself pregnant – then I was old enough to see it through.'

'And then you had Marley.'

I smiled, warmth spreading through my chest. 'Then I had Marley.'

Jacob looked at me for a long moment. I could tell there was something he wanted to say. He pressed his palms flat together, and brought them to his lips. He inhaled. 'Caz is pregnant.'

I nodded slowly. 'How do you both feel?'

'Shit-scared.'

'That's normal.'

'She's thinking of keeping it.'

'And you?'

'I would feel bad, you know, about an abortion. But I . . . I don't want it. I can't even imagine being a dad. Maybe I'll want all that one day, I guess. But not now. I'd mess it up.' He lowered his head, eyes fixed to the floor. 'I dunno what to do.'

'Talk to Caz. Tell her how you feel.'

'She says it's her decision. It's her body.'

We were both quiet for a moment, hearing the clink of cutlery being laid next door.

When Jacob spoke again, his voice was lowered. 'It's not just up to her though, is it? The decision should be mine, too.'

'It doesn't always work out that way,' I told him gently. 'Ultimately it's the woman who has to grow the baby, who has to give birth to it. It's such a huge decision that I can understand why Caz wants to feel in control of it. But it's important she listens to what you want, too. You need to work it out together.'

Lucy Clarke

He looked down at his hands. 'It ties me to her.'
'And you don't want to be tied to her?'
Then his gaze rose to meet mine. 'I don't think I do.'
Neither of us said anything further.
We finished our drinks, our gazes on the water, then Jacob
stood, wiping the heel of his hand across his mouth. 'Cheers,
Isla. Don't mention it to Mum, will you?'

I didn't mention it to Sarah.
Just like I didn't mention a lot of things that happened
in the weeks after that conversation.

136

17. SARAH

DAY THREE, 4 P.M.

'Jacob and Caz just seem so . . . young,' Nick says, leaning forward on the sofa, elbows on knees, hands clasped.

'We weren't much older though, were we?' I say, carefully drying a mug from the draining board, then placing it in the cupboard with the others, handles facing south. Nick and I had been dating for less than a year when I fell pregnant. I'd always pictured having a family, but first I saw a career for myself, a spring wedding with all our friends, a honeymoon somewhere tropical, and later, much later, children. Two boys and two girls.

'I know, but Jacob's still a—'

'Child?' I offer. 'That's how he might seem to us – but it's not how he sees himself. Remember being seventeen? I felt like an adult. I felt like the whole world was out there waiting for me. Isla and I had a thousand plans about what we'd do after college, where we'd travel, who we'd become. Being parents didn't feature in any of them.'

Nick nods slowly as he considers this. 'We didn't tell our parents when we found out you were pregnant, did we?'

I'd forgotten that. 'We waited ages – a month, maybe two, wasn't it? Jacob isn't the only teenager not to confide in his parents. He's probably terrified.'

I remember the sheer white panic I'd felt when my period didn't arrive. I'd checked the dates again and again, praying I was wrong. When I had finally taken a pregnancy test, I'd passed it to Nick without looking at the result. I had watched his hands trembling as he'd angled it towards the light from the bathroom window. Then he'd lowered himself on to the edge of the bath, like an elderly man unsure his legs would hold him. 'You're pregnant,' he'd said so quietly, I'd had to ask him to repeat it.

Later that night, Nick turned to me in bed and said, 'Do you think we should get married?' A question, not a proposal.

'Do you?'

The bed creaked as he'd rolled on to his back, making a pillow of his arms. He thought for a long time before saying, 'Yes. I think we should.'

'Well, okay then.'

A few minutes later, I'd turned towards Nick, my mouth close to his neck. 'Nick,' I'd whispered. 'You know, people will want to know how you proposed. Would you mind if you asked me . . . properly . . . some other time? With a ring.'

A week later, when I visited Nick at the sandbank, there was a picnic rug laid on the beach, and a ring box hidden inside a wicker hamper. *Yes!* I beamed, as Nick slipped a diamond ring on to my finger.

I find myself looking at my husband and wondering, not for the first time, whether he would've married me if I hadn't been pregnant. I ask, quite suddenly, 'Did you feel trapped?'

Nick runs a hand along one side of his jaw and I hear the scrape of his stubble. 'Maybe,' he says slowly. 'Yes, I probably did.' He glances at me, then qualifies, 'It wasn't that I thought *you'd* trapped me. It was just the situation.'

But I had, hadn't I? That was exactly what I'd done.

'The police are here,' Nick says, glancing out of the beach hut into the late afternoon sun.

I move to the open doorway. PC Roam is walking at PC Evans's shoulders, nodding intently at something he is saying. Every few steps she has to jog lightly to keep up. I wonder what they're talking about, if there've been any developments, or whether they're discussing the information I shared about Caz and Robert.

I should put the kettle on, I think. As I turn, I notice Diane hovering in the doorway of her hut, her watchful gaze pinned to the police. When she sees me, her face changes and she smiles tightly, then ducks inside.

'We're the local news at the moment,' I say to Nick, gesturing towards next door.

'Everyone's just concerned.'

I don't bother to argue the point. Instead, I pump water into the kettle with more force than it needs, then light the hob. By the time I've set out four mugs, the police are here.

I notice immediately that PC Roam has more colour to

her face – a light tan. Has she found time to sit in the sun while she's been working on Jacob's case? I have an overwhelming urge to grab her shoulders and yell, *Why haven't you found my son?*

I feel ashamed when she smiles warmly at me, enquiring how Nick and I both are, and whether we're managing to get any sleep. This young woman has been nothing but nice and helpful. But I don't want *nice* or *helpful*. I want efficiency. I want excellence. I want single-minded determination and fierceness. I would never say this aloud – but here it is: PC Roam is a new mother; if her child is anything like Jacob was as a baby, she's probably exhausted and doing a sterling job managing to just get into the office each morning in a clean uniform. When you have a young baby, you are consumed by them – when what I want is for PC Roam to be consumed by Jacob's disappearance. I want her to eat, sleep and breathe this case until Jacob is found.

I drop tea bags into the mugs, splashing milk on top. 'Have you spoken to Caz about the pregnancy?'

PC Evans nods.

'And Robert? Have you interviewed him?'

'Not yet, but we intend to.'

'Robert was out looking for Jacob the night he disappeared. He said himself he was furious with him. I'm not saying, well, that he'd *hurt* Jacob, but he does have a motive.'

Motive. Am I really using words like that?

Nick shoots me a warning look.

PC Evans nods lightly, but I can't help but think he looks a little uninterested – as if he's thinking along different lines.

I hand out the tea, then sit on the sofa beside Nick.

PC Evans glances into his notebook and says, 'We've also interviewed Ross Wayman, who owns the harbour ferry. He's confirmed that Jacob didn't use the ferry on the evening of his disappearance, or any time since.'

Ross Wayman has run the ferry for years. I like his story: he left school at sixteen and headed to the City, where he fell into a banking role. By nineteen he was on the trading floor, cutting huge deals with City folk who had degrees and a decade more experience. On his thirtieth birthday he retired – rumour has it with a few million in his pocket – and disappeared to Africa for the next ten years. He came back when his father died, and moved himself and his mother into an Edwardian house overlooking the harbour. At the time, the old sandbank ferry came up for sale, so he bought it, and he and his mother used to run the business – she collecting the fares, and he captaining it. He must be in his sixties by now – and he's still running the ferry every day. *Eight till eight*, the sign reads, *365 days of the year*.

But just because Jacob hasn't used the ferry, I'm careful not to let myself believe that he's still here. He could easily have walked across the headland; it might take an hour at a good pace – though probably longer in the dark.

PC Evans looks at Nick, then me. 'It's been brought to our attention that the day of Jacob's disappearance fell on the anniversary of another boy's death. Marley Berry.'

My face flushes hot. *Brought to our attention, by whom?* I think of Diane's curious expression as she'd watched the police arrive. By *her?* I can't think of any reason Diane – or anyone – would have for bringing up Marley's anniversary.

'Marley was Jacob's best friend,' Nick explains. 'His

mother, Isla Berry, is Jacob's godmother. She has the hut next door to us.'

PC Evans says, 'I understand that Jacob was with Marley when he drowned?'

Nick nods.

'I'm surprised neither of you thought to mention this.'

'We didn't think it was relevant,' I say.

'Where did it happen?'

There's a pause before I answer, 'Here. This bay.'

PC Evans looks between Nick and me. 'So, just to get this clear, Jacob's best friend, Marley Berry, went missing from this bay. Then on the same day – seven years later – Jacob also goes missing, from the same spot.' He says the words slowly, carefully, imbuing each one with importance.

'Marley didn't go missing,' I amend. 'He drowned.' I will not let him imply that the two cases are the same.

PC Evans responds with another question. 'How was Jacob affected by Marley Berry's death?'

'Devastated,' Nick answers. 'Marley was his best friend. They did everything together.'

'So Marley would've been on Jacob's mind, seeing as it was the anniversary of his death?'

A shiver travels down my spine as I think about the photo in Jacob's wallet. My mouth is dry, but I swallow and answer clearly. 'It's possible.'

PC Evans takes a drink of his tea, then sets the mug on the side table, neglecting to use one of the coasters that I've left out. When I bought them – banana-wood coasters that toned with the sofa cushions – Nick had said with a smile, *You know this is a beach hut?*

PC Evans leans back into the sofa. 'I want to talk in a little more detail about the last time you saw Jacob.' He is looking at me closely. At my eyes. At my mouth. It's as if he can see right inside me, as if he knows exactly who I am, what I'm capable of – and knows the exact chain of events that have led us here.

'What, specifically, do you want to know?' My tone sounds clipped, defensive.

'You mentioned previously that you'd had a disagreement with Jacob.'

My mind's racing to recall what I've told them. 'It was nothing. Just a spat.'

PC Evans looks down at his notebook. 'Someone mentioned that they overheard a commotion in your hut at around 8.15 p.m. They said they could hear Jacob shouting. Then there was a loud thud, followed by the slamming of a door.'

I can feel a slick of sweat building underarm as everyone focuses on me.

It must've been Diane. She'd have overheard us arguing from next door. Did she hear *everything*? I'm sure I'd pulled the hut doors closed during the argument – but when?

'Can you recall what the thud might have been?' PC Evans asks, his gaze fixed on me.

'Possibly a drawer or cupboard closing. Maybe I dropped a book or a bag, perhaps. I really can't remember.'

He nods, expressionless. 'Jacob did slam the door though?'

'Yes!' I laugh, shrilly. 'He slammed the door on his way out. He's a teenager. Life is full of drama. I'm not sure how this helps us find him?'

PC Roam says gently, 'All we're trying to do is understand as much as we can about Jacob's state of mind that evening. Build the picture as vividly as possible.'

'We've had reports that Jacob's behaviour can be disruptive at times,' PC Evans says.

'Excuse me?' Nick's voice is sharp.

'I understand there was a complaint about vandalism – glass bottles thrown against a beach hut.'

Nick's jaw clenches tightly around his words as he tells them, 'It was once. At the start of summer. There was a beach party – they'd all been drinking. Jacob said afterwards they didn't realize anyone was in the beach hut. He apologized to the owner, removed all the glass.'

'We've also spoken to the college, who've told us there were some attendance issues.'

'Yes, but that was just Jacob acting up,' Nick says. 'He's bright. College doesn't always stretch him. His grades haven't slipped – did they tell you that?'

'Yes, we've seen his reports.' A pause. 'Would you describe him as troubled?'

'No, not at all!' I say reflexively.

'And yet Cassie Tyler's statement, when we spoke to her on the way here, referred to Jacob as crying on the rocks, saying, "I'm not a good person. You're better off without me."'

She told them that?

I can see the thoughts stacking up in the police officers' minds: Jacob's a troubled teenager with a disruptive home life, who was depressed over Marley's death, and felt trapped by Caz's pregnancy.

The police don't think Jacob's missing: they think he's killed himself.

When the police leave, Nick tells me he's going for a walk to clear his head. It's a relief: I'm not ready to have a conversation with him that has to include the question, *Is it possible our son was unhappy enough to kill himself?*

I boil the kettle, then fill a bucket with hot water and detergent. Crouching on my hands and knees, I scrub the hut floor, leaning the weight into my shoulder. I drag the sponge back and forth, the skin on my hands turning pink. Do the police really think I haven't considered the possibility of suicide? Of course I fucking have! I've thought of every single possibility, looping them around and around in my brain until my head is so tightly knotted I can barely function.

I've done my research, pawing through article after article on the Internet, as if words and facts can give me back some control. But they don't. They make it worse because now I know that 1,800 missing people are found dead each year – and that three quarters of these are male, and most often the cause of death is suicide.

I clench my fingers into the wet sponge, nails digging into the damp flesh of it. I picture Jacob sitting hunched on the rocks, sobbing, *I'm not a good person.*

I will not – cannot – allow the possibility of suicide to take root, as otherwise I'll be forced to consider what it truly means: that Jacob could be dead – and it'd be my fault.

*

The floor is scrubbed raw. I push myself to my feet, knees red and dented. I rinse out the sponge in the sink, and balance it on the edge of the washing-up bowl, deciding to tackle the hob next. But I make the mistake of pausing – and in that moment my energy drains away with the swiftness of a plug being pulled. I feel it swirling out of me as my knees begin to give. Tears rise over my eyelids.

Before I can stop myself, I'm crouched on the damp floor, sobbing, gasping.

Jacob! Oh, Jacob!

I just want to know. I NEED to know what's happened to you!

'Sarah?'

I lift my head and find Lorrain standing in the doorway of the hut, her palm pressed to her chest. 'Oh Sarah!' She moves towards me, placing her large hands under my elbows, steering me to the sofa. 'It's all right, now. It's going to be all right,' she says, settling beside me, patting my knee with a hand.

'Was it you? Did you tell the police about the glass bottles?'

'Bottles?'

'That Jacob threw. The police knew about it.'

'Course it wasn't,' Lorrain smiles easily. 'As if a few shards of glass would make me blink. You never knew the mischief my twins got up to!'

I haven't met her twenty-five-year-old sons yet, although she's fond of telling people, *They're both gay, can you believe it? The both of them!*

'Listen sweetie, you're going through shit right now, but

it'll all work out okay. You'll see. Now, what did the police say?'

I've only known Lorrain since the start of this summer, so I'm not sure whether she's fishing for gossip, or whether I can trust her. 'I think they . . . they are considering the possibility that Jacob . . . well, that he may have . . . committed suicide.' The words sound strange and alien as they leave my mouth.

'What would they bloody know? Nothing! A fun-loving boy like Jacob? Absolutely not!'

Suddenly I love Lorrain for her beautiful optimism.

'Don't give that nonsense a second thought! He'll turn up.'

She has no knowledge basis to make this assertion on, but I let myself believe it anyway. I wipe my face dry with the back of my hand.

'You eating? Sleeping? Remembering to drink water? Let's pour you a glass now, shall we?'

She bustles towards the sink, pumping water into a glass. 'Here you go. Drink it back. No use you making yourself ill.'

I take the glass obediently.

She gives me a little squeeze on my shoulder and says, 'I'll leave you to it – but you know where I am if you need me.'

I watch her move away, grateful for her visit. As I glance through the window, I catch her pausing on the beach, turning back to look at me, something sharp and inquisitive in her expression. Then, just as quickly, the look is gone, and she turns and walks on, leaving me wondering if I imagined it.

I shake my head sharply and the movement refocuses my gaze. I catch myself in the reflection of the window and barely recognize the woman looking back at me. There are deep bags beneath my eyes that bloom like bruises, and my hair hangs lank and unwashed. The lines etched across my forehead seem deeper, permanent. I run a knuckle beneath my eyes, wiping away the traces of mascara, but it does little to improve things.

Leaning in closer, I angle my head slightly, noting something oddly familiar in my expression. I can't quite grasp what it is. I've a strange sense of déjà vu, as if I've lived this moment before.

I am about to turn away, when I realize.

My whole body turns rigid.

It's not me who's lived this moment before: it's Isla.

My expression is a mirror of hers, seven years earlier, as she pressed her face to the window looking for Marley.

I think of PC Evans's words: 'Just to get this straight, Jacob's best friend, Marley Berry, went missing from this bay. Then on the same day – seven years later – Jacob also goes missing, from the same spot.'

No! I tell myself, my head beginning to shake from side to side. Jacob's disappearance has nothing to do with Marley.

'Nothing,' I whisper at my reflection. 'Nothing . . .'

18. ISLA

A tipping point is the moment at which a series of small incidents become significant enough to cause a larger, more important change. It's that exact moment where everything hangs suspended between the before and after. The hinge that turns your life from something you once recognized and understood – into something startlingly different.

Again and again I return to the events of the day I lost Marley, searching them from every angle. Would it have been as simple as removing one incident, changing one small word or action, and the tipping point might never have arrived? What if Samuel hadn't been there that morning? What if the tide had been coming in, not out? What if Isaac's boat had been closer to Marley rather than Jacob?

I remember it in fragments – glass-sharp pieces that slice. I can't remove any of those shards. I can't go back and unwind. It's impossible to stop the moment when my whole world tipped.

Lucy Clarke

Summer 2010

Marley raced into the beach hut, cheeks flushed, sand clinging to his bare feet. 'We need to make a flag pole for the sand fortress,' he told me breathlessly, salt-mussed hair wild around his face.

I rummaged at the back of a cupboard, pulling out a pack of wooden skewers that we used for toasting marshmallows. 'Would one of these work as the pole?'

Marley grinned, knees bending with excitement. 'Yes!'

Samuel, who'd been staying for the weekend, found a blue-and-white napkin for the flag, and a thinning roll of Sellotape to secure it with.

'Just a minute,' I said, before Marley made to disappear again. 'Sun cream.'

Marley rolled his eyes at Samuel, before planting himself in front of me. I pasted the cream across his smooth back, his shoulder blades like sharp little wings beneath my hands. I spun him round, then dabbed cream across the bridge of his nose and cheeks. 'Hey,' I said, catching his hand, 'I've got something for you.'

He wrinkled his nose as I kissed the tip of it. I watched him run down the beach, the taste of sun cream and salt on my lips.

Then what? How many minutes passed before I checked on him again? Maybe twenty? Twenty-five? Did I really leave it that long? Was I so swept up with new love that I didn't pull my gaze away from Samuel?

If I'd known what I do now, I would have watched Marley

150

every moment. No; I wouldn't have let him leave the hut.
I would've held on tight, pressing my face into his neck,
breathing in the warm scent of my baby.

'I should really get back,' Samuel told me, scooping up my
hair in one hand, and placing a kiss at the nape of my
neck.

I shivered with pleasure.

'I'll try and get back down here in a night or two.'

'I'd like that.'

I'd fallen in love with Samuel for many reasons. For the
way he kissed each of my fingertips as if they were the most
beautiful hands he'd ever seen. For the boyishness of his
laugh. For the unashamedly passionate way he talked about
flowers. And then I fell in love with him again when I
introduced him to Marley. They were friends from the go.
They went on bug hunts and made dens; they ganged up
on me, knowing where my ticklish spots were. Sometimes
Samuel would take him to work with him – he was a landscape gardener – and Marley would help him pull out weeds,
holding them firmly by the base and shaking free the loose
soil.

Samuel slung his bag over his shoulder, pushed his feet
into flip-flops and said, 'Tell the little guy I said bye.'

I raised myself on to tiptoes to press a kiss to his lips.
The soft give of his mouth made my stomach flutter. His
fingers moved through my hair, pulling me deeper into him.

'You are undoing me,' he whispered against my lips.

I stood on the deck to watch him leave, admiring the
long stretch of his legs as he moved across the sand. There

was a smile on my lips as I replayed Samuel's suggestion that, when the contract on my rented flat ended in autumn, we should think about moving in with him. 'Marley will love having a garden,' he'd said. I'd told Samuel that I'd think about it, but I could already feel myself edging towards saying, *Yes.*

I see it, the life I could have had. It's tantalizing, like a heat haze on the horizon, shimmering and beautiful, but just out of reach. There would have been a family home with a striking garden, vegetables grown ourselves. Later, there'd have been a simple wedding, a bunch of wildflowers as a bouquet, Marley dressed in slacks and a loose, open-necked shirt carrying the rings. Maybe there would even have been another baby – I was young enough, then. It was a life that would have been filled with laughter and love and happiness.

But instead, I wasn't watching—
I let my focus slide. It was only for a few minutes.
That's all it takes.

I looked out towards the sea. A small crowd were gathered on the waterline and I idly wondered what they were doing. Just beyond them, Robert was gutting fish, gulls circling above the bloodied soup. I'd heard him bragging about his haul of mackerel earlier, and seen the pinched expression on Neil's face, who'd returned with an empty catch bucket.

Someone in the crowd began hurrying towards the huts. It was Diane. I'd never seen her run before and there was a clear urgency in her jerking, rushed movements – the awkward gait of someone unused to moving quickly. 'Neil!' she yelled. 'Boat keys! Get your boat!'

A moment later, Neil stepped from their hut holding a beer.

'Children! In the water!' Diane yelled, breathless.

My fingers sealed around the deck railing. *Marley!*

I scoured the beach, spotting the sand fortress he and Jacob had been building near the tideline. Buckets and spades lay abandoned on their sides, a wilting flag flapping in the breeze. Panic bubbled in my throat. I glanced across to Sarah's hut, hoping the boys were there, but it looked abandoned – a washing-up bowl planted on the deck, a pair of rubber gloves discarded haphazardly.

The crowd on the shoreline shifted, and I saw what I'd missed before: Sarah was at the edge of the group, further forward than the others. She had her back to me, but there was something odd about the way she was standing. Then I realized: she was up to her knees in water, the hems of her summer trousers soaked.

My blood ran cool. *It's our boys out there.*

I raced down the beach, my breath short. Reaching Sarah, I gripped her elbow, turning her towards me; her face was white, eyes wide.

'The boys.' She took a breath. 'They're in the water.'

Fear spread down my spine, a fingernail dragging across the bone. 'Where?'

'I can't see them . . . the current. They're caught in it. The coastguard's been called. There's a boat already looking for them.'

'They were meant to be making a fort. That's what they were doing. Why did they go in the sea?'

Sarah was silent.

In the bay, Neil was dragging himself on to his boat. A moment later the engine roared to life, the smell of petrol mixed with the salt breeze.

My hand found Sarah's, our fingers gripping tight, the hearts of our palms sealing together.

A seagull screeched overhead, the sound cutting from the sky like metal against metal. The murmur of concerned voices came from behind us on the shore, and then one voice sliced through the rest: 'Found?'

Sarah and I both turned. Diane was staring in the direction of Neil's boat – her mobile pressed to her ear.

I watched her with the focus of a hawk as she nodded slowly. Her gaze shifted to Sarah and me. 'They've found one of the boys.' She hesitated. 'They're still looking for the other.'

'Who?' Sarah and I asked together.

Diane shook her head. 'I don't know.'

I was only vaguely aware of mine and Sarah's hands unclasping – maybe I loosened my grip, or perhaps she let go of me. I tucked my hands deep into the pockets of my dress, my fingers twisting around a loose tissue I found there. Beside me, Sarah's fingertips lifted to her hairline.

I prayed that it was Marley who was safe. He was the stronger swimmer. I'd taken him to swimming classes since he was four months old, holding his little body close to mine as we dipped and splashed in the pool, singing nursery rhymes about crocodiles and rowing boats. Last summer he'd outraced me for the first time. This summer he was twice as fast. He was a strong, confident swimmer. He would survive. He had to.

I'd chosen.
  We both had.
  I'd chosen Marley's life over Jacob's.

The lifeboat was vivid orange. The colour seemed both dramatic and urgent, but also reassuring as the hull boomed against the waves, men in bright suits and helmets scouring the water.

'Everything is going to be fine. Both boys will be fine,' Sarah said in a strangled voice, keeping up a steady stream of narration. 'There's three boats out there now. More on the way. They'll find them both. Look, Robert's going out, too.'

I looked towards the spot on the shoreline where he'd been gutting fish – the catch bucket now gone. Had he found time to put the fish in his fridge before getting in his boat to search?

'Isaac's coming to shore,' Sarah said, pointing towards the dark-navy fishing boat, which had been the first one circling out there. 'He must have one of the boys.'

We watched in silence as the boat drew nearer, our gazes locked on that vessel. The sun was high in the sky, illuminating Isaac standing at the helm. A second figure was hunched beneath a towel or blanket at the stern, head lowered.

Beside me, Sarah gasped. Suddenly she was lurching forwards, stumbling through the water. 'Oh baby! My baby!'

Jacob, not Marley.

No, no, no! That couldn't be right.

I kept staring at the boat, certain Marley must be on board, too. *They should be together!* I watched as Isaac placed a hand at Jacob's back, steering him gently towards the side of the boat where Sarah was opening her arms to him.

'Marley!' I shouted, wading forwards. 'Where is Marley?'

Isaac lifted his head. I know he saw me, heard my question, but he looked away.

A cold pain pushed through my veins. 'Where is my son?'

But there was no answer.

I shook my head, pressed my hands over my mouth. 'This can't be happening,' I whispered. 'This can't be happening.'

Events unreeled around me, as though I was a spectator of a film that wouldn't stop.

Eleven boats joined the search. Ross Wayman re-routed the harbour ferry to help. The coastguard helicopter churned above the sea for hours. They searched until the final blush of daylight had disappeared – and resumed again at first light.

I didn't get to see my son brought back to shore hunched beneath a blanket, wet hair pasted to his head, like Sarah did.

I didn't get to hold my son, to feel the weight of his beautifully lean ten-year-old body, or kiss the smooth curve of his forehead one final time.

I didn't even get to say goodbye.

I stop remembering. Like I say, it doesn't change anything. I've lived through every moment of that day a thousand times. More.

I know every detail. Every element that led to the tipping point.

At least, I thought I did.

19. SARAH

DAY FOUR, 8.15 A.M.

The early sun holds little heat, its thin warmth blown clear by a northerly wind. Walking on the tideline, I stoop to pick up a limpet shell, turning it through my fingers and following the rough grain of its curve. With my fingertip, I dust the sand from the interior of the shell, admiring the pastel whirl of colour.

When Jacob and Marley were young, I'd often take them beachcombing following a big summer storm. We made up a points system, scoring the sea treasures on rarity and beauty. Jacob would race up and down, gathering up driftwood, old rope, the backbones of cuttlefish, and glass bottles, stuffing them into his bucket. Marley never once had the heaviest haul, but could happily spend several minutes in one spot, sieving through the sand in search of a special shell. Then he'd bound to my side and unfurl his palm, as if he was holding a precious stone. 'Look! A cockleshell! Beautiful, isn't she?'

When I glance up, I realize I've reached the rock-line at the end of the bay where Jacob was last seen with Caz. I try to picture exactly where they were arguing, which rock Jacob was sitting on when he'd said, *I'm not a good person*, tears pooling in the corners of his eyes. God, how I wish I could go back in time, hold him to me and tell him, *It will be okay*.

But that's just a romantic idea. If I'd tried to hug Jacob, he'd have turned rigid in my arms, or extracted himself from my embrace. His withdrawal from me happened gradually, like the stealth with which summer pulls away, leaving you shivering into autumn. I should've tried harder to bridge that gap between us. I still can't believe that Jacob had known about Caz's pregnancy for weeks – yet didn't confide in me. Where was my mother's intuition? Why wasn't I alert to something being wrong?

What else have I missed?

I shiver, wrapping my arms around myself. I have the strangest feeling that there is someone close by, hovering in the distance, watching me. I consciously slow my breathing, reminding myself that I've barely slept since Jacob's disappearance and that exhaustion is taking its toll. But when I turn, I see Neil slumped on the rocks at the end of the bay. He meets my eye, and suddenly he is pushing himself to his feet, staggering towards me.

'Sarah . . . I just wondered,' he says, glancing over my shoulder towards the huts, '. . . is there any news on Jacob?' His voice has an odd hush to it, as if he doesn't want to be overheard.

'Not yet,' I say, forcing my tone to sound light.

His frown deepens as he nods.

I'm looking at the bloodshot corners of his eyes, the way he lightly weaves from foot to foot. Am I imagining it, or can I catch alcohol fumes on his breath? It's barely past eight in the morning; he can't have been drinking.

He pushes his hands into his pockets. 'The police must have some idea of what's happened, no?'

When I don't answer, Neil asks, 'Do you think Jacob's run away? Perhaps he was upset about something.'

'Upset about what?' I snap, wondering what Diane's been saying, and how much of mine and Jacob's argument she overheard. She's always made it her job to know everyone else's business – but I didn't realize Neil would be so quick to dig for information, too.

'Nothing. I'm just . . . we're all concerned. Everyone's thinking of you.'

'Thank you,' I manage, before turning from Neil and resettling my gaze on the rocks.

Thankfully, he picks up the cue and leaves. I move slowly forward, trailing a fingertip across the rough surface of the rocks. At the corner of my vision, something dark catches my eye. I look down to see an object tucked between a gap in the rocks.

A shoe. No, a pair of shoes. Trainers.

I bend to reach them, scraping my wrist bone against the coarse rock. My fingers reach the tongue of one of the trainers and I pull it through the gap in the rocks, then dive my hand back down for the other.

I stare at the trainers, heart skittering.

Blue Converse, size eleven, laces tucked beneath the soles, leather tongues pulled up, the back of the heel trodden down, scuffs on the toes.

They are Jacob's.

The trainers are damp with salt, and a fine layer of sand dusts the inner sole. Stuffed into the toe of each shoe is a balled-up sock. I pull them out and a shred of dried seaweed clings to the wool.

I look up, as if he must be nearby and has taken them off to go for a swim—

No! He couldn't have—

'Nick!' I start to say, twisting away from the rocks, breaking into a run. I race towards our hut, holding the trainers awkwardly to my chest, sand flicking against the backs of my calves.

Someone is watching me; I feel it, like a cool hand brushing the back of my neck. I swing round, stumbling to my knees in the deep sand, Jacob's trainers flying from my grip. I scrabble to retrieve them, gathering them to me.

I right myself, standing. But when I look around, there's no one there.

I hurry back to the hut. 'Nick!'

He steps out on to the deck with a piece of toast in his hand, concern widening his eyes. 'What is it?'

I hold out the trainers. 'They're Jacob's! They were by the rocks!'

He stares at them, perplexed, then looks across the beach towards the rocks, his brows drawing together.

'He must have taken them off. To swim,' I say.

I see the moment Nick registers my meaning. His forehead

tightens, lips opening slightly as he blinks blindly into the hazy light.

Nick takes the trainers from me. 'They're definitely his?'

I remember buying them with Jacob in the spring. I'd stood back in the skate shop, pretending to be interested in a display of heavy-soled boots. I knew well enough that the invite to go shopping with my son was for my financial input rather than my style input. An attractive young girl served Jacob; she had a silver bolt through her ear, the hole in the lobe stretched until it was large enough to push a fingertip through. Jacob talked easily with her and I'd admired his self-confidence.

He wore those trainers almost every day, scuffing up the nose when he practised ollying on his skateboard. I reach out and trace a finger along the scuff-marks now. 'I bought them with him. They're his.'

'Where were they?'

'In a gap between the rocks, near where he and Caz had been arguing.' I pause, heart racing. 'He took them off to go swimming, didn't he?'

'We don't know that,' Nick says. His voice is studiously level. 'He might not have been wearing them that night. He could've taken them off earlier in the day.'

I'm trying to think back to that evening. The police had asked me what he'd been wearing, and I remembered the bright-red T-shirt, which was stamped with the image of a globe on the front. He wore it with his favourite pair of beige shorts that had an oil stain on the front pocket from his bike chain. But what about his feet? Over summer he alternated between flip-flops and trainers. Which had he been wearing that night?

I'm suddenly remembering our argument, and how I'd jumped when he'd kicked the drawer in frustration. Then there was the storming of feet across the deck as he'd left, the beach hut trembling as the door slammed shut. Trainers. 'He was wearing them. I remember.'

I picture my son, drunk and angry, hurt and confused, standing on the shoreline alone at night. Did the sea look like the answer – dark and peaceful? Did he want to sink below its surface, stay there? My voice catches as I say to Nick, 'Are the police right? Do you think Jacob—'

'No!' he barks so loudly that I jump.

Nick runs his hands through his hair, his eyes darting across my face. 'Listen, finding these trainers doesn't neces-sarily mean anything. We can't assume he swam out there, Sarah. We just can't. I mean . . . he could've taken them off to pad about in the shallows, or just to walk on the beach.'

I nod, wanting to believe that's possible.

'Was there anything else there?'

'Just his socks balled up in the trainers.'

'No phone? No T-shirt? Because if he went in the water, he'd have taken his phone out of his pocket, and taken his T-shirt off.'

Nick is right, I think, my heart lifting a fraction. He would have done. His phone wasn't in his rucksack, so we've been assuming he had it on him.

But then a whisper of doubt breathes into my ear: unless Jacob was in such a dark place that he no longer cared about what would happen to his phone, his clothes.

We walk back down the beach together, the trainers still in my grip. I'm distantly aware of someone waving, calling out a greeting, but neither of us looks round. Nick strides out a little in front of me, and I realize how much I want him to take control of the situation, to tell me everything is going to be okay. I don't want to think about the way his expression clammed up with worry – he can't falter. He has to believe. I need him to believe.

We return to the spot I found the trainers, and crouch down, searching. I'm not sure whether I want to find something further, or not. I put down the trainers, placing my palm on the rock, looking in its shadow on the sand. I rake my fingers through the sand, and find nothing but the charcoal remains from a barbecue, and the broken husk of a crab's shell.

I move further up the beach, searching, Nick looking at the other side of the rocks. I find a tangle of fishing line, the hook long gone, and a piece of driftwood wedged in the sand.

'Can't see anything else,' Nick says as he clambers across the rocks and comes to my side.

'Nothing here, either.' I press my fingertips against my temples, trying to think. *Why were Jacob's trainers there?*

I'm surprised when Nick answers me; I must have spoken aloud. 'It's possible that he left his T-shirt on the rocks and his phone – and that someone came across them, took them.'

Is that possible? I suppose it is.

I've no idea what to think.

I look at Nick, wanting to find him calm, unruffled.

He returns my gaze as he says, 'We need to let the police know.'

*

I watch as PC Roam places Jacob's trainers within an evidence bag, and seals it. She takes a biro from her pocket and writes something on an exhibit label, which I cannot read. I imagine his name, the case number. The area where the trainers were found has now been photographed and searched by the police.

I stand back with my arms hugged to my chest – if I hold myself tightly enough, I can stop myself from falling apart.

Nick places a hand on my elbow, turning me towards him, into him. I press my face against his chest and close my eyes. But everything is still there. Jacob's trainers. The police. The days he's been missing stacking together like a wall that's getting harder to scale.

'Let's go back to the hut,' Nick says.

We walk like an elderly couple, leaning into one another. 'Everything okay?' Diane calls from the deck of her hut. *Fuck off! Just fuck off and leave us be!*

Nick lifts a hand in response. Even he has no words for Diane.

The beach hut smells vaguely of disinfectant from yesterday's floor-scrubbing frenzy. Nick steers me on to the sofa and I sit with my feet pressed together, hands on my knees. I hear the pump of the water tank as he fills the kettle, then the whoosh of gas as he lights the hob. He pulls out mugs, the jar of tea bags, a pint of milk. I stare blankly at the cream wood-panelled walls of the hut, the navy cushions with their roped trim, the brass porthole mirror that reflects the view of the sea. None of it feels like mine. I am sitting in a stage set. This is a place for family holidays, a place for bare, sandy feet, not the slamming of doors, the trudge of police boots.

I catch sight of my face in the porthole mirror. My skin is pale with dark shadows lingering beneath my eyes. There's a permanent groove between my brows and fine worry lines running across my forehead. I have a sudden urge to launch across the hut and slam my fist into the mirror, to see the glass splinter around me, feel the warmth of blood trickling over my knuckles. My hands tremble on my knees with the desire. Before I can move, Nick has stepped towards me holding out a mug of tea.

As I take it, I begin to laugh. Nick looks at me with alarm as my tea sloshes over the rim of the mug, spilling on to the floor.

'Sarah?'

Even our mugs tone in with the colours of the beach hut. I remember standing at the checkout of the homeware shop, delighted with the purchase. Now I want to shake that smug version of myself, and yell, *What does it matter?* Because all that is important now – all that will ever matter in my life – is that Jacob is found, alive. I need him to walk through these doors and slouch on to the sofa beside me. I'd throw my arms around him, press my face into his neck, squeeze him so tight that I'd feel his heart beat against mine. I wouldn't care that I'd embarrass him, or he'd try and shrug me off; I'd hold on tighter.

'Sarah, are you okay?'

I turn towards the open doors. The police are standing near the rocks; PC Roam has her radio pressed to her mouth, and I wonder who she is speaking to, what she is saying. They think Jacob's disappearance is a suicide – and, in their minds, his trainers are evidence. What do they picture? My son swimming out on a dark night, desperate, alone, drunk. Swimming and swimming into oblivion.

Beyond the police, a young girl and her father are flying a kite, a trail of ribbons dancing on the breeze. The girl's hair is a golden colour and it twists in the wind as she bounces on the spot, looking up at the sky. Everything feels too bright, too vivid.

I put down my tea and press my fists into the sockets of my eyes, making a low guttural sound.

'They'll find him,' Nick says, but his voice lacks the certainty I need.

'How? How will they find him?'

'They're going to do more interviews.'

'They've spoken to everyone.'

'They're bringing more officers in to search the sandbank.' He pauses. 'And the coastguard has been told, too.'

I pull my hands from my face. 'Don't! He's not in the water, Nick. He can't be.'

'I know, I know,' he says gently.

'It's what the police think though, isn't it?'

He doesn't speak but I can see the answer in his expression. I shake my head. 'This can't be happening.'

This can't be happening.

There's a rhythm to those words that I recognize. A chill shivers down the length of my spine as I remember who said them.

20. ISLA

I wish I'd taken a thousand photographs of Marley, and then a thousand more.

I wish I'd recorded videos of him, so I could remember the exact way he ran, and how his hair had the tendency to flop in front of his eyes.

I wish I'd kept the bright-yellow tub I used to bath him in at the beach hut as a toddler, watching him splash and paddle, until his legs were too long to sit in it.

I wish I'd written journals, or made one of those baby books, like Sarah did for Jacob, charting all the tiny details of your child's early life, the date of their first steps, their first word. I'd teased her for it, saying she'd probably buy a special keepsake pot to store Jacob's first milk tooth in, too.

I was the sort of mother who had the naïve confidence to think my child would always be there, that I wouldn't need to hoard memories. We'll make new ones each and every day! We'll live in the moment. I let Marley roam wild on the beach and come back with scabby knees and sun-kissed shoulders. Who had time for annotating every detail of our days together when we were too busy living them?

But now, now I wish I'd recorded everything – because my memories feel dangerously loose, unpinned, like autumn leaves scattering in a cold wind.

Summer 2010

'I've made you a cottage pie,' Sarah said, standing on my doorstep proffering a basket filled with pre-portioned dishes of food. No big ceramic pie dishes for me any more, not in my new life. I stood back in the doorway as she bustled in, stepping over the pile of post I hadn't bothered to gather.

'What's that?' Sarah asked, moving into the lounge where a leather-bound journal was open on the floor.

'A memory book,' I answered, tightening the cord of my dressing gown, as I knew Sarah would make a comment about how thin I'd become. I'd headed the first page: *Marley Berry, 2000–2010*, and had begun to write down memories of Marley, or glue in old photos and special sheets from his school workbooks. I stuck in homemade birthday cards and scraps of his favourite clothes. Gradually I felt the satisfying way the pages began to thicken, the spine cracking. I had no gravestone to visit, nor a special place to mourn: there was only his memory book.

'That's a lovely idea.'

Was it? I didn't want to be collecting memories. I wanted to be *making* them. This wasn't supposed to be my life. Mine was filled with crab nets and wellingtons and kites.

There were treasure maps and wetsuits and flasks of hot chocolate. There were bedtime stories and warm hugs and plasters on knees. My life was supposed to be crammed with noise and laughter and love.

Marley had been missing for fifty-three days. *Missing*: how much longer could I keep on calling it that? In the space where I should have buried my son's body, instead I planted seeds of hope. For weeks I'd grown and tended wild theories about what'd happened to him, nurturing possible explanations as to how he could still be alive. I lived in a desperate hinterland, unable to let him go, unable to move forward.

Drowned, he drowned. That's what everyone was saying. That's what I must say, must believe.

'Are you seeing Samuel this week?' Sarah asked, shouldering off her coat and hanging it on the hook behind the door that only she used.

I shuffled into the kitchen behind her, watching her eyes skirt the piles of washing up beside the sink. She moved aside a tray of breakfast things and set down her basket.

'It's over.'

She turned, surprise lifting her brows. 'But . . . why?'

'I don't love him.'

Sarah looked at me searchingly. After a moment she said, 'That's not true.'

'Isn't it?' I countered, a hand planted on my hip.

'Don't push him away, Isla. He's a good man. He adores you.'

I told myself I let him go. But I didn't. I made him go. I forced him out. I wanted to be alone with my grief. I didn't want to have to try and feel better. I wanted to lurk in its darkness. Crawl through rough-toothed places. I no longer had the heart for light, or love.

I didn't want Samuel. Or Sarah. Or anyone. All I wanted was the boy who had a comforter named Zib. I wanted the boy who unfurled his fingers to show me a shell in the palm of his hand. I wanted the boy who would laugh with delight when I tickled his ribs. I wanted the boy who looked through binoculars at the world, amazed by its detail.

Sarah knew me well enough to sense she should drop the conversation. She turned to the freezer and began making space for the portions of cottage pie. Watching her neat blonde head bobbing around as she rearranged things, I felt the sparks of my anger snapping and flickering. Some days I could feel it building, expanding in me; it was loose and spiked and hot and unpredictable. A writhing ball of flames and fury. I could feel it edging deeper into my body, stiffening my limbs, making knots of my muscles.

'What were you doing?' I asked, my voice brittle.

Sarah turned, one hand on the freezer drawer. 'What am I doing? I'm just putting—'

'No,' I said hotly. 'What *were* you doing?'

Understanding arrived, a flush of pink rising in her cheeks.

I knew I should pull back, but I felt as though I was standing on the edge of a cliff and, rather than step back, I jumped. 'What were you doing when Marley drowned?'

'I . . . I . . .' Sarah brought her palm flat against her breastbone. 'What do you mean?'

The flames travelled through my throat, came licking out of my mouth. 'Why weren't you watching?'

171

Sarah screwed her eyes shut, her whole face twisting and shrinking.

'Look at me! Just fucking look at me!'

Her eyes snapped open. I could read the guilt in her expression as she said, 'I was cleaning. The hut windows. I was washing the salt from them.'

It was so impossibly mundane. So unimportant – she was washing windows while my baby drowned! I knew there was no correct answer that would appease me – what possible response could account for Marley's death? But that! That!

I slammed my head backwards, hitting the base of my skull against the cupboard door, a deep crunch sounding into the kitchen. Pain expanded in my head like heat. I hit it again. And again. And again.

'Stop! Please stop!' Sarah's hands were covering her mouth, her eyes welling with tears. 'I'm sorry. I should have been watching.'

And just like that, the fire in me went out. I found myself sliding on to the tiled floor, my head hanging forwards, cupped in my hands.

Sarah didn't hesitate; she gathered me in her arms and held me there, her tears streaming with my own.

It wasn't only Sarah who bore the brunt of my anger. I was furious about everything: that Jacob lived when Marley died; that, every day, I saw mothers who weren't cherishing their children; that I once had all this love in me – but now it had turned brittle and frozen, like cracked ice.

It felt impossible that Marley was lost. A swarm of questions buzzed constantly in my thoughts: Why didn't the boys tell us they were swimming? Why did no one see what happened? Why did Isaac bring Jacob to shore before searching for Marley? Why can Neil no longer look me in the eye? Why was Robert the first to abandon the search? Why hasn't Marley's body been found?

I distrusted everyone, certain that something was being kept from me. I believed that someone knew exactly what'd happened that day in the water – and was keeping the truth from me.

And I was right.

21. SARAH

DAY FOUR, 9.30 P.M.

The public showers on the sandbank smell of mildew and drains, and I keep my flip-flops on while I wash as quickly as possible. I'm vaguely aware that it's the first shower I've had since Jacob's disappearance; strange how the routines of normal life break apart with such ease, as if they were never anything more than a thin crust holding back bubbling molten mess.

I snap the shower off and dry myself swiftly. I pull my underwear from the hook on the back of the door, cursing as my jeans tumble on to the wet floor. My skin's damp as I wriggle into my knickers, then battle to tug on my jeans, the denim wet and stiff against my thighs.

Leaving the humid warmth of the shower block, I step on to the dark, fresh beach, my wash bag dangling from my fingers. The night air chills my damp scalp, the collar of my cardigan absorbing the moisture from my hair.

Sand cakes my wet flip-flops, making them uncomfortably gritty against the soles of my feet. The sandbank is quiet now, the day-trippers long gone, candlelight flickering in a few hut windows. I see a couple sharing a sofa, books propped in their laps, and I envy the evening that lies ahead for them – the simple pleasure of losing oneself in a book, letting the mind wander, roam, escape.

I can't help but think about the mother I'd read about on a missing persons' website, whose son had disappeared twenty years ago. Has she ever had a good night's sleep since? Has she ever woken and not thought first of him? Has she ever enjoyed a book, a film, a meal, as she once had?

I walk on, my mood low, anxiety beating thickly in my chest. As I pass Isaac's hut, I keep my gaze lowered out of habit. He'll be away on the oil rig, I remind myself, but still, I'm careful not to pause.

My mind must be agitated as I find myself imagining him sitting in his darkened hut, his long fingers linked together, watching. Always watching.

Does he know something? a voice inside me whispers.

I shake my head sharply and continue on. I've almost reached our hut when I notice a cluster of people ahead, their chairs pulled close to a small fire burning in the belly of a barbecue. As I approach, I can hear the first notes of conversation drifting on the breeze. 'Brings it all back, doesn't it? What Isla went through . . .'

It's Joe's voice. I can make him out, sitting beside Binks, drinks in hand. Diane and Neil are opposite them, and there are a couple of other people with their backs to me. On another evening, a lifetime ago, Nick and I would've joined

175

them, dragging over sun-chairs, opening a bottle of wine, throwing blankets over our knees – but tonight I find myself hovering in the shadows, listening.

Neil's voice is low, almost whispered, a light slur to his words. 'I can't shake the image of Isla standing on the shoreline. She looked . . . broken. Hopeless. It was like . . . like you could see the life draining out of her.'

Beside him, Diane says firmly, 'You did everything you could, Neil.'

I watch Neil reach down for the wine bottle by his chair. He refills his glass almost to the brim. Diane looks away.

Binks says, 'I always thought it was a shame Isla never had any more children. She was such a wonderful mother.'

Behind the group, I'm aware of the looming shadow of Isla's hut. Shuttered, empty, almost accusing in the darkness. What if the candles were lit, the doors thrown open, Marley still here, tucked up in bed? A bat dips low overhead. I can feel the vibration of its wings through the night, the air thrumming against my face.

'Too torn up,' Joe says. 'You remember how she was. Fixated, wasn't she? All her theories. All her doubts. You can understand it, course you can.'

Out there, beyond the fire, beyond the beach, the sea sprawls towards the horizon, dark and knowing.

'Theories?' another voice asks – and I realize it is Lorrain, who sits with her back to me.

'About what happened to Marley,' Binks explains. 'The sea never brought him back. She didn't get to see his little body. Impossible for a mother, that. For anyone. She still asks us to talk her through it sometimes, what we saw, what happened. Heart-breaking,' Binks says softly, turning her head towards the water.

'Isla didn't believe he'd drowned?' Lorrain asks.

I can feel the shift in atmosphere at her directness.

'She had . . . questions,' Binks responds. 'Marley was a terrific little swimmer. She had some doubts about the search. Cast a few names around.'

'Like Isaac's,' a booming voice offers.

Robert! I hadn't noticed him before, but now I can make out his broad frame, seated beside Lorrain. He would never usually join our group for a fire – particularly not if it meant being in Neil's company – but from the proximity of his and Lorrain's chairs, I can guess what's drawn him to our end of the beach.

'Why Isaac?' Lorrain asks, an unmistakable note of interest in her tone.

There's a long pause and I find myself holding my breath.

Eventually it's Joe who answers. 'I think,' he says in a slow, considered way, 'that Isaac is an easy person to be curious about. He keeps himself to himself. You'll never see any family or friends at his hut. He likes his boat and his fish – but that's no crime. He was the one who brought Jacob back to shore, after all. I wouldn't like to believe that anything amiss went on that day.'

Neil lifts his wine, gulping back half of it.

'Hard to imagine that Marley would have been seventeen this year,' Binks says. 'Such an angel. Joe, remember the summer he and Jacob made that beautiful driftwood mobile on the beach, just here? They collected shells and stones and feathers and all sorts – then hung them from the wood.'

I remember. Nick had to borrow a drill to make holes in the shells so that the boys could thread string through a trail of them. Why am I lurking here in the shadows; these are my friends, aren't they? I should join them. I'm about to step forward when I hear Lorrain say, 'Must've been hard on Jacob, losing his best friend like that.'

Diane is the one who answers. 'It was difficult that first summer, wasn't it? He didn't talk much. Barely came out of the hut, I seem to remember. He wouldn't go near the sea – although you wouldn't know it now. He's rarely out of the water.'

'What do you make of Jacob's disappearance?' Lorrain asks, her voice a beat quieter than before – but I catch it, the hint of gossip wrapped up as concern.

I stay exactly where I am, frozen to the spot. A mosquito buzzes nearby, a high-pitched drone vibrating close to my ear. I don't move. I am barely breathing. I feel the hot prick of its bite on my wrist bone.

'Strikes me as a little odd that it happened on Marley's anniversary,' Robert says, something provocative in his delivery.

'Why?' Neil asks sharply. 'What's the anniversary got to do with anything?'

I hold my breath, aware of a strange tension crackling in the air.

When Robert doesn't answer, Neil rises from his seat, reaching for a piece of wood. He throws it to the fire, sending sparks into the night.

Lorrain says, 'It's just worrying. It's been what, four days? No one's seen him, not even a glimpse. His trainers even had his socks balled up inside them – like he took them off to swim.' She pauses for a moment. 'But why swim alone, at night, like Jacob did?' Lorrain poses. 'Makes you wonder, doesn't it?'

'Wonder what?' Neil presses.

'Well, I don't know,' Lorrain says, uncertain now. 'Sarah told me the police are questioning whether . . . well, whether Jacob swam out there on purpose. Whether he didn't *want* to make it back to shore.'

'They think Jacob killed himself?' Neil asks. 'On the anniversary?'

'How dare you!' I cry, kicking up sheets of sand as I rush forward. 'How *fucking* dare you! All of you!'

There's the sharp intake of breath as everyone turns. Chairs are pushed back. People rise to their feet.

'Sarah! I'm so sorry,' Lorrain rushes. 'That must have sounded incredibly insensitive—'

'You think Jacob killed himself, do you?' I hiss from the edge of their circle, my wash bag swinging from my fingers. 'You think that Jacob's life was so shitty – that Nick and I had made such a hash of things – that he'd want to kill himself?'

'No, I was—'

'Because you have no fucking clue about who Jacob is or how he thinks! And you!' I say, swinging round to Robert. 'Don't you dare pass comment on my son, when Caz—'

'Let's calm down,' Diane is saying.

'Calm? My son has been missing for four days – and my *friends* would rather sit around gossiping about whether he's topped himself than actually doing anything productive like helping search for him. I know you told the police that Jacob and I were arguing the night he disappeared. Did you enjoy your moment in the limelight, Diane?'

'I'm sorry – but they asked if I'd heard anything. I didn't want to lie . . .'

There's a warm hand on my arm. 'Sarah, love, it's all of our faults. We shouldn't have been talking about Jacob, full stop. We know the strain you're under. No one meant any harm, I promise you.' Reasonable, rational, kind-hearted Joe.

'Joe's right,' Diane explains. 'Jacob is on all of our minds. We're just worried.'

'Really? Nick and I have seen you, Diane, standing on your deck ear-wigging into our conversations. Is it you who's been keeping the police abreast of your little theories about Marley's anniversary?'

'I never mentioned it!' Diane protests, turning to look at Neil.

'That was me.' Binks pushes herself awkwardly to her feet, the blanket covering her knees pooling on to the sand.

The admission wrong-foots me. I stare wordlessly at Binks.

'I'm so sorry, Sarah. I didn't realize it was a . . .' Binks halts as if she's rethinking her choice of words. 'Well, that you and Nick hadn't mentioned it.'

'We didn't think it was relevant,' I say, losing steam.

In the silence that follows, I no longer know what I'm doing out here, arguing with these people. Suddenly I just want my bed. I want to lay my head on the soft pillow, pull the duvet up to my chin, and sleep. I can feel my throat closing, tears threatening. I turn from the group, hurrying towards the beach hut. Their eyes are on my back as I clamber on to my deck, yank open the hut door and disappear inside.

22. ISLA

In the days and weeks after losing Marley, my name and his blew from hut to hut like the salt wind. I felt as if my every movement was watched, speculated on. Although people were kind, concerned, I didn't want to talk. I didn't want to do my unravelling in public. So I began to close myself off, person by person, piece by piece. The only family I could bear to be around was Sarah's. They understood my grief because they shared it. Their company, their memories of Marley, became my refuge.

And that was the problem.

Summer 2011

I sat cross-legged on the sand-dusted floor, holding up a small sky-blue T-shirt with a picture of a whale embroidered on the front. I gathered the cotton in my fingers and pressed it to my nose, breathing in. A fragment of memory loosened:

Marley picking his way over the rocks, barefoot, arms outstretched for balance. He crouches down on all fours searching for something, his flyaway blond hair falling over his face. Suddenly he is springing to his feet, waving his arms and jumping up and down to get Jacob's attention.

I tried to recall what happened after that. Did I go down to the rocks to see what had caught his attention, made his eyes brighten like that?

'Auntie Isla?'

I turned. Jacob was standing in the doorway of the hut.

'Hello, baby. Come in,' I told him, setting down Marley's T-shirt.

He stayed in the doorway, watchful, his dark eyes worried. 'Mummy asked if you'd like to come over for lunch.'

'Lunch,' I said absently, unsure when I'd last eaten. 'Yes. Thank you. I'll come.'

Jacob hovered a moment longer. I thought he was going to leave, but instead he crossed the hut and plonked himself down beside me. He didn't say anything, just gazed at the memory book that was open on the floor. I worried about Jacob, sensing that his grief was something dark and unchannelled that he didn't yet understand. He seemed like a tiny soul, adrift without the anchor of his best friend.

'I'm writing down some special memories about Marley,' I told Jacob, passing him the book. 'You might be able to help me. I'm trying to remember a day when you and Marley were playing down by the rocks. I think you were building a tower out of pebbles and Marley was excited as he'd seen something, or found something, near the rocks. I couldn't remember what.'

'An adder,' Jacob said without hesitation. 'This long.' He measured with his hands.

My face split into a wide smile. 'That's right!' Marley had seen strange tracks on the sand earlier in the day and had been following them wondering what they were, but none of us could decide. Occasionally we spotted adders on the headland, basking in the sun, but we'd never seen one on the sand before.

'We made snake catchers out of old fishing nets,' Jacob went on, his voice growing brighter, 'so we could return the snake to the headland. Marley drew a snake tattoo on the inside of my wrist, and I did the same for him, and we were the Snake Catchers' Club.'

I laughed as it all came back to me. 'I had to redraw Marley's tattoo as he was convinced you'd made it look like a worm.'

Jacob grinned, a mischievous little smile I hadn't seen in months. 'I had!'

Sharing the memory was a balm, a shimmer of gold in the darkness, and I knew later that I'd write it down, secure every detail of it into the memory book.

'I've got something for you,' I said, getting to my feet. I climbed on to the sofa and stretched to reach the top shelf, removing a pair of binoculars. I'd bought them for Marley's eighth birthday; they were lightweight adult binoculars, not kids' ones. Marley would tick off all the birds he'd spotted in a bird book, sometimes adding notes in his beautifully childish hand. 'Marley would've liked you to have these.'

Jacob hesitated, his dark gaze serious again. 'Are you sure? Really?'

'Absolutely.'

He carefully took the binoculars and turned them slowly through his hands. Then he stood up and faced the sea, pressing them to his eyes. A small smile spread across his mouth. 'I can see right into that boat! There's a seagull sitting on the wheel! I can see . . . *everything*!'

He scanned the stretch of the beach, looking at it afresh through the binoculars, narrating what he saw. When he lowered them, he turned to me and threw his arms around my neck.

I felt the warmth of his little body pressed to me; I smelt salt and sun cream on his skin; I felt the boyish softness of his hair against my cheek. I squeezed my eyes shut, holding tight.

23. SARAH

DAY FIVE, 11.30 A.M.

Nick is repairing the hinge on the back door of the beach hut. He mutters to himself about the state of his toolbox, and twice I hear the screwdriver clatter to the ground, followed by a curse. He says something to me, but I don't respond, don't move from my position in front of the window. I'm concentrating on the details of Jacob's disappearance, as if the facts are parts of an equation that only I am able to solve.

Here's what I know: at around eight o'clock on the night he disappeared, Jacob and I argued and he left the beach hut and went straight to Luke's. There, he had several drinks with his friends and Caz, hiding out at the back of the hut when Robert appeared. At eleven o'clock, he walked Caz out, leaving his rucksack behind, telling Luke he'd be back soon. He and Caz stopped to talk by the rocks at the edge of our bay, arguing about the pregnancy. Some time later, Caz returned to her hut alone, and Jacob remained on the rocks, upset.

Four days later, his trainers and socks were found in that very place.

He has not answered his phone.

He did not pack any belongings to leave.

There have been no sightings or traces of him since.

Here's what I don't know: I don't know whether Robert managed to hunt down Jacob later in the evening. I don't know why Caz didn't tell the police she was pregnant. I don't know why Diane and Neil are acting strangely whenever Jacob's name is mentioned. I don't know what happened in the minutes immediately after Caz left Jacob. I don't know why his trainers were by the rocks – but his phone and T-shirt weren't. I don't know where Jacob is now.

'I don't fucking know!' I cry, my fist slamming against the window with a force that rattles the pane.

Nick looks round sharply.

I mumble a low apology, waiting for him to resume what he was doing.

The police believe that one of two things has happened. Option one: Jacob had been drinking all evening with his friends, and then he'd had an upsetting argument with his girlfriend. Perhaps he was already feeling emotionally unstable because of the anniversary of Marley's death. He decided to go for a swim to clear his head, so he removed his trainers and socks and waded into the sea. Maybe it was the alcohol coursing through him that made him over-confident and he swam out too far, or maybe the tide was running particularly hard that night and he got disorientated in the dark. Jacob got into trouble – and drowned.

Option two: Jacob never had any intention of making it back to shore at all.

That is what they believe.

That is what our beach hut neighbours seem to believe.

But I don't.

I can't.

I'm not convinced that he went into the water at all. He would have taken off his T-shirt, taken his mobile from his pocket – not waded in with them. So where are they? He'd had time to remove his trainers, ball up his socks and leave them in the toe of each shoe. That shows he wasn't rushing – that he was doing something consciously. Maybe he wanted to feel the water around his feet, so he paddled for a while – then something distracted him, and he left his trainers where they were, or couldn't find them again in the dark.

The facts swell like a balloon, so my head feels stretched tight.

Then one thought pricks the rest.

'Nick!' I say so suddenly, that I hear the clang of the screwdriver against the door as he spins around.

'What is it?'

'Jacob balled up his socks and put them in his trainers. The trainers weren't just cast aside on the beach – they were tucked out of sight beneath the rocks. He was planning on coming back for them – but knew he'd be a while.'

He looks at me blankly.

'He wasn't going swimming.'

'Then—'

'Jacob was getting in a boat.'

It is so logical, so simple, that I'm amazed we didn't think of it before.

Nick looks at me for a long moment – and then he nods slowly, saying, 'He took his socks and trainers off to wade out to a boat.'

I feel the corners of my mouth turn upwards. 'Maybe someone took him to the quay, or further up the coast. Dropped him off, perhaps?' New questions are pounding forward now. 'Who does he know with a boat? Do any of his friends have one?'

Nick presses his knuckles to his lips. 'Luke?'

I shake my head. 'No. His dad had a motorboat a couple of years ago, but sold it.'

'It doesn't have to be one of his friends. Anyone could have come into the bay.'

He's right. Once the ferry stops running, people use their boats to leave the sandbank, or cross to the pub on the quay. 'Robert could've been out on his. I'm sure I saw Neil going out on his boat that night, too. Let's ask around – see if anyone saw anything.'

We start next door with Diane and Neil.

I rarely step inside this hut and I'm reminded how sterile it feels: the kitchen area is overdesigned with its faux lime-stone worktops and tiled splashbacks. There are no bookshelves or photos on the wooden walls, just a pair of polished wooden oars fixed to the wall that will never feel the wash of the sea.

'Neil's not here,' Diane tells us warily, smoothing down her skirt.

'That's fine. We won't keep you,' I say crisply, the memory of last night's beach gossip hovering between us.

As Nick explains our theory about Jacob boarding a boat, Diane listens in an overtly engaged way, her head bobbing up and down.

'Sounds likely. Very plausible,' Diane agrees.

I ask, 'Neil's boat was in the bay that night, wasn't it?'

'Well, yes. It's there most of the summer.'

'Did he go out on it?'

She hesitates before answering, 'Yes. Briefly, I think.'

'What sort of time would that have been?'

Again, she pauses before answering. 'I suppose around nine o'clock.'

'Where was he going? To the pub?'

'No, I don't think so. Just out.'

'With you?'

'On his own. Sometimes he likes to just get on the water.'

'At night?'

Diane raises her chin. 'Yes. At night.'

Nick asks, 'Did Neil happen to mention seeing anyone else out on the water that evening?'

She shakes her head.

Before we leave, I have a final question for Diane. 'There was a ding on Neil's boat. He spotted it the morning after Jacob disappeared. Did you ever find out what it was from?'

'It's just a small scuff at the bow. Might have been there for days before we noticed it. It could've been the anchor chain rubbing, even.'

'If you do find out what happened,' I say, 'let us know, won't you?'

'Course.' She smiles tightly.

As we walk away from Diane's hut, I whisper to Nick, 'Don't you think that was odd?'

He shrugs.

'Neil took his boat out the evening Jacob disappears – not to go to the pub, not to go fishing – just out.'

'Maybe it's his bit of peace and quiet.'

'Perhaps, but I still want to ask Neil about it directly.'

There's a wariness in Nick's tone as he says, 'You don't honestly think Neil has anything to do with Jacob's disappearance?'

The truth is, no, I don't. I can't think of any reason why Neil would be involved – he and Jacob have very little to do with each other beyond passing the occasional greeting. That said, it doesn't mean I'll let Neil slip from my radar. 'I just want to be thorough,' I tell Nick.

We don't have the chance to discuss it further as we stop next at Joe and Binks's hut to ask whether they saw a boat entering or leaving the bay that night. They apologize for being of little help, saying they were in bed by nine thirty as their grandchildren had worn them out.

We call in at various other huts along the sandbank, learning very little, until we come across Fez, one of Nick's old friends. 'How's it all going? Any news? I've been thinking of you both,' he says warmly.

191

I like Fez a great deal; he's one of those people who never takes himself too seriously. He works as a roadie for nine months of the year, but takes the summer off to spend on the sandbank. But right now I don't have the heart to go over the details of Jacob's disappearance – yet again. Nick steps in, telling him about the trainers by the rocks. 'You know of anyone who was using their boat on Sunday night? Leaving our bay, maybe?'

'Wouldn't be able to tell you. I was in The Rope and Anchor from six. Had a right night of it.' The Rope and Anchor sits on the edge of the quay; it's mostly visited by the local fishermen who unload their catch nearby. In the summer months it's also busy with beach hut owners, who moor by the quay so that they can drink until close and still get back to the sandbank after the ferry stops running.

Fez glances at Nick, saying, 'Was hoping you might've come in for a quick one. Been a while. Thought I saw your car.'

'Probably leaving. Was on my way to Bristol. Work.'

I remember Robert telling me that he'd spent the evening in the pub. 'Robert was there, wasn't he? He went by boat?'

Fez thinks for a moment. 'Yeah, think he did. Had his boat keys with him at least.'

'What time did he leave?'

'You know how bloody prompt those bar staff are – checking their watches, telling us to drink up well before close – it's like they don't want our money.' He sniffs. 'Eleven, bang on. Chucked us all out.'

Enough time for Robert to get in his boat – steaming – and roar back to the sandbank.

And, what does he see when he gets there?

The scene forms clearly in my head. Caz is drunk and weeping on the rocks. She must have looked so vulnerable, so young. Then Robert looks more closely and sees someone else on the rocks with her: the same person who has caused her tears, who has got her pregnant.

Jacob.

'Jacob got into Robert's boat,' I say to Nick the moment Fez leaves. My voice is fast and low as I explain. 'We know Robert was looking for him earlier that evening. When he came back from the pub, he could've seen Jacob and Caz on the rocks – asked Jacob to have a word. The two of them go out to sea to talk. Sounds like Robert was steaming from the pub – and we know Jacob had been drinking, too. What if . . . what if the conversation got heated, and maybe . . . I don't know . . . maybe something happened?'

I can see from the way Nick's jaw tightens that he is considering my explanation, believing it is possible.

'We've got to speak to him.'

'Don't you think we should let the police do that?' Nick counters.

I snort. 'Really? Do you think they'll rush down here?' When I'd shared our boat theory, they'd told me that they'd 'look into it', whatever that meant. 'You saw the papers this morning. Where do you think their resources will be directed?' The front page of *The Daily Echo* was ablaze with the tragic news of a hit-and-run case: a six-year-old girl had been knocked down by a van, and the girl had died in hospital overnight. Right now, solving that case will be the police's priority.

193

'I want to handle this myself. We know Robert. I want to look him in the eye and see what he says.'

Nick looks at me carefully. 'Okay, then. We'll talk to him together. But Sarah,' he says, catching my fingers in his, 'we need to tread carefully. We mustn't go in there accusing Robert, okay? The sandbank is a small place.'

'I know that,' I say tersely.

I want to walk on, but Nick doesn't release my hand. 'You remember how Isla was in the weeks after . . .'

Of course I remember! I was the one trying to pick up the pieces! She tore apart friendships in her search for answers. She barely slept or ate or left the hut. When I speak, my voice comes out in a low hiss, 'Don't you dare compare us. This is different! Everything is different!' I yank my hand from his, and walk on.

When we reach Robert's hut, he's crouched on all fours beneath the deck, a spade in hand. His cheeks are red and his thick grey hair looks windswept. He's zipped into a sailing jacket with a boat racing number stamped across the chest. 'Digging out,' he says, on seeing us. 'Need some extra space for the sails.'

He gets to his feet, dusting the sand from his knees. 'Cassie isn't here if you've come to see her. She's resting at her aunt's house.'

I can't believe I'd forgotten: Caz was scheduled to have the abortion yesterday. A piercingly beautiful image of a baby – Jacob and Caz's baby – stabs into my heart. How could I have forgotten something so important? That baby was part of my son. It could have been part of our family.

I've no idea how I feel . . . 'Is Caz okay? Did the . . .' I falter. 'Did . . . everything go okay?'

Robert sets his cool blue gaze on me. I find myself willing him to say Caz didn't go through with it. She changed her mind. There is still a baby. Still a part of Jacob undeniably here.

'It went as well as can be expected. She's a tough girl.'

I swallow hard.

Nick says, 'Please tell Caz we're thinking about her. We're sorry that she's had to go through all of this . . .'

'Me, too,' Robert says.

There's an awkward silence during which the three of us stand looking at one another. Nick pushes his hands into his pockets and explains that we're looking into whether Jacob boarded a boat the evening he disappeared. 'We're talking to everyone who used their boats that night.'

'Good idea. Most likely one of his young chums gave him a ride to the quay.'

'Were you out in your boat?' I ask.

Robert's gaze moves to me. 'My boat's in the marina. Took it in a few days ago. Needs a new propeller, so I'm keeping it over there until they've got a slot down at the yard. Bloody expensive hobby, boats.'

'When did you take it in?'

'Last week some time.'

'So you weren't out in your boat on Sunday evening – the night Jacob disappeared.'

'Sunday,' he repeats slowly, looking skyward. 'I took the boat into the marina early evening, if my memory serves me, then went over to the pub.' He folds his arms, rolling forward on to the balls of his feet. 'If you're looking into who was on the water, you should speak to Neil. I seem to remember he was out on his boat that night. Goes out every year on Marley's anniversary. Odd, if you ask me.'

Does he? I steal a glance at Nick, who looks equally surprised by the suggestion. Diane certainly hadn't mentioned it earlier – and there was a strange caginess about her answers. Then again, Robert could just be stirring, redirecting our focus.

I ask one last time, 'You're absolutely sure you weren't out on your boat at around eleven o'clock on Sunday night?'

'I'm sure.'

'Thank you for your help,' Nick says cordially. I feel the light brush of Nick's hand on my lower back as he directs me away.

'He's lying! I know he is!' I say the moment we're back inside our hut, the doors closed.

I half expect Nick to defend Robert, so I'm relieved to hear him agree with me. 'I don't think he was giving us the full picture.'

'Then why the hell aren't we still there, demanding to know?'

'Because I want to make a call first.'

'To who?'

'The marina where Robert keeps his boat. They'll be able to tell us exactly when he dropped it off.'

I listen as Nick makes the call, leaving a message on an answerphone with instructions to call him back urgently.

'I'll try them again in an hour,' he tells me.

We both turn towards the beach hut doors at the faint

sound of laughter. Two young boys, their skin tanned to a nut-brown, are digging a hole in the sand, yellow spades plunging into the ground, sand cascading into the air. A spaniel crouches between them, pawing at the hole with equal fervour.

'Wind back the clock,' Nick says, 'and it could be Jacob and Marley.'

'I know,' I say quietly.

Nick turns, the light gone from his eyes. 'How did things get like this? Marley dead; Jacob missing.'

'Don't,' I say, squeezing my eyes tightly shut. I don't want to think of the *how*. Instead I say, 'Do you remember when the two of them built that bivouac deep in the woods on the headland? You helped set them up, showing them what sort of branches to look for and how to tie them together with twine.'

'I let them use my penknife, didn't I? You and Isla went mad!'

'They were only nine!'

'Made a bloody good bivouac with it, though. Remember the grand unveiling?'

I nod. Nick, Isla and I were invited to inspect the den. The boys had stood in front it, chests puffed with pride. We'd hugged our little bark-stained wild-men to us, telling them it was the most wonderful den we'd ever seen. 'Didn't they sleep in it one night?'

'With Isla,' Nick says.

'That's right.' I remember packing Jacob off with a thick sleeping bag and a flask of hot chocolate, thinking, *Poor Isla!*

Nick asks, 'Still no word from her?'

I shake my head. 'I haven't tried her today. Maybe I'll

give her a ring now,' I say, slipping my mobile from my pocket. I punch in Isla's number once again, yet even as I'm cradling the phone to my ear, something inside me knows that she isn't going to answer.

When I hear her voicemail click on, I feel the sting of disappointment. I try reasoning that when Isla's in Chile, we never phone each other – I'm not even sure that she has her English mobile switched on over there.

As I leave her a message, my voice feels tight, a notch louder than it needs to be. I update her on the latest developments, telling her about Jacob's trainers by the rocks, my conviction that Jacob got on a boat, our visit to Robert's hut. I tell her how scared we are. That I'm not sleeping. I want her to understand how serious this is. To understand that I need her.

As I'm talking, her voicemail cuts off.

I listen to the stretched beep of the phone, blinking.

'What is it?' Nick asks, noticing my expression,

I tell myself that my message must have been too long – it filled up Isla's voicemail. Yet a strange chill creeps down my spine; I have a vividly uncomfortable sensation that Isla was staring at the phone in her hand – watching my name flashing on her screen, choosing not to pick up. And then her finger moved to the 'End call' button – and she cut me off.

'Don't be ridiculous,' Nick tells me. 'Isla wouldn't have cut you off.'

Wouldn't she? I haven't told Nick about our argument on the night she left for Chile.

'If she'd heard any one of your messages, she'd have

called you straight back. You said yourself that you don't know if she uses her UK mobile in Chile.'

This is true. Perhaps the stress of Jacob's disappearance is getting to me. Isla and I have argued before and always made up. And, anyway, if Isla has been getting my messages, she'd have called. She cares too much about Jacob not to help.

'Why don't you try emailing her?' Nick says.

'I can't from my phone.' I rarely need to use my email account, so I've never got around to setting it up on my mobile.

'I'll do it,' Nick says, taking out his phone. 'What do you want to say?'

'Just to ring us urgently.'

I watch Nick tapping away. Less than a minute later, he says, 'Sent.'

I stare at him. 'How did you know her email address?'

He shrugs. 'It was in my contacts.'

'Really? Why?'

'No idea. Probably been in there for years.'

'You've emailed Isla before, then?'

A pause. 'Must've done. Or maybe you have from my email account.'

We both know I never use Nick's email.

I look at Nick closely, my gaze searching his face for clues. 'Is there anything you want to tell me?'

Nick's eyes are on me, his expression hardening. 'What does that mean?'

'I think you know.'

He shakes his head once. 'Don't do this, Sarah. I mean it. Let's not go there.'

24. ISLA

An email from Nick pings across the screen of my phone. It's been a long time since I've seen his name in my inbox.

From: Nick Symonds.
Subject: Jacob
Message: Can you ring Sarah urgently? Jacob's been missing for five days. We're scared, Isla. Call us. Nick x

I delete the email. I can't think about Nick.

Instead, I play Sarah's voicemail for the second time. I hadn't meant to cut her off while she was still talking. I'd been holding my mobile, watching her name on the screen, and my thumb must have slipped.

Replaying the message now, I hear the sharpness of her tone and the way she gulps in air between her sentences.

'I need to talk to you. You're the only person who will understand.'

My teeth clench together. Yes, I know what it's like to wake each morning with the sickening lurch of memory: He's not here.

I continue to listen, catching Nick's footsteps in the background. I hear the breathless rush of Sarah's voice as she tells me about Robert and his boat, Neil and Diane, her theories and suspicions. It's amazing to me that she's still not asking other questions – the important ones. She's not even mentioned Isaac's name yet. Not once. But I suppose she can't. Not to me, at least.

Even now she's hiding from the truth.

There's a pause in the voicemail. I can hear the sea in the background – a particular sound that is unique to the sandbank: the cawing of gulls, the light breeze washing through the hut doors. There's something fresh about it, intoxicating. It makes me wistful for the summers we've left behind.

When Sarah speaks again, she sounds distracted – impatient with me for not being there when she needs to talk. I've always been her go-to person; if she's exhausted a topic with Nick, or doesn't think he'll be a sympathetic audience, it's me she talks to.

I listen carefully to the timbre of her voice. By now she must be wondering why I've not returned her calls. Why my phone goes straight to voicemail.

And I think I can catch it – just the tiniest flicker of hesitation.

Jacob's been missing for five days. When Marley had been

---

gone for that long, I'd travelled down every possibility, ludicrous or not. Sarah will be getting desperate for answers. She may just be pulling me into her radar. But it won't be long, I realize.

She is my best friend – the nearest person I have on this planet to family. But Jacob is her son. She will doubt me, I know she will.

She'll begin to question everyone close to her – and she will be right to.

25. SARAH

DAY FIVE, 8 P.M.

I sit at the table with a glass of wine, facing the view. As dusk rolls in over the water, sand martins pour from the sky, soaring and dipping in their chase for insects. Dusk has always been my favourite time on the sandbank, when the day-trippers have left and the beach is returned to us again. But I've begun to dread this peculiar half-light between day and night, where thoughts blur and meld – a shadow becoming a boy, or the cawing of a gull seeming like a panicked voice. As the colour is leached from the sky, I know we're approaching the close of yet another day without Jacob.

Nick stands and clears our supper things. Cutlery slides against china as he scrapes the virtually untouched pasta into the bin. We went through the motions of dinner – cooking, laying the table, placing steaming plates of linguini heaped with parmesan before us – but neither of us had an appetite. We watched the meal grow cold, the cheese congealing in yellowy gluts.

I don't move to help. A tension headache is threatening behind my eyes. I finish my wine without tasting it, and set down the empty glass.

Nick crosses the beach hut, leaving the stacked dirty plates for me to deal with. Clearing up for him means making a pile by the sink. He crouches on the floor by the sofa bed, pulling out Jacob's belongings. Clothes, wash stuff, and magazines litter the beach hut floor.

'What are you doing?' I catch the waspish tone of my question.

'We're missing something. There's got to be a clue.'

I've already been through every inch of this hut, but I don't say anything. I understand Nick's need to do something. He is not a man who coasts. I've never once heard him say, *We'll see what happens.* Nick steers the course of his life; he makes things happen. To not be active in finding Jacob would render him passive – and he'll never be that.

Some time later, light footsteps sound across our deck. My shoulders tense: I don't want to see anyone, not tonight. There's a tentative knock.

I open the door to find Caz looking pale and drawn against the darkening sky. I'm surprised she's even on the sandbank – Robert had said she was recovering at her aunt's. 'Caz, hi. Come in, come in.'

A breeze washes in behind her, tinged with barbecue smoke and the oily scent of fresh mackerel cooking.

There is almost nowhere to sit as every surface is covered with stuff – Nick has piled our belongings around the hut in his search for clues: a large Tupperware box containing mosquito coils and repellents; board games that don't get played as much as I'd like; a first-aid kit that I must remember to update; a pack of scented candles. I push aside a pile of blankets and Caz perches on the edge of the sofa. Nick, rummaging at the back of the hut, lifts a hand in greeting.

I sit opposite Caz, wondering what she's doing here. Did Robert tell her that we'd been to see him? I clear my throat. 'How are you feeling – after yesterday?'

She lifts and drops her shoulders. 'It was the right thing.' Her response is clipped and it's clear she didn't come here to talk about the abortion. 'Any news on Jacob? Dad told me that you found his trainers.'

'Yes, they were by the rocks – just where you said the two of you had been sitting. Was he wearing them when you were . . . talking?'

She nods.

'We wondered if Jacob took off his trainers to swim – but if that had been the case, we'd have probably found his T-shirt and phone, too. So now we're wondering if he got on a boat with someone.'

I look to Caz, as if she may have some thoughts on this, but she just shrugs.

I notice now the puffiness to her eyelids: she's been crying. I get a strange feeling that she has come here to tell us something. I wait, levelling my gaze to hers.

When she says nothing, I ask gently, 'Is there anything you want to talk about, Caz?'

She looks up at me, her gaze moving across my face.

I wait, heartbeat drumming.

205

'Sorry for the chaos,' Nick interrupts, grabbing an armful of things from the sofa beside Caz. As he removes them, I see the small cotton bag he's left behind, turned on its side, the contents spilled on to the sofa. My eyes widen as I realize what the bag contains: a signed copy of an Anita Shreve novel stolen from Diane's bookcase; an Ace of Spades playing card taken from a pristine pack in one of Nick's friends' huts; and there, right beside Caz, are her silver seahorse earrings.

'I don't even know what half of this crap is doing in the hut,' Nick continues, shoving things back into drawers.

I can't take my eyes off the seahorse earrings. They are only centimetres from Caz's thigh. I want to pull her to her feet, usher her from the hut. But I also don't want to draw attention to the items. She hasn't noticed them yet – maybe she won't do.

My heart pounds against my ribcage and my skin feels so hot it is starting to itch.

Caz is looking at me and I realize my expression must be strained. I fix my features into what I hope is a neutral expression. 'So how have you been feeling today?' My voice comes out oddly tight.

Caz stares at me for a moment. 'Okay.'

'Good. That's good. And your mother, how is she? Do you speak much these days? Portugal, isn't it? No, wait. Spain.'

Her brow furrows. 'She's fine . . .'

'That's good,' I repeat idiotically.

I startle at the sound of a phone ringing. I reach towards my pocket – but realize it is Nick's phone.

He answers it, saying, 'Oh, hello. Thanks for calling me back. Yes, that's right. I left you a message earlier today.' He glances at me.

It's the marina, I realize, returning his call.

'Yes, I just wanted to check the detail of something,' he says, moving towards the open doorway, stepping out on to the deck. I can tell he's stalling, waiting until he's out of Caz's earshot before he asks about Robert's boat.

'Probably something to do with work,' I say as I watch Nick moving away along the beach.

I set down my glass of wine and say, in as light a tone as I can manage, 'Here, let me try and make things cosier. I'll move some of this stuff for you.'

As I rise, about to take a step towards the sofa where Caz is, she says, 'Don't worry. It's fine.'

Maybe there is something in my expression – something resolute and focused – as Caz follows my gaze, angling her head towards the items beside her.

And there they are: two beautiful seahorse earrings, curled together by her thigh.

Her glance is casual – casual enough for me to think she hasn't registered them. But then her head tilts slightly towards the earrings, and her gaze intensifies, pinned to the earrings.

I can almost see each of her thoughts as she looks at the earrings, thinking, *I have some just like these.* She lifts a hand to her ear lobe, touching the empty space – perhaps recalling that her earrings are missing. And then I see it, a slight stiffening in her posture as she realizes that the last time she saw them was when I was in her beach hut.

She picks up the earrings. Turns them through her fingers as if inspecting them, looking for the one tiny, irrefutable piece of evidence that these belong to her.

She sees it: one of the backs of the earrings has a gold clasp, rather than silver. She looks up sharply. 'These earrings . . .'

It is not what she says, or even the tone of her voice exactly, as much as the look on her face which tells me she knows.

My mouth is ever so slightly open. I feel like my cheeks are burning red. I swallow. 'I was just going to move those things.'

I move as if to take them from her, but Caz's fingers make a fist around the earrings.

She stands, and for a moment the two of us face one another. We are exactly the same height. We look into each other's faces and it is there, the truth.

'These are mine.'

I have imagined it – all the different ways I could be confronted by the people I've stolen from. I've practised what I'd say: *I must have put it in my pocket without thinking.* Or, *Are you sure this is yours? I have one just the same.* Or perhaps, *I knocked it off the shelf and intended to put it back, but wasn't concentrating.* But now that I'm standing here in front of Caz, my mind is blank.

'Why?' she demands of me. 'Why did you steal them?'

I've no idea how to begin to explain why I do it. Heat crawls over my skin. I feel as if I've just walked into a public place naked: I am humiliated, exposed, ashamed. 'I . . . I intended to give them back,' I say, lamely.

'You could have just *asked*. I'd have let you borrow them.'

I blink. She thinks I wanted to wear them, that I can't afford to buy my own earrings. I suddenly want to laugh, but I know this is anything but funny.

'It's weird. What you did is just . . . *weird*.'

I glance towards the open door, aware of our proximity to other beach huts. This is not a conversation that I want overheard. 'I'm sorry,' I whisper. 'I don't know what happened. I'm so embarrassed. I think it must just be the stress with Jacob. I wasn't thinking, and I . . . I just . . .'

'Sure,' she says curtly. 'I need to get back.'

'Wait . . .'

A deep exhale of frustration. 'What?'

'You came to the hut to tell us something, didn't you? About Jacob.'

'Forget it,' Caz says with a shake of her head.

'Please. If there's anything you know . . .'

'I don't.'

I am kicking myself. I've put up a barrier between us now. She's the last person who saw my son – and now she doesn't trust me. 'You've got this all wrong—'

'Have I?'

'Listen, Caz—'

She stares at me, eyes narrowed. 'Now I understand where Jacob gets it from.'

A mosquito buzzes close to my ear and I swipe a hand through the air.

'Gets what from?' I ask, perplexed. *Stealing?* Has Jacob stolen something of Caz's? I don't know what she's talking about, but Caz is already moving through the door, crossing the deck, climbing on to the beach.

'Got what from?' I call, following her on to the sand.

But she doesn't stop. Just walks on, leaving me humiliated on the dark beach.

I can feel the flame of heat raging in my cheeks. I know I must tell Nick what's just happened, as there is every possibility that Caz will. I picture myself standing before him like a schoolgirl, confessing that I steal; that I've been doing it for years; that I can't stop.

Bewilderment would cloud his face. *You're joking, right?*

No, I just can't do it, not now, in the middle of all this. I'm afraid of where the conversation would lead us. Nick would ask when I first began to steal, why it started, who I steal from . . . And if I pull out that first thread of truth, then everything else is going to unravel.

A door clangs open somewhere behind me. I turn to see Neil stepping from his hut in a flood of light. He's carrying a set of oars underarm, which smack against the doorframe as he strides across the deck and on to the beach.

I want to ask him about the ding in his boat that he found the morning after Jacob disappeared but, before I have chance to call out, I see Diane hurrying from the hut behind him. I catch her pursed lips and closely drawn brows before the darkness steals the details from her face. 'Neil! This isn't a good idea,' she urges, her voice lowered. 'Please! You've been drinking!'

The burst of his reply is startlingly loud. 'I need to think, Diane! Think!'

'Not out there,' she hisses, rushing on to the beach after him.

Neil doesn't break stride, moving towards the shoreline where the tender for his boat waits.

They don't see me in the darkness, and I'm careful to keep very still as I hear Diane whisper, 'Please, Neil. You're worrying me. You need to let this go.' She says something further, but the breeze carries the words out of reach.

'How can I?' Neil demands, his volume unchecked.

Diane is saying something else and I'm sure I catch the word 'accident', but the rest is lost as they continue moving towards the shore.

The intensity of the exchange draws me forward, and I'm following them through the cool sand when there's a hand on my arm.

I swing round. 'Jesus, Nick! You made me jump!'

'What are you doing out here? I just saw Caz storming up the beach. Everything okay?'

'Oh, yes. Fine,' I manage.

'Did she hear my call?'

Call? Then I remember: Nick was on the phone to the marina. 'What did they say?'

Nick guides me back to our hut, closing the door behind us. 'You were right. Robert lied. He didn't take his boat into the marina early Sunday evening. They have an electronic entry system so all the times are recorded.'

'So where is the boat?'

'It's there – but it arrived at one o'clock on Monday morning.'

'Two hours after Jacob was last seen.'

Nick nods. He lays out the facts. 'Jacob was last seen on Sunday evening at eleven p.m. by Caz. Robert left the pub around that time in his RIB. Then, rather than come back to the sandbank like he normally would, he drives his boat to the marina – but somehow it takes him two hours to get there. Why? What was he doing in that time? And why did he lie to us about it?'

We walk the length of the sandbank by torchlight. The anonymity of the darkness is reassuring; only the path ahead of us lit, no one able to see who we are or where we're going.

When we reach Robert's hut, the lights are on, blinds open. Caz is standing near the sink, scooping up hummus with a handful of tortilla crisps. Robert sits forward on the sofa, hunched over some sort of tool. I wonder if she's told her father about the earrings.

They both start as Nick raps hard on the door.

Robert strides to the door, yanking it open with a force equal to the knock.

'We were hoping to have a word,' Nick says.

Robert hesitates, but only for a moment. Then he steps back, making an expansive sweep of his right arm. He shuts the door behind us.

Caz glares at me, but I hold her stare, chin lifted. If she wants to confront me about the earrings – then so be it. I'm more than prepared to deny it. As it turns out, I'm rather good at that sort of thing.

'To what do we owe this pleasure?' Robert says, loosely folding his arms across his chest.

Caz hasn't told him, I think.

'We've just received a call from the marina where your boat is kept,' Nick informs him.

'*My* marina called *you*? How very interesting.' Robert looks calm, completely unruffled. I can picture him in business dealings: the easy slip of the truth, the slow smile, then the ruthless thrust of a deal.

'They informed us that your boat was taken in at one a.m. on Monday morning. Two hours after Jacob was last seen.'

Robert smirks. 'You've been checking up on me.'

'When we came to see you earlier, you told us that you dropped the boat into the marina early Sunday evening, before going to the pub.'

'Must've got confused. Happens at my age, doesn't it, Caz?'

She shrugs.

'One in the morning,' Nick says. 'Odd hour to return a boat to a marina.'

'It's a twenty-four-hour facility. Flexibility is the very point.'

I step forward. 'Fez tells us you were at The Rope and Anchor until eleven. You left by boat. Then two whole hours passed. What happened in that time?'

Robert's lips narrow as he smirks at me. 'Why don't you tell me what *you* think happened, Sarah?'

'All right. I think it goes something like this: earlier on in the evening, you found out Caz was pregnant and you were upset. You went in search of Jacob, but when you couldn't find him, you took yourself off to The Rope and Anchor instead. Am I right so far?'

'Is she right so far, Caz?' Robert asks, drawing her into his little performance.

Caz only shrugs.

'What happened after that, Robert? Did you have a skinful at the pub, get back in your boat and return to the sandbank – only to find Jacob and Caz on the rocks, arguing? Did you blame Jacob for the pregnancy, haul him on to your boat? Decide to shake him up a little?'

He smiles, white teeth flashing at me.

'Maybe it wasn't only Jacob that you were hauling about,' I say, enflamed. 'I saw the bruise on Caz's cheek.'

Robert's smile vanishes. He takes one step forward, his forefinger pointed, gun-straight, at my face. 'Be. Very. Careful.'

'I told you, I fell,' Caz says, with a disgusted shake of her head. 'Dad would *never* hit me!'

'What about Jacob? Did you hit him?'

'Wouldn't waste my energy on that fuck-up.'

'Watch yourself,' Nick says, ice in his tone.

'Just tell them, Dad,' Caz says, a note of anxiety creeping into her voice. 'Tell them why you were on the boat!'

'Not that it's any of your business what I was doing with my boat that night, but here it is: I'd had a bit too much to drink and didn't put my lights on. When I came into the bay, I bumped into Neil's boat. Wasn't on its normal mooring. Gave it a bit of a knock.'

The ding in his boat.

'You know how he is about that boat – it's like it's a bloody family member. So I slipped off. Thought I'd nip the boat back to the marina and he'd be none the wiser. Last thing I need is him mouthing off to Marine Patrol about me being under the influence.'

'What about Jacob?' I say.

'What about him? Jacob hasn't stepped foot on my boat. I doubt he'd dare after what he's put my daughter through.' He folds his arms. 'Happy now?'

I press my lips together.

'Oh, and by the way,' Caz adds. 'If you're wondering why I came to see you earlier, it was to tell you that the letter Jacob wrote – the *love* letter – wasn't for me.'

This new piece of information catches me by surprise. I look to Nick, certain I'm missing something. 'It must be.'

Caz pulls it from her pocket, holding it in front of my face. Her finger taps the last line. '*Last night was amazing*, he wrote. I wasn't with him that night. I wasn't even on the sandbank!'

My head shakes from side to side. 'Then, who was it for?'

'No idea.'

Robert puts an arm around Caz's waist. 'He gets my daughter pregnant. Tells her to have an abortion. Then buggers off, leaving her to go through it on her own. And now – *now* – we find out he's been messing around with someone else. Lovely boy you've brought up there.'

I go to say something, but Robert hasn't finished.

'So, rather than barging into our hut, accusing us of God-knows-what, I think it'd be best if you both piss off. Don't you?'

26. SARAH

DAY FIVE, 10 P.M.

Nick and I return to our hut and retreat into the silence of tasks. Nick fixes the leg of one of our fold-out sun-chairs, and I busy myself cleaning out the kitchen cupboards. With methodical care, I place each of our mugs on to a tea towel, then take a damp cloth and run it along the smooth white insides of the cupboard, removing the fine traces of sand that line every surface of a beach hut.

On the walk back from Robert's hut, we called the police to inform them about Caz's claim that Jacob's love letter wasn't intended for her – but they only seemed vaguely interested. Caz was assuming Jacob wrote the love letter on the night he disappeared and, therefore, the line 'Last night was amazing' refers to an evening she wasn't on the sandbank – but the police pointed out that he could have written the letter at any time since it wasn't dated. I make a mental note to check with Luke to see if there was anyone else on Jacob's horizon.

I return each mug to the cupboard, trying to shake loose the thread of thought. When the last mug is put away, the cloth washed, squeezed dry and hung over the neck of the tap, I turn from the sink, wondering what to tackle next. My gaze travels dispassionately over the square wooden interior of our hut. Really, it's just a shed. A wooden shed on a beach, beautified with some duck-egg-blue paint and a few nautical furnishings. How can this *shed* have such a presence in our lives? It was the glue in mine and Isla's early friendship; it was the place where I fell in love with Nick; the beach home we made with Jacob; the bay where Marley died; and now the place where Jacob was last seen. Without really knowing I'm doing it, I drag my fingernails across the painted wood panelling, the rasp of my nails scraping through the hut.

Nick turns, and stares at me.

Ask me! Ask me what I'm thinking! Ask me how scared I am right now! Ask me something . . . anything . . .

He sighs as he puts down the screwdriver, then announces he's going to bed.

'I need some air,' I mumble, grabbing a cardigan and leaving the beach hut.

The relief of being outdoors hits me. I walk instinctively towards the sea's edge, where I pause, filling my lungs with salt air and closing my eyes.

If anyone should know what has happened to Jacob, it should be me. Where's my mother's intuition?

Standing there, a cool, creeping sensation slides across

my skin, as if I'm not alone. I open my eyes, staring into the darkness, wondering if there's anyone out on the water; a boat with no lights, perhaps, or a kayaker gliding silently across the water. Did Neil go out in his boat after all? I can't make out any shapes or movement, but the sensation of being watched doesn't fall away.

I turn then towards the beach huts, a chill travelling down my spine. Is someone's face pressed to a window, their breath moist against the glass, peering into the darkness? I shiver, hugging my arms around my middle. I'm being ridiculous, surely. Yet, as I stare at the beach huts, I can't help but wonder whether someone inside one of these huts knows what has happened to Jacob. My gaze travels slowly between them. I can see Joe and Binks sharing a sofa, reading beneath the light from their gas lantern. The warm glow is kind to them and from here they look contented, relaxed. My thoughts wander to our hut, where I can see Nick folding out the sofa bed, his long back rounded as he reaches down to tuck in the sheet. He looks exhausted, defeated. I should go back to him – we should be getting into that bed together, holding each other till sleep comes. But then I see him pull his phone from his pocket. His head dips low to it and I can sense his concentration. I wonder what's caught his attention – a message, an email? He finishes whatever he's doing, and then a moment later he is moving towards the window and, as if looking directly at me, he pulls down the blinds, shutting me out. I stand there for a moment, frozen to the spot.

I blink and look away. Next door, Diane and Neil's hut is illuminated by the spotlights Neil installed at the start of summer. Diane sits alone with a book on her knee, but her gaze is directed towards the window. I think of the strangeness of her and Neil's earlier conversation on the beach. There was something off-kilter – almost frantic – about Neil, and it reminds me of the oddness of our exchange down by the rocks a few mornings ago when he was asking about Jacob. In the harsh glare of the downlights, I notice how strained Diane looks. I wonder if she is watching for Neil, waiting to see his boat returning to shore.

I draw my gaze away, letting it resettle on Isla's boarded-up hut, a shadow in the row. There was a time when her hut was a place of solace – the space where I felt most at home. I find my legs carrying me across the beach, towards it. I climb the wooden steps on to her deck and place my hands flat against the shutters that board the windows. I can feel the rough texture of aged plywood. I want to unlock the doors, slip inside the hut, light the tall candles that stand in the necks of wax-covered wine bottles, and then sink back into her sagging sofa bed and smoke. I know the exact smell of this hut: sun-warmed wood, a slight mustiness locked in the old cushions, the spice of incense lingering in the patterned throws.

Years ago, before there were husbands and children, we'd huddle into opposite corners of her sofa, our legs stretched out alongside each other's, and we'd share a joint. I always rolled them, packing the tobacco tightly and crumbling the edges of the pot, my fingertips smelling pungent. We'd pass it between us, a golden shimmer of lip-gloss kissing the butt, and we'd talk about the future.

A lawyer. That's what I'd wanted to become back then.

I had pictured it so clearly: me in a fitted pencil skirt and blouse, carrying a smart leather handbag as I swept into the office each morning, chatting easily with the other staff. I would have specialized in family law, nothing explicitly corporate, rather blending my knowledge of the law with the complexities of relationships.

I had just begun the second year of my law degree when I discovered I was pregnant. Sometimes I wonder who I'd have been if I'd finished the course. It's not that I want to undo the life I have now, but sometimes I just want a different me. A braver one. A more fearless me. A bit more of the old me.

I pull out my mobile, then sink down on to the deck, my back pressed against the cool wood of the beach hut doors. I dial Isla's number in the darkness. I'm nostalgic for the past. I'd like to sit here with my eyes closed, talking about the evenings when we used to run down to the shore naked and high, skinny-dipping in water lit up with phosphorescence. I want to talk to Isla about what's happening right now. I want to hear her tell me that everything's going to be okay.

But the phone clicks on to voicemail.

I think of all the times after Marley's death that I slept with my mobile beside me in case she needed me in the middle of the night. I think of the meals I cooked and took round to her, making comforting casseroles and lasagnes and nutritious stews. I think of the evenings that I left my own family and went to her flat to keep her company, because she had no one else.

'Fuck you!' I hiss into the unanswered phone, then sling my mobile across the deck.

My fists meet the deck in a thud of frustration. Tension pulses in my temples and clamps tight across my forehead. I exhale hard – almost a grunt. *Why aren't you answering? Why haven't you called back?*

There are jagged parts to our friendship – there always have been – and one of those rough little spikes catches against the edges of my heart. *What do you know, Isla?*

I cannot ignore the symmetry of what's happening: Jacob has disappeared from the same beach as Marley, on the same date, but seven years later. It feels like there must be a connection between the two events, which I don't fully understand.

I wonder whether I should talk to Nick about it – at least put a voice to the thought. I know how absurd it would sound when spoken aloud, and how quick Nick would be to defend Isla. He'd tell me that Isla would never hurt Jacob – and I would believe him. She is Jacob's godmother. She is my best friend. We are like sisters.

'It's not possible,' I whisper into the night.

I hear a noise. A scuffle. It almost sounds like it's coming from inside Isla's hut. It must be the wind twisting through a crack, or the wood cooling after a day in the sun – yet my senses are immediately heightened. I get to my feet, pressing my face against the shutters, testing whether I can peer through the cracks.

'Jacob?' I say, my lips moving against the wood.

Ludicrous. Of course I'm being ludicrous!

But what if . . .

Could he be inside? What if – this entire time – he's been

hiding out here, right next door to us? We have Isla's spare key, just as she looks after ours, so it's possible that Jacob could have let himself in. Isla's hut was a refuge for Jacob. Whenever the two of us argued, Jacob would skulk here to lick his wounds.

My heart is thundering against my ribcage. It's madness, but I need to be sure. Quickly, I return to our hut. I'm pleased to find Nick already asleep, a single candle burning on the kitchen side. In the low light, I skirt the sofa cushions that Nick's tossed to the floor, then I locate the key box, which is tacked to the inside of a cupboard. My fingers move clumsily across the keys for the shower block, the gas bottle locker, the underneath of the hut – and then I find Isla's spare, which is attached to a stone with a hole through its centre by a browning piece of string.

I close my fingers around the key, then push it into my pocket before creeping from the hut – careful not to disturb Nick and provoke questions. As I pass him, I see his mobile beside the sofa bed, face down. I pause, heart drilling, itching to pick it up and scroll through his messages. It wouldn't be the first time. I shake my head sharply. I don't want to be that woman – that wife.

I pull my gaze from his phone and leave the hut, closing the door quietly behind me. Outside, the sea seems louder as the waves crumble on to the shoreline, and then are sucked back out again. I return to Isla's deck and search for the keyhole with my fingers. I should have thought to bring the torch.

I eventually manage to slot the key into the lock, and turn it with ease. I pull the door back, and step inside.

'Isla?' a male voice says.

I freeze. Did the voice come from inside the beach hut? I take another step into the darkness. 'Jacob?'

Nothing.

'Isla?'

I swing round to find Ross Wayman behind me.

'Oh. Sarah. Sorry – I saw Isla's hut open and thought she was in Chile, but—'

My heart races as I say, 'Yes, she's still in Chile. But she called. Earlier. Wanted me to check on something.'

'Oh?' I can feel Ross Wayman's gaze on me.

What, though? What should I be checking on? 'A book! She left a book behind that she needs for her class. Said I'd post it on to her. She left in a rush.'

'I dropped her at the quay. She did seem distracted.'

I feel a beat of relief that he believes me.

'You'll need a torch,' he says, glancing at my empty hands. 'Here. Use this.' Ross Wayman pulls a slim torch from his pocket, which he twists to turn on.

I have to go through with this now. It's an utterly ridiculous pantomime. I take the torch and step into the hut, as Ross Wayman holds the door open.

I scan the torch across the wall, locating the bookshelf. It's above Isla's sofa, which I clamber on to, my feet sinking into the sagging cushions. I direct the torchlight at the row of books, making a show of looking closely at the titles.

'And how are you, Sarah?' he says, a dark figure in the doorway.

I've never been alone with Ross Wayman. I only know him from the short exchanges we have on the sandbank

223

ferry where we talk about the weather, the tides, Jacob's upcoming shifts.

When I say nothing, Ross Wayman adds, 'It must be a very distressing time for you and Nick.'

I murmur a sound of agreement.

'If you don't mind me saying, this summer on the ferry . . . I felt Jacob wasn't in a very good way . . .'

'Oh?'

'He was quieter. No chitchat with the customers. A short fuse. Missed a couple of shifts, too. No apology, just a shrug. I don't know if he said, but he was on a warning. Turned up stoned a couple of weeks back. Denied it of course, but I'm no idiot. Said it was his last chance before I got another kid to help.'

I shake my head. I had no idea. 'He never said.'

'Course he didn't. You're only his mother.'

I know this is just a quip, but somehow it feels like an accusation.

'Anyway, I'm only telling you because when I was a young man his age, I acted up plenty. Felt like I had the weight of the world on my shoulders. I like to think Jacob's just gone to ground, is taking some time out. That he'll be back.'

I'm facing the bookcase, tears hot in my eyes. 'Thank you,' I say quietly, unsure how I feel. I'm grateful to hear that Ross Wayman believes Jacob is unharmed – and yet, I feel uncomfortable that this man, who I hardly know, understands more about my son's state of mind than I do.

I climb down from Isla's sofa, the torch beam dropping to my side.

'No luck with the book?'

Last Seen

'Oh. No. Couldn't see it.'

'Probably best to search again in the daylight.'

I nod.

He takes the torch from me and directs the beam over the door while I lock up the hut. Then he bids me goodnight.

I return to my beach hut, where Nick still sleeps. The candle has burned almost to the wick; I watch the flame make its final dance, before the light finally shrinks, dies.

225

27. ISLA

Summer 2013

I struck a single match, cupping it carefully in my hands and dipping it into the base of the kindling. The young flames danced and stretched as I blew gently on them. Soon the thinnest twigs had set alight and I sat back in the cool sand, looping my arms around my knees.

It had always been a point of pride to light a fire with a single match. My mother had taught me how to find the best materials, arranging them in just the right shape so that the first flame can feed on the oxygen. We used to light fires in our garden on dry evenings, sipping peppermint tea with thick blankets draped around our shoulders. *Living outside-in*, my mother used to call it. That was the mark of a good life, in her book – spending as much time as possible outside.

With my back to the beach huts, all that lay ahead was

the glow of the fire and the grey-blue blanket of sea. It was high tide and small waves folded on to the powder-dry sand. Stretching my legs towards the fire, I felt the first blush of heat against my bare toes. A sand flea leaped away from the flames, disappearing into the shadows.

'Thought it was you.'

I started, swinging round and finding Nick standing at the edge of the fire. 'Want company?' he asked, holding up a bottle of wine and two glasses.

'Sure.'

Nick sat beside me and poured two glasses of red. He'd always had a lovely way of doing things for me without being asked, as if he knew exactly what I needed.

'Sarah in bed?' I asked, taking the wine. Without seeing the label, I knew Nick would be drinking Châteauneuf-du-Pape; he opened a bottle every Friday to welcome in the weekend.

He nodded, but didn't say anything, and I sensed there might have been an argument. I didn't ask. It was safer not to know the inner workings of their marriage.

He settled his glass in the sand and leant back, stretching out his neck. 'God, it's nice to be at the beach.'

'Tough week?'

'No more than usual.' With his gaze on the water he said, 'Do you remember that first summer? Wasn't everything easy back then? We'd make a fire and stay out all evening, drinking rum and cokes, rolling into bed at dawn.'

'Or rowing over to the pub in that bloody awful boat you salvaged – which gave me splinters in my thighs.'

'Only because your dresses were so short!'

I smacked his arm and he laughed.

'They were good times, weren't they?'

I nodded.

Then he shook his head, as if he didn't want to even think about it. 'Anyway. What about you? How are you, Isla Berry?'

I smiled. When we were dating he used to call me by my full name, as if he found something sweet about the pairing of the two words. I picked up a stick and poked at the fire, rolling one of the branches into the centre of the flames. Sparks lifted, weaving into the night.

How was I? If Marley had been alive, he'd have been beside me, perhaps toasting marshmallows in the flames, watching the edges of them bubble and caramelize into a charred, sweet crust. 'I don't know how to answer that question any more.'

'Answer it honestly.'

I looked at him. 'You sure?'

He nodded.

'Okay.' I took a deep breath. 'There's a Marley-shaped hole in my life – and it doesn't get any smaller. I don't think I *want* it to get smaller. It'll be three years this summer – but I miss him just as fiercely.'

'Does it make it harder, being here?'

I drew in a breath, thinking about the question. 'Yes . . . and no. I feel closest to him here. He loved it, didn't he? The beach, the bird life, lying in the hut listening to rain, playing cards with Jacob, crabbing on the jetty . . . all of it.' I took a drink of wine, then planted the glass in the sand. 'But it's harder too because the sea is right there. Right in front of my fucking eyes, all day, every day. Taunting me. I want to trawl it. I want him out of it, back with me.'

Nick didn't say anything. He just waited.

'You know what scares me? I feel like I'm losing who I am. I'm sure I used to be someone braver than this; someone who saw possibility everywhere. But now . . . I don't know . . . it's like the world's lost its colour, lost its appeal. I don't seem to have any . . . energy.' I shook my head sharply. 'Shit, listen to me. Sorry. You don't need this.' I picked up my wine, sand sprinkling across my lap, and drained the glass.

Nick reached across with the bottle and refilled it. 'Isla, you're still *you*.'

I turned, looked at him through the darkness.

'You lost your mum at nineteen – but you didn't let it stop you, did you? You made bold, hard decisions: you bought this hut, then you went off and travelled the world. The rest of us stuck to well-carved paths – university, careers – as we didn't know what else to do. But you were out there doing things your own way, being brave. Then you fell pregnant with Marley – and look how you handled that. You didn't take an easy route. You had him on your own – and were an incredible, inspiring mother. Sarah and I often talked about how naturally it came to you, how both our boys adored you. And then this was thrown at you – losing Marley. God, I wish so much it hadn't happened, because Marley was just . . . such a wonderful, special boy.' I could hear the smile in his voice as he said, 'I still think of the day the two of them made those seaweed scarecrows. What did they call them?'

'Scare-gulls.' Joe had paid them a pound each to keep the

gulls off his boat for the morning. The boys had covered themselves in seaweed, and prowled the deck like sea monsters, terrifying the gulls – and probably making far more mess than any birds would have done.

'His imagination, Isla! Wasn't it incredible? I was sure he'd be a writer one day, or a director of arthouse-type films.' I heard him draw a deep breath. 'It's bullshit that he's been taken so young. It's bullshit that you have to live with that pain – but Isla, you're doing well. Truly, I mean that, you are. You're still here – still sitting in this bay, not hiding away from it. You're working, you've got this hut, you—'

'But I'm sad, Nick. All the time.' I didn't have the words to explain it – the hollowness, the sense of something being permanently off-balance inside me. 'I don't feel like *me* any more.'

Nick's fingers reached for mine, interlacing in the familiar way they used to. 'You're still you, Isla. I promise.'

I looked down at our entwined hands. He'd always had beautiful hands. Long and well proportioned. 'Who is that, though?' I whispered.

'It's the girl in the sherbet lemon yellow beach hut who looks life square in the eye and doesn't turn away.' He squeezed my hand tight.

It would be so easy to lean into him, to breathe in his familiar smell of soap and aftershave, to let my head rest against his chest. I wanted it. I wanted to sink into him and let him hold me, let him take care of me.

We stayed there with our fingers locked together until there was the lightest vibration in the sand, a slight disturbance in the air. I knew without looking up that it was Sarah.

I slipped my hand out of Nick's, sliding it through the cool sand to my side.

'This,' Sarah said, three weeks later, walking into my beach hut and slapping a brochure on the coffee table, 'is where you're going.' She stood, hands on hips, with a slightly manic grin on her face. Was she nervous? Excited?

I put down my coffee and picked up the brochure. It had an image of two towering granite peaks overlooking a white-tipped mountain range. Patagonia in southern Chile. I'd been talking about going there for years – ever since I'd spent an evening with friends of Joe and Binks who'd told me rich tales about a summer of hiking there. They'd described the desolate beauty with such vividness that I'd promised myself that – one day – I'd walk in those mountains, too.

'I've booked it,' Sarah said, flipping over the brochure to where there was a plane ticket paper-clipped to the back.

'You've done what?'

'You heard.'

'But I can't afford it—'

She waved a hand through the air. 'It's a gift.'

'I couldn't—'

'Your flight leaves in a month. That gives you four weeks to strop about and tell me you're not going, you can't go, you can't take the time off work (which, by the way, you can: it falls in the school holidays). It gives you time to ring me up in a panic about what to pack, to tell me you've decided you won't accept the ticket after all, and to worry that you won't be fit enough to manage the hiking. And then, in exactly one month's time, when I drop you at the airport, you'll realize that you have no choice and you'll go anyway. And enjoy it.'

I hesitated. 'The dates . . . what about—'

'You'll be back here for the anniversary,' she said, sitting down beside me. 'Your flight lands two days before.'

Could I do this? Go to Chile? It was so generous of them both. I could imagine them talking together, concocting the plan. I pictured Nick telling Sarah about our conversation around the beach fire a few weeks ago – and Sarah coming up with the idea of Chile. *She's always wanted to go.* At nineteen I wouldn't have needed anyone to buy me a plane ticket, make the plans for me. I would've just gone.

I remembered Nick's words, *You're the girl in the sherbet lemon yellow beach hut who looks life square in the eye and doesn't turn away.*

Sarah took both my hands in hers, squeezing them tightly. 'Isla, please. Say you'll go.'

Sarah had been right, I thought, six weeks later, as I stood in front of a looming meltwater lake, with the sun hitting my face. Completely, utterly and annoyingly right.

I absorbed the view, breathing in crisp mountain air. I could hear the crunch of hiking boots against earth as the rest of the group carried on, but I wanted a moment on my own. The lake was milky with sediment, hunks of melting ice glistening in the midday sun. It was a stark sort of beauty, raw and imposing.

I slipped off my pack and crouched to the ground, the footsteps of the group fading. There were just five of us, including our Danish trek leader, Ole, who wore his thin blond hair in a topknot so you could see the tattoo of a mountain lion at the base of his neck. We camped together, ate together and hiked together – and yet I didn't feel crowded, each of us happy to carve out moments alone in our days. At night I shared a tent with a Frenchwoman, Tabeth, who worked at an international school in Santiago and used her holidays to explore, camp and hike. She was ten years older than me – divorced, fit, and full of an infectious amount of energy.

'Thank you,' I whispered into the still air, thinking of Sarah and Nick. They'd done this for me.

In the past, when Nick was working, Sarah, Jacob, Marley and I used to be an inseparable little foursome – our perfectly balanced square of two mothers and two sons. We would take it in turns to go crabbing with the boys, giving the other a chance to sit down with a book; we had four hands between us to apply sun cream or prepare a quick lunch for our hungry wolves; we could team up and play beach football, the boys squealing with delight and outrage at our crooked tactics.

But when Marley died, one side of our square disappeared and the rest of us didn't know how to hang together. When I went next door to Sarah's hut, Jacob no longer jumped excitedly to his feet, ready to play; when Sarah would help wrestle a shivering Jacob from his wetsuit, I would just stand on the sidelines; when Nick arrived from work, he'd no longer find another family bustling about in his beach hut sharing stories of their day – but just me, wretched and lonely, worrying I was in the way.

I tried to retreat from them, give them space as a family

– but Sarah wouldn't have it. I'd tell her that I wouldn't be joining them for a barbecue, so she'd plonk the barbecue on my deck and light it there. In truth, I needed Sarah. I needed her bossiness, her interference, her relentless refusal to let me be swallowed by grief. She made sure I ate, washed, slept, paid my bills, kept up my work. On the worst nights she slept in my bed alongside me. She couldn't have wanted that role, not really. Every moment spent looking after me was a moment away from her family.

Standing before the meltwater lake, I found myself remembering the way she'd slapped down the brochure of Chile, the plane ticket attached to the back, a strained smile on her face. Was she nervous that I'd say no? Or was there another reason? The spiked tip of a doubt entered my thoughts, scratching at the moment.

I shook my head sharply, pushing away the ungrateful thought. Sarah had done this for me – that was reason enough. I pulled on my pack and jogged to catch up the others.

28. SARAH

DAY SIX, 12.30 P.M.

I am gazing at my half-drunk mug of coffee when PC Roam and PC Evans arrive unannounced.

A wave of dread rises in my chest. I scramble to my feet, sloshing cold coffee on the floor. 'What's happened?'

'No news,' PC Evans says, holding up his narrow palms, as if to show he comes in peace.

'Shed any light on Jacob's love letter?' I ask hopefully. I've already quizzed Luke about it, but he was totally stumped, telling us that Jacob never talked to him about anyone except for Caz.

'None as yet. Actually, we were hoping to speak with your husband.'

'Nick? He's in town. Picking up a gas bottle. I doubt he'll be back for another hour.'

A look passes between the officers.

I can feel my heart rate quickening. 'Please. If you've got something to say, just say it.'

PC Evans asks, 'The night Jacob disappeared, do you know where your husband was?'

'Yes, he drove to Bristol. He had a pitch the next morning, so he stayed over. At the Miramar Hotel, I think.'

'Do you remember what time he left the sandbank?'

I hear myself sigh. We've been through all of this. 'He left Jacob's barbecue about six thirty, maybe seven, then drove to the hotel.'

'And did he stop anywhere on the way?'

'No. He went straight there. He wanted to run through the pitch – then get an early night.' I remember how strained he'd looked all weekend, his focus drifting away from the celebrations, lost to work.

'The hotel have told us that your husband didn't check in until one thirty in the morning.'

I shake my head. 'The drive would only have taken a couple of hours.'

'Perhaps he stopped somewhere.'

'Stopped? But where?'

PC Evans says, 'That's what we want to find out.'

We hear Nick at the back of the hut, heaving the new gas bottle into position. There's a clank of metal, a loud curse, then the shifting of objects. I picture him leaning over the bottle trying to muscle it into the tight space. There's another curse, and then finally the clunking of the wooden locker shutting. I want to tell the police officers, *My husband never swears at Jacob. It's DIY. He has a volatile relationship with it.*

When Nick finally walks in, there's a sheen of sweat across his forehead. 'It took me—'

He stops short when he sees the two police officers sitting on the sofa opposite me, empty glasses of water in front of them.

I watch him wipe his forehead with the back of his hand. He must notice the way we are all staring at him, expectant. 'What is it?' He turns to me. 'Has something happened?'

PC Evans is blank-faced as he says, 'We'd like to know where you were on the evening that Jacob disappeared.'

I watch Nick's expression. It doesn't falter. 'I've already told you.'

'They checked, Nick. You didn't arrive at the hotel until one thirty.' My arms fold across my body. 'You left here at six thirty.'

He presses his lips together, his gaze shifting to the left. It's what he does when he's trying to think himself out of a situation.

'So where the fuck were you?'

Nick stares at me in amazement. I almost never swear. 'Answer me!'

There is a pause. 'I was on the quay.'

If you stand at the back of our beach hut, you can see across the harbour to the quay. Occasionally he'll have a drink at The Rope and Anchor with some of the men from the sandbank – but he wouldn't have left Jacob's birthday early to go to the pub.

'Who were you meeting?' I ask.

But I already know the answer. I know exactly who else was on the quay that night, who goes there every year on the same day, who'd been sitting around our family table hours before.

I know who he was with.

I think I've always known.

'You were meeting Isla, weren't you?'

I stand rigid, staring at Nick. My breathing is shallow – my gaze pinned to his face. I feel as if I'm bracing for impact.

The very first time I met Nick, he was sitting on the deck of Isla's beach hut, waiting for her. His long back was pressed against the closed door of her hut, and he looked relaxed, content. When he saw me approach, he shaded the sun from his eyes with a hand and stared at me for a moment. 'Sarah, right?'

I had smiled. 'Right.'

I climbed on to the deck and slumped down next to him, leaning against the sun-warmed wood. 'So, where is she?'

'Walking the headland, maybe. Or in town, perhaps.' He smiled easily, without worry.

I glanced at him sideways, taking in the strong line of his jaw, the closely shaven skin, the smart polo shirt he wore. He was handsome, clean cut, polite. Isla spoke of him casually, like a new healthy food she was trying to include more of in her diet.

Nick, on the other hand, was intoxicated with Isla. Within minutes of meeting me, he'd asked a series of thoughtful questions about me; I didn't flatter myself that he was particularly interested in me – he just wanted to understand me, to better understand Isla. I thought it was smart of him because, even then, to work out one of us, you needed to know the other.

Isla was his first love. She burst into his world with her summer tan, her long golden legs, and that air of lightness that makes people want to grab on to her even more tightly.

Everyone remembers their first love, because it's tied into something sentimental to do with the person you were in your youth. It's hard to extinguish it completely, because it would be like extinguishing part of yourself. And I worry that it's particularly hard to extinguish when your first love happens to spend every summer in the beach hut next door.

For years I've grappled with an unsolvable problem: I want Isla close to me, yet far away from Nick. It is an equation with no balancing answer.

From the moment I first kissed Nick, I wondered whether I was making a mistake. I didn't want to be caught in Isla's shadow, questioning whether Nick loved me as passionately, or desired me as deeply. And perhaps I did feel a little like that in those early months – but then we had Jacob. The landscape of our marriage deepened the moment Nick placed his palm on my stomach and felt our baby kick. The love he felt for our child was locked into our feelings for each other and, for a long time after Jacob was born, I didn't worry about his feelings for Isla.

But then Marley died.

Everything shifted. His death undid all of us in different ways, and I'm not sure we were ever stitched back together in quite the same way.

I hear someone clear their throat and I turn, forgetting

that the police are still here. My voice is crisply polite as I ask, 'Please could you leave us for a few minutes?'

They look at one another. PC Evans says, 'Nick, we'd like to see you at the station later. Get the correct details of that evening.'

Nick nods, but doesn't speak. His eyes are on me.

I wait until I am sure we are alone and then I ask, 'You met Isla on the quay, didn't you?' I now recall Fez saying he thought he'd seen Nick's car parked there and that he'd been expecting him to be in The Rope and Anchor.

'I saw her, yes.'

I lift my chin. 'You're having an affair.'

'With Isla?'

'Yes, *Isla*! Of course, *Isla*! It's always been *Isla*!'

Nick moves past me towards the beach hut doors. For a moment I think he's going to storm from the hut, disappear; instead he yanks the double doors shut. Then he swings around and faces me, eyes shining. 'There's no affair!'

He's lying, he has to be.

'Why were you together? You said you were going straight to Bristol.'

'I was meeting someone else.'

Someone else? 'Who?'

Nick sighs deeply. 'Your mother.'

I blink, dumbfounded, the remark throwing me off course. 'My mother? I don't—'

'The business, Sarah. It's screwed, okay? It's absolutely screwed!' He exhales hard. 'Your mother was giving me a loan.'

I know our finances are tight – they have been for months. That's why we rent our house and move into the beach hut in summer. We've discussed the option of a loan in the past, but we can't get anything more from the bank, Nick's parents have their money tied up in investments, and his brothers don't have enough to spare. My mother has never been an option because I won't be indebted to her. 'I . . . I can't believe you'd do that behind my back.'

'I was looking after our family. We all win, Sarah: your mum feels like she is helping; I don't lose the business or have a bloody heart attack from the stress; you and Jacob get to keep your home. We all win,' he repeats. 'Except that I knew you'd say no to the idea because of your bloody pride!'

I'm quiet for a moment as I begin to see that Nick hasn't been telling me the full extent of our financial problems. 'How much did you borrow?'

There is a long pause. When Nick speaks, his voice is low. 'Seventy thousand.'

My eyes widen. 'Jesus, Nick! Seventy thousand! How the hell are we going to pay that back?'

'I intend to pay it all back – with interest. But your mother . . . she is calling it a gift. She says the money would come to you anyway – better that we have it now when we need it.'

'I don't believe this!'

Nick glares back at me, eyes flashing. 'Lucky your mum came to my rescue. I didn't win the pitch, in case you're interested. Found out yesterday. It's only thanks to your mum that my staff still have jobs.' The bitterness in his tone is new and unsettling.

I gather myself enough to ask, 'Where does Isla fit in? You said you saw her.'

He shrugs. 'She saw me with your mother. I asked her not to mention it to you.'

'So *she* knew what was going on, too?'

'*She?*' Nick repeats. Then he laughs, a sharp note of disbelief. 'You know what's mad? That you are more shocked that I'd take a loan from your mother, than if I'd told you I'd been sleeping with Isla.'

'Have you? Slept with her? I need to know, Nick. I need you to tell me honestly: since we've been together, have you ever slept with her?'

Nick throws his head back, gripping a fistful of hair. He makes a raw, guttural exhale of frustration. 'For God's sake, Sarah! How can you even ask me that?'

The question, seeded in my head years ago, has now grown roots that seem impossible to pull up. I can hear the emotion in my voice as I say, 'You were in love with her.'

'Yes! I was! And I will *not* apologize for that! But we broke up because it wouldn't have worked—'

'No. The relationship ended because *Isla* left you. I was there that summer, Nick. You were heartbroken!'

'My God, are we really going to do this? Right now, when our son is missing?' The veins in his neck stand proud as his chin juts forward. 'I was twenty-one! That was over two decades ago! It doesn't matter who "ended" the relationship: it would have ended at some point because it wasn't right – we weren't meant to be together long term. Isla and I both know that. You, *you*, are the only one who doesn't!' He slams his fist into the beach hut wall. The force of the punch causes the double doors to swing open on to the deck. 'For fuck's sake, Sarah! When does this stop?'

I want to tell him to lower his voice – that people will hear – but I don't have a chance as he's saying, 'Do you know what it's like to live with someone looking over their shoulder at you – distrusting you? You set me a thousand little tests, ready to judge whether I'm going to slip up. When I hug Isla, I have to be sure it's for just the right length of time – not too short so as to look rude, but heaven forbid I should hug her for a moment too long.'

I draw back, stunned by Nick's venom.

'I know you check my phone.'

My face heats with embarrassment. It's true: I did three weeks ago. And a few weeks before that, too. Sweat is building under my arms. I'm aware of Isla's hut right next door – and even though she's thousands of miles away, I wish Nick would whisper. 'Please, Nick—'

'There's always a test – a measurement. *How much do we love you?* But what if we can't meet your standards? What then? Will you cut off Isla? Will you cut me off? Just like you've done to your poor fucking mother.'

The statement knocks the wind from me. I place a hand against the counter to steady myself. 'I didn't *cut her off.*'

'Course you did! You've told me how she'd always loved your sister more. That Maggie was the favourite. You said your mother would rather surround herself in memories of Maggie than make new ones with you.'

'It's true.'

Nick's gaze is pinned to mine. 'Is it? Your mother was grieving. She lost her child. Maybe you didn't cut her enough slack. You're so easy to slight, Sarah. Maybe your mother was hurting so much she didn't have it in her to give the level of affection that you demanded. Maybe she couldn't measure up to your strict quota of how deeply you need to be loved.'

My mouth opens and closes, but no words come out.

'You know what your constant doubt does? It makes people search for emotions they don't have. You should be careful with that, Sarah. Very careful.'

I think of the accusation I'd fired at Isla when I last saw her. What am I doing to the people I love? My legs feel as if they're going to desert me as a sob heaves through my body. 'I'm sorry.'

Those two simple words of apology drain the tension from the hut.

Nick exhales a long, shaky breath. 'Jesus, Sarah. You need to trust me.'

I cover my face, shocked at myself – shocked at how far I've let things go. For so long I've wondered if something was going on between Nick and Isla. The worst thing is, I'd decided that if it was, I would let it. I would let Isla have an affair with my husband – because I owed her.

My son lived. Hers didn't.

29. SARAH

DAY SEVEN, 11 A.M.

Wind gusts across the sandbank, sweeping the sand smooth. Heavy clouds roll in from the sea, and rain doesn't look far off. The beach is empty as I hunch my shoulders against the salt wind, my hands stuffed into the pockets of my fleece. White sea foam quivers on the tideline and wheels in the air like flung bubble bath. A high tide has washed in a decomposing jellyfish, its milky tentacles tangled with seaweed. I step around it and carry on walking.

Right now, where I want to be is at home. I want to be able to lock the front door and lie in my bedroom with the blinds lowered. I don't want to hear the excited shouts of children playing cards in beach huts, or the whistle of kettles boiling for families sitting down to tea and plates of biscuits. The sweetness of summer days and nights here feels like a distant memory – almost unreal – as if the beach huts are just a setting inside a glass jar, like a snow globe that has been tipped on its side.

The tenants renting our house leave in two days. Until then, this is where we have to be. Nick has gone into the office to sort out a work problem. As he pressed a cool kiss on my cheek, all I could think was: *How do you have the headspace to focus on anything but Jacob?* I managed to hold my tongue: things are fragile enough between us as it is.

I've tried calling Isla again. I rang in the middle of the night and listened to her recorded voice asking me to leave a message – so I did. I told her everything that's happened so far. I talked into the emptiness, explaining. I need to explain it to someone.

She didn't call back. She didn't ring and tell me that it's okay, it'll all be okay.

But then, I don't deserve her reassurances.

I look towards Isla's hut, and am surprised to see a woman sitting on the deck, her back to me. The narrow shoulders and the slim frame are so familiar that the hairs prick on the back of my neck.

I squint to see more clearly.

No, it can't be.

As I approach, the figure turns.

My mother sits neatly with her feet placed together on the lower step. She looks diminutive in a light summer coat and tailored trousers, hair tousled by the wind. She hasn't been to the sandbank in years.

Seeing me, she stands, a hand half rising to wave. Her gaze moves over my face, perhaps taking in my red, puffy eyes, the hollows beneath my cheeks. I haven't washed my hair in days, and I'm wearing a tired fleece thrown on over old jeans.

'Oh, Sarah,' she says gently, surprising me by stepping forward and wrapping her arms around me. She smells, as she always does, of perfume and face powder and breath mints.

Perhaps there is some part of us that never forgets the embrace of our mothers; the tension I've been carrying in the knots of my spine, the tightness of my shoulders, softens, releases slightly in the space of her arms. Tears follow, a stream of them running down my cheeks. My mother holds me tight, one hand smoothing back my hair. As a girl I used to have nightmares, and I remember the dip of the bed as my mother would climb in beside me, leaning her head back against the wall, eyes closed, stroking my hair until I fell asleep.

Eventually I gather myself, wiping my face dry and tucking my hair behind my ears. My mother takes my hand and leads me into the beach hut, directing me to the sofa. We sit together, my mother upright as a needle, her knees touching mine.

I begin to talk, explaining all that's happened over the past few days, sparing almost no details.

My mother listens closely, her expression neutral. When I'm finished, she looks me squarely in the eye and says, 'Life can be messy, Sarah. It can be ugly, painful, and complicated. But you mustn't cower from it. Jacob is a strong, intelligent young man. He'll be okay.' She pats my knee, then stands. 'Tea.'

I watch the white caps dancing on the waves as I hear

my mother negotiating the cramped beach hut kitchen. After a struggle with the water pump, the kettle is filled and she lights the hob. There's no teapot here, and I hear her adding an inch of boiling water to both mugs, warming the china before serving our tea.

'How is Nick?' my mother asks, handing me my tea and a plate with small buttered squares of malt loaf, which she must have found in one of the cupboards. I can't remember the last time I ate anything, and I place a piece in my mouth, chewing lightly as I watch a curl of stream drift upwards from my tea.

'He's gone into the office.'

My mother nods. 'Everyone needs an escape hatch.'

Yes? Then where's mine?

My mother says, 'I understand he's told you about the money I gave him?'

'Yes.'

'I'm sorry if that . . . caused problems.'

I shrug. 'It was very generous, but I just—'

'Don't want my help?' My mother says this with an arched eyebrow, but there is a light smile on her lips.

'Something like that.'

We finish our tea without speaking, but the silence is strangely comfortable – nothing like the long silences that have punctuated the latter years of our relationship. I realize why my mother's presence is so comforting: she understands. She has lost a child. She knows exactly what this is . . .

'Isla,' she says suddenly, in that clipped way of hers that makes Isla's name sound like something distasteful. 'What does she have to say about everything?'

'She's in Chile. We haven't spoken.'

'You haven't called her?' she says, surprised. 'I thought the two of you were still joined at the hip.'

'I've called, and emailed, but I've not heard . . .'

My mother's nostrils flare in disapproval.

'Maybe she's not got phone reception,' I say, feeling oddly defensive, falling back into old patterns. My mother has never warmed to Isla; I've often wondered whether she resented the long hours I used to spend at Isla's house when I was a teenager, preferring the noise and vibrancy and warmth that waited for me there.

She makes a tutting sound.

'What?'

'After all the support you've given her over the years . . . and she can't even be *bothered* to pick up the phone.'

'We argued. Just before she left.'

My mother watches me closely. 'About what?'

I look down at my hands, unsure how to explain. It's more than jealousy – and I've spent enough time in the early days of our friendship experiencing the sawn edge of that emotion to recognize the difference – no, it's more that when I look back over the shape of our friendship, I realize with a sudden shock that I have been the compass circling around the sharp point of Isla's life. Now that I really think about it, I see with startling clarity that that has always been my role. Years ago, when Isla's mother died, I dropped everything to be there for her – but then she just upped and left, went travelling without so much as a backwards glance. Even my wedding to Nick felt like an apology, something to be cele-brated mildly so as not to rebuke Isla. When our boys were born, I was the one who suggested Isla should move in with us after her Caesarean, because what else could I do? Isla had no one – and there I was with Nick.

I can't help wondering if it will always be me who supports her, me who picks up the pieces. When Isla returns to the sandbank each summer, she expects a whirlwind of attention, to be absorbed back into the fold of our family. I prepare her hut, stock her fridge, cook most of her meals – and then at the end of summer she disappears, a migrating bird, back to her life in Chile.

I realize I've not answered my mother's question.

Still watching me, my mother says, 'If the two of you argued, I'm sure you had your reasons. I'm not trying to find fault with Isla . . . it's just, well, over the years I think she could have been a better friend to you. That's all.'

I think about this for a long while. Maybe it's true of us both.

My mother stays for the afternoon and I feel an ache of reluctance as I walk her back to the ferry. I know I'll be spending the rest of the evening in the beach hut, listening to the slow ticks of the clock in the growing darkness.

The narrow wooden jetty bounces beneath our feet as we walk to its end. I can see the ferry in the distance only just leaving the quay, and I know it'll be a few minutes still. A cool gust of wind pushes my mother's hair back from her face and I see how thin it has become at the sides. Something about the glimpse of her pale scalp, the soft-grey roots, makes my heart feel heavy.

'Thank you for coming,' I say.

'Of course,' she says with a light wave of her fingers, as if it is nothing.

I think of what Nick said yesterday – that I set a thousand tests for him, wanting him to prove the strength of his love for me, over and over again. He told me that I judge my mother with equally fierce standards, making it impossible for anyone to reach the mark of how deeply I need to be loved.

'Do you remember Maggie's favourite toy?'

My mother turns to look at me, eyebrows arched in surprise. *Maggie*: my sister's name is rarely spoken between us.

'Of course,' she answers after a moment. 'The miniature iron horse. Black Beauty.'

I take a breath. 'I took it,' I say, my heart pounding at the admission. 'I stole it from her room.'

My mother considers me closely. 'I know,' she smiles.

'But . . . I remember you asking me if I'd seen it. I told you I hadn't.'

'I found it in your coat pocket a few days later.'

'You never said anything.'

'What was there to say? It was important to you, so you took it.'

'No.' I shake my head. 'It wasn't important to me. I took it because I wanted *you* to notice me. I wanted you to see that I was still there, living, even though Maggie was gone.'

'Oh Sarah,' she sighs, sadly. 'I know I wasn't much of a mother to you in those years after Maggie died. Or a wife,' she adds, almost to herself. 'I don't know how to explain it, other than to say that when Maggie died, for a time I lost part of myself. It was the part of me that loved and laughed . . . saw beauty . . . knew joy. For a time,' she repeats, 'I'm not sure I could *feel*.'

I understand. With Jacob gone, it's like something core and essential has been removed from me, and I don't know if it's possible to function without it.

'Did you blame me?' I whisper, the question taking me by surprise. 'For throwing the ball?'

My mother thinks for a moment. 'Honestly? Yes, I think I did. I blamed you for throwing it.' She takes a breath. 'I blamed your father for not giving you both a lift to school that morning, like I'd asked. I blamed the driver for going too fast and not stopping in time. I blamed Maggie for not looking where she was going. But mostly I blamed myself for not protecting her. I was Maggie's mother.'

The comment reminds me of something Isla once said: *Marley was my son, and I let him drown.* She took the responsibility for his death as her own because it was her job, as his mother, to protect him.

The jetty bounces as a family move along it, joining us to wait for the ferry. My mother and I fall quiet again. I lean against the railing, looking down into the dark wind-ridged harbour, thinking of the times Jacob has sat here, bare legs dangling towards the water, a crab-line trailing from his fist.

When the ferry arrives, I give my mother a fierce hug, then move down the jetty and on to the beach. I turn to wave her off and, as I do, the wind swings behind me, whipping my hair forward. For a moment his image is blurred and I think it could just be a stranger moving in my direction. But I recognize the thick dark hair, the slope of his shoulders.

Isaac.

I've lost track of what day we're on. He must be returning to the sandbank at the end of his work rota. His focus is square on me – and there is no smile, no light in his eyes.

Does he know?

I need to talk to him, to tell him. My heart skitters in my chest as I wait, feeling the sand shifting beneath my feet.

But when Isaac reaches the beach, he looks right through me, as if I'm no more than a ghost.

30. ISLA

I've always been wary of Isaac. How could I trust the man who, seven years ago, brought Jacob back to shore, wet and shivering and terrified, but left my boy?

There was something amiss about that day, I knew that from the start. A fragment missing from the story. Over the years, I've been searching for it – asking questions, listening closely, watching, waiting . . .

Summer 2012

I leaned against the foot of the headland, layers of compressed sand and stone warm against my back. I closed my eyes and tried to ignore the pounding at my temples. My mind was foggy – the residue of the sleeping tablet I'd washed down the night before with a bottle of wine. At least I had slept. That was something.

The September sun held a pleasing warmth that pressed

close. The call of a song thrush drifted from somewhere above. The new school term started today and the sandbank had emptied overnight, the beach lying quiet and untrodden.

Today Marley would've been starting Year 8. I should have been laying out a freshly ironed uniform, making sandwiches with their crusts cut off, slipping a bar of chocolate into his lunchbox as a treat.

Sarah and Jacob would be doing the school run right about now. Perhaps she was stuck in traffic, or was standing at the school gate checking Jacob had his sports kit with him, or maybe she was pressing a kiss to his cheek before she returned to her house, her day, her life. I could feel the burn of envy in my chest.

We used to do it together, the school run. Sarah did the mornings and I did the afternoon pick-up. I loved watching our boys bustling out of their classrooms with their shirts untucked, their hair wild. On Fridays I'd stop at the newsagent's and treat them to an ice cream or some sweets, enjoying their laughter and chatter about the weekend ahead.

Now I pictured Jacob sitting alone in Sarah's car, the back seat empty.

I bent forward, sucking in a deep breath.

When I looked up, my stomach contracted. Isaac's boat was gliding into the bay, the engine quietening. I watched him move around the deck, bending low to grab the anchor, then slinging it from the stern. It hit the water with a deep splash. I hated that boat. I wanted to smash it up, burn the thing, so I'd never have to see it come back to shore without Marley in it.

It wasn't just Isaac's boat – there were a hundred triggers;

the sound of Diane's voice calling out to Neil; the roar of Robert's boat engine; the stir of air disturbed by a helicopter.

I watched as Isaac rolled up his shorts, then hopped over the side of the boat into the shallows. He waded to shore with a large catch bucket and planted it on the tideline. Then he took a knife from his pocket and sliced it along the pale silver belly of the first fish. I watched as he scooped his fingers into the fish, pulling out the guts and tossing them into the shallows, the water turning a soupy red.

The gulls were quick to arrive, circling and diving in a cloud of wings, looking for their prize of entrails or fish heads.

I moved towards the shore as if sleepwalking, my steps slow and unsteady. 'Hello, Isaac.'

He started as I appeared at his shoulder. 'Isla. Hi.' His tanned face was heavily lined, a fleck of fish blood caught on the collar of his shirt. 'How are you?'

How was I? Did anyone really want to know the answer to that? Without Marley I was a wheel that has no axis around which to rotate. My life slid and spun without direction, without anything to keep it centred. But Isaac didn't want to hear this. He wanted me to say something pat, reassuring, like, *I'm getting there.* Instead, I told him, 'I've been thinking about that day again. Marley was such a good swimmer – a natural in the water. I still . . . I don't understand what happened. I just need to . . . to understand it.' I'd become the sort of woman who spoke too hurriedly, whose tone was thin and serious, whose gaze darted around when she spoke.

Isaac threw the fish he was holding back into the catch

bucket. He returned to the waterline to rinse his hands, then dried them on the hem of his sun-bleached shirt. He turned and faced me. 'I was out bass fishing when I heard a scream.' He spoke with a gentle, patient voice. And he *was* patient: this wasn't the first time I'd asked him to walk me through exactly what had happened. I'd asked everyone who'd been there that day: Jacob, Sarah, Neil, Diane, Joe, Binks, Robert, the coastguards. Everyone. I'd hounded the coroner into leaving the case open for as long as possible: 'There's *no* body. How do we know he's dead for certain?' But it was Isaac who bore the brunt of my questioning. After all, he was first on the scene. He was the one who brought Jacob back alive – but not Marley.

'I thought it was the gulls – yet something made me reach for my binoculars just the same. I saw the boys. Just one of them at first – then the other. Been separated a little by the current, I suppose. It was running hard because of the springs. I went to help the nearest boy – Jacob. If I'd had a life ring – God, how I wish I had – I could've thrown it to him, then gone straight to your boy. But I didn't.' He sighed heavily. 'I scrambled to the side of the boat, threw in some rope, tried to get Jacob to reach for it. But it was too far away, so I circled back round, tried to get in as close as I could. He was panicking, slipping right under. I managed to grab his arm, pull him on board – but it all took time. Another boat was coming by then. I pointed towards where I'd last seen Marley, but I couldn't spot him. I hoped they would. I got Jacob on board and decided I should get him to shore – he was in shock, had swallowed a lot of water. I didn't know if he was okay or not. Once I dropped Jacob

31. SARAH

DAY SEVEN, 10.45 P.M.

The springs in the thinning mattress dig into my ribcage as I shift, rolling on to my back. I stare into the darkness, listening to the slow draw of Nick's breathing, envying him for sleeping while I lie alone with my thoughts. Time has become something fluid and shifting. A minute can drag, stretching out endlessly – and yet somehow seven days have passed since Jacob was last seen. How is that possible when it seems only a heartbeat ago our family was sitting together in the sunshine, celebrating his birthday?

I'm unguarded as a wave of fear crashes over me: what if we've lost him? My knees draw up and I curl on to my side. I couldn't bear it. I couldn't bear never to see him again. Not to feel the warmth of his body in my arms. He's my baby.

I crawl out from under the covers, my skin slick with sweat, and crouch on the floor by Jacob's drawer. I slide it open and place my hands inside, my fingertips searching out the feel of fabric. I lift something up – a T-shirt, a jumper perhaps – and press it to my face, inhaling deeply.

Oh God! Jacob!

I keep my eyes squeezed shut, breathing him in.

From the bed, I hear Nick stir, murmuring something. I feel tender, as if the skin has been flayed from me by our confrontation about Isla. I can't face climbing back into bed, lying side by side careful not to touch one another. I stay silent.

As I place Jacob's clothing back in the drawer, my fingers meet something cool, rectangular. I explore the shape of it, realizing it's the tin with Jacob's weed inside. I lift it out, carefully opening the lid, and am greeted by the strong herbal smell.

I get to my feet, pull a jumper over my pyjamas and move to the doorway, the tin enclosed in my grip.

'Sarah?' Nick says something else, his voice fuddled by sleep. I don't wait to hear it; I slip from the hut barefoot.

Outside the night is cool and I swallow the air in long gulps. There's a crispness to it that makes me think autumn will be coming soon.

The moon is almost full tonight as I move along the beach. No one is about, except for a night-fisherman in the next bay. I plonk myself in the sand, opening the tin. The thought of that first warm intake of smoke, the sweet flame rushing through my lungs, feels like a hunger. My fingertips tingle, almost itch, with the desire to hold a joint.

Just a toke, I think, to help me sleep. My head will feel clearer tomorrow if I'm finally able to get some rest.

I take out a Rizla and the weed and begin to skin up, fingertips moving deftly across the paper – a dance they haven't entirely forgotten. I lick the edge of the rolling paper, sealing it tight, then click Jacob's lighter, the flame flaring in the darkness. I inhale deeply, immediately coughing, surprised by the fierce heat in my throat.

I can't help myself; I am laughing. Here I am, a forty-year-old woman sitting in her pyjamas, smoking her son's stash in the middle of the night.

I tilt my chin upwards, eyes closed, and inhale again. My ligaments, my muscles, the tendons and sinews stretching around my body soften a little.

Pushing myself to my feet, I tuck the tin in my pocket and wander towards the water's edge, wondering how many times I've crossed this stretch of beach in my life. First it was as a girl, when Isla and I would bunk off from drama club and barrel into the sea together. Then later with Nick, my stomach rounded from pregnancy. Then all those times since: holding Jacob's hand as he was learning to walk; chasing after him and Marley as they dragged body boards to the shore; then, later still, bringing drinks or snacks to him and his friends who'd lounge on the beach.

When I reach the shore, I don't stop. My feet keep on moving, sinking into the water.

It's only when I feel the sea bed softening, the slimy touch of seaweed against the soles of my feet, that I pause.

I stand in the shallows listening to the water rushing around me, the joint burning bright between my fingers.

Looking towards the dark horizon, I have a tipping sensation, as if everything good is behind me.

At the edge of the bay, the night-fisherman sits on a low stool, his rod set up on a tall tripod, the line disappearing out to sea. Behind him stands a tent, lit by a lantern, where his dog shelters, curled on his side. I've seen this fisherman come to this same spot, every Sunday, for years. I've often wondered what motivates him to leave the warmth of his home, hike through the darkness with his dog, then quietly set up his equipment on the empty beach. Perhaps it's because, for the night, he is a wild man, catching food for his family, having space and quiet to sit with the darkness and listen to the sea. Perhaps night-fishing isn't only about what is caught, but about that feeling of space, of quietude, as he watches the world swim around him.

And then I wonder . . . what does he see?

Before the thought is fully formed, I'm turning, moving towards him, my feet pressing into the cool folds of sand.

Aware of me, the fisherman looks up, removing his hands from his pockets.

In all the years I've seen him here, we have never once spoken.

'Were you fishing here last Sunday?' I ask without preamble, my lips feeling pleasantly numb.

He stands, lifts his chin. He is tall, imposingly so now that he towers a whole head above me. 'What?' he asks, his voice low and gravelly.

I realize I'm still holding the joint between my fingertips. I drop it to the ground, toeing sand over the glowing tip.

'The Sunday just gone. You were here, weren't you?' I remember standing at the window of our hut after my argument with Jacob, and noticing the glow of the fisherman's lantern as he set up for the night.

'Yeah. I was here.' There's a defensive note to his tone.

'My son went missing that night.' I turn, pointing behind us. 'The rocks were the last place he was seen. He was with his girlfriend. They were arguing. Did you see him? He's tall, dark-haired. Seventeen. Do you remember?' I make myself stop talking and wait.

His gaze flickers back and forth over my face. I feel the light tick of unease in the base of my throat.

'On the rocks – yes. Raised voices.'

My heart quickens. He saw them!

'Enid was watching them.'

Enid?

He glances over his shoulder towards the dog.

I feel bolder, encouraged that he's seen something. 'What time was it?'

He sighs. 'Probably an hour or two after we got here. Close to eleven, I suppose.'

'Then what happened? Did you see him after that?' I speak as calmly as I can manage, when really I want to grab this man by the shoulders and shake the answers from him.

'Didn't notice, I'm afraid.'

No! Wrong answer!

I stay calm. Take a breath. 'Did you see them leave the rocks?'

'Couldn't say. It just went quiet. Sorry, I can't help.' He puts his hands back in his pockets.

I feel my chest deflate. He's not told me anything new, other than confirming what I already know. Jacob was arguing on the rocks with Caz around eleven o'clock.

'Boats,' I say. 'Did you see any boats that night?'

He sounds narked as he says, 'Yeah – that over-sized RIB was churning up the water as usual. Been at the pub, I expect.'

'Robert's boat? A grey RIB?'

'That's right.' He makes a low clicking sound at the back of his throat.

'Any other boats in the water that night?'

'Just that old fishing boat.'

A fishing boat? I'm trying to think. 'That one?' I say, pointing to Neil's dory.

'Nah, not that one. The other one that comes past sometimes. Looks like an old tug boat. You'd know it if you saw it.'

I shake my head to show that I'm at a loss.

'Navy. With a wheelhouse.'

My heart begins to pound as I ask, 'The boat – is it called *Offshore*? It's usually moored up in the harbour.'

'That's the one.'

My stomach tightens. I know the boat. I've been on it before.

So has Jacob.

It's Isaac's boat.

'Think he must've been out flounder fishing. Had the torch going.'

'Was he alone?'

He pauses for a moment, thinking. 'No, he was with

264

someone. I remember him holding the nose of the boat in the shore break, while someone climbed on.'

I feel a shiver travel down my spine, my skin tightening. 'My boy. Was it my boy?'

The fisherman lifts his shoulders, doesn't answer. But he doesn't need to. Now I see it all clearly: Jacob was out on the water with Isaac.

Isaac's hut faces the harbour. It's set slightly back from the others, and the unpainted wood has faded to a bleached grey. I haven't stepped inside this hut for years.

The blinds are drawn, but a glow of light bleeds from their edges. I glance over my shoulder, checking no one is about, then climb the wooden steps on to his deck. My knuckles rap against the hut door – three sharp knocks.

The briny scent of the harbour feels thick in my throat as I wait. I catch the sound of a chair being pushed back, footsteps across the hut, then the door is thrown open. The draught sucks the roll blind out of the hut towards me, so it flaps in the breeze like a wagging tongue. Isaac wrestles it out of the way, peering at me. 'Sarah?'

'I need to talk to you.'

He stares at me for a moment, perhaps taking in the jumper thrown hastily over my pyjama bottoms, the strained look on my face. Then he steps back, and for a moment I think he's going to shut the door, but instead he rolls up the blind. 'Come in.'

Inside, the hut smells of cooked mackerel and potatoes. Two used pans are settled on the small hob. On a foldout table half a glass of beer rests on a drinks mat beside a fish dinner. *Who eats dinner at this hour?* There is a hardback book face down on the table; I glimpse the title: *Wordsworth's Collected Poems.* On the wall behind Isaac, I take in a framed chart of our coastline, and another glass-fronted print of the landing sizes of local fish. Above, two wooden shelves are filled with rows of books and a selection of pottery. The hut is neat and homely, barely changed from the way I remember it.

I stand with my back to the door, my head spinning from the joint. There is little room, so Isaac positions himself behind the chair he has just vacated.

Two gas lanterns emit a low hiss, a lightly sulphuric smell mixing with the stronger scent of fried fish.

I stare at Isaac, wondering, *Would he hurt Jacob?* I can't believe that he would. But then, I don't know this man. Not really. That very first time I came to the sandbank with Isla, when we'd swam in our underwear, body-surfing the waves into shore, I remember seeing him – although we didn't know each other's names back then. He'd been fishing from the rocks, just a teenager himself, and I recall the interest in his dark gaze as he watched me stretching my arms up to the sun, letting the heat dry the water from my skin.

When I speak, my voice is commanding and too loud somehow for the space. 'Jacob went missing from the sand-bank last Sunday evening.'

Isaac holds my gaze.

'He was seen getting into your boat.'

I watch him closely. His Adam's apple moves as he swallows – but he says nothing.

My heart pulls tighter. 'Isaac? Is that true?'

The stillness of his expression unnerves me and my palms begin to sweat. I am imploring him, silently begging him, to tell me there's a mistake and that Jacob never boarded his boat.

'Yes,' he says eventually, the word swallowing the air from the hut. 'It is true.'

Isaac glances down at his hands, which are gripped around the back of a wooden chair, his knuckles white. He rolls his tongue across his lower teeth. 'None of this was . . . planned. I wish to God I'd never been on the water that night—'

'Tell me what happened!' I interrupt, my voice firm as stone.

'I will. I am . . . I need you to understand . . . it was just . . . it happened all wrong. He was . . . angry, upset . . . I couldn't explain properly.'

'Explain what?' I've gone very cold. I am standing perfectly still, barely breathing, waiting. I can feel the grains of sand against the bare soles of my feet, pressing down into the aged lino. I watch Isaac, the quick, agitated movements of his hands, the darting eyes, the way he sucks his lips to one side as he speaks.

'Fuck! Fuck! Fuck!' he suddenly shouts, the chair he is gripping lifting off the floor.

I shoot backwards, my elbow connecting with the hut door, which jars open, the door swinging out wide into the night, a light breeze winding around my neck.

Isaac holds the chair aloft, his forearms trembling, and I am waiting for him to launch it across the hut, watch the spindles crack and splinter in a shower of wood – but a beat later he lowers the chair back down and then slumps on it, his head hanging forwards, his elbows on his knees.

'Sit down,' he instructs me.

I obey, moving from the doorway and lowering myself on to the edge of the sofa.

'I was going out night-fishing,' Isaac begins, his voice shaky. 'I was loading the boat when I saw Jacob sitting on the rocks. He was upset. I . . . I didn't know whether to leave him or not.' Isaac scratches the side of his face roughly, leaving behind red rivers of nail marks. 'But then Jacob looked up. Looked right at me. I asked him if he was okay. He didn't answer one way or another. Just wanted to know if I was going out on my boat. If he could come.'

I am waiting, feeling the drumbeat of my heart.

'I told him he could fish with me, if he liked. We waded out to the boat, and as he scrambled on board, his mobile fell into the water. He never made a fuss. Never said anything – just looked up at the sky and laughed, like it was topping off his day.'

His mobile, I think, *that's why the police haven't been able to trace it.*

'We motored away from the bay, and I put the lines out. Gave him a spare rig and we fished for a while without talking.' Isaac's gaze is set on a point in the distance, as if he is looking out beyond the open hut door, into the night. An uncomfortable sensation pricks at my skin as I picture the two of them together on the boat, the waves rolling beneath them, night enclosing them. 'Right out of the blue, Jacob turned and said, "It's my birthday." So I told him, "Happy birthday, Jacob."'

Isaac shifts, pushing himself more upright in his chair, the wood creaking beneath him. 'Jacob said to me, "You knew that, didn't you?" I agreed; said I did. Told him that his birthday falls on Marley's anniversary, so I always remember it. Jacob didn't say anything for a long time, just kept his hands steady on the fishing rod. A while later he asked, "Why did you save me that day?"'

My hands clench into fists at my sides. I press them deep into the sofa, my throat tightening.

'So I told him that anyone would have done what they could to have helped . . . but he was riled up, demanding to know more . . .'

My airways feel compressed, as if I can't quite draw enough breath. I turn my face towards the open doorway. Outside there's the lightest dart of movement. A shadow moving between two huts. Instinctively my gaze swings in pursuit, straining to see into the darkness. But there's nothing except black, empty space and the low gurgle of the shifting harbour.

I turn back to Isaac, picturing Jacob firing questions on the boat, an explanation rising up in Isaac, the words stacking on the tip of his tongue. Jacob had come to him looking for answers – and Isaac's promise to me would've faded into nothing.

'I don't care what you said. Just tell me he's safe! Please, tell me you dropped him to shore. That's all I care about – that he's alive. Safe.'

Isaac stares at me, his dark eyes hooded. Then he closes them, his head lowering, shutting me out.

'Don't! Don't you dare!' I shout, suddenly on my feet. I

32. ISLA

*At first I didn't see it. I was looking so closely at Isaac –
searching for the missing fragment of what had happened
to Marley – that I didn't notice the oddness of Sarah's
behaviour around him. Something unspoken hovered on the
edges of their exchanges that I couldn't quite tune into.*

Summer 2014

Jacob was playing keep-me-ups on the beach, bouncing a
football off alternating knees. He cut a lonely figure in the
evening sun, his knees jerking like a toy soldier marching.
Marley used to play this with him for hours, each of them
diving dramatically after the ball to keep it from the ground.

Jacob mishit the ball, which flew through the air towards
the shore. Isaac, who'd been digging in the low-tide sand
for bait, glanced up. In one swift movement, he let go of

his spade and headed the ball almost vertically into the air. As the ball dropped back down towards him, he brought it under control on one knee, then booted it back to Jacob. His skill was so surprising and impressive that Jacob caught the ball, then whooped with delight. I watched him jog over to Isaac and persuade him to play.

Isaac's agility was impressive and I watched with interest, wondering where he'd learned to play. A few minutes later, Isaac kneed the ball wide, and Jacob made a heroic dive for it, but just clipped the ball – sending it flying into the shallows. As they both laughed, the sun hitting the side of their faces, Sarah appeared, striding down the beach towards them. 'Dinner's ready, Jacob!'

'But, Mum—'

'Grab the ball before it gets washed out.'

Jacob waded into the shallows, scooping up the ball, then walked back out towards Isaac – a hand held up for a high-five. Isaac hesitated, then slapped Jacob's palm.

As Jacob and Sarah walked away, I noticed how Isaac's gaze followed them both. He watched all the way until they slipped out of view within their hut.

I closed the book on my knee and stood. Sarah had invited me to join them for supper – so I went to the fridge, grabbed a bottle of wine, and made my way next door. As I climbed on to their deck, I heard Jacob saying, 'Thought dinner was ready.'

'I said I was about to start dinner.'

'No, you said—'

'Does it matter?' Sarah snapped.

Jacob's head jolted up. 'Yeah. Does, actually.' He crossed

the hut and strode out on to the deck, passing me as I entered. 'Wouldn't rush,' Jacob huffed. 'Food's not even started.'

Inside, the kitchen was bare, nothing was cooking. On seeing me, Sarah took out two glasses and poured the wine I'd brought. Her hand trembled as she passed me my glass.

'Just saw Jacob playing football with Isaac,' I remarked.

'Oh?' Her voice was sharp, as if she was expecting me to say more.

I looked at her closely. 'You okay?'

'Fine. Yes, fine.' She took a long drink of her wine.

'Don't you want Jacob playing with Isaac?'

She gave me a strange sidelong glance, then looked away, saying, 'Jacob's had too much sun today – I just thought it was time he came inside.'

I studied her face as she busied herself taking a bag of rice from an overhead cupboard. Rumour had it that Isaac lived in his beach hut all year round, under the council's radar. With the exception of a few friends on the sandbank and the men he'd drink with in the pub, I never saw him in anyone's company. The truth is, if he hadn't been out there on the water the day Marley drowned, I wouldn't have thought twice about him. It's unfair of me really, but had Isaac reached Marley first, if it had been Marley he'd hauled on to his boat, soaked and panting and terrified – I would have loved him. I would have thought he was the most wondrous man in the world. I would have bought him gifts, cooked meals for him, thrown my arms around him whenever I saw him.

Which is why, as I looked at Sarah, I found it odd that she never did. Isaac saved Jacob's life, yet Sarah seemed to shrink from his company.

33. SARAH

DAY EIGHT, 6 A.M.

Ninety-eight steps from the top of the headland to the sandbank. I wish there were more, because every step brings me closer to returning to our hut. To facing Nick.

I've walked all night, following old tracks I haven't taken in years, carving out forgotten pathways in the bleached moonlight, while Jacob's image spun round and round in my mind. Exhaustion burns bright behind my eyes and clenches at my skull. I'm still dressed in pyjamas, my hair wild, my bare feet cut and caked in dirt, but it's strange how none of it matters now.

By the time I reach our hut, I'm trembling. I imagine going inside, waking Nick, watching as he pushes himself upright in bed, his head angled to one side as he listens. I should have come here the moment I'd staggered from Isaac's hut . . . but I just . . . I needed time.

Climbing on to our deck now, I'm surprised to find the hut doors thrown open. I turn towards the sea, half expecting to see Nick's shape in the water – but our bay lies unbroken beneath an overcast dawn.

Inside, the sofa bed is still laid out, the imprint of Nick caught in the dip of the mattress and the light curve of his pillow.

'Nick?' I croak, my voice sounding weak.

But the only reply is my own shallow breathing.

I'm wired: eyes burning, thoughts singeing. I move to the sink and pour a glass of water, gulping it back greedily. I set the glass down with a clatter and, as I turn, I notice a large, smooth pebble on the kitchen counter, grains of sand dusting the work surface beside it. I step towards it, placing my fingertips on the cool chalky contours of the pebble. Then I see there's a note.

I slip the white sheet from beneath the pebble. It's not Nick's handwriting. The note must have been left on our deck secured by the pebble. I bring the paper towards my face like a scientist trying to understand an unusual specimen.

Sarah,
We MUST talk about Jacob. I need to explain! I'm so sorry.
Isaac

A flare of hot panic surges through my body. Looking back towards the open doorway, I know exactly where Nick has gone.

I race from our hut, every fibre of my being screaming, *No! Not like this! Please, not like this!*

All around me, the sandbank is murmuring awake. Curtains are being drawn, hut doors thrown open, kids in pyjamas padding on to the beach, bleary-eyed parents setting kettles to boil and assessing packs of bacon and loaves of bread.

Diane pauses from shaking out her duvet, watching as I run past, sending sheets of sand kicking out in my wake. I thunder past Robert and Lorrain, who're standing in the gap between two huts, looking at me curiously. I don't care who sees me! Let them look!

I am panting hard by the time I catch sight of Nick. He can only be thirty feet ahead of me, but he's climbing the steps of Isaac's hut.

'Nick!' I cry, my voice shrill, desperate.

He doesn't turn. He can't have heard.

'Wait! Nick!' I shout, louder this time.

A woman nursing a baby scowls at me from the doorway of her hut.

I lurch on, a sunken pebble stabbing into the heel of my foot. 'Nick!'

But he is already at Isaac's door. I see his hand lift, his fingers curling into a fist. He knocks.

I'm too late, I realize, as I watch the door open, Isaac stepping out.

Both men turn as I enter the hut.

Nick is dressed in shorts and the faded green T-shirt he likes to sleep in. His hair sticks up at the back and there is a tiny patch of toothpaste at the edge of his mouth. He looks at me, a light dip in his eyebrows – and there is something unbearably vulnerable about him. I want to go to him, take his hand, lead him away.

There's a strange calm in the hut, like the sea flattening off with eerie quiet in the moments before a squall tears across the surface, whipping waves into white peaks. Everything seems still, details enhanced. A cobweb wavers in the corner, the husk of a dead fly trembling at its centre. A cluster of flying ants crowd the top corner of a window, and above them the grey imprint of a dead moth stains the roll blind. Nick's gaze travels to my right hand and I realize I'm still holding Isaac's note.

'What's going on, Sarah?'

I force myself to meet his eye. 'It was Isaac's boat. That's the boat Jacob boarded the night he disappeared.'

Nick's gaze swings to Isaac. 'What? Why?'

Isaac stands at the back of his hut. He's wearing the same clothes as he was last night and I wonder whether he's slept. His eyes dart towards me, then back to Nick. 'I was going out fishing . . . Jacob saw me. Asked if he could come.'

Nick glares at Isaac for a long moment, then glances sideways towards me. 'The letter,' he says, his voice lowered, 'Jacob's love letter. Was it for—?'

'No!' I answer quickly. 'Absolutely not. Nothing like that. No, Jacob was upset after arguing with Caz and just wanted to get off the sandbank. Isaac happened to be there.' I take a breath. 'Jacob got on the boat and they fished for a while. But . . . there was a conversation . . . an argument.'

'About what?'

I move the words around my mouth, trying to decide which one to use first. Each of them feels wrong, misshapen somehow. My skin is burning beneath my clothes. What's happened is because of me, my choices, and I have to explain. I take a deep breath, open my mouth to speak, but Nick is turning away, stepping towards Isaac.

'What were you arguing about?' he demands.

'Jacob was . . . upset. He wanted to get off the boat, but we were a kilometre offshore by then. I wanted him to calm down so we could work things out. But he just . . . he wouldn't listen. He dived. He dived from my boat.'

Nick's eyes narrow. 'No,' he says, shaking his head. 'Jacob wouldn't do that. You're making it up!'

Isaac speaks hurriedly. 'I yelled to Jacob. Tried to throw the rope out to him. But he was swimming away. Just swimming, and swimming. I grabbed a torch, tried to keep him in the beam – begging him to swim back to the boat – but he wouldn't answer me. I lost sight of him . . . so I started up the engine, calling out the whole time, circling in the water.'

Isaac told me these same details last night, but hearing them a second time is no less painful. I cannot bear to picture Jacob swimming away from that boat in the pitch dark of night, distraught, alone.

'There was no swell, very little current running. I thought he'd be okay, I really did,' Isaac says, his voice wavering. 'He's a good swimmer, I've seen him . . . but . . .' He trails off.

'No, no. That can't be it. That's not what happened,' Nick says, his tone raw, desperate. 'It can't be. You'd have called the coastguard. The police. You'd have told us! We'd have known!' He's shaking his head violently. He swings round to face me. 'It doesn't make sense. Does it? None of it is right.'

'I searched for hours . . .' Isaac says. 'I thought he must have made it back—'

'Jacob was in the fucking sea!' Nick is saying. 'You should have called the coastguard! Got a search party together. Rung the fucking police! Told us!'

'I saw Sarah the morning after, didn't I?' he says, eyes on me. 'I tried to talk to you – but you said you were meeting Jacob. I thought everything was okay – that he'd made it back safely. So I left the sandbank – went to the oil rig for work. I didn't know Jacob was missing, I—'

There's a blur of movement, a rush of footsteps, and all of a sudden Isaac is being shoved backwards. Nick has him by the scruff of his jumper and is shoving him up against the wall of the hut.

Air expels from Isaac's lungs like he's been punched. His eyes bulge.

'Nick!' I cry.

'Why was Jacob on your boat? He'd never dive off! You pushed him, didn't you? That's what happened!'

Isaac tries to shake his head.

'What did you do to him? Tell me!'

His voice is squeezed into thin gasps of words. 'Didn't . . . touch him . . . I swear!'

'Then, WHY? Why did he dive?' Nick forces, his fingers digging into the skin at Isaac's throat.

I watch as the colour in Isaac's face rises to a puce.

He's going to choke. Nick is going to choke him to death.

'He can't breathe!' I plead.

Nick doesn't even register me. 'WHY?'

'Truth . . .' Isaac gasps. 'I . . . told him the truth.'

'Let him go! Please, Nick! I'll tell you what happened!'

Nick's eyes flick briefly to me. His grip loosens slightly and Isaac flounders, gasping for air.

'What . . . what are you talking about?' he says, still holding the neckline of Isaac's jumper.

Blood thunders in my ears.

Isaac's voice is low, trembling, but he returns Nick's gaze. 'Jacob's my son, Nick. And I told him.'

Nick is saying something, but I can no longer hear. His hands fall to his sides as he steps away, his forehead creased in confusion. *What?*

Each beat of time slows. I see the sun-damaged skin on the backs of Isaac's hands stretch, then gather, as he rubs the red skin at his throat. I notice two peas, fat and round on the work surface, beside a tray. I smell pepper in the air and something like sawdust, too. I catch sight of the faded navy pillow embroidered with the tentacles of an octopus, which I'd once laid my head on.

My hearing comes rushing back as Nick says to Isaac, '*That's . . . insane!*'

He turns to me and I imagine how I must look: slack-jawed, my face drained of colour, arms hanging limp at my sides. I'm aware of Nick's head tilting to one side, assessing me.

Then his eyes widen and he is taking a step back, shaking his head from side to side. 'Sarah?'

Nick's voice is a boy's now: scared, desperate, high. 'Sarah?'

Over the years I've often thought about telling Nick – and Jacob – the truth. But how could I hurt the very two people I love the most? I was the one who'd made the mistake. I was the one who would live with it.

That's what I told myself, at least.

But now I look at Nick's ghost-white expression, the fear in his widened pupils. He blinks rapidly, caught in the dazzling headlights of shock. 'I'm not Jacob's father?'

I think of how he used to hold Jacob as a baby, walking him around the house with one arm over Jacob's front, so Jacob could be upright, facing outwards. He was so proud. I fell in love with him all over again seeing the tenderness he had for his son. Nick would go for long walks on the beach, Jacob strapped to his chest in a sling, legs dangling, two tiny fists gripped around Nick's forefingers.

How can I have done this to him?

I can feel my lips stretched thin as I talk, the warm air of the hut heavy in my throat. 'I'm so sorry, Nick. You're not his father.'

He makes an awful choking gasp, as if he's trying to breathe underwater. 'No . . . no!'

I still can't believe it happened. Sometimes I'm able to pretend that it didn't. It was almost eighteen years ago and I've allowed the memory to become distant, blurred – like looking the wrong way into a pair of binoculars. But now, standing right here in this hut – where it happened – it's all coming into sharper focus.

I tell Nick, 'There was a night at The Rope and Anchor – years ago. My birthday. We'd been drinking since lunchtime, and you and I, we were fighting about Isla. I left the pub on my own . . . missed the ferry . . . and Isaac was there in his boat.' I'm filled with shame as I remember how I'd clambered on board in my tiny summer dress and gold sandals, smelling of perfume and alcohol. Isaac's gaze travelled over my tanned legs, my nipped-in waist, the low cut of my dress. When he met my eye, he flushed lightly, then turned away. But I didn't want him to stop looking – I liked it. I wanted him to look harder.

'I don't know what to say, Nick. We ended up going back to his hut.' This hut. 'I was drunk, angry with you, hurt. It happened that once. Never again. There was nothing to it, I promise you.'

'You fell pregnant,' Nick says, staring at me in disbelief. He rubs a hand down his cheeks and I hear the rough scrape of stubble. His fingers move to the back of his neck, plucking roughly at his skin. 'And you . . . you never told me. You let me believe the baby was mine . . . My God, you let me propose to you, marry you, stand at your side in that birthing room as Jacob was born. I cut the umbilical cord! I cried as I held him for the first time. You said – you said when I handed him to you – *He has your eyes, Nick.* My fucking eyes!'

'Oh God,' I whisper, hands covering my mouth. 'I didn't know, Nick! Honestly, I didn't know at first. Not for definite.' When I discovered I was pregnant, the possibility that the baby was Isaac's was little more than the light brush of a wing fluttering over my thoughts. When Nick cut the umbilical cord and lifted a red-skinned Jacob into his arms, any doubts I'd had vanished into the sunlight of parenthood. It was Nick who sang 'Twinkle Twinkle' over and over again to soothe Jacob to sleep; Nick who took him to football practice every Saturday morning; Nick who played Monsters for hours, chasing Jacob up the beach with his T-shirt pulled over his head, roaring. Nick was Jacob's father. 'It was only when we couldn't fall pregnant again that I started to wonder.'

There's a tremor at the edge of Nick's left eye, a pulse beneath the skin, flickering and quivering as he looks at Isaac now. 'You told Jacob this on the boat?'

He nods slowly.

'How could you? I can't . . . I can't . . .' He turns, lurching past me, unable to meet my eye. I watch as he stumbles from the deck, the back of his neck a bright, livid red.

'I'm sorry, Sarah.'

The sound of Isaac's voice behind me makes my skin turn to ice. I turn. 'You're sorry? It was cruel . . . unthinkably cruel to tell Jacob like that. He'd been drinking. He was in the middle of the sea with nowhere to go. It should have come from me, not you! After all these years, why then? You didn't think about anyone else – not what it'd do to our family, or—'

'Did you ever think about me?' he says, stepping closer, his face only inches from mine. I can smell the wool of his jumper. 'I've had to watch my son grow up from a distance, never able to tell him the truth, never able to get to know him. You denied me that, Sarah.'

'Nick's a good father. Jacob didn't need another.'

Isaac's mouth twitches. His voice is low, his eyes on me. 'I loved you. Did you know that? That's why I kept quiet about being Jacob's father – because I didn't want to hurt *you*.'

Loved me? My head shakes minutely. Had I seen that? I'd known he was attracted to me. I'll admit that there was something appealing, flattering, in the way he had always looked at me – as if everything else ceased to matter. But for me, it didn't run any deeper than that. What happened between us that one night was reactive, impulsive, a way of protecting myself against all those tiny hurts and slights that were stacking up as I tried to negotiate a relationship with Nick in Isla's shadow.

'I'm sorry,' I say. 'You never told me how you felt. You barely even talked to me about Jacob.'

'And that suited you.'

'I won't pretend it didn't. But you never once suggested that we tell Jacob the truth, did you?'

He looks at me with that dark unreadable gaze that I've so often seen in my son. 'Because you didn't want me to. Everything I've done, every decision I've made, has been for you, Sarah.'

'*For me?*' I laugh, incredulous. 'How was taking Jacob out on your boat, telling him that you're his father, for *me*?'

'It wasn't planned. It felt . . . like he'd been waiting to talk. He seemed . . .' Isaac looks as if he's struggling for the right word. 'Lost,' he says eventually. 'He seemed lost. Like he didn't know himself. I thought that maybe if I explained . . .'

'What did you expect? He dived from your boat because

it was too much – you gave him no choice. And then . . . then you left him out there.'

'I searched for hours!'

'You should have called the coastguard. Told us.'

'I was protecting you—'

'No! You were protecting *yourself*. You were the last one with Jacob. You didn't want the police to involve you. Who's to even say Jacob dived from your boat? How do we know you didn't push him?'

Isaac looks appalled. 'How can you even say that? I never wanted any of this. I didn't want to tell Jacob like that. I didn't want Nick to find out.'

'Then why the hell did you come to our hut? Why leave a note for me?'

Isaac's brows draw together. 'What note?'

'This!' I say, pulling it from my pocket, slamming it down on the table. 'This fucking note!'

Isaac takes a step forward, his eyes lowered as he looks closely at it. He rubs the back of his neck, his gaze not leaving the note.

Sarah,
   We MUST talk about Jacob. I need to explain! I'm so sorry.
   Isaac

After a moment, Isaac looks up, his gaze meeting mine. 'Sarah,' he says, his voice quieter now, bewildered. 'I didn't write that note.'

34. SARAH

DAY EIGHT, 7 A.M.

My legs somehow carry me in the direction of our beach hut. I'm aware of the hems of my pyjamas dusting the tops of the sand, leaving the faintest thread of a trail. *Isaac's note. Who wrote it, left it outside our hut?*

Exhaustion is a colour, a blinding white, burning my eyes. There's a surreal quality to everything, as if I've been awake for days. I find myself standing on the deck, my palm pressed against the wooden exterior, my nose almost touching the window. Nick is inside, towards the back of the hut. His hands are locked together, pressing into the worktop, his body rounded forward, shoulders shaking. He is, I realize with horror, crying. His face seems to have folded in on itself; his mouth is open, lips pulled back, teeth bared.

The door handle is cool in my grip as I turn it, stepping quietly inside. 'Oh, Nick . . .'

287

I half expect him to rear upright, voice raised; but he doesn't move, doesn't even lift his head. A choked, awful sound continues to twist from his mouth.

I sink heavily on to the edge of the unmade sofa bed, taking the weight of my head in my hands.

Sometime later I hear the rub of fabric against the hut wall as Nick slides to the floor, the buttons on the back pockets of his shorts clinking against the wooden floor.

'All these years,' he says, his voice shaky. He clears his throat, starts again. 'All these years, you suspected me of cheating.'

I lift my head, looking towards him. He sits on the floor, legs outstretched, head tipped back as if he's studying the ceiling. A glistening trail of tears winds into his stubble.

'But it was you who cheated.'

'I know . . . I know I did . . . and I'm so desperately sorry for it. It was before we were married and I—'

'No,' he interrupts, turning his head to look at me for the first time. His eyes seem paler, almost blank. 'You cheated me of Jacob. Of knowing he was *my* son.'

I feel my teeth pressing together on the inside of my cheeks. That's exactly what I've done.

'Can you imagine what Jacob must have felt on that boat when Isaac told him? Because I can, Sarah. It's like your whole world is being tipped – tipped and then shaken so fucking hard that you're disorientated, battered, and you look up – and the person who's done it to you, is the person you're meant to love more than anyone in the world.'

The metallic taste of blood fills my mouth. I can feel

the clamp of my teeth around my cheeks, the softness of the flesh as it splits.

'That's why Jacob dived off the boat. He would have done the same whether he was a hundred feet from shore, or a hundred miles. He would've dived.'

I tip back my head, looking up at the mezzanine. Through the neat parallel lines of wood, the screws and the timber framework, lies Jacob's bed. His duvet is still laid out on the mattress, two pillows plumped and waiting for him, the sheets holding his smell in the weave of their cotton.

'He's our boy, Sarah. Our boy. How could you let that happen?'

Every cell, every sinew in my body feels stretched taut, set to snap. 'He could have made it to shore,' I rush. 'It's possible, isn't it? Isaac said there was no wind, very little current. He's a good swimmer. He would've made it.'

Nick stares at me. 'If it were me – right now – if I were in the water, I'm not even sure I'd want to.'

'Oh God! Please don't, Nick! Don't say that!'

'Eight days, Sarah. It's been eight fucking days! Where is he? No one's even glimpsed him!'

'He could've made it to shore – then run. He wouldn't have wanted to come back to the hut. He needs time. It's going to be okay, Nick. It'll be okay.'

Nick looks at me as if he has no idea who I am. 'It can never be.'

An hour passes, maybe two. We talk. We don't talk. I boil the kettle. Let it cool again. Neither of us eats anything. I keep expecting Nick to walk out, leave. But he doesn't. He stays. Asks questions. Squeezes the bridge of his nose as he cries silently. He tells me to call the police. I explain everything to PC Evans, whilst Nick listens from the edge of the hut, his hands gripped to the wooden sides of the chair he's sitting on.

I change into jeans. Clean my teeth. Drink a glass of water. None of it helps.

'Were you ever going to tell me about Isaac?' Nick says some time in the afternoon. The inner corners of his eyes are pink and lightly swollen.

'No, I don't think I was.'

'Why?'

'You are Jacob's father. That's how I saw it. I didn't want to tell you *or* Jacob, because I didn't want either of you to doubt the importance of what you are to each other.' I close my eyes for a moment as I remember the tiny butterfly-wing flutters when Jacob first moved inside me, and the warmth of Nick's palm as he'd circled my stomach. I look at him. 'I wanted, more than anything, for Jacob to be yours.'

His gaze is searching, scrutinizing, as if he's trying to work out who I really am. 'When did you know? For certain?'

I swallow. 'We had that set of fertility tests at the clinic.'

His voice is wary as he says, 'You told me everything was fine.'

'I know. I did. But, well, the tests showed that the sperm wasn't . . . the right quality to—'

Nick's eyes widen. His head shakes from side to side. 'My God! You – you actually made up the results? *My* medical results!'

'I'm so—'

'Don't!' he says, standing. 'Just don't speak. Don't say anything.'

I press my knuckles against my mouth, feeling bone against teeth.

Nick swings round. 'How did Isaac know he was Jacob's father? Did you tell him about the fertility tests?'

'No! Of course not! He didn't know, not for a few years at least. But I suppose . . . over time, he began to wonder. He knew when Jacob's birthday was. Knew the dates worked. And there's a . . . likeness,' I say, thinking of the heaviness of their brows, the darkness of their eyes.

I tell Nick how, years ago, I'd been standing on the shore-line in the thin morning light, watching Jacob splashing through the shallows, wielding a fishing net. Isaac appeared at my shoulder, his shadow falling across me. He said nothing, but his gaze followed mine to where Jacob continued to play. I was aware of the proximity of him, a disturbance in the air between our bodies. Eventually he'd said, 'He's mine, isn't he?'

'Don't be ridiculous!' That was all I'd said. Maybe it was my tone, the knee-jerk defensiveness, or the way my eyes darted away from his face, but he knew. He knew I was lying. He'd turned to face me, his whole body square to mine. I couldn't catch my breath. He fixed his dark gaze on me. I felt exposed, as if he could read something buried deep inside me. I wanted to turn away, run – and yet I stood before him, frozen to the spot.

'I'd never do anything to hurt you, Sarah.' He let a pause hum between us. 'But please, don't ever take Jacob away from the sandbank. Promise me.' Then he added, 'Otherwise, I'll be forced to tell Nick.'

Nick is silent for a few minutes, lost in thought. 'Isaac guessed,' he says quietly, 'but I didn't.'

I watch as he pockets his wallet and phone, then gathers an armful of clothes, stuffing them into a bag. 'I need to get off the sandbank,' he says without looking at me.

'Okay,' I manage. I have no right to ask where he'll go or for how long.

He flings the hut doors open and the breeze comes rushing in, causing the white cords of the blinds to dance and swing, tapping a rhythm against the windows. He stalks across the beach, a bag on his back, the wind raking through his hair.

I watch until his shape becomes faint, lost to distance, then I curl up on the sofa bed, drawing my knees towards my chest. When Jacob was a few months old and was able to sit up on his own, I used to prop him on this bed in a throne of cushions, and he'd sit contentedly, watching as I pottered in the hut, cooking dinner and chatting to him lightly. As a mother, all I've ever wanted is to protect Jacob. Yet somehow I've managed to fail him on an incredible, terrifying scale.

If he has drowned . . .

My arms wrap around my knees, hunching against the thought. I can't let that voice in. I need to hope. I want to believe that there is a possibility, a chance that he survived.

I have to.

Time grinds on. I listen to the sounds of the world beyond the hut: the high pitch of a dog whistle being blown in the distance; the low vibration of a plane; the buzz of insect wings against glass; a boat engine straining.

292

The air turns thick, stuffy. I force myself to my feet, and drift towards the hut doors, pushing them open. I'm surprised to find dusk has arrived, velvet-grey. I pad across the deck but make it no further. Slumping down on to the bottom step, I dig my heels into the cool, damp sand.

Running a knuckle back and forth across my lips, I think about the strangeness of the note that was left in our beach hut. Isaac claimed he didn't write it and, if he's telling the truth, then it begs the question: who did?

Names spring into my thoughts. I wonder whether it could be something to do with Robert. Or, Diane, even. Or Lorrain, perhaps. But even if one of them had overheard something about Isaac and myself, why leave a note for Nick that would devastate us?

I shake my head, trying to push aside the train of thought. My nerves are raw. I need sleep. Everything is spinning away from me, out of my grasp. I can't seem to straighten any of my thoughts.

Waves are breaking on to the shore, low rumbles like distant, settling thunder. I am tuning into the sound, letting my breathing fall into rhythm, when I hear raised, urgent whispers nearby.

I turn my head, trying to make out where they are coming from. It takes a few seconds to understand that, next door, Diane and Neil's voices are escaping through the small side window that is ajar at the side of the hut, just a couple of feet away from where I sit. I straighten, lifting my gaze so that I can see through the window.

Neil is standing with his back to me, arms held out at his sides, gesturing expansively. I can't see Diane, but it's clear from the way Neil leans forward as he talks, hands opening and shutting in quick movements at his sides, that there's an intensity to their conversation.

I catch a word that holds me in its grip: *Jacob*.

My whole body becomes alert, poised, my hearing keen.

Diane's voice pushes from somewhere within the hut, her delivery rooted and firm, as if these words are often repeated. 'You need to stop fixating on this.'

I watch as Neil shakes his head, hands rising in front of him. 'How can I? It was my fault. I need to tell her. I should have said something immediately.' His words are sliding, slippery things, well oiled by alcohol.

'You don't know anything—'

'I *know* I was driving the boat too fast! I *know* I'd been drinking! I *know* I was reckless—'

My fingers curl into fists at my sides, the nails embedding in my palms.

'I won't believe that. You're not a reckless person, Neil.'

'No?' He spins round, suddenly lurching into view. The bright downlights in their hut illuminate his narrowed lips, his wildly darting eyes. His hands fly to his head, clasping the back of it and – just as swiftly as he came into view – he disappears, the vibrations of his footsteps crossing the hut. Whatever he says next must be mumbled as I lose most of it, except for the words, '. . . prove something to Robert!'

I rise to my feet, taking a step forward so as to place myself closer to the window. My fingertips press against the outer slats of Diane and Neil's hut, as I peer through the glass, my nose inches from the open window.

Neil is in full view now, sitting at the edge of their sofa, his head hanging forward, so that I can see the thinning patch of hair at his crown. Diane crosses the hut in a dressing gown, her expression weary, exhausted. She sits beside Neil, putting a hand lightly on his back. He bends towards her, as if blown by wind, his head leaning against her chest. The next words are whispered, lost.

I'm aware of the pads of my fingertips pressing against something lightly sticky, but dry, as I strain to listen. A spider's web. I want to pull my hands back, wipe away the clinging cotton sensation, but I stay rooted as Neil lifts his head, his eyes screwed tightly shut as he says, 'I still can't get the noise out of my head. I remember it exactly, the sound of the hull hitting something. The clunk.'

'You don't know it was him.'

I feel the blood swirling away from me.

'I should have told her.'

'Told her what? You heard a clunk. It could've been a fish, a piece of driftwood, a buoy marker – anything.'

I am suddenly thinking of the strangeness of Neil's interest in Jacob's disappearance, and Diane's hesitance to answer questions about Neil's whereabouts the night Jacob was last seen.

'He was in the water,' Neil says. 'That clunk – it was his head hitting the hull. I killed him.'

35. SARAH

DAY EIGHT, 7 P.M.

I am trembling from head to foot. Neil's words are a seismic quake, ripping through me.

I killed him. I killed him. I killed him.

Fragments of information shuffle and reform like tectonic plates aligning, until I see it all with glaring clarity.

Jacob dived from Isaac's boat and was swimming in the sea at night.

Neil was out on his boat, drinking, driving too fast.

He heard a clunk – the hull connecting with Jacob's head.

Neil returned to shore. Told no one except for Diane.

I must have been holding my breath, as suddenly I am gasping in air, lurching through the sand, clambering on to the deck of Diane and Neil's hut, yanking their door open.

Diane shoots to her feet, her face white. 'Sarah? What are you doing—'

My focus swings to Neil. The inner edges of his eyes are bloodshot, a grey pallor to his skin. He is breathing heavily, the smell of scotch souring on his breath. 'You . . . you killed him!' My voice is hoarse, choked with fear.

He steps back, eyes widening.

'Please,' Diane is saying, her palms opening towards me. 'Please—'

'How could you?' I cry at Neil.

'Oh God! I'm so sorry. It was an accident. I should have told her. I know, I should've . . .'

Her? My mind stalls, not following.

I look to Diane, but she is saying, 'We don't even know if anything happened. Let's just slow down.'

'Isla deserved the truth,' Neil says.

I shake my head. 'Isla?'

Neil continues, 'I was searching for him. I wanted to help. But instead . . . I hit him! I killed Marley!'

Marley. His name spins through my thoughts, disorientating me. 'Marley? Not Jacob?'

Diane's eyes widen. 'Oh God, Sarah! You thought . . . you thought we were talking about Jacob—'

There's a hot pain behind my eyes as I blink rapidly, seeing the truth unspool before me . . . *Marley*. Neil was part of the rescue effort, the second boat on the water after Isaac's. Had he been drinking? I have some vague memory of it, an unsuccessful fishing trip, drowning his sorrow with a few beers on the deck of his hut. When he went out to search for the boys, he was driving fast, with urgency.

'I was trying to help,' Neil tells me. 'Marley was out there all on his own. I wanted to save him. Bring him back to her. But I was going too fast, I know that. It was stupid, childish, but I wanted it to be me, not Robert, who rescued him.' Suddenly he is coming towards me, clutching my hands, squeezing them tightly in his hot grip. A vein in his temple pulses as he says, 'Do you think it was me? Do you think I hit him?'

'You'd have seen him, Neil,' Diane answers. 'If you'd hit him, he'd have come up. You'd have known.' These words sound well worn, like they've been said again and again.

Neil doesn't release me. 'But do you, Sarah? What do you think?' Desperation radiates from him.

I try to form an answer, make my mouth move around the shape of words, but I can't speak. I yank my hands from his grip, then rush from their hut.

'Wait!' I hear Diane calling after me, her footsteps hurrying across the deck.

I am already on the beach when she catches up with me. 'Sarah! Please! Just listen.'

I pause, my legs unsteady.

She gulps in air as she tells me, 'Please understand – Neil isn't himself. He's blown all this up in his mind. It's not as it sounds.' She lowers her voice. 'It's got out of hand . . . he's drinking too much, letting his mind play tricks on him.' She shakes her head. 'It's my fault. I should have told him to speak to Isla years ago, when it was just a tiny niggle. He told me about it the day it happened. It was nothing then – just the breath of a thought. "Think I clunked something out there . . . boat seems fine though." That's what he said. He was relaxed about it. Thought it was a buoy marking a lobster pot or something. You know where he was when he heard the clunk? Right out east – about five hundred feet from the yellow buoy that Marley and Jacob swam to. There's no way Marley would've been that far over. Not on a running tide. Neil knows all this, he really does.' She sounds exhausted, wrung out. 'But every anniversary it gets worse, like the idea of it has grown into something more than it is. He goes out on his boat, thinks about it, gets himself worked up. Then this summer, well, I think . . . Jacob's disappearance has brought it all back, you know, what with him disappearing on the anniversary, it happening in the same bay.'

It is not the same! I want to scream.

'Neil has worked himself into a state that Jacob has disappeared because he feels . . . I don't know . . .' she grapples for a word and comes up with 'responsible'.

My throat feels tight, choked.

'I'm sorry if . . . if I've given the impression that I've been . . . overly interested in your affairs, speaking to the police about Jacob. It's just – I wanted to reassure Neil that Jacob's disappearance had nothing to do with Marley, with the anniversary. I need him to let this go.' She glances over her shoulder towards the hut, where Neil is slumped on the sofa. 'I wish I'd made him talk to Isla at the time. Now the possibility of it has grown and distorted into something it wasn't.' Diane reaches out, a cool hand on my forearm. 'Sarah, I just want you to know, if I thought there was *any* chance Neil had hit Marley, any chance at all, I would've told Isla. I would never have let her suffer like this. But I know his boat didn't hit that little boy. Marley drowned. That's all there was to it. He drowned.'

*

My hands are still trembling as I pull open the door to our beach hut.

I blink and look again. Somehow Nick is inside, sitting on our sofa. I don't understand. My head is whirling. Whirling. Didn't he pack a bag, leave a few hours ago? How is he back here already? How much time has passed?

Seeing my expression, he asks, 'What is it, Sarah?'

'I . . . I thought Jacob was . . . Neil said he was out in his boat, and I thought . . .' My sentence trails away. I take a deep breath, then try again, recounting the conversation with Diane and Neil.

Nick's brows draw together as he listens. When I've finished, he asks, 'Neil really thinks he hit Marley?'

I nod.

'My God, he's been nursing that guilt all this time. But surely Diane is right – there's no way Neil's boat could've hit him. He was too far away. He'd have seen him.'

I nod because I agree.

It wasn't Neil.

My voice is a whisper as I say, 'I thought they were talking about Jacob. I thought Neil's boat had hit him . . . I honestly thought we'd lost him, Nick! I couldn't bear it . . . I couldn't bear it if he's—'

Nick interrupts. 'PC Roam called me. She's on her way here. That's why I'm back; she wants to talk to us both.'

I straighten, suddenly alert. 'About what?'

'She wouldn't say.'

We're only kept waiting a matter of minutes. When PC Roam arrives, she casts a quick glance first at me, then at Nick. I wonder what she sees: us sitting on opposite sofas, hollow-eyed, silent. Now that she's heard about Isaac, does she think I deserve everything that's happening? She threads her fingers together in front of her, then parts them, smoothing down imaginary creases along the sides of her trousers. 'I have some news about Jacob,' she says carefully.

My skin tightens.

Nick's gaze travels towards mine. Our eyes lock and I see it – the fear in his face that mirrors mine.

In that moment it doesn't matter what's happened between us, it doesn't matter about biology and DNA, or a night in a beach hut seventeen years ago. Right now, we are just two parents filled with dread as we sit before a police officer, waiting to hear what's happened to our son.

36. ISLA

Everything was different this summer. I noticed the shift from the moment I landed – and I believe Sarah did, too.

Sarah always picks me up from the airport. I've never asked her to, but it has become just one of those things we do. She meets me at the arrivals gate, wrapping me in a fierce hug, then leads me to her car, asking about my flight, Chile, work. The moment we pull away – Sarah driving too fast and too close to the other cars – the questions stop and her stories begin: I slide back into her world with a rainbow of tales about the sandbank, mutual friends, the minutiae of the grievances and triumphs that pepper her days. 'Oh. The twentieth?' she'd said this time when I called. 'I'm on a spa day. Miranda's birthday. She thinks we're too old to celebrate by getting blindingly drunk, so we're going to have our toes painted instead. You okay to grab a coach? I'll be back at the hut by the evening. I'll do a meal.'

It was a small thing. Certainly nothing to get upset about.

But I can't help but wonder if it set the tone of what was to follow.

This summer

The coach dropped me off in a wheeze of diesel fumes. It was a relief to stretch my legs, and I felt shaky and light-headed as I hauled on my backpack and began to walk through town.

Ravenous after the long journey, I stopped at my favourite bakery, treating myself to an almond croissant and a pain au chocolat. I was opening the bag of still-warm pastries, their buttery smell making my mouth water, when a brown Ford pulled into a car parking space ahead of me. I was vaguely aware that I recognized the vehicle, but before I'd had time to process the thought, the driver stepped out.

I froze. A tiny gasp of air escaped my mouth.

Samuel. He hadn't seen me as he pulled the keys from the engine and straightened. I took in the familiar frame of his body, still lean and muscular. His once-long hair had been cut short, and I could see a peppering of grey near his temples.

A powerful shot of longing took me entirely by surprise. I took a step forward, my tongue pushing to the front of my mouth to say his name—

But the passenger door swung open and a woman with glossy dark hair stepped out, wrapping a primrose-yellow scarf around her neck. She was smiling, two spots of high colour on her cheeks.

I looked back to Samuel, who was now opening the rear

passenger door. He was talking, his generous mouth curving into a smile. Then, in a careful, practised movement, he extracted a child from a car seat, lifting it into his arms.

A boy with a thick mop of blond hair.

A deep pain cracked in my chest, my ribcage compressing. I sucked in air, struggling to breathe.

I thought of the hours Samuel had spent playing with Marley. How he could turn anything into a game: he'd wrap our circular drinks mats with tinfoil and bury them in the sand as pirates' treasure; he'd create obstacle courses out of driftwood and seaweed for Marley to race through; he'd use skimming stones to clang the iron posts at the end of the rocky groynes. He had loved my boy.

But now he had his own.

He was turning, looking up. I couldn't let him see me. I couldn't stand on the roadside with my old battered backpack on my shoulders, my skin washed out from the flight, and congratulate him on his new family.

I spun round, diving into the nearest shop. I heard the tinkling of a bell, breathed in the thick, musty smell of second-hand books, caught a greeting from the shop owner. I hovered at the edge of the shop window, heart ricocheting, as I watched Samuel's thick hands snapping a buggy into position, taking the bag the woman held, all of them talking and moving and smiling, like a well-choreographed dance. Samuel leant down and placed a kiss on the crown of his son's head.

The same mouth that had kissed Marley. That had spoken my name. That had promised me, his face wet with tears, his fingers gripped hard around mine, that he would wait for me.

And he had.

He'd written long letters and sent books of poetry he thought I'd like. He emailed pictures he'd drawn to make me laugh. He left wildflower bouquets on my doorstep, and photographs of the renovated house he still wanted me to move into. He left phone messages and sent emails.

And then, eventually, he'd stopped.

I arrived on the sandbank, relieved to find Sarah had already opened up my hut, removing the winter shutters and airing out the place. She'd arranged a bunch of flowers in a jam jar, with a note saying, WELCOME HOME! She'd signed all three of their names – *Sarah, Nick, Jacob* – with a kiss beneath each.

Their beach hut was closed, and so was Joe and Binks's next door. Standing in my empty hut, exhausted and shaken, I found myself pulling Marley's memory book from its drawer, and pressing it to my lips. The book never came with me to Chile: it was for here, the beach hut. This was the place where I allowed myself to swim back through our memories, cloak myself in them.

No, I wouldn't open it yet. I wasn't in the right frame of mind. I carefully returned the memory book to the drawer, then grabbed a rug and a novel, and took them on to the beach. I lay near the shore, the book shading the sun from my eyes. My breathing began to settle as the sea air rolled in and out of my lungs. Within minutes the soporific sound of the waves had pulled me away from the page, towards a sleepy place. I felt the drag of my eyelids closing, the book lowering to rest on my face. I could smell the pulp and ink of the pages, feel my breath warm and moist against it. Just a moment, I said to myself. Just half a minute.

There were dreams. Dreams of Samuel, my face pressed into the warmth of his neck, but when I pulled away it was Marley's face, wet and cold, staring back at me.

I woke with a start to find a man calling my name. I sat up, disorientated, the book sliding from my face. The man was standing right in front of me, bare-chested and tanned. I squinted against the sun.

'Auntie Isla.'

I blinked. *Jacob?* My gaze travelled across his face. The proportions had changed. His dark eyes were set beneath strong brows, his chin had squared off and there was something more defined to the angles of his face. It'd been two years since I'd seen him and the change was staggering.

I pushed myself to my feet. He was taller than me now.

'Jacob!' I said, my face breaking into a grin. Then I threw my arms around him, squeezing him tight. 'I missed you!'

I became aware of the warmth of his bare skin against mine, and the hardness of his muscles in his arms and back. I held tight, feeling a rise of emotion. Jacob had always been my marker for Marley. It forced me to see the passing of time. If Marley were still alive, he'd be turning into a young man, too.

'Good to see you!' Jacob said, letting me go. His eyes were bright, his voice animated.

'I can't believe it's you! Just look at you! What has your mum been feeding you?'

He smiled, shrugged.

There was a new confidence about him in the way he

held my gaze, held space. It threw me off balance, somehow. 'Hey, I've got something for you back at the hut,' I said.

I left the rug on the shore, and we walked up to my hut. Inside, Jacob flopped on to the sofa, in the spot he always chose by the door, one leg drawn up.

I rummaged in my backpack and pulled out a brown paper package tied with string. I always brought a gift back for Jacob, something special I'd pick up during the months I was away. It had become a ritual over the years, and it gave me pleasure to search the market stands and shops, looking for exactly the right thing. I'd scour antique bookstores, artisan stalls selling local instruments, or clothes weaved from sheep's wool, allowing myself to think the gift was for Marley. It had become a test to see whether I still knew who he'd be at this age, whether he'd like the gift or not.

I passed the package to Jacob, suddenly panicking that it was too babyish for him – that I'd got it wrong. Maybe he wouldn't be interested any more.

Jacob untied the string and tore off the paper, pulling out the carved figure of a bird. He held it up, his face serious. 'A kingfisher,' he said, tracing a finger over the polished mahogany. His brow creased as he studied the curved lines and details of the carving. Then he looked at me and said, 'It's incredible.'

I felt the warmth of pleasure spreading through my chest. He leant forward and hugged me. 'Thank you, Isla.'

As his arms wrapped around me, my eyes closed and I breathed him in, letting myself believe – just for half a moment – that it was Marley.

*

We had a beer on the deck of my hut. They'd been in the cupboard since last summer – out of date and warm – but Jacob didn't complain.

'So, how's college?'

'You know, all right.'

'Still skating?'

'Yeah, got myself a longboard at the start of summer. I'm done with tricks.'

'Because of your ankle? Your mum told me you broke it last summer.'

Jacob nodded. 'Sand in the wheel bearings.'

'Nasty. And what about your folks; how are they?'

He shrugged. 'Dad's stressed with work. Or a lack of work, I think. But he's all right.' He took a swig of beer.

'And your mum?'

'On my case the whole time.'

I was going to ask him more, but his attention was caught elsewhere. I followed his gaze down to the beach. A beautiful girl with a shock of bright blonde hair was walking along the shoreline, her body tanned and lean. I faintly recognized her. 'That's not Robert's daughter, is it?'

He stood. 'Caz!'

She turned, shading the sun from her eyes. The moment she saw Jacob, she grinned.

I glanced at him. His face was unguarded, his eyes bright.

'Go,' I told him. 'Take your beer. We'll catch up later.'

I watched Jacob jog down the beach with long, easy strides. When he reached her, he said something that made her laugh and she bashed him playfully on the arm. Then their hands threaded together – and they kept walking, their backs to me.

I watched them for a while, thinking, *You don't realize it, but you have everything ahead of you.*

Sarah and Nick arrived at the beach laden with bags of food and drink. 'We're celebrating your homecoming!' Sarah said, holding up two bottles of champagne.

She put them down, then hugged me tightly. 'Jesus, Isla! You're back! It's so good to see you!'

Then Nick stepped forward and hugged me, too. 'Isla Berry!'

It'd been two years since I'd seen him – and I couldn't help noticing how much he'd aged. His skin was pale for midsummer and his hair was a little longer than usual, as if he'd forgotten to get it cut. 'Looks like you brought summer with you,' he said, lifting his hands to the sunshine.

'Been an awful summer so far,' Sarah added. 'You probably heard. Wettest June on record.'

'Let's hope July and August make up for it,' I said.

Nick asked, 'You're here for two months?'

'Just under. I fly back the morning after Marley's anniversary.'

He left Sarah and me to catch up while he lit the barbecue on the deck, scraping the grill clean with a metal spatula.

Sarah and I stayed in the kitchen, threading chunks of chicken, cherry tomatoes and button mushrooms on to bamboo skewers. When I told her about seeing Samuel, Sarah's face immediately coloured. 'Shit, I'm so sorry! I should have warned you. I didn't think—'

'You already knew? I can't believe you didn't tell me!'

'I didn't want to upset you. Or tell you over the phone.'

'Since when did you stop telling me things because you don't want to *upset* me? You know how much I hate that.'

'Oh honey, I wasn't thinking. I just . . . you weren't here and I thought . . . Well, it doesn't matter what I thought. I made a mistake. I'm sorry. I should've told you.'

Her admission put out the flame of my anger. 'It's not your fault. He was always going to meet someone.'

Sarah smiled at me sadly. She washed her hands, then poured champagne into two glass flutes.

'Well,' she said, handing me one, 'I'm sure they're desperately unhappy and will have a calamitous break-up very soon.'

'Here's hoping,' I said, clinking glasses and forcing a smile.

From the deck I heard Nick bellow, 'And here he is!' clapping Jacob on the shoulder as he loped in. 'Look who's inside,' Nick said, nodding in my direction.

'Old news,' Jacob said with a light smile. 'We've already caught up.' He grinned at me, then went straight to the kitchen, pouring himself a pint of water, and swallowing it in a few gulps.

'Have you and Nick been feeding him growth hormones? I'm pretty sure that last time I saw Jacob he only came up to my knee.'

'I think it's all the calories in beer, isn't it Jacob?' Sarah said.

'How would I know? I'm not eighteen yet.' He grinned.

I took a sip of my champagne and soaked up the family atmosphere. It was comforting – like pulling on a favourite warm jumper and hugging it tight to my skin.

'So,' Jacob said, his gaze full on my face, 'how's Chile?'

I followed him on to the deck and we sat in the evening sun, talking. Nick closed the lid of the barbecue and perched on the edge of the table, listening. I told them about one of the hiking trips I'd taken in my free time, driving the van down south to a national park. 'I was the only person there. It was eerie how deserted the place was. I'd expected the trails to be well used – but it was just me. I hiked all day until I reached this glacier I'd read about. It was incredible seeing it up close – there was no snow, just rocks and ice. It just stood there – like a huge white skyscraper, glistening in the sun.' I told them other stories, too, about the beaches that are constantly pounded by swell, and the street dog I'd adopted and named Feral Williams, who'd left my apartment infested with fleas.

When I glanced up, Sarah was standing inside the hut, a tea towel bunched in her hand, watching the three of us. Her lips were pressed together, and there was a tightness around her eyes. When she saw me looking, her eyes softened, a light smile flashing across her lips. 'More drinks, anyone?'

'Another beer, please,' Nick said.

'Same for me,' I said, finishing my champagne. 'Hey,' I said to Jacob, 'how was your camping trip last summer? Heard you toughed out the rain.'

When I'd arrived on the sandbank last year, I'd been so disappointed to learn that Nick and Jacob were away in Cornwall for the whole duration of my visit. If I'd known I'd miss them, I'd have changed my dates.

'Made a pact, didn't we?' Nick said to Jacob.

'Yeah. We're never sharing a tent again. Dad snores like a buffalo's arse.'

'And Jacob messed about on his phone all bloody night. Shining the screen in my eyeballs.'

'So it was a great success, then.'

'Hmm,' Nick said, raising his eyebrows.

Sarah returned with ice-cold beers.

'Gutted we missed you though,' Jacob added.

'I know. Me, too,' I agreed.

'Shame your flights changed,' Nick said. 'If we'd had more warning, we could've gone camping earlier.'

'My flights didn't change. I was always coming for the last two weeks of August. I booked them months in advance.'

Nick's brows drew together. Then he turned to Sarah. 'I'm sure you said Isla had to change her flights or something.'

'Did I?' she said, seemingly perplexed. 'Must have got the dates muddled. You know what I'm like.'

Yes, I do know what Sarah's like. She's efficient, organized, and doesn't make mistakes like that.

I've thought a lot about that exchange since. If Sarah gave Nick the incorrect dates – booked their two-week holiday over the exact span of my trip – it was certainly no coincidence.

Sarah made light of it, saying she was pleased to have me to herself for a change. But now I realize Sarah didn't want me to herself; she just didn't want me near her family.

37. ISLA

This summer

'What did you do to those cashew nuts?' I asked, stretching up into the cupboard to put away the final plate, a damp tea towel over my shoulder.

'Roasted them in sesame oil and honey.'

'Incredible.'

Nick was away for the night, so Sarah had cooked for Jacob and me, and I'd brought the wine.

'Ready for dessert?'

'Always,' I said, hanging the tea towel over the handle of the oven door.

'Jacob?' Sarah called up into the mezzanine, where Jacob was changing ready to disappear to a beach fire with a group of friends. 'You having dessert?'

A thud sounded from above. 'No!' he hollered.

'Let's have it on the sofa,' Sarah said to me.

I crossed the hut with my wine and sank into the cushions, tucking my feet to one side. Candles twinkled in glass jars and the smell of warm chocolate filled the air. As Sarah sliced a tray of brownies into generous squares, my attention was absorbed by a song on the radio. 'Billie Jean' was playing, and the chirrupy rhythm released a memory of Marley imitating Michael Jackson's fluid moves, sliding backwards from his heels to toe, then threading his fingers together and making energetic waves with his linked arms. Sarah had the song on an old CD and used to play it in her kitchen for Marley, while the rest of us hooted with delight as he entertained us.

My chest ached with a fierce longing to see him moonwalking across this hut, to hear him burst into fits of giggles, for Sarah to clap her hands together in delight and announce, 'Everybody, it's Marley Jackson!'

I looked up, catching Sarah's eye, smiling at the unspoken memories.

She glanced back with her head angled to one side. 'Did you want more wine?' she asked, perplexed.

I shook my head lightly. She'd forgotten. How could she have forgotten Marley's love for this song? I swallowed, inexplicably hurt. I knew I could remind Sarah about the track, but the moment was lost, the warmth of the memories draining away.

Jacob's bare legs descended the wooden ladder, the smell of freshly sprayed deodorant wafting after him. If Marley were alive, they'd be going off to the beach party together, the two of them teasing each other as they ambled from the hut, beers clinking at their sides.

Jacob caught my eye, then clasped his hands together in front of him and made a waving motion of his arms – wearing the same concentrated expression that Marley used to. Then he moonwalked across the hut, bare feet dragging across the sand-gritted floor.

It was so perfectly unexpected, so exuberantly executed, that I snorted with delight.

Jacob grinned back at me, dark eyes sparkling. 'Marley Jackson will be dancing to this somewhere,' he said, his voice low, a smile in his tone.

I pressed my lips together, nodded.

'What is it?' Sarah asked, turning to look at us both.

Jacob shook his head as if to say, *Nothing*. Then he moved to the doorway, departing with a casual wave. 'Catch you later.'

I watched Jacob stroll down the beach, slipping his mobile from his pocket, head bending towards the screen. I could feel the grief opening up in me, a dark space unfurling. I wanted Jacob to come back, sit with us, talk to me about Marley. He was my link, my marker, the strongest connection I had left to my boy. My gaze travelled instinctively to an aged cream photo frame on the wall, beside Sarah's *Hut Sweet Hut* sign. For years it'd housed one of my favourite pictures of Marley and Jacob, taken when they were eight or nine years old. They'd just returned from an afternoon's fishing and were holding a mackerel in each hand, faded lifejackets bunched up around their ears, Marley's nose wrinkled as he squinted into the sun.

As the song ended, I realized that the photo frame show-

315

cased a new image of Sarah, Nick and Jacob sitting on the deck of their beach hut, drinks raised to the camera.

'You changed the picture?' The words came out sharp, high.

Sarah stepped towards me, her gaze following mine. Her voice was over-bright as she said, 'Binks took that at the start of summer. I look a bit like I'm storing food in my cheeks – but it's about the only one that's ever been taken of the three of us.'

I could feel my jaw tightening, a tingling at the ends of my fingertips. 'There used to be a picture of Marley and Jacob here.'

Pink blotches rose instantly to her cheeks. 'I'm so sorry, Isla,' she said, pressing her hands to her chest. 'I didn't think when I changed it over. I had a whole load of photos printed at the same time and updated all our frames.'

'Where is the photo?'

'I've kept it. Of course, I have. How bloody thoughtless of me changing it! Sorry.' She sounded genuinely so, and I felt bad for making a point of it.

'I'm just being over-sensitive.' I shook my head, blowing out. 'It's this time of year. I work myself up into a state.'

'Let me switch the photo back. I do love that one of Marley and Jacob.'

'No, don't. You should have one of your family.'

'At least let me give you that photo of the boys. I've got it somewhere. You make a start on dessert and I'll dig it out.'

I washed down a few mouthfuls of brownie with my wine, but my appetite had vanished. Eventually Sarah located the photo, wiping it with her sleeve before handing it to me. The picture was sun-faded from its years in the frame, Marley's face bleached as pale as a ghost's. I carefully smoothed out the creases, then pressed the photo into the breast pocket of my shirt, feeling Marley close to me.

I stayed just long enough for Sarah to finish her dessert, then I thanked her and made my excuses, returning to my hut.

It was midnight when I laced up my running trainers, then switched on my head torch, slipping from the beach hut. It was one of the many freedoms my life allowed: there was no sleeping child to leave, or husband to comment, *Where are you going at this hour?* It didn't matter what time I ran, or how long I was gone for, or why I went.

Night on the headland was quiet. There was a low hum of insects, the occasional swoop of wings, but mostly there was just the sea – the tide sliding away from the shore, the moon luminous and ghostly, bleaching the landscape grey.

The small circle of light cast by my head torch danced two paces in front of me, like a star I could never catch. I could feel the welcome burn of heat in my calf muscles as I ran, earth and stones shifting beneath the soles of my trainers. I pushed away the image of the faded photo of Marley and Jacob, focusing on the fierce pump of my heart. I was breathing hard, but wouldn't slow. Minutes later came the sharp glass fingers of a stitch cutting between my ribs. I should have dropped my pace, waited for the pain to ease – but instead I pushed on harder. I welcomed the burning stitch – focused on it.

When I was pregnant with Marley, I read an article about childbirth and how it was possible to manage the presence of pain by channelling your thoughts to a different sensation in the body. It worked on the idea that if the non-pain-carrying nerves are active, they can override some of the pain signals. The pain is still physically present – there's no way to lessen it – yet you're better able to deal with it.

Over the years, I've wondered if it's the same with emotional pain. Losing Marley never becomes less painful, but I am able to channel that pain more effectively. There are times when I prefer to wrap myself in memories of him, say his name aloud and share stories of him so that he feels real and present to me. And there are other times when the pain is so dark and thick, it feels like this great pressure within me that is going to explode. That's when I run.

I reached the end of the headland and jogged down the stone steps that led on to the beach. I sucked the night air deep into my lungs, tasting scents of earth and salt. Heat fired through me, a slick of sweat pooling at the base of my back and between my breasts. My breathing was rasped and hard, and I liked the physicality of it.

The sea was right there ahead of me – both enemy and friend. I knew I had to be in it. I made a final sprint to the water's edge, coming to a halt in a spray of sand. Further along there was the glow of a beach fire, but other than that, the beach was mine.

Panting, I removed my head torch, then bent forward and pulled off my trainers and socks, feeling the heat and swollen veins in my feet. I wriggled out of my vest, shorts and underwear, then tugged out my hair band, losing it to the sand.

I was still breathing hard as I waded in, diving forwards and losing myself to the inky water.

There, everything silenced. There was just the black-cool dark, my limbs moving fluidly through it. I could feel my nipples hardening beneath the water, feel the sea covering every inch of my hot flesh. I broke through the surface with my face tilted to the night, a slick of wet hair dripping down my spine.

I kicked around in the water, floating on my back and watching the stars, until my skin was chilled and puckered like goose flesh.

Eventually I waded out, wringing the water from my hair. I pulled my vest and shorts straight on, not bothering with underwear, which I stuffed into my trainers, and carried them swinging at my side.

Walking along the shoreline with the warm night wind behind me, I felt the boost of endorphins that exercise always rewarded me with. The stars were bright, dancing. As I grew closer to the beach fire, I could see a group of young men standing around it, bottles of beer in their hands. I smelled dope in the air and smiled to myself.

'Isla!'

I turned. A figure was standing at the edge of the fire, calling to me with the glow of a cigarette between his fingers. It took me a moment to realize it was Jacob. It shouldn't have been such a shock to see him here drinking and smoking with his friends – yet there was a part of me that still believed he was the boy who slept in the bunk above Marley's, the promise of a hot chocolate and a Roald Dahl story being enough to make him beam.

I should have simply waved, then walked on. I could have poked fun at him the following morning that I'd busted him smoking. But I didn't. I waited as he jogged towards me.

Away from the flames we stood in the darkness.

He stepped close to me. 'Isla,' he said again.

He took a drag of his cigarette, then breathed out away from me, flicking the butt into the sand.

I said nothing.

He reached out and touched my wet hair. 'You've been swimming.'

'And you've been drinking.'

He grinned. 'How was the water?'

'Refreshing.'

I could feel his gaze travel down my body; my clothes clung to my wet skin. My nipples were hard and erect with the cold. 'Beautiful night for it,' he said. He told me about the phosphorescence that had lit up the waves earlier when he'd swum, alcohol loosening his words.

I glanced over his shoulder towards the fire where his friends waited. They weren't watching, and Jacob didn't seem in a hurry to return.

'I love the beach at night,' Jacob said. 'It's ours, isn't it? No tourists, just a few of us from the huts.'

I nodded.

Jacob reached out and placed the back of his hand against my upper arm, his fingers warm against my cool skin. 'You're cold. Come to the fire.'

'I'm fine.'

He held my gaze.

'I'm going back to the hut.'

'Shall I walk you?'

I would have loved someone to take me by the hand, lead me back to the hut, put me in bed and tuck the covers under my chin.

'Jacob!' I heard one of his friends calling to him. 'Who are you talking to?'

'You'd better get back to the fire.'

'He doesn't matter.'

There was silence between us.

'I'll walk you.'

It was a statement this time, not a question.

'Goodnight, Jacob,' I said. I turned and set off alone.

38. SARAH

DAY EIGHT, 4.15 P.M.

Outside, wind gusts across the beach, a cloud of sand lifting into the air. I want to feel the coarse sting of it, taste the salt and chalk in the air, feel the chill of the cooling wind.

I have some news.

PC Roam stands with her back to the hut doors, as if blocking our exit. I'm sitting on the sofa opposite Nick, but my position feels all wrong, head angled awkwardly to look at her face, my throat stretched. I need to be next to Nick. I need his hands around mine.

I am about to move, when PC Roam says, 'We have a positive lead.'

Air leaves my lungs in a rush. 'A lead . . .' I say, my gaze flicking to Nick. *A lead, not a body. A lead!*

'We have run some checks with the Border Agency. Jacob's

322

passport has been used . . .' PC Roam is still speaking, apologizing that they hadn't picked this up sooner, that border checks are typically only a priority in high-risk cases, but all I want to know is:

'Used by him?'

'We believe so.'

'Jacob's passport has been used,' I relay to Nick, even though he, too, is right here in the hut.

My mind spins with new thoughts. Jacob must have made it to shore, then taken off, wanting to disappear, to get out of the country. This is good news. This is excellent, wondrous, incredible news! We can find him! Bring him home! Explain! We will all be okay because Jacob is alive!

'Where is he?' Nick asks.

I am already picturing somewhere in Europe, or possibly further flung, like Australia. Somewhere he could easily blend in – New Zealand possibly, although, what about money?

PC Roam answers the question. 'Jacob is in Chile.'

'Chile?' I repeat.

Nick's eyes narrow. 'Jacob's in Chile?' He pauses. 'With Isla?'

My mind works fast, trying to unravel the knot of why he is there, how he is there. I picture him scrambling out of the dark sea, sodden clothes clinging to his body. He'd have been in shock, reeling. Nick and I would be the last people he'd want to turn to, so he'd have thought of the one person who he could rely on, who he trusted, who would do anything to help him: Isla.

She'd have already left for Chile by then, but there was nothing to stop him following her out there. I've seen how spellbound he becomes listening to Isla's stories of the wild, wave-pounded coastline, and the startling jagged peaks of the mountains. Perhaps he pictured himself there, romanticized it, till it became the perfect solution.

'Where in Chile is he? Can we speak to him?' Nick is asking.

'I'm sorry; we don't know.'

'How did he get to the airport? What about his passport? How did he pay for it?' Nick fires.

PC Roam says, 'These are all things we're looking into.'

Possibilities turn through my head. Jacob had no money on him – we found his wallet in his backpack, and the five hundred pounds cash he'd taken out for Caz's abortion was safe in the beach hut drawer – so did he borrow money from someone else? He'd have had to pay for a bus or taxi to the airport, plus the flight.

Then there's his passport. I'm almost certain he wouldn't have been carrying it on him, so he must have returned to our house to fetch it. Had he walked there? It is twelve miles from the sandbank – so it would've taken him several hours. Unless he was helped? But the police have already spoken to his friends and no one claims to have seen him since the disappearance. I keep all our passports together in a document file at home, so he couldn't have—

I'm halted in my thoughts. All our belongings are stored in the garage. He knows where we keep the spare key. He could easily have let himself in unseen. Suddenly, I think of it: the box file lying on its side on the concrete floor, the contents spilled out. That's the file that contains all our important family documents – our passports, travel insurance documents, mine and Nick's wills. I'd assumed the file had toppled over, but now I am picturing Jacob searching for his passport, knocking it over in his hurry to leave.

PC Roam is saying, 'We've checked Jacob's savings account again, and still no money has been withdrawn since his disappearance. I wanted to know if it's possible that he had any cash or savings that you didn't know about?'

'My mother gave him some money last Christmas – but that's the cash we found in his drawer. Apart from his wages from the ferry job, he has little other money. Certainly not enough for a plane ticket.'

'We're aware that Jacob's godmother, Isla Berry, lives in Chile. Is it likely that he'd have gone to see her?'

'Yes, yes I think it is.' Jacob knows the name of the international school where Isla works, and would have been able to find out her address. He could've followed her out to Chile, turned up on her doorstep.

'Isla Berry hasn't been in touch?'

I shake my head.

'Is it possible that Jacob has begged Isla not to say anything?'

Nick rubs his hand back and forth across his brow. 'No. Isla would know how worried we'd be – Sarah's left lots of messages. Isla would have called us.' Yet there is something in Nick's expression – a flicker of doubt.

PC Roam says, 'We've called her workplace – Santiago International School – but she is not due to start back until next week. Now we're trying to get in touch with the landlord of the apartment she rents.'

'What if Jacob arrived in Chile,' I say, 'but never found his way to where she lives?'

I picture Jacob stepping out of the airport, bewildered and exhausted. Would he have tried to get a taxi or coach to take him to Isla's address? He doesn't speak any Spanish; he's never travelled. Did someone notice him, a naïve, fresh-faced English boy?

'How are you planning on tracking him down?' Nick asks. 'Have you contacted the Chilean authorities?'

'I have to warn you,' PC Roam begins, 'that I don't think they'll get involved, as there's no reason to believe that Jacob left the UK unwillingly. As he's over sixteen, I'm afraid the Chilean police wouldn't see any reason to begin searching for him. However, we will see if they are able to send someone over to Isla Berry's apartment. Ask her to contact us.'

'That's not enough!' I say, my voice rising. 'What if he's in trouble? When did he fly? How long's he been there?'

'He flew last Monday.'

'Last Monday,' I repeat. 'That's the day after he disappeared. What time?'

'Let me just check for you,' PC Roam says, pulling a notebook from her pocket and flicking through the pages.

Nick gets to his feet and paces the hut. 'When did Isla leave?'

'The day before Jacob. Sunday. You bumped into her when you were meeting my mother. What time was it?'

'Around nine, I'd say.' He draws a hand over his mouth, thinking. 'But she said her taxi wasn't booked for another couple of hours.'

It was then a two-hour drive to the airport, plus checking

in. Which means she would have flown in the early hours of Monday morning.

'Here we are,' PC Roam says, arriving at the relevant page in her notebook. 'Jacob was on the 04.45 flight from London Heathrow to Santiago, Chile.'

I look at Nick, my stomach falling. 'He left at the same time as Isla, didn't he? They went together.'

39. ISLA

From the vantage point of hindsight, it should be easy for me to look at the pieces of our friendship and decide exactly where the first cracks began.

Take a china vase, for example, once beautiful and prized, that lies broken on a tiled floor. The vase might have shattered at the moment the china hit the floor, but perhaps there was a weakness there from the beginning. The kiln might have been a degree too hot; the vase might have been knocked years before, leaving a tiny hairline fracture, barely visible to the eye; maybe it was the position it was placed in – too near the edge of a table or mantelpiece – so that there was an inevitability to its destruction.

Or, what if the vase smashing into a thousand fragments was no accident? Maybe that vase, once beautiful and whole and adored, didn't topple to the floor – but was thrown.

This summer

I pushed aside Marley's memory book, and stood. The soles of my feet fuzzed with pins and needles and I stamped on the spot to try and encourage the blood to flow back into them. Dusk had crept up on me and I realized the hut had fallen into darkness. I shivered, and pulled my cotton scarf from a hook on the wall and wrapped it around my shoulders, then set about lighting the candles.

Once that was done, I poured myself a gin and tonic and fetched a novel. The gin slipped down with ease, but I couldn't focus on the book, my thoughts swimming away from the page towards Marley. Tomorrow would be the seventh anniversary. Hard to believe that it'd been seven years since I'd hugged him, breathing in his warm biscuit smell.

I snapped the book shut and stood. I had to get out of the hut. I grabbed a bottle of red wine from the rack, picked up Jacob's birthday card that I'd written ready for tomorrow, then went next door. I was hoping to find Sarah and Nick with the candles burning, the radio on, one of her huge pasta dishes bubbling on the hob, the smell of melted cheese thick in the air.

'Hello!' I called, crossing the deck with wine in hand, feeling a little light-headed from the gin. The double doors were thrown wide open, yet the hut was in darkness. With a lurch of disappointment, I remembered Sarah telling me that they were having dinner with friends of Nick's who were renting a beach hut at the far end of the sandbank. They'd invited me to join them, but I'd said no, lacking the energy to be in the company of strangers.

I was about to leave when I noticed Jacob stretched across the sofa, eyes closed. Large headphones were clamped over his ears and his thumbs were tapping a rhythm against his bare chest.

In the half-light he could, so easily, have been Marley.

I stood there, transfixed by an urge to place my fingertips on his chest, feeling the warmth of his skin and his heart beating beneath my palm.

Jacob's eyes flicked open.

'Sorry, I didn't know you were—'

He pushed himself upright, pulling off his headphones. 'Isla.' He smiled. When Jacob smiled, it transformed his whole face, softening the darkness of his eyes.

'I came to find your mum – but I just remembered she's out for dinner.'

He glanced at the wine in my hand. 'Yeah, but come in.' He stood, crossing the hut towards me, and removed the bottle from my hands before I had a chance to protest. He set the wine on the kitchen side while he slid a pack of matches from his pocket and lit the gas lantern. A warm glow from the flame illuminated his face as he opened the cutlery drawer and took out a corkscrew.

'It's screw top,' I said.

He grinned at me, twisting it off deftly and sloshing wine into two glasses, filling them almost to the top.

He passed me one, then grabbed a bag of crisps from the cupboard and tore the bag open and put it on the coffee table, like we were sharing crisps in a pub. I took a seat on the sofa, unwinding the scarf at my neck. Jacob pulled on a T-shirt, then sat beside me, drawing one of his legs on to the sofa, his knee angled towards me.

I took a drink, pleased for the warmth of the alcohol as it slid down my throat. Without realizing, I sighed.

Jacob watched me closely.

We often spent time together, but not at night, not drinking wine on a sofa. I became acutely aware of the raised beat of my heart. I wanted Sarah and Nick to bustle in, grab themselves a glass each and join us. I looked towards the open doors, where the moon hung suspended above the sea, laying a silver trail.

Following my gaze, Jacob said, 'Remember those moon walks you used to take me and Marley on?'

I smiled. 'I'd let you stay up late and we'd tramp over the headland.'

'No torches. That was your rule.'

'So your eyes could adjust,' I said. 'Plus, it made you eat your carrots.'

Jacob laughed. 'You used to make a flask of hot chocolate and we'd sit up on the bluff listening to the crickets and natterjacks. You'd tell us those stories about the smugglers.'

I felt the warmth of the memory. Jacob and Marley loved interrupting to ask questions about the smugglers, wanting to draw out any horrible, boyish details – like the fights on the boat, the ghastliness of the living conditions, the spookiness of the night runs they'd make.

'I miss him,' Jacob said.

I turned, looking squarely at Jacob. In the glow of the lantern, I could see the seriousness of his expression, the sadness that lingered in his eyes.

'Me, too,' I said softly.

'Seven years tomorrow.'

I nodded. 'And your birthday, too.' There was a pause. 'Is it hard – that it's on the same day?'

'It links us, doesn't it? The dates. I like it.'

I hadn't thought of it that way. Looking at Jacob I wondered if I'd underestimated the loss he'd suffered.

Jacob said, 'D'you remember crabbing? We'd tie bits of bacon to string and spend hours dangling them from the quay.'

'Marley used to name every crab.'

'They were *such* good crab names – like old men: Alfred, Billy, Egbert, Frank. I'd tip my bucket of crabs back in the harbour, but Marley used to place each one back in turn, waving them off. 'Nice to meet you, Harold! Send my regards to Marjorie! Crawl safe, Albert!'

I could feel the first prick of tears in my lower lids. Jacob seemed to sense the moments when I needed to talk about Marley – and those when it was too much.

'So anyway,' he said, changing the subject, 'I wanted to ask you about Chile. I can't believe you leave tomorrow.'

'Me neither.'

'You planning to do much travelling?'

'Hopefully – if the van's engine is still going. I've got a fortnight before I start work, so I'm hoping to drive south, go hiking in the mountains.'

'Patagonia?'

'I'm not sure I'll make it that far. But I've heard about a beautiful national park where I might start. The trails hug the coastline and you can camp out on the beaches.'

'So you wouldn't sleep in the van?'

'Most of the time, yes. But I've got a tent, too. It's just a one-person thing, more like a bivouac. Last summer I hiked to a mountain lake. It took me eight hours, but when I got there – this lake – God, it was something else, like a blue jewel tucked into these wild, dusty mountains. No one else there. I spent the night right by the lakeside. Watched the sun go down.'

'You had it all to yourself.'

I could see that it sounded romantic to Jacob – and it was – but as I'd lain in my tent alone, all I'd been able to think of was how much I wanted someone to share it with.

'Maybe I'll visit, sometime.'

'I'm not sure your mum would be keen on the flight.'

'I meant on my own.'

His gaze held mine squarely, watching my reaction. His eyes travelled over my face, resting on my mouth. I finished my wine and said, 'Thank you for the company, Jacob. It was just what I needed.'

As I moved to stand, Jacob noticed the birthday card I had propped at my side.

'Is that for me?'

'Oh yes. Thought I'd leave it here in case I didn't catch you tomorrow.'

'Can I open it now?'

I hesitated. 'Sure.'

He tore open the envelope and pulled out my homemade card. As he looked at it, I wondered if I'd made a mistake. I'd used the photo of him and Marley, which Sarah had removed from the frame, and made a small collage of things I'd found on the beach; a shell, a sliver of sea glass, a thread from a rope.

'Isla, I love it!'

'There's something inside.'

He opened the card and pulled out two tickets – day passes for a festival on the Isle of Wight, where I knew one of his favourite bands was performing.

'Seriously?' he beamed.

'Yes, seriously. Thought you and Caz might fancy it.'

He threw his arms around me. 'You are amazing. Thank you!'

He turned the card over and studied the front of it again. 'This is why Mum said you wanted the photo.'

I hesitated. 'How do you mean?'

'Mum said you'd asked for the photo back.'

Sarah had told Jacob that?

Something dark and cold slithered through me, stealing the warmth from the evening. Jacob must have asked why the photo of him and Marley had been replaced – and she'd told him I'd wanted it. But it was a lie: it was Sarah who no longer wanted a picture of Marley in their beach hut.

The gin bottle was where I'd left it on the side. I rooted around in the cupboard beneath the counter but I was out of tonic, so I drank it with soda and a dash of elderflower cordial to sweeten it. It tasted surprisingly good. I poured another.

I slouched on to the sofa with it and lit a roll-up. I only smoked occasionally – and almost always outside, but I couldn't make myself move – couldn't see the point. As I smoked, I watched the candlelight flickering over a framed photo of Marley I kept on the driftwood shelf. The evening sun was warm on his features; he squinted against it, holding a shell towards the camera. I'd seen the photograph so many times that the memory had become worn and frayed, losing its original shape. I let the features of his face blur as I tried to reimagine him as a teenager, Jacob's age. I pictured dark skinny trousers, thick-tongued trainers and band T-shirts, his blond hair grown long and falling in front of his eyes. I would love to see who he'd have been now. Even if he'd turned into a sullen thing, I wouldn't care. I wanted those slammed doors, those moody grunts, the heap of dirty laundry. I had missed out on all of that. I wanted the good and the bad. I wanted anything. Just one more chance to press a kiss to his cheek, to breathe in the smell of his hair. I would give anything – do *anything* – to hold him in my arms one last time.

I finished my cigarette, then wobbled to the kitchen to pour another drink, realizing how hard the alcohol had hit me. I couldn't remember when I'd last eaten a proper meal. I stood there, gin and tobacco sour in my throat, letting the tears roll down my face. In another three years, Marley would've been dead for as many years as he'd been alive. The thought terrified me.

There was a knock on the hut door. Jacob stepped inside holding up my scarf. 'You left this.'

'Oh,' I said, wiping at my cheeks. 'You needn't have—'

Jacob's face creased with concern. 'Shit, are you . . . okay?'

I didn't trust my voice. I nodded, tears dropping from my chin.

Jacob moved closer. 'Isla?' His expression was desperately pained. He looked awkward, uncomfortable – every bit the teenager. I wanted to smile for him, reassure him everything was okay, but then he reached out and wrapped his arms around me. I could smell the sweet boyish scent of sweat lifting from his skin, and I clung on to him, my fingertips digging into his hard muscles. Tears ran from my face, trailing down the neckline of his T-shirt. I could feel the warmth of his skin against my cheek and I closed my eyes.

'I'm sorry, Isla. I'm so sorry,' he whispered over and over, his grip tightening around me.

When you've had a child, you carry them inside you for the first nine months, and then in your arms for months and months beyond that. I used to wonder how many times a day I'd kiss Marley as a baby, butterfly kisses on his cheeks, on the soft skin on the soles of his feet, my lips on his smooth white belly, kissing his tiny fingers, the soft skin at his neck, in the smooth dip between nose and forehead. As he'd grown older, I'd had to lessen those kisses. Sometimes I'd laugh, pinning him down, smothering him with them, and he'd jokingly protest, but I could see his delight. And then they stopped. All that love, all those kisses I could no longer give to him. Where does that love go? I imagined it as something physical – like hot water that freezes in a moment, hardening, cracking, splintering into shards. That was what happened to it. I was full of that ice now. Numb with it.

And here was Jacob, holding me. Warming me. I wanted to turn his fingers in my hand. Examine the boyish nubs of his fingertips. I wanted to plant kisses on each of them.

Suddenly becoming aware of myself, I staggered back. In my hurry, I caught my hip on the corner of the kitchen counter, knocking the bottle of gin to the floor. The glass shattered, fragments flying across the hut in a slosh of gin. I crouched unsteadily to the ground, alcohol vapours turning my stomach.

My head was spinning and I could feel the room starting to slide away from me.

'Here, I've got this,' Jacob said, placing his hands under my armpits and helping me to my feet. Then he fetched some kitchen towel and the dustpan and brush.

I tried to pour myself a glass of water, but even the action of holding a glass steady seemed beyond me.

When Jacob had cleared up, he looked at me clinging on to the counter and I saw the sympathy in his expression. 'We need to get you in bed.'

I nodded. Bed. I needed to sleep. I tried to think what to do next. How to pull out the sofa bed. I needed to get changed. Clean my teeth. It seemed too much.

Jacob took charge, folding out the bed, grabbing the duvet from where I kept it stuffed in the bunks. The bunks where Jacob would sometimes sleep with Marley. They always slept so well at the beach – Sarah, Nick and I used to eat dinner together on the deck, the two boys sleeping soundly only feet away from us, their low snores emanating from the bunks.

'Stay,' I said. I wanted Jacob to sleep in the bunk so I could hear the slow rhythm of his breath in the night when I woke.

Jacob guided me to the bed, and I seemed to crumple into it. I was still wearing my clothes as I felt the coolness of the duvet being pulled over me.

Jacob's footsteps crossed the hut, then I heard the soft

fizz of the gas lanterns being turned off. The hut fell dark and quiet, just the low hum of the fridge behind me and the drum of waves. I listened for Jacob and could hear the shallow draw of his breath. Then there was the rasp of his T-shirt being pulled over his head and dropped to the floor with a whoosh of air.

I was surprised when I felt the give of the bed as Jacob climbed in, the metal springs creaking beneath his weight. He slipped beneath the covers, moving himself until his body was pressed lightly against mine. He wrapped an arm around me, drawing me into him, his fingers finding my hand and closing around it.

A faint awareness radiated somewhere beyond me that Jacob wasn't supposed to be in this bed. The bunks. That's where he and Marley always slept.

And yet – there was the hardness of his body against mine. My head swam with the warmth of his skin, the feeling of someone next to me. The hollow ache in my chest lessened. I turned into him, wanting to sink deeper into his warmth.

In the darkness, my fingers moved to his face, tracing the line of his cheeks, running my fingertips along his jaw, over his lips.

I felt his breath against my fingers as he whispered my name in the dark.

40. SARAH

DAY EIGHT, 5 P.M.

'The same flight?' Nick is saying, running a hand across his mouth. 'Jacob and Isla went to Chile . . . together?'

Only an hour ago I would've bargained anything to hear that Jacob was alive, but the relief of knowing he's in Chile has been replaced by a new fear.

'I just . . . I can't even begin to fathom *why* Isla hasn't been in touch?' Nick says. 'I understand why Jacob would go to Isla for help, but there's just no way,' he says, his left hand slicing decisively through the air, 'that she'd have let Jacob go to Chile without telling us. She knows exactly how worried we'd be. She knows that we'd get the police involved.' His hands open. 'So what are we missing?'

'Jacob could've boarded the same flight as Isla without her knowing,' I pose. 'The planes are so big, aren't they? They could have been seated in entirely different sections.'

Nick considers this for a moment, but then says, 'Why would Jacob go to the trouble of travelling to Chile – and getting the same flight as Isla – if he didn't want to see her?'

'Maybe he knew she wouldn't let him come with her. Perhaps he'd decided to wait until he'd set foot in Chile – surprise her at the airport when it was too late for her to say no.' I press my lips together, shake my head, already dismissing my own theory: 'Isla would still have called us the minute she realized Jacob was there.'

'Unless he begged her not to tell us. Made her promise.'

'No, she wouldn't make that kind of promise to him. This is too serious. Absolutely no way.' But then I am thinking about how things were between us when Isla left . . . what was said.

'What is it?' Nick asks, noticing my hesitation.

'I don't know . . . it's just . . . that night Isla left, things were . . . strained between us. We had words after the barbecue.'

'No matter what you'd said to each other – Isla still wouldn't do this. She just wouldn't.'

PC Roam's voice is low as she asks, 'Is there any possibility that their relationship was . . . romantic?'

Our heads snap up. 'No!' we both say.

PC Roam says, 'We never discovered who Jacob's love letter was intended for—'

'You think it was for Isla? That Jacob was . . .' I can't even bring myself to say it . . . '*infatuated* with her?'

'It's possible,' PC Roam says gently.

But she's my age, I am thinking. His mother's age! The possibility of it makes my stomach churn with disgust. I glance towards the window. Outside wind rakes the darkening sea, whipping the water into ridges, boats straining against their anchors. The light misting rain has been blown away by the wind, but heavy storm clouds are gathering on the horizon.

When I turn back, I can see from Nick's expression that he is considering it, wondering if it's possible. He takes out his phone and scrolls to the photo he took of the love letter. He crosses the hut and we look at it together.

I am thinking about the way Jacob has always looked up to Isla. She treated him like an adult – and perhaps when he was with her, he saw himself as one.

He thought it was love – so he wrote to her telling her, *It is love, I know that!*

That's why he was upset on his birthday, as Isla was leaving for Chile.

That's why he defended her with such vitriol when we argued on the night he disappeared.

That's why he went to her. To Chile.

A boy's infatuation with an attractive older woman.

I scan the letter, my eyes travelling to the final line.

There it is, like a knife twisting into my flesh . . .

Last night was amazing.

My breath catches in my throat.

What if it wasn't a one-sided infatuation?

What if . . . they were lovers?

I stand with the palms of my hands pressed against the window, the skin flattened against the cool glass. To someone passing I must look like a woman desperate to escape.

PC Roam has returned to the station to see if she can track down Isla. She's already informed us that she's seen the payment details for Isla and Jacob's flights. Both tickets were paid for on a credit card registered to Isla Berry. Her flight was booked nine weeks ago, and Jacob's was paid for two hours before the plane departed.

I'm aware of Nick pacing somewhere behind me. He's speaking in a low voice – whether to himself or to me, I can't be sure. What I am thinking is: Isla cradled Jacob as a baby, laying him across her forearm while stroking his back to ease his wind. She took him blackberry picking, bringing him home with his lips stained purple, blackberries squished into the tiny pockets of his shorts. She cried in his first nativity play when he said his one line, sounding like the proudest innkeeper that Bethlehem had ever seen. She made up fantastical stories, Jacob and Marley always the heroes, as the boys sat entranced on her lap. It's not possible that she and Jacob have become . . . lovers.

I breathe out hard, casting my eyes upwards. Hooked to the wall next to our bookshelf, I see Jacob's binoculars. Something catches in my thoughts. In a flash, I'm reaching up for them. I flick off the lens cap and step out on to the deck. The wind snatches the door and it flings open, smacking against the side of the hut. Inside the tea towels are blown from the side, the kitchen roll flutters and Jacob's birthday cards fly to the ground. Nick strides across the hut, glaring at me. He yanks the door closed.

I press the binoculars to my eyes, then follow the direction Jacob had been looking in the last time I'd seen him using the binoculars. I'd assumed he was staring at Caz, who was sitting on the shoreline between two boys, but now I remember that Isla was standing at the sea's edge talking to Joe and Binks after her swim.

Jacob had been watching Isla, not Caz.

It was Isla he was in love with.

Did she know?

Did she love him, too, and that's why she'd let him join her in Chile? Is that why she isn't answering our calls?

A wave of nausea pushes through me and I let the binoculars hang from my neck as I reach for the railing, gripping it tightly with both hands, the wood coarse beneath my palms.

For years I've worn myself ragged worrying that Nick has been in love with Isla. I became obsessed by it, the idea flaming bright like a wicked heat singeing the edges of our marriage. Yet it isn't my husband who is in love with her: it is my son.

The first drops of rain fall, plump and heavy. Nick watches from the window, his thumb joint tapping against his collarbone, making hollow thuds. I lean back into the sofa, placing the heel of my hands against my eye sockets. I know almost nothing about Chile. When Isla first travelled there, I searched out the country on a world map and was intrigued by the narrow strip of land that wound almost the entire length of the western coast of South America. It's so vast and huge and unknown to me, that I feel dizzy at the knowledge that Jacob is somewhere within it.

I try and picture Jacob boarding a plane alongside Isla. Did he sit by the window, watching England shrink and disappear beneath him? He's flown with us to Italy twice, and he travelled to Switzerland once with the school, but he's never been on a long-haul flight. I picture his legs bunched up against the seat in front. Would he have been nervous? Would Isla have held his hand? Would he have talked to her about Isaac? About me?

Are they together now? They could be travelling north into the scorched salt flats that Isla's shown me photos of, or perhaps they are headed south, tucking themselves into the cool folds of the mountains. They could be anywhere – and we'd have no way of finding them.

When I look up, Nick is glaring at me, his gaze cold.

'What?'

'He's out there because of you. You and Isaac. You know that, don't you?'

The words punch me in the gut.

I watch as Nick snatches up his mobile, scrolling through his contacts. 'What are you doing?'

'Calling her.' His face is flushed as he strikes the screen with his fingertip, then presses the phone to his ear, jaw clenched. As he paces, I count his steps: three forward, then he turns on the spot. Another three steps back. Turn.

His tone is a lethal whisper. 'What the fuck are you playing at, Isla? We know Jacob's in Chile with you. The police have told us.' He sucks in his breath. 'We found a letter Jacob wrote to you – a fucking love letter!' He shakes his head in disgust. 'You've heard Sarah's messages, so you know *exactly* what we've been going through. Why haven't you called? We're reeling here, Isla. Reeling—' His voice cracks so suddenly that it takes us both by surprise.

He ends the call, flinging the mobile on to the sofa. Then he sits heavily, his hands cradling his head.

I move to him, placing my arms around his shoulders, drawing him towards me. His muscles are locked and I wait for the moment when his body softens into my embrace. But it never comes: he shakes his head, pulling away.

I sit there beside him feeling hollowed out. Through the rain-smeared window, I can see the edge of Isla's hut – a dark shadow in the dusk. *How could you?* I think. Nick's phone is beside me, Isla's number still on the screen. Without pause I pick it up, press call, my throat tightening with all the words I want to say.

As I hold the phone to my ear, I realize something is different. I'm not hearing the same ring tone that I've heard every other time: seven rings, then the click of her answer-phone. This time I hear a series of long beeps. The phone is engaged.

The hairs on the back of my neck stand on end as I realize. 'She's listening to your message.'

Nick looks up.

'She's playing it back, right now. She's there, Nick. She's listening. She's heard every single word.'

41. SARAH

DAY EIGHT, 9 P.M.

Dusk thickens into night. Nick stands at the window, his breath making small clouds against the glass. I watch from the sofa as he leans his forehead against it. In a low, careful voice, as if he's talking to himself, Nick says, 'She's not in love with him.'

'Pardon?'

'Isla. She's not in love with Jacob.' He pushes away from the window, and turns towards me. 'How could she be? Jacob's still a boy. She's seen his table manners; she's heard how rude he can be when he's tired; she knows you still do his laundry and that I give him pocket money. Isla's forty. She's travelled the world; brought up a child; had a career. She's *lived*. I just don't believe she'd fall in love with Jacob.' He pauses, the pad of his thumb travelling back and forth along his lower lip. 'This is about something else.'

346

Nick is right. The hum of the fridge kicks in and I listen to the vibration of it, counting in my head.

He looks at me searchingly. 'What was going on with you and Isla this summer?'

'Sorry?'

'Something was off. There was an odd tension between you. I felt it.'

I draw a sofa cushion across my stomach, my fingers tracing the piping as I say, 'I'm not sure . . . it feels like we've been pulling apart.'

Nick asks astutely, 'Who was doing the *pulling*?'

I can feel heat building in my chest. I'm not sure how to answer, how to put my feelings about Isla into words when I barely understand them myself. After some time I say, 'Me, I think. Mostly me.' I exhale a long breath, looking down at the cushion as I work out what it is I'm trying to say. 'When Isla comes back here every summer, I've started to feel . . . I don't know, uncomfortable, perhaps.'

Nick lifts one eyebrow.

'It feels like I'm sharing you all with her. You and Jacob. I know that sounds strange – but it's as if I have this . . .' I search for the right word, my fingers opening, '. . . obligation to Isla. She has no one – and I've got you both.'

Something I've said seems to trigger a new direction of thought in Nick. His hands meet together in a prayer, which he draws to his lips, eyes blinking rapidly. 'Marley . . .' He lifts his gaze and looks at me. 'That's what this is all about. *Marley.*'

Marley. I picture him, the beautiful little blond-haired boy I've been trying not to think of. Nick is right, I know he is.

He's given voice to a thought that's been inside me for days, twisted tightly. Now Nick is hooking it out, pulling it slowly towards the light, forcing me to look.

'You and Isla argued the night Jacob disappeared. What happened, Sarah? All of it – I want to know every detail.'

He watches me so closely that I can feel beads of perspiration gathering on my top lip. The hut feels impossibly hot. I shift, uncomfortable, spotlighted. I get to my feet and move to the sink, pouring myself a glass of water. I swallow it back, a light taste of earth caught in the water. I wipe my mouth and set the glass back down.

'Sarah?'

'It was awful. We both said things . . .' I shake my head. 'I started it. I know I did. I made a scene about those festival tickets. But they weren't the problem, not really. I just . . . I was just so furious!'

'Why?'

'I wanted Isla at the barbecue. We talked about it, didn't we? How much good it'd do Jacob to have a *normal* birthday this year. Make a bit of a fuss of him. Not let Marley's anniversary overshadow things. I was so pleased he was going to Luke's for birthday drinks. It seemed like a turning point, like Jacob felt he deserved to have fun on that day.' I lift my shoulders. 'Maybe it was too much to ask of Isla – expecting her to join the family barbecue, sit at our table, smiling and laughing, and celebrating for Jacob. How could she do that?' I rub a hand over my face. 'So she was distant, sad, I get that, I really do. But then Jacob made that toast to Marley. It should have been lovely and touching, but somehow it just reminded me how it'll always be there –

how Isla will always be there, right on our doorstep, every fucking summer!'

I realize my hands are clenched into fists, my knuckles white, and Nick is staring at me, eyes wide, as if I'm a stranger.

I try and soften my expression, uncurl my fingers – but it is too late, Nick has seen.

42. ISLA

If I look back at the events of this summer, each one is like a piece from a puzzle – and Sarah holds them all in her hands. I could put them together for her and Nick, show them how they fit. But then, why should I? When Marley died, I begged Sarah for help, desperate to understand what'd happened. She never once said: 'Sit down, Isla. Let me tell you what I know.'

This summer

I woke curled on my side, knees bunched towards my chest, as if cowering from a blow. I drew a hand across my face, rubbing my eyes open with my thumb and forefinger. As I adjusted to the dimness of the beach hut, a glass of gin eyeballed me from the side, sending a wave of nausea pulsing through me. Then my gaze reached a bundle of fabric on the hut floor. It took me a moment to place it as Jacob's T-shirt. My cheeks flared with heat.

I scrambled out of bed, launching myself towards the sink. My back arched as I retched, the tendons in my neck straining. I clung to the edge of the sink, panting, staring at the trail of vomit dribbling towards the plughole. Jesus Christ!

I wiped the back of my hand across my mouth, then poured a large glass of water, rinsed my mouth, and swilled the rest down the sink. I crossed the hut, grabbed Jacob's T-shirt and shoved it into an overhead cupboard. I stood there – palms pressed against the closed cupboard, heart racing, thoughts leaping and crackling like flames.

I needed to get out of the hut. Pushing my feet into flip-flops, I pulled on a pair of sunglasses, then left. The empty beach told me it was still early. The realization made my heart sink a little further: it meant more hours to wade through. Today would be the seventh anniversary of Marley's death. I felt like hell.

I walked fast with my eyes down, and it was only once I'd reached the headland, climbing to the very top, that I let my pace slacken. My gaze found the bay where Marley was lost, as if it were the compass point that every other direction was marked by. It was too early to give in to tears, so I turned from it, forcing myself to walk on.

Over the years, Marley's anniversary had become filled with small rituals: collecting treasures from his favourite parts of the sandbank to put in a glass jar; reading his memory book cover to cover; eating fish and chips on the quay for dinner; setting sail the jar of beach treasures from the quayside. I don't know if they helped, or made the hours pass more quickly, but they gave the day a structure of sorts.

I buried myself in activity, searching for just the right

things to go in the glass jar: a chalky, slim pebble from the bay where Samuel had taught Marley how to skim stones; a lost feather from the marsh where he'd liked to watch egrets stalk the muddy flats; a mussel shell from Troll Bridge, one of our favourite crabbing spots. I managed to avoid seeing anyone as I walked the length of the headland, slipping off the main paths and pushing my way through the dense woodland, where dwarf oaks and wild rhododendrons grew. My head throbbed with the low voltage of a hangover and I could feel my stomach twisting, churning.

After two or three hours, when my thirst won out, I returned to the hut, pulling the doors firmly shut.

Sarah must have been watching for me, as I'd only been inside a moment when she arrived. 'Don't think you're escaping me.' She came towards me, wrapping me in a hug.

Jacob's T-shirt: had I moved it?

'Seven years. I'm not going to ask if you're okay. Of course you're not. But just know that I'm right here if you want to talk, or cry, or remember, or forget. Whatever you need, okay?'

I'd shoved the T-shirt in a cupboard, I remembered with relief.

When we pulled apart, Sarah told me, 'We're doing birthday dinner at five. I know today is hell for you. I know that. But please, Isla. Please come. Just for an hour. You're leaving tonight. We won't see you for a whole year. I need to drink you in. It'd mean the world to Jacob to have you there. I want this birthday to be a special one.'

I looked up at her. She didn't know.

'And it's only us – no big party. Us and Nick's parents.

Last Seen

I'm making pavlova.' She squeezed my hand. 'So you'll be there?'

I spent the afternoon packing up the beach hut. The chores suited me; I sorted through tins of food, restacking those that would last until next summer and piling up those that wouldn't to pass on to Sarah; I shook out the bedding and squeezed it into two bin-liners so that it didn't turn damp over the long winter I'd be away; I emptied the bin, scrubbed the hob and bleached the sink. Jacob had come to the hut once – but as I'd seen him crossing the deck, I'd grabbed my mobile, and pretended I was on a call, mouthing to him, *See you at the barbecue.*

By the time my belongings were buckled into my backpack, it was half past five. I could hear Nick and his father out at the front of their hut, talking as they tended the barbecue. I could do this. I'd just go for half an hour – enough time to say my goodbyes. With the distraction of the party, it'd be easier.

I changed into the only clean top I had left, swept my hair into a low knot, then grabbed the bottle of wine I'd been chilling in the otherwise empty fridge.

Nick's father was the first to see me as I stepped out of my beach hut barefoot, moving next door to theirs. He slipped his arm around my waist. 'Isla, darling girl. Wonderful to see you! You look beautiful, just beautiful!' He kissed me on both cheeks before releasing me.

The air smelt of firelighters and newly burning charcoal. Nick turned a row of pink sausages with a pair of tongs as he said, 'So pleased you decided to come.'

353

Nick's father asked, 'Are you home for long?'

'Actually, I'm leaving in a few hours – back to Chile.'

'Chile. That's where you've been teaching for the last few years, isn't it?'

I nodded. 'Four years.'

'Good on you! It seems to be treating you well. You must stop in and see Stella and me one of these summers when you're here. Tell us about all the wonderful adventures you're having.'

'I'd like that,' I said, although in truth I couldn't picture it.

Nick glanced at the bottle of wine in my hand and said, 'Go inside, grab a glass.'

I climbed on to the deck, swiftly scanning the hut – but thankfully Jacob wasn't indoors. The hut smelled of roasted garlic and rosemary, and I knew the oven would be filled with stuffed red peppers, and a tray of those herby roasted potatoes Sarah always made. My stomach twisted uncomfortably: I wasn't sure I could eat.

Sarah was rinsing a bunch of coriander at the sink, and Nick's mother was checking her phone. 'Isla!' she said, looking up. 'I didn't know you were joining us. How delightful.' I leant forward, accepting the kiss she lightly planted on my cheek. 'Hasn't Sarah gone to such a lot of trouble?' she said, casting an arm around at the kitchen side, which was lined with colourful bowls of Greek salad, pomegranate tabbouleh, couscous with roasted vegetables. 'I offered to bring something but she wouldn't hear of it. Likes to do it all herself.'

Sarah wiped her hands on a tea towel, then took the wine from me and gave me a quick, tense hug. I noticed something white caught in her hairline. 'Here,' I said, reaching to remove it. 'Feta.' I dusted the crumbs into the sink.

'Oh.' Sarah smoothed back her hair firmly, then returned to the coriander, tearing it over the salad.

I felt dislocated, out of sorts, like everything was too busy, too loud. I didn't want to be here. I wanted to be alone, the doors of my beach hut pulled to, the memory book on my lap. Looking up, I noticed the row of birthday cards that had been arranged on the shelf. I smiled to see the one I'd made was at the centre of them, Marley and Jacob's faces beaming into the hut.

My beautiful boy, I wish you were here with us.

'Lovely card,' Stella said, noticing me looking at it. 'Homemade are always the most special. I've still got every single card my boys made me when they were growing up.'

I smiled.

'Jacob told us about the festival tickets,' Sarah said. Her tone was crisp.

There was the scuffle of feet above us in the mezzanine, and I looked up to see Jacob's bare legs moving easily down the wooden ladder.

'Thought you'd got lost up there,' Stella said.

'Just replying to some birthday messages,' he said, jumping down from the third step, then slipping his phone into his pocket. Jacob's gaze met mine. 'Auntie Isla.'

I could feel heat building in my cheeks. 'Happy birthday.'

Jacob continued to stare at me, and I found myself turning towards the balcony, saying, 'Lovely weather for your birthday.'

Lovely weather?

'Pour Isla a glass of wine, will you?' Sarah said to Jacob.

'Course. Nana, would you like one, too?'

'I shall wait for my meal.'

When Jacob handed me the wine, he held on to the stem for just a split-second, making sure our fingers touched. He looked me in the eye, then smiled, his face open and warm.

'I'll take this on to the deck,' I said quickly. 'See how the barbecue is getting on.'

Nick carried the wooden picnic bench down towards the waterline, and the rest of us followed with bowls of food, plates, cutlery, drinks and glasses. It was low tide and the afternoon was still and bright – a breeze would have lifted the heavy tang of baking seaweed from the air.

The six of us began settling around the table, Nick's father looking to me as he patted the space beside him. I squeezed on to the bench between him and Nick, digging my bare feet into the sand.

Opposite me, Sarah was squinting against the sun as she dished out the tabbouleh, her movements rushed and jerky. A sheen of sweat clung to her brow, and her cheeks were high with colour. Her tone was clipped, overly bright, as she instructed people to 'Dig in before the meat goes cold.'

Nick's father tore off a hunk of garlic bread, plunging it into the hummus, which was already forming a yellowing crust in the heat. 'Lovely to be back down here,' he said through a mouthful.

'Doesn't change, does it?' Stella said, gazing along the length of the beach, which was dotted with families beginning to pack up their towels and sun tents ready to take the ferry home.

'I remember,' Nick's father said, 'what a surprise Stella and I got when we first met you, Isla. We were desperate to see who'd bought the hut next door, weren't we? We were expecting some middle-aged yachting type – and then there you were,' he said, nudging me lightly in the ribs, 'a wisp of a thing, all long legs and willowy arms, with this steely look of determination on your face, as if you were about to set the world on fire.'

I tried to smile, but the girl he'd described seemed like a stranger to me.

Sarah picked up her wine glass.

'How are you getting on with your work?' Stella asked. 'Nick tells me you're doing very well at the international school.'

'I love working with the children – seven to eight year olds.'

'A lovely age,' Stella agreed.

'We had to take you under our wing, didn't we?' Nick's father said, returning to his thread. 'You barely knew how to boil an egg back then. Lived on those packet noodles, didn't you?'

'Still does,' Sarah added.

I looked up, wondering if I were the only one to notice the tightness in her voice.

'Good for you, I say! Life is to be lived out here,' Stella said, casting an arm wide. 'Not in the kitchen.'

'There's something to be said for wonderful home-cooked meals,' Nick added, loyally.

'You boys didn't go hungry though, did you?' Stella said. 'There was always food in our house.'

'Yes – we just had to cook it.' Nick smiled warmly at his mother.

I toyed with the food on my plate, wishing I hadn't agreed to come. When I looked up, Jacob was watching me.

Everyone's attention was caught by a sandy-haired man in a pair of red trunks, who burst from between two beach huts, chased by a pack of young children, who came bounding after him in a flurry of legs and sand. The man steamed towards the shoreline, and dived clumsily into the shallows with an almighty splash. The children screamed, delighted, dancing on the shoreline. When the man surfaced, he shook the water from his thinning hair, hooting. 'Glorious! It's like the Caribbean!'

'Darling, you haven't had one of the steaks,' Sarah said to Jacob, leaning across the table and pushing one towards his plate.

'No, thanks.'

'They're your favourite. There's blue-cheese sauce.'

Jacob took another bite from his sausage bap, shrugging.

I realized Jacob, like me, had barely said a word. His face looked drawn, tired.

Sarah sat back down and picked up her wine.

Nick's father said, 'Let's have a toast. To the birthday boy. Seventeen today! Happy birthday, Jacob. Go forth and set the world alight!'

The rest of us reached for our glasses, calling happy birthday across the table and clinking them against Jacob's beer bottle.

'I'd like to make a toast, too,' Jacob said, looking across the table to me.

I felt my pulse quicken, unsure.

'I'd like to toast Marley. Seven years today. Always missed, never forgotten.' He raised his beer. 'To Marley.'

Tears sprang up at the corners of my eyes. My throat closed around Marley's name as I touched my glass to Jacob's.

Nick's father patted my hand gently. 'Brave girl, you.'

'Lovely,' Nick said quietly to Jacob, a hand resting on his shoulder.

The toast was left to settle for a few moments, and then conversation gently resumed, Nick telling his father about his upcoming pitch, and Jacob answering Stella's questions about whether he would be applying for university.

I glanced at Sarah; her mouth was set in a tight line, her food untouched. The two of us would normally fall into easy conversation, yet I could feel the anger radiating from her. Was it me? Was she annoyed about the festival tickets I'd given Jacob? Jesus, I couldn't deal with this. I picked at the rest of my meal in silence, and refused the dessert that was heaped in towering portions into bowls. Afterwards I said, 'I'll clear,' and I carried a stack of bowls into the kitchen. I was already pumping water into the washing-up bowl when Jacob and the others appeared.

'I'll help dry,' he said.

Nick clutched his heart. 'Did our son just *offer* to help?'

Jacob rolled his eyes, then picked up a tea towel, moving to my side.

I could feel the proximity of him, the heat of his skin beside me.

Thankfully Stella shooed him away, plucking the tea towel

from his hand. 'Go on, birthday boy. Scoot! Have fun with your friends. They're waiting for you.'

He looked reluctantly at the group of teenagers who'd emerged from a hut somewhere and were loitering around on the shoreline.

As Jacob left the hut, he came close to me, whispering, 'I need to see you – on our own – before you leave.'

I pulled the ply-board shutters from beneath my hut, and dragged them on to the deck. Next door, Sarah was angling Nick's forearm towards her so she could read his watch-face. 'It's only six thirty.'

'Best I go now. Beat the traffic. Then I'll get to the hotel early enough to give me time to run through the pitch.'

'I'll get you some cake for the journey.'

As she went inside, Nick saw me struggling with the shutters. 'Here,' he said, coming over to help.

'All packed and ready?'

'Yep.'

'Do you look forward to it – returning to Chile? Or is it a wrench to leave?'

I thought for a moment. 'Both.'

He stacked the shutters against the hut, offering to help me screw them into position.

'I'm fine. You get off. You've got a pitch to prepare for.'

He checked his watch. Nodded.

Sarah returned to their deck with a slice of cake wrapped in a napkin. 'Here you are,' she said, placing it on his overnight case.

Nick thanked her, then turned to me. 'I guess this is goodbye then.' He threw his arms out wide and I moved into them. 'Thanks for coming this afternoon,' he said quietly. 'I know how hard today is for you. We really appreciate it. You're a star.'

I knew without needing to look up that Sarah would be watching from their deck.

I could feel his arms beginning to loosen. 'Safe travels, okay?' He pulled away, giving me a boyish little pat on the shoulder.

It took me an hour to put all of the shutters on the windows, and I managed to stab my thumb with the screwdriver in the process. By the time I hauled on my backpack, I was exhausted and clammy.

Goodbye, I whispered to the hut, running my fingers down the wooden door, feeling the grooves and splinters in the wood, as if imprinting it on my memory.

When I was ready, I climbed from the deck and crossed the sand to Sarah's hut. She was standing in the kitchen area, a glass of wine in hand. The hut was immaculate; no sign of the earlier bustle, except for the leftover dishes of food clingfilmed on the side.

'You're off?'

'Afraid so.'

She nodded. Said nothing else.

'Lovely barbecue.'

'Shame there was so much food left over.'

'Oh, I've got more food for you here,' I said, handing

over the bag of perishables that I'd cleared from my cupboards.

'Thanks.'

There was an awkward silence that I felt compelled to fill. 'Do you think Jacob had a nice time?'

'His birthday is always . . . difficult.'

Perhaps Sarah was waiting for a response from me – some acknowledgement that I understood that Marley's anniversary was hard on Jacob. Of course I knew it was, but I wasn't about to apologize for it.

Sarah shifted, refolding her arms. 'I wish you hadn't bought him those festival tickets.'

'It's just a day pass. I thought—'

'We said he couldn't go to Glastonbury earlier this summer – so now what are we supposed to do? Back down and let him go to this one?'

'There are two tickets. You or Nick could go with him.'

'Oh yes! I can imagine how that'd go down with Jacob!'

'I don't see what the big deal is. He's seventeen.'

Colour burst into Sarah's cheeks. 'The *big deal* is that your gift undermines me. Jacob is *my* son. I am the one who makes the decisions about what is or isn't appropriate. Look, I know today is difficult for you—'

'This has nothing to do with the anniversary. It's about *you*!' I retaliated. 'You've been off with me all day. It's clear you didn't want me here—'

'Oh, come on! I was the one who invited you. I practically had to force you to come.'

'But you didn't make me welcome, did you?'

'Everyone else was doing *such* a good job of that.'

My eyes widened. 'You're . . . jealous?'

'Don't be pathetic.'

I looked at the shelf where Jacob's birthday cards were arranged, mine placed at the back. I plucked it free, holding it up to Sarah. 'You told Jacob that I'd asked for this photo back, didn't you?'

'What?' she snapped, with a dismissive shake of her head.

'He told me, Sarah,' I said looking her full in the face. 'I never asked for this photo – it was you who decided to replace it. So why lie to Jacob?'

Sarah folded her arms. Said nothing.

I could feel my anger unravelling, hot and swift. 'And what about you giving Nick the wrong dates last summer?'

'That was a mistake.'

'Was it? Or was it that you didn't want me here at the same time as Nick and Jacob?'

'Now you're really being ridiculous.'

'Pathetic *and* ridiculous?'

'If you must know, I took down that photo of Marley and Jacob because I wanted one of our family on the wall. Is that wrong of me? We can't tiptoe around you for ever, Isla.'

I drew back, stung. 'That's how this friendship feels to you? Like you have to tiptoe? We've been best friends for over twenty years. You're the one fucking person who should know me well enough that you don't need to tiptoe. The one person I should be able to be *real* with.'

Tears stung at the edges of my eyes; I couldn't be here any longer. I turned, grabbed my backpack and left her beach hut.

Sarah didn't call me back. Didn't attempt to apologize. She let me walk away as if that was exactly what she'd wanted.

43. SARAH

DAY EIGHT, 9.30 P.M.

'I didn't call after her, didn't apologize. I just let her go,' I say, finishing recounting the argument to Nick.

He has been sitting very still, a frown deepening across his brow. 'That's the last time the two of you spoke?'

I nod.

His thumbs tap together as he thinks. 'I still don't see it. Your fight wasn't enough to provoke Isla into doing something as drastic as taking Jacob to Chile.' He looks up, his gaze meeting mine, assessing me. The air in the hut hums between us.

There's something new in the way he looks at me since he discovered Isaac is Jacob's father. It's as if he no longer knows who I am, or what I'm capable of. I feel stripped bare, disorientated by the wariness in his gaze. I want to take his face in my hands, tell him, *It's me, Nick. I'm still me! Everything I've done has been to protect this family!*

But I don't move, because Nick is saying, 'There's more, isn't there?'

My stomach turns over. Maybe he does still see who I am.

'Yes,' I say, slowly. 'There is.'

I scanned the contents of the fridge: there was a bottle of white wine open from the barbecue, and half a bottle of prosecco. I chose the prosecco, pouring myself a tall glass, hands trembling. I drank the first one standing up. Then I refilled my glass and tipped that back, too.

I had moved on to the white wine by the time I heard Jacob's footsteps lumbering across the deck. 'Oh. Everyone's gone?'

'Your dad had to leave for Bristol. He asked me to say goodbye. Nana and Pops had to get on, too.'

'Auntie Isla?'

'Left about half an hour ago.'

'For Chile?'

'Yes.'

His expression darkened. 'But . . . she didn't say bye.'

I apologized on her behalf, making an excuse about her being rushed, while silently cursing her lack of consideration. 'Did you have a good time at the barbecue?'

'Yeah.' Jacob crouched down to his drawer, pulling out his rucksack.

'I've put up the rest of your cards.'

He grunted without looking up.

'Would you like a drink?' I asked, hopeful. 'I could make

you a sausage sandwich if you're hungry? There are plenty of leftovers.'

'I should get to Luke's.'

'Nice of him to put on a party for you.'

'It's not a *party*. We're just gonna be hanging out.'

'*Hanging out*, not *a party*,' I said, writing the words in the air with my fingers poised around an imaginary pen. 'Another bullet-point to add to my "How To Talk To Teenagers" thesis.'

I hoped Jacob might crack a smile, but he actually shuddered at my attempt at humour. I took another slug of wine, finishing the glass. 'Oh,' I said, sitting forward to set the glass down. 'Did you like your birthday present?' Nick and I had stretched ourselves to buy him a set of ten driving lessons.

'Yeah!' Jacob's face brightened as he moved to the shelf where our birthday card was. He plucked down a card. 'The line-up is amazing. It's, like, the best day of the whole festival, easy!'

Isla's card, not ours. The crush of hurt was far more painful than I should have allowed it to be. I knew I should let it go, but I couldn't stop myself: 'Isla should've talked to your father and me before buying those tickets.'

Quick as a fox, Jacob turned on me. 'What, so you could say *no*?'

'So we could have a discussion about it. We'd agreed no festivals until you're eighteen.'

'You and Dad agreed. I didn't.'

'Isla should have checked—'

'Checked? She can buy me whatever she wants! She's my godmother.'

'And I'm your *mother*,' I said, standing to face him.

'This is bullshit!' Jacob slammed the heel of his foot back against the drawer, a loud thud vibrating through the hut.

'Watch it,' I warned, aware of the raised beat of my heart.

He flung out his arms suddenly and I flinched. 'So Isla did something nice. She gets me. Why turn it into a big deal?'

'I don't *get you*?'

He looked at me square in the face, his dark gaze unnerving. 'No, Mum. I don't think you do. I don't think you ever have done.'

My breath caught in my throat. 'It's hard to be the *cool* one, like Isla, when you're cooking and cleaning and running around after a family all day, don't you think?'

Jacob's gaze narrowed. 'Don't *you* think Isla wished she had a family to do all that for?'

'Oh, I don't know,' I said, under my breath. 'She seems fairly settled into ours.'

Jacob's eyes widened.

I stepped towards him. 'I'm sorry, I don't know why I said—'

'Because you're jealous!'

The crack of my palm against his cheek filled the hut.

Jacob stood there, slack-jawed, holding his face. 'You . . . you hit me?'

'Jacob, God! I'm so sorry. I didn't mean—'

'You hit me?' he said again, shocked.

'Please, just let me explain.'

His mouth twisted as he hissed, 'You know what you are? You're a liar!'

'What?'

'You heard. You lie to people – that's what you do. And guess what?' he snarled, eyes blazing. 'I'm just like you. I'm just fucking like you!'

My blood ran cool. 'What are you talking about?'

His voice was ice, his gaze unflinching. 'You know.' He grabbed his rucksack, stalked past me, and slammed the hut door so hard that the timber trembled in his wake.

I think back to the whispered conversation I had with Isla seven years ago, in the dark hours after Marley drowned. I remember her standing by the hut window, a sentinel with bloodshot eyes and skin as pale as fright. Her face seemed to have caved in, dark hollows beneath her eyes. She grabbed my hands in hers, bony fingers digging into my flesh. 'How did it happen? I don't understand? Tell me, please Sarah, tell me every detail.' So I let her hold on to me as I began the story, the one I'd repeat time and time again, until I could almost picture it being real. Being the truth.

Only it wasn't.

I can hear the rain pounding against the hut roof – or perhaps it is my heart drumming. I shift, sliding my hands beneath my thighs. I force myself to look at Nick, to go on, to tell him everything.

44. ISLA

This summer

I turned the jar slowly through my fingers. In the moonlight, I could just glimpse the edge of a skimming stone, the white softness of the egret feather, the shadow of a sprig of heather. Pressing my lips against the cool curve of the glass, I whispered Marley's name, then cast the jar into the air, a flash of moonlight glinting as it spun through the darkness, before hitting the water with a light splash. It bobbed for a moment, as if unsure which way to travel. Then the outgoing tide seemed to gather around it, pulling it away from the quay, out towards the open water. Had any of the jars, I wondered, my fingers wrapped around the railing, washed up and been found? In a sense, I hoped they'd hadn't: there would be a cruelness to it – that a jar tossed to sea washed up safely, when Marley did not.

I breathed out slowly, remembering how Marley and I

used to sit here on the quay, legs dangling towards the water, a parcel of fish and chips warm in our laps. Marley loved making up wild stories of the people across the harbour in their candlelit huts – a mysterious family from another planet; a fisherman who kept his catch in an aquarium in his beach hut; a band of smugglers who had been trapped in time.

The warmth of the memory faded before I was ready, my thoughts dragging me back to the brittle argument I'd left behind in Sarah's hut. I could picture her pacing right now, a glass of wine gripped in a fist. She'd be stewing, her lips pursed with that indignant little expression she wore when she felt wronged. I could feel the itch in my fingers wanting to reach out, right across the harbour, and grab her by the shoulders, asking, *Today? Did you really have to pick today?* I was leaving – all she'd needed to do was bite her tongue and I'd have been gone for another year. But she couldn't let it slide. I'd seen it building all summer, those old insecurities circling, hawk-like, waiting for the opportunity to swoop.

There was a burst of laughter as a group of people entered The Rope and Anchor, light spilling on to the dark quay. A moment later, the door swung shut, swallowing the noise behind them. I imagined the warmth and chatter that waited inside, the bottles of spirits lined up on the back wall of the bar, the burn of rum sliding down my throat.

My fingers slid free from the railing, fastening around the straps of my backpack. I knew where I was going.

I ordered a double rum, neat, and drank it standing at the bar, my backpack leaning against my legs. I kept my back to the room, aware there were familiar faces in here tonight: Fez, Robert, the guy that works the crab shack. I didn't want company. I wanted to drink.

I checked my watch. There were still two hours until my taxi would arrive. I ordered another rum, which was pushed across the bar to me, the glass warm and damp from the dishwasher.

The pub smelt of chips and malt vinegar. The spirit bottles behind the bar glinted under the glare of downlights. I picked up threads of conversations that weaved around me, let them go again. My thoughts were agitated, jumpy, and the alcohol did nothing to soften them.

I took out my phone and was surprised to find four messages from Jacob.

6.45pm. When's a good time to see you? I want to say bye before you leave. Jx

8.15pm. Your hut is locked up. Tell me you haven't left? Jx

8.55pm. Where are you? I can come to you. I have to see you before you go!!!

10.10pm. So you've left. That's it, is it? You've just fucking left!

I ran a hand across my mouth. I selected all four messages, pressed *Delete*, then slipped the phone back into my pocket.

A man with a black moustache and a suntanned face appeared at my side. 'Waiting for someone?'

'Just leaving actually,' I said, hauling on the backpack.

'Shame. I was going to offer to buy you a drink.'

I exited the pub, the briny smell of the quay sharp in my nostrils. Everything felt wrong: the pub, the argument with Sarah, leaving things as they were with Jacob. I'd call the taxi company, ask them to come earlier. I'd rather spend the extra hour waiting in the airport than being here.

As I moved along the quayside, I saw Nick up ahead. The sight of him felt reassuring, soothing. 'Nick!' I called – before I realized he wasn't alone.

He was talking to a smartly dressed older woman, who had her back to me. I hesitated, unsure, remembering him leaving the sandbank an hour before me, claiming he needed to get to Bristol to prepare for his pitch.

The woman Nick was with turned towards me. It was Sarah's mother.

I watched as he said something to her, then kissed her cheek briefly, before hurrying over to me. Up close he looked agitated, flushed.

'I thought you'd left for Bristol?'

'Yes . . . well, no, actually I'd arranged to meet Sarah's mum. But, well,' he shifted on the spot, 'Sarah doesn't know.'

'Whatever's going on, I don't need to know about it,' I said, lifting my hands in the air, stepping back.

Nick's gaze flicked across my face. Then he hung his head, and for an awful moment I thought he was going to cry. Instead he took a breath and straightened. 'I'm close to losing the business, Isla. A month away from bankruptcy.

Even if we win tomorrow's pitch, it's not enough.' He paused. 'Sarah's mother is giving me a loan.'

I had no idea things were that bad.

'Sarah doesn't know – she'd never accept help from her mother. Please, don't tell her you saw me.'

After a moment, I nodded.

'Thank you, Isla,' Nick said with meaning, catching my hand. 'I really appreciate it. Sorry – I know it puts you in a difficult position.' I thought he was going to let go of my hand, but instead he drew it towards him, pressing it against his chest. I could feel the beat of his heart against my palm and the gesture was so oddly intimate that I caught my breath. 'Sorry for involving you in my shit. I know how tough today is for you. Sorry we didn't get a chance to talk properly. I feel like . . . I don't know . . . there's never enough time. Not to really talk. So, well, anyway, I just want you to know even though you'll be in Chile, I'm still here if you need me. Email me, won't you? We used to, didn't we? I liked that, knowing what you were doing, how you were feeling.' He shook his head. 'Sorry, I'm being sentimental. Think the pressure's getting to me.' He laughed. 'Anyway, all I mean is, I'm here – if you need anything.'

He was so like the Nick I used to know. *My Nick*. I didn't trust myself to speak, so I leant my head forwards, my forehead resting against his, noses almost touching.

We stayed like that for a moment, and then I felt Nick's hands begin to release mine.

I didn't want him to let go, not this time. I turned my face towards his, pushing on to my tiptoes and pressing my mouth to his. I felt his surprise; a slight retraction.

A beat later his lips began to move with mine, the kiss deepening. His hand moved to my face, drawing me into him.

I could feel the warmth of his breath as he whispered, 'Isla Berry.'

Sarah was right not to trust me. After all, she knows me better than anyone.

45. SARAH

DAY EIGHT, 10 P.M.

Rain drums against the hut roof, bleeding wet trails down the windowpanes, while the wind sucks and rattles at the beach hut doors. Beyond it all, I'm aware of the deepening groan of the sea.

Nick has left, stalking out on to the beach, telling me he needs space to think over what I've told him. I didn't try to stop him.

Huddled in the corner of the sofa, I stare blindly into the wet night, wondering if there is someone out there, watching. Someone else who knows what happened seven years ago. My thoughts stretch and contract, exhaustion blurring the edges of reason. The strangeness of Isaac's faked note won't leave me and I keep wondering whether there is someone here, on the sandbank, who is in touch with Isla. Someone who knows she has Jacob – and has been keeping it from us? I feel utterly powerless knowing she holds every card. I want to weep and scream; I want to pound at her hut, tear it to the ground; I want to fly to Chile and hunt her down.

In the back of my mind, a quiet, logical voice asks: *What is the most precious thing in Isla's world? What does she value more than anything?*

It only takes me a moment to realize what it is – and then I'm up on my feet, striding across the hut, my thoughts snapping and firing.

I open our key box, flicking past the keys for the shower block, the gas bottle locker, and our spare – but I can't find the one I'm looking for. My fingers tremble as I search through them a second time. I know we have Isla's spare key – I only used it a few days ago – but oddly, it's not in here. My fist slams down on the kitchen counter. *Where the hell is it?*

I yank out the drawer where we keep homeless odds and ends, and rifle through old coins, a tube of mosquito repellent, a pencil torch, a screwdriver, the browning instruction manual for our gas fridge, a painted pebble I bought from a group of young girls selling them from the deck of a beach hut. It's not here either.

Maybe I put the key in the pocket of whatever I was wearing the night I used it. I'd climbed out of bed, so I would've been in pyjamas. I whirl towards my clothes drawer, pulling out my folded pyjamas. I turn out the thin pockets and pat them down – but there's no key. I fling everything out of the drawer in case the key has slipped out, but it's not there.

The rain is drilling against the hut roof and it feels like the noise is inside my head. I can feel my legs begin to weaken.

I am moments away from giving up, from sinking to the floor, defeated.

I take a deep breath, then I shake myself into action, slipping on my raincoat. I return to the kitchen drawer, grab the screwdriver and pencil torch, and step out into the night.

Rain rivers from the eaves of Isla's hut, running down the collar of my coat as I hunch over the door lock, water trailing down my spine like a damp fingertip. The wooden deck is wet and cool beneath my bare feet.

I've never broken into a place before and I've no idea what I'm doing. On television it looks simple, a quick flick of a screwdriver and the lock opens – but it's harder than that. I point the torch at the lock, and try jiggling the screwdriver in the keyhole, hoping it'll act as a key. Nothing happens; there's no resistance.

Next I try edging the screwdriver into the gap between the doors. I need both hands, so I grip the torch between my teeth, and then hold the screwdriver tightly. I'm thankful that Joe and Binks are in the Lake District for a couple of nights. If anyone sees me, I've no idea how I would explain. I can only hope that the weather will keep people indoors.

Rain slides into the corners of my eyes as I agitate the lock, and I have to keep stopping to wipe my face. Just when I am beginning to think it is hopeless, I feel the first give, a slight loosening in the door. I keep the screwdriver in place and wiggle the handle vigorously. My teeth press hard against the thin metal torch. Then suddenly, the handle snaps down and the door is opening.

I stare in amazement. It worked! I drop the screwdriver

into my pocket, then with a quick glance over my shoulder, I slip inside the hut, pulling the door behind me.

There is silence, apart from the sound of my own breathing and the rain against the roof. Water drips from my raincoat, puddling on the floor at my feet. My skin is clammy beneath my waterproof and I wonder what the hell I'm doing in here. I shiver. I want to light the gas lanterns, but Isla will have shut off the gas before leaving. I don't worry about people noticing my torch beam: there are shutters across the windows, so nothing but a sliver of light will be visible.

I cast the beam of the torch around, taking in the sofa and bookshelf above it. I've spent so many nights in this hut – lounging on the sofa with a bottle of wine, smoking on the deck, laughing in hushed whispers, knowing our boys were tucked up in the bunks – that it's strange to be here now as a trespasser. Guilt stirs at the edges of my thoughts – until I remind myself of what I know: Isla has taken Jacob to Chile. She hasn't returned a single one of our calls. She knows exactly what she's putting Nick and me through.

I shine the torch towards the kitchen area. She's left the place tidy; the surfaces are clear except for a newspaper folded on the side, and a glass left beside it. I so rarely see her hut this neat that, for a moment, I panic, thinking she's left for good – taken everything with her.

I need to keep focused. I begin searching through her drawers, looking for the one thing I've come for. I'm not surprised by the chaos I find tucked within them – beach towels shoved in alongside old tubes of sunscreen, the drawers cluttered and dusted with sand. I find books, and shells, and sun hats crushed out of shape. I pull open one drawer and find it's neater than the rest. There are a pile of children's books, a box of toys, and several small outfits that once belonged to Marley. I pick up a pair of red swim shorts, the material soft in my damp fingertips. What am I doing in here?

Shame surges through me as I think of Marley's small hand searching out mine. 'Auntie Sarah? Look!' He'd led me to the deck of this hut, showing me a trail of shells he'd laid out in a spiral. He'd picked up the first and held it to my ear. 'Listen . . . It's the sea!' He played with those shells for hours, not just listening to the secret hush of the waves, but pressing them close to his mouth and whispering back.

I loved that boy.

I'd give anything to turn back time.

Carefully, I return his clothes to the drawer, emotion thickening my throat.

I set my mind on the task ahead, doubling my efforts. I move on to the cupboards, searching through bedding, tins of food, spare clothes of Isla's. In one cupboard I find a T-shirt that I recognize. I hold it up. It's a pale-blue T-shirt with the skate brand *DC* printed on the front.

It's Jacob's.

I squeeze it beneath my fingers, bury my face in it to stifle a scream of outrage.

She has him! She has my baby!

I slam shut the cupboard with such force that the wall shakes. As I swing the torch round, I notice the bookcase. I step closer, running the torch across the spines of the novels. It'll be here. Of course it'll be here! Marley and Isla loved reading together; I used to envy the way Marley would curl up beside her, happy to sit still for half an hour at a time, contentedly listening. She used to buy him exercise books and he'd create his own magical tales, filling the blank pages with stories in his tiny neat hand.

I climb up on to the sofa and scan the bookshelf, the torchlight passing over a selection of children's books, thrillers, two hardback autobiographies, and a cluster of romance novels. There, at the end, larger than the other books, is a journal covered with fabric. I know immediately that I've found what I'm looking for.

I reach for the book, carefully removing it from the shelf and holding it in my hands: Marley's memory book. It is the beating heart of Isla's grief – more precious to her than anything.

And now I have it.

I lower myself on to the edge of Isla's sofa and set the memory book on my lap. The spine creaks reverently as I open it. As I run the torch over the pages, I see that the memories are dated and ordered, Isla's writing neat and precise. The recollections are vivid and beautiful, capturing the essence of Marley so sharply it's as if the words are breathing life into him.

I pause on a page titled: *The disappearing kite*. It's an account of an overcast summer's day when the boys must have been about seven or eight. Isla and I had taken them up to the headland to fly a new kite I'd bought them. The wind was up, gusting off the cliff top and making it tricky to keep the kite under control. Jacob, being the faster of the two boys, was the runner, speeding along with the kite in one hand, and then flinging it skyward with a heft of energy. Marley worked the strings, head craned upwards, squinting at the dipping and fluttering kite. On one of the launches, Marley was so focused on looking up that he didn't see the branch at his feet, and stumbled over it. A gust seized the kite, whirling it aloft, the lines whipping out of reach. The boys were laughing and shrieking in delight at the misadventure, running and pointing as the kite disappeared over the headland, stolen by the wind.

I remember the day – not so much for the event itself, but rather from Jacob's retelling of it. Earlier this summer I'd seen Jacob sitting on Isla's deck, sharing this story with the sun on his face, a brightness in his eyes. Isla had been sitting forward, head angled towards Jacob, absorbing his words like each one was a gift. I wonder whether Jacob felt like the keeper of Isla's happiness – he could bring Marley's memory to life better than anyone.

Is that what happened? Jacob saw how happy he made Isla, and thought it was love?

I turn the pages, flicking through more and more memories, passing small illustrations that Isla has sketched alongside the entries. They are basic, often a little childish, and the sight of them makes my eyes sting with tears as I think of what she's lost.

I stop abruptly, eyes widening.

I sit back. *No*, I think, shaking my head.

The torch beam quivers on the page in my trembling grip.

The memories and recollections of Marley stop in August 2010, the month Marley drowned. But the memory book doesn't end there. After a blank double page, there is a new title.

It reads: *Jacob.*

My gaze skitters and slides across the pages, racing to understand. Isla has transcribed dozens of moments she's shared with Jacob. The memories begin the summer after Marley died and lead right up until this summer.

Sweat beads across my forehead as I read these meticulously recorded moments: Jacob, age thirteen, strutting across the deck of Isla's hut doing an impression of his science teacher, Mr Melody; Jacob racing across the headland clasping an old Quality Street jar to collect tadpoles in; a hazy afternoon sprawled on a rug by the shore with Jacob playing Top Trumps. They are simple memories that would be forgotten by most people.

But not by Isla.

She has been keeping them for years. Recording every interaction. Securing them in ink. Filling page upon page with memories of my son.

My hands shake as I dial Isla's number.

I know she won't pick up, but she'll listen to my message, hear me say that I have the memory book in my possession – and will destroy it unless I hear from her within the hour.

Across the hut, something catches my attention. A pale-blue light has begun to flash on a shelf above the kitchen counter. I stare, perplexed. The light pulses in a steady rhythm, illuminating the underside of the shelf above.

I'm on my feet, moving towards it. My phone is still

pressed to my ear and I hear Isla's answerphone clicking in, her voice filling my head. The flashing in the corner of the hut suddenly stops – and I realize what I'm seeing. A mobile phone.

I reach for it, seeing my own name emblazoned on the illuminated screen: *Missed call, Sarah mobile*.

My brain feels syrupy, slow to understand. Isla's mobile. Does this mean Isla hasn't been ignoring my calls – she just hasn't received them? She must have left her mobile behind when she flew to Chile.

Is it possible that I've got everything wrong, somehow? Maybe Jacob took the flight to Chile with Isla, promised her that Nick and I knew where he was, said it was okay with us – and she believed him. Surely she'd have called us still, just to check. It doesn't feel right.

I'm suddenly aware of how exhausted I am, that I haven't slept properly in days. I just want my boy back. I want to hold him in my arms, explain things.

Looking at Isla's phone, I wonder whether Jacob's called her. Perhaps there'll be a clue in her messages. I look at her call history and am expecting it to show me a host of missed calls from my number and voicemails that haven't been played, but as I scroll through her call history, I see that all my messages have been played.

A chill shivers down my spine. I turn on the spot in the heavy darkness. I feel in my pocket for the torch, but I must have left it on the sofa. I know I'm standing in the kitchen area, near the hob. I use the light from the screen of my mobile to locate one of the knobs on Isla's cooker. I press it in and hear the hiss of gas as the ring flames to life.

I step back, the hut illuminated.

Isla wouldn't leave the gas on over winter.

I crouch to her fridge, open it. The light comes on and I blink into the fridge. There is milk and cheese, fruit and yoghurts. I pick up the milk, open it. It smells fresh. I find the sell-by date – it doesn't go off for another five days. Isla couldn't have bought it before she left.

Then I stand, directing the light from the mobile's screen on to the newspaper on the counter. I scan the cover.

Today's date.

My breath is short now, rasped.

Everything is beginning to come into focus. I move towards the sofa and pick up the memory book ready to leave. I need to get out of here.

But as I move, I hear the creak of the door opening behind me.

I whirl round, my voice unsure as I stare into the darkness. 'Nick?'

46. ISLA

When you look at the life ahead of you, there are moments stretching into the future that you could never predict or anticipate. I could never have conceived that, a week ago, I would be flying to Chile with Jacob, or that, seven years before, I'd be listening to a coastguard saying he was calling off the search for Marley. Not that. Never.

And not this.

I never wanted this.

When I said goodbye to the sandbank with my plane ticket in hand, I meant it. I'd planned to leave the tensions of the summer behind and get back to my life in Chile.

But that didn't work out, did it?

It was so very strange returning here, crossing the headland in the early hours of the morning when it was shrouded in darkness. I felt alert, each of my senses heightened; it was as if I could feel my heart pumping the blood around my body, a deep pulse of it moving through my chest, my wrists, my neck. When I reached the hut, I stood inside with my palms pressed against the shuttered windows, watching the morning yawn awake through the gap in the plywood.

That's when I saw her. Sarah was standing at the water's edge, arms hugged to her chest, her back to me. I experienced a strange, dislocated sensation, as if I were looking at myself seven years earlier. I'd stood exactly where she was as I'd watched the rescue boats carving empty circles in the water in their search for Marley.

Then Sarah had turned – looked straight at me.

My chest constricted and I went to step back from the doors, but then I realized: Sarah couldn't see me. But I could see her. Her skin was bleached of colour, and her hair hung lank around her unmade face. There was a blankness about her expression that I recognized in myself: she looked haunted.

What I thought was: *Now you know.*

47. SARAH

I hold my breath as the door opens behind me, the roar of rain and waves washing into the hut. Then a light footstep moves inside.

I want to believe it is Nick – that he saw the flash of torchlight in Isla's hut and came to investigate, but I know from the slimness of the frame beneath the raincoat that this is not my husband.

The figure pulls the door closed, then unzips the coat and hangs it from the back of the door handle. The person turns, facing me in the darkness.

Isla.

My mind is stumbling and tripping in its race to understand. Isla is not in Chile, she is standing right here in her beach hut, only feet from me. There are a hundred questions I want to ask . . .

Or perhaps there is just one: 'Where is Jacob?'

Isla pulls something out of her jeans pocket – and is

suddenly crossing the dark hut towards me. I jerk backwards, catching my hip against the edge of the counter, a hot pain shooting through me. Isla merely passes me, moving into the kitchen area. I hear the sliding of cardboard, then a quick rasping sound, and a match flares to life. Isla directs the match towards the gas lantern; a warm orange glow fills the hut and we're bathed in light.

I stand opposite her, blinking. I don't know what I am expecting to see; a monstrous version of Isla with wild eyes and a distorted expression – but that's not what I get. This is just . . . Isla. Her damp hair hangs loose around her face, the thighs of her jeans are soaked to a dark navy, her feet are bare and caked in sand. She's wearing a cream cotton top with a soft crocheted neckline that I bought for her birthday two years ago.

'You broke into my hut,' she says.

'I have your spare key.'

She shakes her head. 'I have my spare key.'

It takes me a moment to understand. I couldn't find Isla's spare key because she must have taken it back. Which means she's been in *our* hut. A steady beat of fear builds in my chest.

Isla's gaze travels to Marley's memory book, which I am clutching to my chest. 'What are you doing with that?'

I tighten my grip. 'Where is Jacob?'

Isla's expression is level, emotionless, as she lets silence answer me.

A shiver travels along the nape of my neck. 'My God,' I say, my voice whisper-thin. 'What have you done?'

'I think the more interesting question is, What have *you* done, Sarah?'

48. ISLA

Over the past week, I've only seen Sarah from afar, or heard her voice, played back on my voicemail. Seeing her up close like this makes my breath catch: there's a deep vertical line running between her brows, and the circles beneath her eyes are so dark they look like bruises. Anger or fear tightens the muscles around her mouth; her top lip twitches. She is wearing an oversized raincoat, water sliding from it to the floor. She is shivering but doesn't seem to notice.

'The police think you're in Chile.'

'I flew back six days ago. I've been here.'

'*Here*? That is . . .' Sarah turns, taking in the hut, the boarded-up windows, '. . . madness!'

Actually, I liked it. There was something soothing, quietening, about being here unnoticed. I've been free to fall into step with the sandbank, feeling its rhythm, taking long walks across the headland at night, watching the bats swoop, hearing the scuffling of foxes leaving their dens, watching the moon turn from a deep orange to silver-white as dusk moves towards dawn.

'All those messages I left you . . . You've been right here – listening to them?' Incredulous. Breathless.

'Yes.' I was the fly on the wall that no one knew about. When the doors of Sarah and Nick's beach hut were left open, I could hear them only feet away from me – their phone calls, their conversations with the police, their arguments. When there was little wind and the sea was tame, I could even catch the clang of metal pans on the hob, the drone of the water pump as the kettle was filled, the clink and scrape of cutlery. I knew when they cooked, when two plates were laid instead of three, when uneaten meals were scraped into the bin. Invisibility is a strange feeling – both liberating and lonely.

I wondered if Sarah had somehow sensed me here. I'd see her on the beach, her gaze hovering in this direction, as if trying to decipher a message in the faded wood of my hut. I was surprised when she let herself in – I'd forgotten she had my spare key. I'd been out walking over the headland, like I've been doing most nights, and returned to find her and Ross Wayman standing in the doorway. I'd watched from a distance, certain she'd notice something that'd give me away, like the still-warm kettle, or the bowl of fresh fruit on the side. But I suppose we all see what we want to see.

'Why?' Sarah asks, quite rightly. 'Why have you been here all this time? What the hell is going on? Where is Jacob? Is he safe?'

Her questions can wait. 'Isaac,' I say firmly. 'That's where we'll begin.' My voice is level, cool. I barely sound like myself – and perhaps that's how this needs to be. 'You never told me he's Jacob's father.'

Sarah's back stiffens. 'Because it's got nothing to do with you.'

'You've always acted strangely around Isaac. Jittery, that's the word, like you're uncomfortable when he's near Jacob. That struck me as odd when you owed *everything* to Isaac for saving Jacob's life. Maybe I should have worked it out – but I suppose I didn't, because I'd never have imagined that you'd been lying to Nick and Jacob for all these years, too.'

Sarah glares at me. 'I don't need to explain myself to you.'

'Everything that happened the night Jacob disappeared started with *you*.' I pause for a moment. 'I've been watching you stalking the sandbank, throwing around accusations and blame – but when have you once stopped to ask yourself what *your* part in all of this was?' I fix my gaze on hers. 'It's time you took responsibility.'

Sarah's eyes widen. 'My God! Last night . . . you followed me to Isaac's hut, didn't you? I thought I saw someone outside . . . You were there, listening!' Her head shakes in disbelief as she realizes. 'It was you, wasn't it? The note . . . the note Isaac was supposed to have written – you wrote it! You manipulated things so Nick would find out—'

'He deserved the truth.'

'He deserved to hear it from me. *Me!*'

'When would that have been, Sarah?'

Her gaze narrows, bewildered. 'Is that what this is about? Nick? Are you still bitter that I married him? Do you honestly think you have some claim to him because you were lovers twenty years ago? That's it, isn't it? You can't bear that I have a husband and a son – and you have no one.'

The punch of her words hits in my stomach, winding me. 'This is between you and me.'

'Is it? Then why involve Jacob?' Sarah takes a step towards me so that we are standing only inches apart, her face tilted towards mine. I can smell the sourness of her breath as she pleads, 'Where is he? Just tell me, please, I'm begging you. Is Jacob safe?'

'That was all I wanted to know about Marley, too. Do you remember all those times I came to your hut, sobbing? I was desperate for answers. Desperate for someone to tell me what happened on the water so I could understand, let go.' I pause, look her in the eye. My voice is arctic as I say, 'Only, you made me wait seven years for my answers.'

49. SARAH

Blood pulses just below my skin. I'm still wearing the rain-coat, and beneath it I'm clammy, sweating, the plastic pinching against my bare neck. I have to get it off. I can't breathe in here. I step away from Isla, keeping the memory book clutched awkwardly in one hand as I shrug off the coat. A few strands of loose hair must have got caught around the zip and I feel them tearing from my scalp as I shuck the wet coat on to the floor.

I suck in air, shoulders heaving. The hut is thick with the scents of sweat, mildew – and something else; an earthy smell like damp, rotting wood.

The rain continues to pound against the hut roof, insistent, loud, as if it's banging to be let in. I feel trapped in here – the hut boarded up, no moonlight or fresh air filtering in. Just the burn of the gas lantern, our black shadows cast against the wooden walls.

My palms are damp as I grip on to the memory book,

holding the weight of both our sons in my hands. Isla stands with her back to the lantern, her face in shadow, just wisps of hair backlit golden. I don't know this Isla. She's a stranger to me. I'm no longer sure who she is – or what she's capable of. My mobile is in the pocket of my raincoat. I could ring the police, or call Nick. But I sense it would be the wrong move; instead, I say what Isla is waiting to hear. 'I'm listening.'

'The night Jacob disappeared, do you know where I found him?' Isla begins. 'He was crouched on the quay, right by the harbour edge. He was soaking wet. Shivering like a dog. He could barely speak.'

Oh, Jacob!

'Do you know how far offshore Isaac's boat was when Jacob dived?'

I shake my head.

'Almost a kilometre away. It was even further to the quay – but Jacob chose to put himself at greater risk, swim further to the quay, because he couldn't stand the thought of going back to the sandbank where *you* were. I can't even imagine how terrified he must have been swimming in the pitch black. He knows the danger of the sea better than anyone. But somehow he made it.'

I swallow, reminding myself to breathe. He made it. That's what I need to remember. Jacob made it to the quay, alive.

'I dug through my backpack for a towel and clothes he could wear. He was shaking so hard I wanted to call an ambulance, but he told me no, he would be okay. My taxi for the airport had arrived, so I put Jacob in the back seat, telling the driver to put the heating on full. I knew something had happened on Isaac's boat, but he didn't say what – not immediately. He just said he couldn't go back to the sandbank – and asked if he could ride with me as far as Winchester. He told me he had a schoolmate there. It was on the way to the airport, so I agreed.'

Winchester . . . Yes, he did have a friend there. The boy's family had moved there a couple of years ago. Oliver, I think his name is.

'He said he needed to stop at home first to get some clothes from the garage. So that's where we went. When he was in there, I stayed in the taxi and called you to let you know Jacob was with me, he was safe.'

I blink, surprised by this detail. Then I remember I'd seen Isla's missed call. 'You didn't leave a message. Why didn't you ring me back?'

'When Jacob climbed back in the taxi, he began to talk, telling me Isaac claimed to be his father. He asked me if I thought it was true. I thought about how you'd always dreamed of having a big family – yet when you and Nick couldn't conceive again after Jacob, you seemed to give up without a fight. It had never made sense to me, as the Sarah I knew would have done everything in her power to have another baby: she'd have had every medical test under the sun; she'd have taken out loans to pay for IVF; she'd have put herself forward for medical trials. But instead, you just accepted it – as if you knew there was no hope.'

'Isla—'

'And then there was the oddness of how you've always acted when Isaac's nearby. So I thought, yes, it was probably true – and I told Jacob this.' Isla's head shakes slowly from side to side. 'He sobbed, Sarah. Just like he used to when he was a little boy. I cradled him in my arms, this hulking teenager sobbing his heart out. I can't begin to understand how you could've done that to him. Lied about something so . . . vital . . . all these years – and then left him vulnerable to being told in the way he was.'

Until I had Jacob, I didn't know that when you have a child, their hurt becomes your own. Only it is magnified. Each of those tiny slights they feel – the knocks in the playground, a disdainful look from an older kid, the heartache they experience as teenagers – are felt twice over. Imagining Jacob's devastation when he learned the truth about Isaac squeezes the breath from my lungs.

Despite everything, I'm oddly thankful that Isla was the one who was with Jacob. He couldn't have come to Nick or me – and the one other adult he could turn to, trust in, would've been Isla.

But then what? What did she do with his trust?

'As I was sitting in the back of that taxi, I was desperately trying to reframe everything, and that's when it hit me.' Isla looks me square in the eyes. 'I'd always wondered why, when Isaac came across our two boys struggling for their lives at sea, he'd chosen to go to Jacob first, not Marley. That question had plagued me. I'd asked Isaac, over and over, to talk me through exactly what happened on the water. And finally I saw the answer: he'd gone straight to his son.'

'Isla—' I begin, but she cuts me off with a shake of her head.

Her gaze bores into me. 'I realized that if you hadn't cheated on Nick and screwed Isaac, *my* son might have been the one who was still alive.'

Oh God, I can see it now, the distorted equation Isla made in that taxi, wanting to lash out, punish me. 'You told Jacob he could go with you to Chile because of what happened with Isaac. Listen, Isla, I promise you—'

'No,' she interrupts. 'That's not what this is about.'

'Then—'

'Jacob told me, Sarah. He told me everything.'

I freeze.

'I know what happened the day Marley drowned.'

No, he can't have! Panic crawls beneath my skin like the scurry of beetles.

I've always known that you can only keep something hidden for so long. The day-to-day mechanics of life willingly offer distractions – yet all the while, it is still there hidden inside you. You know there will come a time when that tightly bound secret is going to start to shift, to breathe, to pulse. When the bindings begin to loosen and that darkness you've been concealing starts to move again, it takes on a life of its own and there's nothing that can be done to stop it.

I feel the blood leave my head, draining out of me. I'm cold, weightless.

Isla knows.

And if she knows the truth, what has she done with Jacob?

50. ISLA

'I want you to tell me what happened that day.' I need to hear it in her own words.

Sarah looks straight at me, fear caught in the edges of her eyes. The air in the hut has grown heavy with anticipation. I catch the faint scent of the gas lamp as it flickers and whirs, its glow spilling across the sharp angles of Sarah's face. She opens her mouth as if to speak, and then shuts it again. I can tell she's thinking of how best to slide away from the question, stall for time.

Eventually, she says, 'I honestly don't know what you're getting at. I've told you before that I was washing the hut windows – that I didn't realize the boys were in the sea.'

Incredibly, she seems sincere. I wonder whether she's become so adept at lying over the years that she's managed to convince herself it's the truth. 'How about I remind you what happened?'

I tell her it exactly as Jacob had told me while the two of us sat buckled in the back of the taxi, the heating on full, the rear windows steaming with condensation. I'd been trying to comfort him about Isaac, when he'd pulled away, his jaw tightening. 'Mum's been lying to you.'

There was something so serious, so loaded in his tone that I felt my spine stiffen. 'Jacob, what do you mean?'

He'd looked away then, running the heel of his hand over the window, clearing a patch of condensation. The glow of streetlamps punctuated the darkness at steady intervals as we sped through the night.

'Jacob,' I'd said, placing my hand on his forearm. 'Please, what are you talking about?'

He'd turned towards me – and I knew before he'd said a word what this was about. It was all there on his face. 'Marley?'

Very slowly, he'd nodded. 'It was Mum's fault.'

I look at Sarah now. Beads of sweat glisten on her brow. 'Jacob told me everything,' I say. 'I know what happened in the minutes before he and Marley went for a swim. They'd finished building the sand fortress, and then went back to your hut to get a drink. As they walked in, Marley knocked over the bowl of water that you'd been using to clean the windows. Is that true?'

Sarah nods, eyes flicking over my face.

I can picture Marley drifting into the hut, his bare feet still looking too large for his narrow legs. He wouldn't have been concentrating – his head was in the clouds half the time – and I can imagine him knocking into the bowl, sending water sloshing across the hut. Jacob had said Sarah

Last Seen

was angry, and I can imagine the heat of embarrassment flushing pink in Marley's cheeks.

'You told them to get out from under your feet, play on the beach. When they complained they'd been doing that all morning, you said, "Go and swim, then!" You made it into a competition, didn't you, telling them to swim out to the yellow buoy marker? You said there'd be a prize for whoever got back to shore the quickest. A Snickers bar; that's what the prize was, wasn't it? A fucking *Snickers*!'

Sarah listens, her face white.

'With you there were always running races, obstacle courses, prizes for the best drawing, the first one to finish their dinner. Everything was a fucking competition! You're the same with me – always competing, as if you can only know your worth by measuring it against someone else. I can just picture you setting the boys off. Did you draw a line in the sand, tell them: *On your marks, get set, go?* And then what? They speed down the beach, hurdle through the shallows and start to swim. But you . . . you turn away. Our boys were confident in the water – but they were only ten! Why weren't you watching? Where were you?'

When Sarah doesn't answer, I continue. 'You were finishing cleaning the windows. You got distracted – went to the standpipe to fetch fresh water. Forgot to check on them.' I swallow, feeling the emotion swelling into my throat. 'You *forgot* to watch our ten-year-old children swimming to a buoy marker forty metres from the shore. You *forgot* to watch our boys – and because of that, Marley drowned.'

I hear her breath catch.

'You could say it was a mistake – a moment's carelessness.

We've all done it, haven't we? God knows, I wish I'd checked on them more often that morning. So I could have forgiven it, Sarah. I think I truly could have.' I take a breath. 'But what I find impossible to understand is why you never told me.' I shake my head as I say, 'It wasn't a lie by omission. You didn't just leave that detail out. You *made* Jacob lie to me, too! You told him that the competition was a secret. You prepped him to tell me that it was Marley's idea to swim around the buoy marker – when I knew, *knew*, Marley would never have suggested that! You laid a threat for Jacob, saying that if I found out the truth, I'd blame you. That you and Nick would have to sell the beach hut – wouldn't be able to return to the sandbank ever again.'

Sarah covers her mouth with a hand, her free arm wrapping around her middle.

'What kind of mother does that to their son?' My voice shakes as I say, 'You should never have sent them out into the sea. You should've been watching them. But you *forgot*. Forgot about our children! You carried on cleaning your fucking hut, while my baby was drowning. And then . . . and then you lied about it! Made Jacob lie about it, too!'

I snatch a breath, my mouth twisting around my words. 'You've known for years that I blamed myself. I thought I should've taught Marley better to not swim without asking me. I punished myself for not watching – for being with Samuel when Marley was drowning. Jesus, Sarah, you saw that I pushed Samuel away – that I couldn't bear to be with him because of the guilt. But it wasn't my fault, was it? It was yours.' I suck in air, my lungs tight. 'But *you* – your life gets to carry on. You have Nick. You have your boy.

402

You are part of a family. Everything that I should have had – you kept it all, when you'd cost me mine. And you didn't even admit your part in it, or say sorry . . .' My voice cracks on that word.

'Listen—'

'Listen? I was ready to listen seven years ago. I was begging you – begging Isaac – begging Jacob – begging everyone who'd been there that day to try and help me make sense of things. I sold myself a thousand theories of what happened. And all along, *you knew*!' My fingers grasp at the roots of my hair. 'You came to my flat, bringing meals, books, magazines. I thought you were being a good friend. A best friend. But you did those things out of guilt, didn't you?' I jab a finger in the direction of the memory book Sarah still grips. 'And now that – that is all I have left. Memories!'

I step forward to reach for it, but Sarah draws back, tightening her grip.

My tone is lethal, punctuated. 'Give. Me. The. Book.'

She shakes her head. Swallows. 'Not until you tell me if Jacob is safe.'

My eyes widen in disbelief. 'You've still not said sorry. After everything that's happened – after everything you've done, you can't even bring yourself to say, *It's true. I'm sorry.*'

Sarah lifts her chin. 'I've looked through the memory book, Isla. There are pages and pages of memories about Jacob. Why? Why do you need to keep his memories? What have you done?' She is yelling now. 'What the hell have you done?'

'You don't deserve a single fucking answer!' I hiss.

The sound of tearing rips through the hut. It takes me a moment to understand. I look down and see that Sarah is shredding pages out of the memory book, screwing them up and tossing them to the floor.

'Stop! Stop it!'

'Where is he, Isla?' she demands, yanking out another page, the thick cream paper crumpling in her fist. 'Where the hell is my son?'

I watch, horrified. It's everything I have left of Marley – and she is destroying it in front of me. I launch forward, grabbing for the memory book, but Sarah snatches it out of reach, and I am unbalanced, falling forwards. I reach for Sarah, bringing her down with me. We crash to the floor, my cheekbone smacking against her shoulder as we land.

I find myself on top of her, and she is pushing, trying to shove me from her. Rage seethes through me and I grab her wrists, pinning her arms down. She thrashes beneath me, her teeth bared. 'Get off!'

I feel the heat of her skin beneath my fingers, see the veins pulsing in her neck. She strains and writhes, her hair tangled across her face.

'You've taken everything!' I spit.

'So you took my son?' Sarah yells back. She jerks an arm free of my grip and it comes swinging towards me, her fist connecting with my jaw. There's a hot burst of pain. Metallic notes fill my mouth.

My hands go to my lips, fingertips meeting something hot, wet. Blood.

Beneath me, Sarah's body slackens.

We are both silent, staring at one another in amazement. *How? How did we get here?*

At the edge of my vision I can see the memory book splayed on the damp floor, loose pages ripped and scattered. I think of my beautiful little Marley with his sun-kissed face. I imagine him sitting in the corner of the hut, looking quizzically at his mother and Auntie Sarah.

A deep wave of shame floods me. I drag myself off Sarah, slumping against the hut wall.

Slowly, she pushes herself up so she is sitting, too. 'Are you . . . okay? Your lip . . .'

Silence beats between us.

Sarah stares at me in the growing quiet. When she speaks, her voice is a whisper. 'Jacob was in love with you, did you know that?'

I think about the question for a moment. 'Yes, I did know.' Not at first. I was slow to read the signs. But as the summer wore on, I could sense his feelings had shifted. I know I enflamed things with my hunger for closeness, letting him misinterpret it as attraction. I should never have allowed him to stay the night in my hut. I came dangerously close to crossing a line that I'd once thought was so much clearer to see. I look Sarah in the eye when I tell her, 'Nothing happened between us. Never.'

'But you took him to Chile.'

'Because he asked me to. He needed *me*. For the first time in years, I felt like . . . like a mother again.'

Sarah presses her palms together. Her voice trembles as she says, 'I took your son, so you're taking mine. Is that it?'

I stare at Sarah, understanding the precise undulations of

pain she feels, the unbalancing sensation of not knowing whether your child is safe, of feeling like your whole world is disorientated. I swallow the blood that's filling my mouth. 'You treat me like I'm a trespasser, like the beach hut, the sandbank, Nick, Jacob – it's all yours. You never talk about Marley any more. He thought the world of you, Sarah. Your family. But you were quick to forget. You took down his photo, replaced it. You forgot the small details of who he was. His dance – his Michael Jackson dance – you'd forgotten it. Only Jacob remembers.' I drag in a breath, my throat thickening with tears. 'You, Nick, and Jacob were *everything* to me after Marley died. All I had. But you didn't want me to be part of that. Have you any idea how it felt knowing you'd lied about Nick and Jacob's camping dates just to keep me away?' Tears pool in my eyes, making my vision swim. 'You were pushing me out. So I wrote down those memories of Jacob, as I knew I wouldn't have many more. I let him come to Chile with me because he was hurting – we both were. I wanted to look after him.'

'He's in Chile, still? He's safe?'

I look at Sarah. There are tears streaming down her face. 'Yes, he's there. He's safe.'

Her eyes screw shut as she breathes out heavily.

I push myself to my feet, wiping the blood from my mouth with the back of my wrist. I gather up the memory book, smoothing the pages between my fingers. After a moment, Sarah reaches for the torn sheets that litter the hut floor. She gathers them carefully, passing them to me. As I reach for the final one, her hand moves over mine.

I look up, our eyes meeting.

'I didn't know that's how you felt. How you saw things. I'm so sorry, Isla. I'm sorry for everything I've done.'

When I'd arrived in Chile with Jacob, there had been no plan as to what would come next. Numb with shock, I barely remember the three-hour drive south, or packing Jacob off on a trekking trip with a friend who runs wilderness expeditions. I do remember Jacob begging me to come with him, but I'd told him I had to work – that the space would be good for him. I agreed I'd pick him up afterwards; we'd talk then. I waved him off but, instead of returning to my apartment, I found myself at the airport spending the last of my savings on a return flight to England, knowing I needed to confront Sarah face-to-face.

When I arrived on the sandbank, there was Sarah standing on the shoreline, desperate to know what had happened to *her* son. It was as if our lives had flipped – and I found myself watching, riveted. I only intended to stay hidden for a few hours, a day at most, yet . . . there was part of me that wanted to let her suffer. I wanted her to understand.

But I let it go too far, I know that. I'm not proud of the person I've become. It's up to me to end it.

Now I take Sarah's phone and dial the number for the mobile I'd pressed into Jacob's hand before leaving him. It'll be late afternoon in Chile. I imagine Jacob with the lowering sun on his face, standing in the mountains, hiking boots laced up, a pack on his shoulders.

I hand the phone to Sarah.

There is a question in the dip of her eyebrows.

I nod at her. 'It's him.'

She grips the phone to her ear, her other hand pressed to her chest.

I watch as she pushes open the hut doors, stepping out on to the deck. The rain has stopped now. The night is bright with stars, the sky washed clean. She presses her back against the deck railing, her face turned towards the light.

Lit by the soft glow from the gas lantern, I can see from Sarah's expression the exact moment Jacob answers. The icy fear that's held her prisoner melts in the sunburst of his voice. Her knees buckle and she grips on to the railing. 'Oh, my baby! It's you! It's you!'

It's a moment I will never have in my life: the reuniting of a mother with her son.

51. SARAH

Hearing his voice is like stepping out of a nightmare into the golden light of a dream.

'Jacob! Jacob!' I repeat over and over, the two syllables of his name having never felt so wonderful on my lips.

In clipped sentences he tells me he's safe. He's in Chile. Hiking. With a group.

I am grinning and crying, and still repeating his name.

In the blinding relief of hearing his voice – knowing he is alive, breathing, safe! – I'm slow to notice the strangeness of his tone. Somehow he sounds older, detached, changed. I press the phone closer to my ear, as if I can draw him nearer to me. But his voice remains hesitant, distant from me. I'm a mountaineer ascending a peak, suddenly seeing I am still miles from the final summit. I realize just how much distance lies between us now.

In his silence, I attempt to explain about Isaac, but when he doesn't respond, I falter, uncertain. I hear his breath coming in quick bursts, his footsteps crunching against earth. I try and picture him walking with a backpack on his shoulders. Are there new muscles in his shoulders, stubble dusting his chin, a tangle of unwashed hair? We have only been apart for days, but I feel like years have moved between us.

'How did you get this number?' he asks.

'Isla.'

'She's been in touch?'

'I'm with her.'

'Where?' he snaps. 'Where are you?'

'On the sandbank. Isla's here, too.'

'But – I thought she was here. In Chile.'

'She wanted to talk to me.'

'She flew back? I can't believe she . . .' I hear him curse several times, the words muffled as he holds the phone away from his mouth.

I wait for him to return to the line, ears pricked as I try to gauge what he's doing. More than a minute passes without a word, and I can feel the stutter of my heartbeat as I begin to think he's cut me off. 'Jacob? Jacob?'

Nothing.

'Are you there? Please, Jacob . . .'

His voice is low, hushed. 'Has she told you?'

'Told me what?'

There's a pause. 'Isla blames you for Marley's death.'

I glance inside the beach hut, where Isla stands with her back to me, her face lifted towards a photo on the wall. 'Yes,' I say finally, 'she told me.'

A weighted silence beats between us.

Jacob's voice is a whisper. 'Does she know it's a lie?'

Isla chooses that moment to turn, to look directly at me.

She cannot hear Jacob, yet her gaze seems to bore into me, her skin ghostly white. The deep hollows beneath her cheekbones sharpen her features, making her eyes seem larger, questioning.

Seven years ago, a whispered promise in a darkened beach hut, tears wet on our faces.

I lower my voice as I answer. 'No. She doesn't.'

There's a pause. 'Are you going to tell her?'

52. ISLA

When there are so many words to choose from, so many places to begin, I wonder what Sarah is saying to Jacob. Where they will start.

I begin to gather up the few things I have into my backpack, knowing I'm done here. The anger that's been flaming bright since the night I left with Jacob has burned out, but what is left in its place, I can't say.

I turn off the gas lantern and the hut falls into darkness.

I lock up the beach hut and slip the keys into my pocket. Outside, the waves beat against the shore, a restless rhythm.

Sarah has left the deck and is standing on the dark beach, talking quietly into the phone, her eyes on the ground.

With my coat pulled around me, I tuck the memory book under my arm and cross the deck. I pause for a moment, placing one hand against the hut, the wood damp beneath my palm. I lean forward, press my lips to the wood, tasting earth, and salt, and the layers of the sandbank.

Then I push away, climbing down on to the rain-pocked sand. I pause at the narrow gap between our two huts that our boys once made into their Secret Sand Tunnel. I remember them whispering together in their private hide-away, as if the rest of the world couldn't reach them there.

With the dark sea at my back, the harbour sighing before me, I think: what we've lost. What we've all lost.

As I'm about to move off, Sarah looks up. Our gazes lock. Her eyes are wide in her pale face. She holds her phone away from her ear, stepping forward. 'Isla, wait.'

She stares at me, her fingers outstretched, as if she wants to hold on to something that's just out of reach.

I'm not sure what more there is to say. The truth hangs between us now, immovable, insurmountable.

Her mouth opens and closes. She glances at the phone in her hand and then back to me.

'Isla—'

413

53. SARAH

I'm not sure what to say next. What to do.

The phone throbs hot in my fingers, Jacob still on the other end of the line. I can distantly hear his voice, faint and panicked, blurring with the murmur of the sea.

Isla and I stare at each other, layers of history folded between us. My mouth opens and closes around the choices that lie before me. If I let her leave, it is over. We are over.

Jacob's questions pound in my head. *Does she know it's a lie? Are you going to tell her?*

I think of Isla on the water's edge seven years ago, the moment we had stood with our hands locked together, waiting for news of our boys. All this time, the events of that day have been sealed off, buried between Jacob and me. But now, as he waits for my answer on the other end of the line, as Isla stands in front of me, a question in the dip of her brow, I can feel the memories being unearthed, pulling me right back into the grip of it.

I circle the wet rag over the window, working loose the trails of salt. The rush of feet pounds on to the deck as the boys come barrelling in, Marley clipping the washing-up bowl, sending water sloshing across the hut floor.

'Sorry!' Marley says, leaping from foot to foot to avoid the puddle.

'Good one!' Jacob laughs.

I count to three. Smile. 'Never mind. The floor could use a clean.'

I grab the beach towels that are thrown over the deck railing, and lay them over the puddle. 'I expect you two are after some lunch?'

Jacob opens the fridge, asking, 'Can we have a Snickers?'

'After lunch. I'll finish up the windows, then do you both sandwiches. Go and play for quarter of an hour. I'll call you when it's ready.'

I hear them laughing and teasing one another as they dash back down to the beach, while I mop up the spilt water. I hang the towels out to dry, then refill the plastic bowl with soapy water and get to work finishing the windows. It takes me fifteen minutes, maybe twenty, but it's worth it. I can see the reflection of the sea dancing in the polished glass, a quiver of sunlight shimmering on the windows.

I'm not sure what exactly makes me turn towards the water, but an unsettling feeling moves through me. Instinctively I scan the bay, then the shoreline, looking for the boys.

But all I see are two spades cast aside at the water's edge, their sand fortress abandoned.

The skin on the back of my hands pinches as I yank off the rubber gloves, my gaze not leaving the beach. Sand shifts beneath my feet as I begin to jog, lightly at first, towards the water – a hand shading the sun from my eyes. Diane is already there, pointing. 'The boys are swimming. I think they're in trouble.'

I find them, two tiny dots in the water, so far from shore that panic seizes my chest. 'Oh my God!'

Everything seems to be happening in broken fragments. I am standing on the shoreline with Isla, our hands laced tight, fear marching in our hearts. I am hearing Neil's boat engine roar as he thunders out of the bay. I am watching Isaac's boat return with only one of our boys on board. I am wading through the shallows towards Jacob, who shivers beneath a blanket, his lips a purplish blue. I am cradling him, holding him, saying *Thank God! Thank God you're safe!* Then I am turning, aware of Isla alone on the shore, her hands balled into fists, her eyes filled with terror.

I guide Jacob into our beach hut. He doesn't speak. Not a word. The paramedics say it's a reaction to the trauma and advise me to keep things as normal as possible, not to push him to talk, telling me he'll do it in his own time. It could take hours – or days.

I bring him mugs of hot, sweet tea, and crumpets with melted butter and cinnamon sprinkled on top. I open a Snickers bar and place it beside him. I dab antiseptic cream on the cuts on his knee and hand from where he must have been hauled onto Isaac's boat. I wrap a fleecy blanket around his shoulders and pull out his favourite books. But he doesn't eat, or drink, or talk, or read. He just sits, staring at something I can't see – his dark eyes still.

Nick rings. His voice is tight with worry as he waits at Bergamo Airport, despairing that there are no flights till morning. When I put the phone on speaker for Jacob, I hear Nick saying, 'Mummy's told me what happened today. You're such a brave boy, Jacob. We love you so much. I'm going to be home soon. This will all be okay.' I watch Jacob's face closely, but his expression never changes.

Hours pass, but he says nothing. When dark falls, I ask if he'd like to sleep in my bed, but he starts climbing the ladder to the mezzanine at the top of the hut. I follow him up, but he turns his back on me when I try reading him a story and I descend the ladder, winded.

Twenty minutes later, when I poke my head into the mezzanine to check on him, I'm relieved to hear the slow draw of his breath as he sleeps.

I know Samuel will be next door with Isla, but I need to be with her, too. I've seen the searchlight from the helicopter disappear, the beach grow quiet. It is unthinkable. Completely unthinkable. As I slip out of our hut, I hear Jacob's scream. It's a piercing, heart-shattering sound. I fly back inside, catching my shoulder on the doorframe. My skin is throbbing and hot as I scramble up the wooden ladder in the dark.

Jacob is curled in the corner of his bed, his arms clenched around his head, knees balled to his chest. 'It's okay, you're safe. I've got you,' I say, pulling him into me. His little arms wrap around my middle, his hands gripping on to the fabric of my jumper. I rock slowly, whispering over and over, 'It's okay, baby. You're okay. You're safe now.'

I free one of my hands and use it to tug the blind cord, letting moonlight flood in through the porthole window. Then I return my hand to his back, rubbing in slow, soothing circles. After a few minutes, Jacob goes still in my arms and I wonder if he's fallen back asleep, but then I hear his voice – barely more than a whisper. 'It was my fault.'

I wait, wondering if I'm imagining it.

When he doesn't speak again, I ask, 'What did you say, baby?'

'It was my fault. I pushed him under.'

A prickle of unease licks at my skin. 'Jacob,' I say, very calmly. 'Why don't you tell me what happened?'

'I wanted to swim to the marker buoy. Some people did it yesterday – I thought we could do it quicker. It's not even that far. It was easy on the way out. When we got there, we were talking, drifting.' He sniffs, pushes his hand over his face. 'When we went to swim back . . . I don't know, it was further. The huts – they looked tiny, Mummy. Like . . . like those Monopoly houses.'

'You'd drifted with the current.'

He nods, like he understands. 'I tried to swim – to be calm – but it felt like we weren't moving at all. Like we'd never make it. We started shouting . . . I don't know. I can't remember. I couldn't breathe. Couldn't think. I wanted to get out. I grabbed Marley's shoulders. I just . . . I needed to rest, to breathe. But, I don't know . . . the weight of me . . . he went under. When he came up, he was thrashing around, shouting at me. I swallowed so much water. I was choking, spluttering, and I grabbed him again. He . . . he went under again. I just needed to catch my breath. I was going to let go. I knew I had to. But I didn't. I didn't let go. I held him down. Kept holding him and holding him . . .' He breaks off, tears streaming down his face, his body shuddering against mine. 'He didn't come up.'

Jacob is trembling, clinging to me, his skin fever-hot. 'I'm sorry, Mummy. I'm sorry. I'm sorry.'

I try gently shushing him, my lips against his salt-thickened hair, rocking, rocking. 'It's okay, baby. Everything's going to be okay. It wasn't your fault. It was an accident. A terrible, terrible accident.'

He's heaving with panic, his face wet with tears, his fingers pawing at me. 'Please don't tell Daddy!' he cries. 'Or the police. I'm a bad person. They'll take me away – don't tell them, please! Promise!'

'I won't, I won't,' I soothe reflexively.

He presses his face to mine, our cheekbones clashing, his tears sliding down the side of my neck. 'Promise, Mummy? You have to promise you won't tell anyone. Not even Auntie Isla.'

One of the hardest things about being a parent is the choices – those crack-sharp decisions you have to make in a blink of an eye. There's a window of time when your child looks to you to know what is right. But what if you don't know? What if you have absolutely no idea what to say? What if you are as bewildered as they are?

I feel the rabbit-like race of Jacob's heart as he waits for my answer. Strangely, what I think about is Maggie: her lying on the roadside, her skirt ruched around her waist, a neat pool of blood warm on the tarmac. Then I see the grey void of my mother's gaze as we'd watched Maggie's coffin lowered to the ground, her hands clenching into closed fists as I tried to reach for her.

I breathe in the sweet warmth of Jacob's skin. My lips move against the side of his face as I whisper, 'I promise. I promise I won't tell anyone.'

*

As I look at Isla now, tears slide unbidden from the corner of my eyes.

'Mum? Mum? Are you there?' I hear distantly from the phone still held in my hand.

Did I make the wrong decision back then? Should I have told Isla the truth?

I remember all those nights as a teenager when I'd sit on the swing chair in Isla's old garden, talking and smoking with the awning pulled down. Or later, when we'd huddle around beach fires, talking until dawn. I spoke a lot about Maggie. After she died, when my mother looked at me, there was this blankness in her expression – as if she could no longer see who I was. All she saw was me throwing a ball into the road – and Maggie chasing after it. She blamed me for Maggie's death. She wasn't being cruel. She just . . . couldn't help it. I told the truth – and spent the rest of my childhood living under its shadow.

I couldn't bear that for Jacob. If Isla had known Jacob had drowned Marley, she'd have looked at him differently, felt differently about him – I know she would have. People on the sandbank would've talked. What happened that day was an accident – yes – but if Jacob had stayed calm, not panicked, then Marley would still be alive.

It's a brutal fact, but it's the truth.

Isla needed our family more than ever after Marley drowned. How could we have supported her if even just a part of her held Jacob responsible? At the time, I truly thought it was the right decision, not just for Jacob, but for *Isla*, too. But then . . . Marley's body didn't wash up – and it left all that room for her to . . . hope. To search for answers. To look for explanations. I had no idea the damage the lie would cause. But by then it was too late.

I swallow. I had to either watch her suffer the anguish of never truly knowing what'd happened to Marley – or let Jacob suffer the agony of being blamed.

I chose to protect my son.

'Isla,' I say again, as she stands on the dark beach, her backpack on her shoulders. 'I'm sorry.'

And I am. I am desperately, desperately sorry for everything she's suffered, for everything I've kept from her, for making a decision that is a bullet to our friendship – but sometimes the truth is more painful than the lie.

She looks at me for a long moment. Then nods. 'Me, too.'

I watch her leave, slipping between our two huts, disappearing into the night.

I glance at the phone still held in my hand. Eventually I draw it towards me, my lips moving against the mouthpiece. I tell Jacob, 'I made you a promise.'

54. SARAH

SEVERAL MONTHS LATER . . .

The beach lies silent beneath a jewelled blanket of frost, the sea shivering under the sun's early light. I stand on the deck of our hut, shoulders hunched against the cold, a mug of freshly brewed coffee cupped between my hands. I've tramped across the headland to get here, sending warm clouds of breath into the morning.

I take a sip of the hot, milky coffee, scalding my lips. *Coffee for one*, I think, echoing a worry I'd had last summer, a lifetime ago. I lift my face to watch as a gull cuts across the sky, wings stark white against the weak blue morning.

My fingers travel over the smooth, rectangular *For Sale* sign nailed to the deck of our beach hut. We hand the keys over to the estate agent this afternoon. I asked the office not to give me any details of who's buying it: I'd rather not know.

Last Seen

Climbing down from the deck, the hard-packed sand crunches underfoot like fresh snow. I turn once, looking back at Isla's hut, which stands frostbitten and faded in the winter light. I only hear her news second-hand: she's left Chile and is living on the west coast of Ireland, where she's retraining as a Reiki practioner. The strange thing is that, even after everything we've done to each other, I still miss her. But we can never go back, I know that.

Nostalgia swells around me as I think of the warm memories that tide-mark our beach huts: the years of sandy footprints tramped between our decks, fingerprints greased with sun cream on the door handles, ring marks from hot mugs of tea or glasses of wine placed on the windowsills. There is the afternoon I lay in the sand next to Isla, our pregnant stomachs resting in carefully sculpted grooves; there's the evening swim we took as the tide lolled and the wind stilled; there's the day our boys showed us the bivouac they'd built, their sun-tanned chests puffed with pride. Those are the memories I'll hold tight to, pressing them close, like beautiful shells slipped into a pocket.

I pull my gaze away and continue moving towards the water's edge, wanting a final look at the sea. There's no one around except for a young fisherman hunched against the cold on the rocks; I smile lightly, then walk along the shoreline in the other direction.

Jacob moves into my thoughts, as he so often does. He has a meeting with his counsellor this morning. I hope Nick gets him out of bed on time; in fact, I hope Jacob decides to turn up this week. He needs to start talking to someone, and he's made it clear that that person won't be me. As the months pass, I'm beginning to understand more about why he lied to Isla about my part in Marley's death. I'd hurt him in the deepest possible way over Isaac, and he was lashing out – wanting to hurt me back. He needed Isla to have a reason to say, *Yes, come to Chile with me.* So he chose a lie that positioned him in the light, and me in the dark.

It hurts, of course it still hurts, but he is my son and I have to believe that we'll come out the other side of all this.

I'll see Jacob later tonight when I visit him and Nick – knocking on the front door rather than letting myself in with the key I can't quite bring myself to remove from my key-ring. I like Wednesdays. I prepare a meal for the three of us – there's fresh beef waiting in my fridge, which I'll cook with shallots, garlic and plenty of red wine, taking round the casserole steaming hot.

The other nights of the week are quieter, harder on my heart. Once or twice a month I meet Nick straight from work. I enjoy arriving in the smart clothes I wear to my job as a legal secretary and having new things to talk about that aren't the running of a home. I make Nick laugh more than I remember ever doing – but we won't be reuniting; in fact, the first set of divorce papers are due to be submitted to our solicitors next week. We have talked about trying to save our marriage, but the trust is gone. I admit that on the nights when I wake alone in those strange, silent hours before dawn, I sometimes wonder if, several years from now, I'll catch sight of him across the street, or in a restaurant, or on a beach – and he'll be with Isla.

I'm living at my mother's for now. I'm forty-one years old, single, and I've moved back home with my mother –

but I like it. My mother and I are closer than we've ever been, and this gives me hope for my relationship with Jacob.

My pace slows as I notice someone moving along the beach towards me. Their shape and stride are familiar and I pause, hugging my arms to my chest.

'It's true, then?' Isaac says, coming to a stop in front of me. I haven't seen him in months. He looks tired, paler in the winter light. 'You're selling your hut. Leaving.'

'It's not the same here any more.'

He nods as if he understands this only too well, and I wonder how these last few months have been for him. He pushes his hands into the pockets of his coat. 'How's Jacob?'

'Living with Nick.' It's not much of an answer, but it is the best I can do.

'If he ever . . . you know, wants to see me . . . I'd like that. I'd like that a great deal.'

I nod. 'Thank you. I'll tell him.'

A slow silence stretches around us. 'And you, Sarah. How are *you*?'

I shrug lightly. 'I'll be fine.'

Isaac watches me closely, as if he's reading something hidden in my eyes. 'You're a good mother, Sarah. You know that, don't you?'

My gaze drifts to the space between us. 'Am I? I'm not sure anyone else would agree.'

I hear the shift of sand beneath Isaac's feet as he moves closer. 'People here have been talking about that day on the water with Marley and Jacob.'

Course they have. It was one of the many reasons why I know selling the hut is the only decision.

'They think you sent the boys out swimming. Set a competition for them to reach the buoy marker. The rumour is you forgot to watch them – that's why Marley drowned.'

I shrug again, not wanting to get into this with Isaac. I've made my bed.

'But I know that didn't happen.' Isaac's dark gaze is square on my face. There's something unsettling in the intensity of his expression, a familiarity that reminds me of Jacob. 'I saw what happened, Sarah.'

I'm slow to understand – to register his meaning.

'From my boat. I saw what happened between Jacob and Marley.'

My breath shortens. 'You can't have.'

'I worried a lot about whether I should have told you – but I didn't want Jacob to get into trouble. I didn't want to hurt *you*.'

I see it then, the depth of feeling he's always held for me.

'But you knew all along, too,' Isaac says.

I nod, feeling the pulse of a connection between us: we were both carrying Jacob's secret, protecting him.

Isaac's gaze slides away to the sea, as if considering something in the soft patterns of the swell. 'Has he ever told you why he did it?'

It's an odd question – when the answer is so obvious. 'He was ten. He got dragged by the current. Panicked. Tried to save himself by holding on to Marley. It was a tragic accident.'

Surprise registers in Isaac's features.

A beat later, he has adjusted his expression and nods lightly. Yet as I watch him, I catch a flicker in his eye, a light creasing around his brow. It's the same look I've seen flit across Jacob's face when he's hiding something. 'What is it, Isaac?'

'Is that what Jacob told you? It was an accident?'

'Yes.'

He lifts a hand, scratching at his scalp.

'Isaac?' I repeat, my voice rising. 'What aren't you saying?'

He considers me for a long moment, his lips pulled to one side. He shakes his head, as if to close the subject.

I'm afraid now. 'Please! What did you see?'

He won't look at me. Won't speak.

I step forward, my hand fastening around his arm, making him look up. 'Please, Isaac,' I beg.

'It's true that the boys were caught in a current,' he begins slowly. 'But that's not why Marley drowned.'

'I don't understand . . .'

'They were arguing.' He pauses, swallowing hard. 'Jacob hit Marley. Held him under.'

'No,' I say, instantly. 'You're wrong!' Yet somehow, my heart goes cold.

'I was right there in the boat,' Isaac says quietly, yet firmly. 'He drowned Marley.'

My head is shaking back and forth. Absolutely not. There's no way he'd have hit Marley. 'He loved Marley. They were like brothers . . .' I counter, but my voice comes out as a whisper.

Jacob cried when Marley went on a school trip to the Isle of Wight because they wouldn't see each other for five nights.

Marley spent an entire term in woodwork building a

driftwood clock – and gave it to Jacob the moment it was finished.

Jacob asked for walkie-talkies for his eighth birthday so the two of them could speak to each other before bed.

Marley wrote a short story about being washed up on a desert island, illustrating it with beautiful images of two boys – one blond, one dark-haired, both heroes and best friends.

'You've got it wrong! Jacob was panicking and Marley came to help him. He held on to him.'

Isaac's head shakes slowly. 'Jacob was shouting at Marley. That's what made me look over, grab the binoculars. I couldn't hear what they were saying – but I saw it all. He punched Marley – then he held him down.' He swallows. 'I couldn't get to them – not in time.'

My head spins as Isaac's words whirl and twist, a raging current dragging me out of my depth. I am thinking, *No, no, no!* Yet something seems to slot into place, an aligning of sorts.

'But why?' I ask. 'Why would Jacob do that?'

Epilogue

JACOB

I sit hunched between the rocks, a winter coat buttoned to my chin. Light clouds of breath disappear into the chilled air. My scalp itches beneath the woollen hat that's pulled low to my brow. I'm anonymous. I could be anyone beneath these layers of clothes, sitting alone on the beach.

Except, I know. I know exactly who I am.

What I've done.

I shift slightly, angling my gaze towards our beach hut where my mother stands, a mug cupped in her hands. I should have guessed she'd be here, making her goodbyes before the keys are handed over this afternoon. Just like I've got mine to make.

She looks smaller, lonelier these days. I feel a tug of

something deep in my chest as I watch her, and have to drag my gaze away.

Slipping a hand inside my coat pocket, my fingers meet the smooth curved surface of a jar. I know precisely what's sealed within it: a page torn from a book showing two shorebirds in faded watercolour – *Oystercatchers, Male 1. Female 2*; an oak leaf, crisp brown but perfectly shaped; a sprinkling of sand from this bay; a packet of fiery bubble gum balls bought in an old-fashioned sweet shop. Tucked at the centre of these things is a slip of paper, a single word written for Marley: *Sorry.*

I can't look at the sea without remembering.

I've been over and over that moment – the way Marley's head snapped back as my wet fist connected with his face. Blood poured from his nose, hideous red rivulets of it that dripped from his chin, swirling into the water. I didn't mean to do it – I'm almost sure I didn't – I just needed him to stop!

My teeth grind together, but I won't let myself flinch from the memory. I hold it still in my mind. Force the full beam of my thoughts to centre on it.

It'd been my idea to swim out to the yellow buoy marker; I told Marley that I'd checked with Mum and that she'd keep an eye on us. We reached it with ease, but Marley seemed preoccupied. He wore this odd expression he gets when there's something worrying him. I asked what was up, dragged it out of him. Secrets were safe between us – we shared them, never kept them from each other.

We trod water as he told me he'd found a letter to his mum pressed into the back of a book in the beach hut. A love letter. 'It's from *your* daddy.'

I shook my head, told him he was making it up, but we both knew Marley never lied. He started quoting bits: *Isla Berry, I'll always love you. Always. You're what makes my world spin. Whatever happens, you are it for me. Everything.*

There was this buzz about him, as if he was . . . I don't know . . . part shocked by the discovery, part elated. When I looked up, I saw how far we'd drifted from the buoy marker. I could feel panic starting to rise; I wanted to be out of the sea, away from Marley. In my silence he just kept on talking and talking, telling me more details of the letter. Marley had never met his father and I could see the idea of him sharing mine – *my* daddy – taking shape in his thoughts.

I needed him to stop. Just stop talking! I felt the cartilage of his nose against my knuckles, saw the blood spurt from his nostrils.

He was coughing, crying, grabbing for me. I knocked his arm away, slipped beneath the water myself. I remember the thrashing of legs and arms, wild eyes, shouting. I grasped his shoulders, used my weight to push him under. I didn't want to see his face, bloody and scared, or hear him saying those words any more. But when I let go, Marley didn't come up. I was treading water, spinning round, searching, desperate . . . but he . . . he wasn't anywhere. I looked. I know I did. I couldn't catch my breath. Kept slipping under. And then there was a boat . . . a rope in the water I couldn't quite reach . . . someone shouting for me. Then a hand around my arm, the sensation of being hauled upwards, away from the sea.

What I remember is sitting at the back of that boat, staring at the lobsters in their dark pots, certain it must all be a mistake. Marley had to be okay. He was my best friend. I blinked and looked down, noticing the red swelling rising across the back of my knuckles. I slid my hands beneath my thighs. *No! No!*

Now my fingertips push down into the solid, freezing grit of the rocks where I am sitting. I'll never get it out of my head – the shock and horror in Marley's eyes as I gripped his shoulders, pushing him under.

Something inside me took over; something I didn't even know lived in me.

But it does, I understand that now.

It's a shadow I can't outrun.

In a sick twist of irony, I found out years later that Dad and Isla had been lovers in their teens. For all I know, that letter could've been written during their relationship, Isla slipping it into the back of a forgotten book.

Now I watch as Mum climbs down from the beach hut deck, stepping on to the sand, moving towards the shoreline. I'm more like her than she knows.

Suddenly she glances up, looking this way. My skin flares hot. I could be anyone – a fisherman setting up camp for the morning, a walker pausing to rest – but for a moment I think she recognizes me and my chest swells with hope. I want her to. I want her to come towards me, put her arms around me, tell me I'll be okay.

She smiles lightly, fleetingly, then slides her hands into her coat pockets. My chest constricts as I watch her move along the shoreline in the opposite direction.

Once she's out of sight, I push myself from the rocks and walk towards the sea, my breathing uneven. At the shore I remove my trainers, setting them neatly together. Next I take off my coat, a note folded carefully inside the breast pocket, and place it on top of my trainers.

The wet creeps into the fabric of my socks, biting at my skin as I take the first step into the sea. I wade forward, eyes on the horizon, the glass jar gripped in white fingertips. My skin flinches and contracts as the sea climbs up my jeans, clings to my calves, my waist.

I pause, drawing back my arm, my whole body shivering. Then I launch the jar high into the air, watching it twist towards the waiting sea.

I take a breath. The sandbank lies behind me, the winter horizon ahead. As the sea bed shifts beneath my sinking feet, I wait to feel the shadow falling away.

Author's Note

Longstone Sandbank is based on a stretch of coastline on the south coast of England where I spend much of my time. I've chosen not to name the real location because it allows me to take a few artistic liberties.

A Q&A with Lucy Clarke

What was the inspiration for *Last Seen*?

I had an image of two women standing on a shoreline, hands gripped, scanning the water for their young sons. When I tried to zoom in more closely on this image, I could tell from the clasp of the women's hands that they were best friends, and I began to wonder what would happen if only one of their boys was brought back to shore alive. What then? Could their friendship survive? How would it shift and change over the coming years? That was my starting point.

Why did you choose to set your novel in a series of beach huts?

I've grown up spending my summers in a beach hut, so it's a lifestyle I love and know intimately. The stretch of beach where our family hut stands became the inspiration behind the fictional setting of Longstone Sandbank. I liked the idea of exploring how this idyllic, peaceful setting could hold a darker edge. There's an intensity to summers when you're living in such close quarters – particularly as most beach hutters have owned their huts for years, so there are layers of history locked within the community.

In *Last Seen* a toxic female friendship lies at the centre of the story. Why does this relationship interest you?

I've always been intrigued by the bonds between women – mothers and daughters, sisters, best friends – and particularly how the shape of those relationships can change over time. In the novel, Sarah and Isla have been best friends since childhood, but I wanted to explore what happens when that bond is pushed to the edge of its limits.

What is your typical writing process? Do you have any writing rituals?

My husband and I co-parent, so we split each day in half: I write from 8am – 12.30pm, and then spend the rest of the day with our two young children. Because writing time is limited, I *try* to be very focused, so I turn off my phone and the internet and get my head down. I can write anywhere as long as I've got a pair of headphones and a good playlist, but my favourite writing spot is definitely the beach hut. I don't set myself a daily word count, I just do what I can. Some days are productive and the words seem to flow. Other days – many, many other days! – are a battle of coaxing and teasing the words onto the page. Tea helps. As does chocolate. Or a blast of sea air.

When you start writing a novel, do you know how the story is going to end?

When working on a new book idea, I typically spend the first few weeks brainstorming the plot and fleshing out my characters. So yes, in theory, I will have a loose idea of how the story will end. However, the reality is that the ending usually turns out to be completely different to my original plotline! Once I'm truly immersed in the story, and begin to live and breathe my characters, they tend to direct things in ways I hadn't imagined. The last two chapters of *Last Seen* only came to me in the final month or two of writing.

Dive into these other breathtakingly suspenseful novels by Lucy Clarke

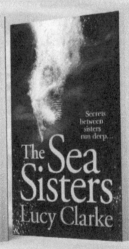

All available to buy now